DISCARD

3-99

AT ANY PRICE

Recent Titles by Brian Freemantle from Severn House

BETRAYALS
DIRTY WHITE
GOLD
THE KREMLIN CONSPIRACY
O'FARRELL'S LAW

AT ANY PRICE

Brian Freemantle

This title first published in Great Britain 1998 by
SEVERN HOUSE PUBLISHERS LTD of
9–15 High Street, Sutton, Surrey SM1 1DF.
Originally published in 1982 under the title *Chairman
of the Board* and under the pseudonym of *Jonathan Evans.*
This title first published in the USA 1999 by
SEVERN HOUSE PUBLISHERS INC., of
595 Madison Avenue, New York, NY 10022.

British Library Cataloguing in Publication Data

Freemantle, Brian, 1936-
     At any price
     1.   Suspense fiction
     1.   Title
     823.9'14 [F]

     ISBN 0-7278-2241-1

Printed and bound in Great Britain by
MPG Books Ltd, Bodmin, Cornwall.

For Allan and Colleen, with love

Prologue

During the flight from London Harry Rudd explained the emergency and was the first to disembark when the aircraft landed at Logan airport. The pilot radioed ahead so immigration formalities were waived and because Rudd didn't have any luggage there was no customs delay. Walter Bunch was waiting directly beyond the automatic doors, in the public section of the Boston arrival building. The lawyer moved to put his arms around him but Rudd shrugged his friend away. "How is she?"

"Bad, Harry. Very bad."

"Christ!" said Rudd.

Bunch had ignored the restrictions, parking immediately outside the exit. Rudd got in beside his friend and held himself stiffly, against any emotion, jarring with the movement of the vehicle. He blinked at the blurred kaleidoscope of headlights and neon that flashed in upon him as they left the complex and picked up the city road.

"The baby's dead," said Bunch.

"I don't care about the baby."

"I thought you'd want to know."

Neither man spoke for several minutes. Then Bunch said, "The gynaecologist says there was no way of knowing it would happen."

"I should have been here."

"There wasn't any delay: she was with her father."

"I still should have been here."

Rudd was forward against the windscreen, recognizing Charles Street and then the black outline of the hospital forming ahead in the darkness. He had the door open before the car stopped, running into emergency reception and babbling his name to the clerk. He wanted to find his own way but she insisted on summoning a houseman and Rudd stood with his hands gripped

1

against the counter. Only seconds passed but his control went.

"Where the hell is he!"

The woman, who was used to it, didn't reply.

"I said where is he!"

"Here." The houseman was used to it, too. On the way to Angela's room he talked of breech birth and haemorrhage and blood count but later Rudd couldn't remember the conversation although he tried, desperately, because he wanted to remember everything.

It was functionally bare, an intensive care unit cubicle, just a bed and monitoring equipment ticking and flickering, and everywhere an odour of cleansing disinfectant. He had expected to see her in pain but she was lying still and appeared quite peaceful. There were drips feeding into either arm and another tube protruding from the side of the bed, connected to some part of her body. Her black hair, usually so lustrous, but sweat-soaked now, seemed to have been arranged on the pillow but it didn't make her beautiful because of the colour of her face. Her skin had a strange, unnatural texture, shiny and waxy yellow, like the candles that she lit when she prayed to the Virgin Mary for them to be happy forever. Rudd, whose church-going had been because she wanted it, pressed his eyes tightly and tried to believe and said, the sound hardly coming, "Please. Please help."

After several moments he opened his eyes and said: "Angela."

There was no reaction.

"Angela, I'm here." He went forward in sudden fear and then saw that almost imperceptibly the bedclothing was rising and falling with her breathing. He heard the door behind and turned to see Bunch enter.

"She's sleeping, that's all," said Rudd. "Just sleeping. I won't wake her."

"No," agreed his friend. "Better not to."

Rudd lifted a chair quietly across to the bed and sat down. Gently, anxious not to disturb the arm into which one of the drip needles was taped, he felt out for her hand; her fingers lay cold and flaccid in his.

He pressed softly, and said, "I'm here, darling." The hand remained still. If she was so cold, why was there the sheen of

2

perspiration on her face? He wanted to dry her forehead with a tissue but didn't, suddenly frightened of doing anything more than lightly touching her hand. From movies he had seen he supposed one of the bleeping screens was a cardiac monitor: the green dot was crossing in a regular, bouncing pattern.

"Her heart's strong," he said.

"There's a cot for you in the room next door," said Bunch.

"I'm staying here."

"There's no purpose."

"I'm staying!"

Throughout that first night Rudd sat unmoving, forward in the chair, oblivious to the cramp or the efforts of Bunch to make him leave, leaving the room only when the doctors insisted. Then he stood right outside the door, unaware of the taste or even of drinking the coffee that Bunch handed him. This formed the pattern of the following day: quitting when the staff demanded, the rest of the time tensed forward in the chair, willing some movement from the still, resting, cold but sweat-flecked face.

Herbert Morrison arrived early in the morning, entering the room without any acknowledgement and leaning over his daughter, whispering "Come on, baby: wake up. It's Daddy."

"She's very tired," said Rudd.

The older man ignored him.

"I should have been here," said Rudd.

Morrison didn't turn.

"I won't forgive you."

"Shut up." Still Morrison didn't turn.

The feeling that had broken through, just briefly, at the reception desk surged through Rudd. He thrust up, wanting physically to hit the man, to hurt him, not caring who he was or how old he was, just wanting to see that waterfront hard, arrogant face split and bleed. And then he forced himself down in the chair, not looking at Morrison but at Angela. Not now; not here. Later. Morrison must have heard the movement and guessed the intent. He hadn't moved.

For an hour Morrison stood appearing unaware of Rudd, finally leaving without bothering to look at his son-in-law. He returned early in the afternoon. Again he didn't speak, just standing by the bedside. This time Rudd didn't say anything

3

either. He could no longer feel anger, he could no longer feel anything.

Morrison had just left when Angela's eyes opened, slightly. Rudd whimpered, saying her name again, and when there was no response he grabbed the summons button and kept it depressed until a nurse and the doctor hurried in. He had to leave and when Bunch brought the coffee this time Rudd laughed and said she was going to be all right and Bunch said sure, he'd always known she was going to be.

It was longer than the other times before the gynaecologist came out and when he saw the man's expression, Rudd's excitement deflated. Sympathetically the doctor attempted to explain that involuntary spasms came with unconsciousness and that was all the eye opening had been, a muscle reaction. Rudd went back into the room and took up the chilled, damp hand and sat, waiting. He closed his eyes, trying to remember the formal prayers that Angela had known so perfectly but couldn't, so he whispered again, "Please. I'll do anything, but please," not knowing if it were possible to strike a secular bargain with God.

Angela died that night.

Without recognizing it, Rudd had been listening to her even breathing and suddenly he couldn't hear it any more and the green ball on the heart machine was crossing in an even, unbroken line. The staff came running again and didn't bother to eject him this time, flustering about the bed with stimulants and injections and heart massage. It was an hour before they turned, the tension seeming to go from all of them at the same time.

"I'm sorry," said the gynaecologist. He must have said it many times but he still made it sound sincere.

Bunch was there as he had been throughout, and this time Rudd allowed the arm around his shoulders because he didn't know what to do or where to go. They were in the corridor but still close to Angela's door when her father came running from the reception area. He must have heard the news because he was already crying. Morrison stopped in front of them, barring their way.

"You killed her, you bastard. You killed her," shouted the older man. "Jesus, you're going to suffer."

4

Rudd tried to hit him then, lashing out in a wild, flaying punch that would have missed even if the doctor and the nurse hadn't intruded.

"Bastard," yelled Morrison again and this time he tried to hit back but now Bunch was between them as well, forcing them further apart. The lawyer snatched at Rudd's arm, hauling him down the corridor, and the hospital staff prevented Morrison from following.

"I didn't kill her," said Rudd. The shock was already moving through him so the words came out dully. "He sent me away . . . I didn't kill her."

"It was just grief," said Bunch. "He didn't mean it."

Bunch was wrong.

Herbert Morrison had never meant anything more sincerely.

1

Sir Ian Buckland decided it had been a mistake to agree to the meeting, despite Condway's insistence upon its importance. Friday, after all. And Condway knew damned well he always went out of London on a Friday, just as Condway invariably did. And sooner than this, too. What the hell was there that couldn't wait until Tuesday? Nothing, Buckland knew; absolutely nothing. Buckland looked needlessly at the desk clock, establishing that Condway was more than half an hour late. Either testing the humidity of some Havana-Havana or debating with the sommelier the superiority of the Vintage Dow against a 1969 Warre.

Buckland sighed. Fiona had said she understood when he'd telephoned, but he thought he'd detected an edge to her voice. It was still new enough for him to care about upsetting her. Bloody man.

Buckland thrust up and began pacing the chairman's office which was his by title but hardly by occupation, needing positive movement in his irritation. It was a large room originally designed by his grandfather and panelled still in dark Victorian teak, creating the impression of frames. In each square there was either a photograph or a print of one of their hotels throughout the world, London to the immediate right, Europe next, then Africa and finally India. Along the outer wall, where the windows overlooked Leadenhall Street, the shipping fleet was in modelled convoy, seven glass-encased liners steaming majestically back towards the desk that Buckland had vacated.

He walked jerkily trying to reassure himself the day could still be salvaged. Another fifteen minutes and he'd abandon the confounded man altogether. He could be at Fiona's by three and down to the Hamble by late afternoon. The yard were expecting him and knew it was more than their worth to close before he got there; he could have the yacht out into the Solent and into refit sea trials before the evening. And then an uninterrupted weekend with a woman who made love as if she'd invented it and was anxious to share the secret.

He was striding purposefully back towards his desk and the door that led to the outer office when the intercom sounded. He was annoyed that he hadn't made the decision earlier, to avoid being trapped. He punched the button and hoped Condway would detect the annoyance in his voice. If he had there was no indication of it having made any impression when the deputy chairman entered the room with his steady, measured tread. Lord Condway was plump, white-haired and port-mottled, the sort of British business director chosen as much for a lineage of four centuries as for his business acumen. The man carried a cigar still four inches long; he paused by Buckland's desk to dislodge a ring of white ash.

"You said two o'clock, George," reminded Buckland.

"Unavoidably delayed," said Condway, without an apology.

"I've an appointment."

Buckland remained standing. Condway nodded, settling himself expansively in one of the soft leather armchairs fronting the desk. "Necessary that we talk this through, Ian," he said.

Reluctantly Buckland settled himself behind the desk. "What?" he demanded. If Condway could be discourteous, so could he.

Condway moved his head again, absent-mindedly, suddenly interested in the burn of his cigar. "We've got a good finance director in Henry Smallwood," he said.

"What the hell are you talking about?" said Buckland. Smallwood was their most junior director, a round-bodied, round-faced man: even his spectacles were circular, making him appear exactly as Buckland regarded him, a clerk.

"Came to see me yesterday," disclosed the deputy chairman. "Something he can't understand in the accounts."

Buckland sighed, looking at the desk clock again. "Couldn't this have waited until Tuesday, George?"

Condway raised his eyes from the cigar, shaking his head. "There's a company cheque with your signature on it, Ian. For £635,000, made out to Leinman Properties and provisionally entered under investment."

7

Buckland's annoyance leaked away. "It was a private matter," he said shortly.

Condway shook his head again and Buckland was reminded of his housemaster at Eton: he'd smoked cigars and drunk port and been patronising. "It's a company cheque," said the deputy chairman.

"Buckland House *is* my company!"

"No it's not, Ian. And you know it. It's a public company with public investors. The only Leinman Properties Smallwood can find in the company register own casinos in Curzon Street and Hertford Street."

Buckland laughed dismissively. "It was a debt," he said.

"A gambling debt?"

"Yes."

Condway sat regarding him expressionlessly for several moments. When he spoke it was slowly, for the words to be understood. "You've committed a criminal offence, under the Company Acts."

"What!"

"A charge could be brought against you, under the fraud provisions."

"That's ridiculous."

"That's the law," said Condway, with quiet persistence.

"Your interpretation of it? Or Smallwood's?"

"My interpretation," said Condway. "Smallwood wanted to know if it was an executive decision we'd made between us in the absence of the full board and omitted to have entered into the minutes."

"What did you say?" demanded Buckland.

"Condway hesitated again. Then he said, "I told him I had a vague recollection but that I'd have to check my notes."

"It *could* have been an executive decision," said Buckland, seeing the way out and grabbing for it. "We only need three directors to agree."

"Was it your intention to attempt to get £635,000 through the company books?" asked Condway formally.

Not his housemaster, corrected Buckland. His father. The tone had always been like this, slightly weary, vaguely superior. Condway had served on the board under his father and Buckland

8

knew the deputy chairman made comparisons, as they all did.

"It was an oversight," he insisted. "I happened to have a company cheque book on me and it was the convenient thing to do. . . ." He stopped, conscious of the other man's concentration. "An oversight," he repeated.

"It could be listed as an executive decision on a director's loan," said Condway. "Could you repay it?"

"Of course."

"Now?"

"That's offensive."

"I'm being practical. And trying to avoid some public embarrassment," said Condway.

From the top, right-hand drawer of his desk Buckland took his personal cheque book and hurriedly completed an entry. In his annoyance he tore it out badly, leaving part of the counterfoil still attached, which made the gesture seem petulant. Slowly Condway reached forward for it and said, "I'll see it goes to accounts this afternoon, with a memo. There'll need to be a retroactive minute, which will mean board discussion."

"I understand," said Buckland. He looked obviously at the desk clock: he was more than an hour late for Fiona.

"It *is* an offence," said Condway.

"You've made your point."

"I just felt it was worth repeating," said Condway. He was unable any longer to maintain the white ash at the top of his cigar and it snowed down on to the carpet.

"You're driving too fast."

"I want to cast off before six," said Buckland. "After that the water starts to drop."

"You're in a rotten mood, too," accused Lady Fiona Harvey. She had a little-girl voice: occasionally, when she was excited, it actually came out as a squeak. Usually Buckland found it attractive but today it grated.

"Something awkward at the office," he said. "I'm sorry."

"I had a letter from Peter's solicitors today. They've given me a week to get out of the flat."

"I thought it was yours, under the terms of the settlement,"

9

said Buckland. She was bloody lucky there'd been a change in the British divorce laws, making an irretrievable breakdown the only grounds necessary. Sir Peter Harvey had proof of six different men with whom she'd committed adultery and a scandal would have been inevitable.

"It's one of the things that's got to be sold, for the division of the family property."

"What are you going to do?"

"I don't know," she said. "It's a bloody nuisance." She moved her hand across into his lap and began caressing him. "I could always move into one of your hotels, I suppose: would I get preferential rates?"

"How could I explain the visits?" he said, laughing with her. He shifted on the seat, making it easier for her, feeling himself stir under her touch. He'd never known anyone as sexual as Fiona.

"What did you tell Margaret?" she said.

"The truth," said Buckland. "That I was going to Hamble to put the yacht in the water."

"But forgot to mention me?"

Buckland smiled quickly to her. "She regards you as a close friend," he said, "though not that close."

"She called me the other day about the children's charity. Time to start organizing things, apparently."

"She's very efficient," said Buckland.

"Not in everything," said Fiona, moving her hand harder against him. "I'm better at this."

It was her favourite ride and Lady Margaret Buckland tried to make it at least once a week, to the very top of the rolling hill which gave the best view of the Cambridgeshire estate. She reined in and then stood in the stirrups, picking out the boundaries. Further than the eye could see in at least two directions and only just visible in a third: it was right that the family should be proud. It was a pity that Ian didn't appreciate it more.

She turned the horse for a full view of the mansion. It stood laid out before her, square and solid, like a man with his legs astride, confident of its own importance. The falling sun sparked off some of the windows, making images of tiny fires. The horse's head dropped and she let it graze, leaning back assuredly in the saddle. She wished Ian were coming down this weekend. Weekdays were all right because she'd adjusted to fill them, but the weekends were for him and when he stayed away there was a vacuum. A good word, vacuum; an empty vacuous life. Far away, in the direction of Cambridge, she heard a clock bell strike what sounded like a half hour. Time to get back, she thought. Back to the formalized sherry with Ian's mother and then formalized dinner and then the formalized sessions of bezique. Duty, she thought. Dear God, how she hated duty!

Henry Smallwood had a fat man's agility and went quickly into the offices of Samuel Haffaford and Co. John Snaith, who was a partner in the merchant bank and their nominee upon the Buckland House board, was waiting in the foyer and came forward, hand outstretched.

"It's good of you to see me, so late on a Friday," said Smallwood.

"You described it as urgent," said Snaith. "The chairman's waiting for us upstairs."

"I think it is urgent," said Smallwood. "I think something very serious has happened."

2

The flight path of the Lear jet brought them in from the West, over the silver thread of the Potomac. Harry Rudd had a brief view of a neatly patterned city and then the plane dipped further for its approach to Washington National airport. Rudd refastened his seatbelt for the landing, feeling again the stir of curiosity at the senator's approach for a meeting. Rudd rarely moved unprepared and within a day of the suggestion, through politicians whom he employed as lobbyists in the capital, he ordered a file on Warren Jeplow, to go further back than his chairmanship of the Ways and Means Committee and ten-year membership of the Foreign Relations Committee. The conclusion had been that Jeplow was the doyen among the Washington professionals, a committee and caucus room manipulator with a reputation rivalling Lyndon Johnson's. Certainly a man for whom it was worth flying down from New York to have breakfast, without the mention of specific reason.

Normally Rudd travelled with a personal assistant and usually with Walter Bunch as well, to provide legal advice. But discretion had been a word used frequently during the arrangements so Rudd disembarked alone from the executive jet, told the pilot to be ready within three hours, and hurried across the private section of the airport to the waiting limousine. It was a company car and driver, moved down overnight, so no gossip would come from a rental agency. The early morning commuter traffic was building up but it was still not at its peak: they'd arranged eight o'clock and it was still only seven-forty-five when the vehicle moved into Georgetown. Rudd stared out at the ghetto of the privileged and supposed there was a vague similarity with Boston's Beacon Hill. He wasn't attracted by the tradition of either. He preferred the upthrust buildings and shoulder-bumping of New York; that's where the money was,

12

the personal electricity, and the risk-taking. Not that he considered himself a risk-taker. *Fortune* magazine had described him as an edge-of-the-chair entrepreneur which he'd considered an exaggeration. Rudd, who was honest but not conceited, knew himself very well. He was a businessman and a good one. And good businessmen didn't take foreseeable chances.

The house was three-storey and brick, with a small rise of steps leading up from the sidewalk. Over the lintel and higher still, protruding from the wall, were television security monitors, so that any caller would be visible from inside the house. Rudd depressed the bell and stood self-conciously, aware he was under scrutiny. There was hardly any delay and Jeplow personally opened the door. Although the biographical file had been a warning, Rudd was still surprised by the senator. He represented Texas and saw himself as a Southern gentleman. The flowing moustaches which bisected his brightly pink face were completely white, matching the hair which he wore long, to create a patrician effect. The clothes were expertly tailored, the jacket cut to suggest a frock-coat: from photographs, Rudd knew that for evening wear Jeplow often used a stock instead of a black tie.

Jeplow took Rudd's hand in both of his and said, "Welcome, sir. Welcome to my house." Jeplow made it a prolonged greeting, staring straight into Rudd's face. Finally he stood back, gesturing to their right, to a circular entrance. The breakfast room was heavily furnished with what Rudd guessed were antiques, a large oval table and heavily stuffed chairs, with brocaded curtains and patterned silk walls. One was dominated by a display of photographs, charting Jeplow's political life. Rudd recognized Kennedy and de Gaulle and Churchill, each with Jeplow close at hand. The serving sideboard was against the far wall, with covered silver chafing dishes.

"A Southern breakfast, sir. Bloody Mary's and grits. You like grits, Mr Rudd?"

"Well enough," said Rudd. He decided Jeplow wore politeness in the same way as his hair, for effect. Rudd wondered if he was going to like the man. He took his drink, raising his glass to respond to the politician's toast.

"Appreciate your coming all the way down from New York," said Jeplow. "And so early."

13

"I was interested in your suggestion that we meet," said Rudd honestly, wanting to bring the conversation on course. Jeplow had made the drinks himself, just as he had opened the door. Rudd guessed he'd dispensed with his staff for the same reason that he'd brought his own car down from New York.

"Why don't you sit there, by the window?" invited Jeplow, refusing to be hurried.

Rudd did, looking down at the setting. Damask individual cloth, hallmarked silver and crystal glass, he saw. Jeplow enjoyed living well.

"Allow me to serve you, sir," said Jeplow. "There's kedgeree, kidney, ham. And eggs of course, fried or hashed.'

"Ham," said Rudd. "Hashed eggs. And grits." Jeplow was obviously determined the meeting would go at his pace. Would he have rehearsed it, like a speech?

The senator offered the plate and freshened Rudd's glass and then served himself. When he sat, he wedged the napkin flamboyantly into his collar.

"I've made a study of you, Mr Rudd," announced the politician. "Of you and your company."

"It's a pretty well-known corporation," said Rudd. He'd let Jeplow make the running.

"Through you, sir," said Jeplow, as if seizing an important point. "Through you. You've a reputation on Wall Street, with every justification. To take a Boston motel chain with a $3,000,000 turnover to a $500,000,000 multinational leisure conglomerate in ten years is pretty impressive, sir. Pretty impressive."

So was Jeplow's research, thought Rudd. The senator wasn't offering flattery: he was listing the figures to prove his own professional attention to detail. What sort of deal was he going to offer?

"I'm proud of it," said Rudd. He supposed he was, now. But pride hadn't been the motivation in the beginning. Business – and his complete and utter involvement in it – had been the refuge after Angela's death.

"Rightly so," said Jeplow. "Rightly so." He gestured towards the covered dishes. "A little more, perhaps?"

Rudd shook his head, not wanting any interruption.

14

"A history of expansion," said Jeplow, as if offering a motto.

"And one I hope to continue," said Rudd. He could detect a glimmer of light, far away.

"In the last few years the trend seems for you to have gone beyond this country, to the Caribbean and Mexico and Europe. The Middle East, even."

"Because the opportunities were better," said Rudd. Rudd recalled from the file that the senator was coming up for election, and that for the first time in fifteen years he was confronting a serious challenge. He said: "Were the opportunity to present itself here in America, then I'm sure my board would respond to it."

"Pleased to hear you say it, sir. Very pleased indeed." Jeplow sat with his head forward, the mane of hair full around his face. After several minutes' silence he looked up and said, "Ever considered expansion in Texas, Mr Rudd?"

Anticipating the question, Rudd shook his head at once. "We've two hotels already in the state," he said. "And we got those by takeover, not initial development. You represent a rich state, senator: I would need a premium price on city land if I were to consider new property." It was negotiating time, thought Rudd; he felt the excitement begin.

The silver head went down again and this time Jeplow spoke looking into his glass. "I noticed you came in a car with a New York licence plate," he said.

Rudd decided that beneath the artificial exterior Jeplow was a clever man.

"I've noticed your staff are working elsewhere," said Rudd. Wanting Jeplow to know he matched the preparation, he added: "A cook, a gardener, a maid and a chauffeur, I believe."

Jeplow raised his head smiling a smile that didn't have any humour in it. "I think we understand each other, Mr Rudd."

"I understand there are certain negotiations where discretion is essential," said Rudd.

"It's development land that's at a premium," said Jeplow. "I know of sites in, say, Dallas, Houston and Corpus Christi zoned for open space that is being offered at a quarter the cost."

"For public benefactor purchase," pointed out Rudd. "What use to me is land, no matter how cheap it is, if I can't build upon it?"

15

Jeplow shrugged. "One of the excitements about politics are the variables," he said. "Conditions change and when that happens, there's the need to alter decisions which were made years ago, without any anticipation of what might happen in the future." Jeplow became aware that both their glasses were empty. He refilled both.

"Anyone who owned land that was rezoned for development would have a very definite advantage," conceded Rudd. It had been a worthwhile trip. He said: "Even with that benefit, however, there would still be considerable cost, building in three cities."

"How long does it take to develop a hotel complex?" asked the politician.

"There's no recognized period," said Rudd. "But from development consent I like to see an operation under way within a year."

"And how much local labour can be absorbed?"

"The construction can mean work for anything up to a thousand men," said Rudd. "And there are, of course, ancillaries, like design by local architects and material purchase. Once a hotel is in operation, we budget for a working staff of 200, but again there are ancillaries . . . laundry, food supply, even though we are largely centralized."

This time Jeplow's smile was different, an expression of satisfaction. "What would you budget, for five hotels?"

The number surprised Rudd but he didn't show it. "It's not possible to be specific," he said. "I'd estimate $200,000,000." Conscious of Jeplow's frown, he went on. "That's why the consideration for development would have to go beyond land purchase."

Jeplow sat back in his ornate chair, fixing Rudd again with that politician's look of instant candour.

"How far beyond?" he asked directly.

Rudd hesitated. There'd be a lot of public officials in the state capital dependent upon Jeplow remaining in Washington. He said, "A state tax lay-off, for the development. And if we went for loans through Texas banks, which would again benefit the local economy, I'd have to have fixed term interest or roll-up."

"Roll-up?" queried Jeplow.

16

"No month-to-month interest payment during construction," said Rudd. "The interest is calculated at the conclusion of the development, when there is an income to put against it."

"I'd hoped land purchase would be sufficient inducement," said Jeplow.

Rudd knew he was in the stronger position. He shook his head. "I would have to have it all."

It was several moments before Jeplow replied. "If it could be arranged, what would your attitude be to constructing five hotels in the state?" he asked.

Rudd recognized that it was time for specifics: he recognized, too, that he had nothing to lose if Jeplow rejected him. "With land purchase, tax lay-offs, and proper funding through Texas banks, I would be happy to build five hotels within your state," he said. "Without any one of them, I wouldn't consider it."

"That's not a bargaining position," protested Jeplow.

"We're not bargaining, senator," reminded Rudd. "We're having a hypothetical conversation."

"The re-zoning is happening very soon," said Jeplow. "Within a month."

"I could buy it in that time," said Rudd. "But you couldn't give me the assurances I want in such a tight period."

"There'd be a profit on the land, even if nothing else worked," said Jeplow.

It was a good argument, thought Rudd: he won either way. "Only if I purchased the right land."

"Do you have a pen, Mr Rudd?"

Rudd lifted his briefcase on to his lap, opened it, and took out the notepad and attached pen. Succinctly, without any reference, Jeplow dictated the locations and in the case of Houston their designation numbers on the local planning map. Rudd wrote without interruption, capped the pen and returned it and the pad to his briefcase.

"If I were ever asked about this breakfast, I would insist it was purely a social occasion," said Jeplow. "No one would doubt me: I'm highly respected in this town."

"I'd say the same," said Rudd. "I'm highly respected, too."

He was back at Washington airport with thirty minutes to

17

spare on the timing he had given the pilot; it was the way Rudd liked to do business.

The headquarters of Best Rest occupied the top four floors of a skyscraper block built on reclaimed land at the bottom of New York's Coenties Slip. Rudd stood at the window of the chairman's office, with its panoramic view of the East River and Brooklyn beyond, watching a line of barges being hauled up river by a fussy tug. Suddenly its entire length was shadowed by a commuter helicopter arriving at the downtown heliport. His mind moved away from that morning's Washington meeting, concentrating upon the insect-like machine. Herbert Morrison could arrive for board meetings on time if he used a helicopter from La Guardia instead of risking the traffic on the Triboro Bridge, thought Rudd. But he knew his father-in-law would be late that afternoon, just as he was late for every meeting. His resistance had now degenerated to the level of petulance.

It had been different in the early days. Then the opposition had been constant and unremitting, to everything proposed or suggested. Rudd had had to fight because Morrison had the support of a board as angry and bewildered as himself at the overnight shift in share control that Angela's death had caused. Morrison had been implacably determined, prepared to use anything, do anything, to change her will. There had actually been a court action threatened, with papers issued, before Morrison had finally given way to the legal pressure that the bequest was incontestable. And accepted that he had lost a company as well as a daughter. It had never been intended that way. Being responsible, Angela had called it, insisting that they make matching wills. And in hers she had left him not only her own Best Rest shares but those that she had inherited from her mother. He had already been allocated five per cent, just before the hurried wedding because of Angela's pregnancy. With an additional thirty per cent Rudd had been elevated literally overnight, from deputy company accountant and junior board member forever fettered in a prison of Morrison's creation to predominant holder.

Rudd shrugged aside the reminiscence, turning back into the

18

room. The chair and desk were unostentatious, chosen because Rudd was a small, compact man who thought people looked ridiculous trying to achieve stature from their surroundings. He pressed the call button and at once Edward Hallett came through the linking door from the outer office. The personal assistant was a bespectacled, studious-looking man who worried too much; lines were already etched into his forehead and around his eyes. He carried a stiff-backed leather folder which he opened as soon as he sat down; Rudd thought he looked like a young curate, about to deliver his first sermon from carefully prepared notes.

"Good meeting?" asked Hallett

"I think so," said Rudd cautiously. "Certainly worth pursuing." He handed over the zoning references that Jeplow had provided, identifying them with the appropriate cities. "I want the sites fully investigated," he said. "Access routings, public services, everything. I know it's open land at the moment, but don't bother about that."

Hallett sat head-bent, making notes in his folder.

"What else is there for today?" asked Rudd.

Hallett turned to the diary. "Apart from the board meeting, only tonight's dinner with Mr Bunch and Prince Faysel."

Rudd nodded. The idea of how further to use Jeplow's approach had occurred to him on the return from Washington and he was glad that the Saudi Arabian would be attending the meeting. Rudd had brought Faysel on to the board five years before, wanting the Saudi-backed investment fund for the liquidity to expand into the Caribbean and the Middle East. The arrangement was reciprocal, giving Rudd a place upon the general committee of the Arab investment board. It was a concession made only to four other Westerners – all bankers – and was a recognition of Rudd's ability to find a way of involving the prince and surplus Arab funds in a Western business operation without offending the Islamic law forbidding *riba*, the paying or charging of interest upon money.

It had taken almost six months of talks with international lawyers and then Islamic legal experts for Rudd to evolve the scheme. It was thick with legal jargon and Arabic terms like *modaraba* for contract and *modareb* for managing trustee, but quite

19

simply it consisted of a profit-sharing arrangement. Instead of purchasing shares in the normal way, Faysel and the investment trust committed their money for management within the Best Rest group: while interest was forbidden, enjoying profit from someone else's successful management was not. In their five-year association, Rudd had never caused the Arabs a loss.

"The board will expect to hear something about the stock-holders' report," warned Hallett.

"Let's go and tell them," said Rudd, rising.

Hallett held back, following Rudd into the boardroom. Like Rudd's office it was an uncluttered, functional workplace, just a table and chairs, with a smaller table for Hallett and the secretariat. It was adjacent to the chairman's office, retaining a view of the river but with a fuller expanse of uptown Manhattan: there was a nicotine stain of smog building up on the skyline.

As Rudd had anticipated, Morrison's chair was still empty. Prince Tewfik Faysel was placed to Rudd's immediate right. Next to him sat Walter Bunch. Rudd had roomed with Bunch, just off the campus as Boston University, before setting up home with Angela, when he was studying accountancy and Bunch international law. Bunch had been the best man at the wedding, the person they'd gone to beach cook-outs with and who had promised to look after Angela when Morrison pulled the trick which had separated them almost immediately after the ceremony. And he had always been there, ready to help, after Angela's death.

Bunch was a polish-faced, smiling man of quick, impatient movements and untiring enthusiasm. He still wore his hair in a college boy crewcut and the business suits seem restrictive. Bunch was a man for jeans, sweatshirt and loafers, and skateboards and frisbys with the kids. There were two, at boarding school in the Hamptons. Bringing Bunch into the company had been Rudd's first positive demonstration of strength when he gained control of Best Rest. Morrison had opposed, automatically, and been supported by the rest of the directors. Rudd had only narrowly avoided defeat. With the exception of Morrison, the others had had to admit their opposition wrong. Bunch had been the lawyer involved in every negotiation during their expansion, sharing with Rudd the success of their development.

20

Next to the lawyer sat Patrick Walker. Like Morrison, the ancestry was Irish. The two men had started out together with a saloon on the Boston harbour-front just off Atlantic Avenue, Morrison serving and Walker doing the books in between the ordering. Officially Walker controlled them still, as company secretary, although the work was now done by an industry of accountants and lawyers two floors below. He was a red-faced, wire-haired man who looked at least ten years younger than his sixty-seven years. He wore widely cut suits of a thick cloth that had been fashionable twenty years earlier and he had remained unaffected by the half bottle of Irish whiskey that was his rumoured daily consumption. Rudd suspected it was more.

Further around the table was Eric Böch. An immigrant from Nazi Germany, Böch was the only survivor of the original Best Rest board apart from Morrison and Walker. He was a fat, indulged man who smoked cigars from stumpy holders and wore diamond rings on the little fingers of each hand. He was as interested as the Irishman in profits, but for different reasons. Böch's concern was to maintain his lifestyle of company limousines and company planes and suites in any one of the company hotels throughout the holiday resorts of the Caribbean, Mexico or Hawaii.

Harvey Ottway was the seventh member of the board. He was a thin, disordered man, of sharp, uncertain smiles, anxious never to offend or misunderstand. He had the habit of listening to whoever was talking to him half turned, as if he were hard of hearing, head nodding every so often in gestures of assent. He had been president of Belle Air and had parlayed his position on the board as part of the takeover deal, three years earlier, which had given Best Rest their own airline to service their holiday complexes from New York, Chicago and Los Angeles.

With the exception of Morrison, a pliable, acquiescent board, thought Rudd, looking round the table. As this impression came to him, the door from the outer office opened and Herbert Morrison thrust in. If the shuttle from Boston had been on schedule, Rudd knew the man would have told the driver to take his time, to enable him to make an entry like this.

"Sorry I'm late. Got stacked over La Guardia and then caught

21

in the traffic on the bridge." The apology was to the rest of the board, not to Rudd.

Herbert Morrison was an overpowering man, more than six feet tall, bull-shouldered and large-handed, his age suggested not by the greyness of his hair but by his once bright red hair fading to sandy-grey. It was easier to imagine him as a tavern keeper, shirt-sleeved and aproned, with pitchers of beer splayed from either hand, than as the president of a world-wide hotel chain. Which he'd never wanted to be, remembered Rudd. At the time Angela's death projected Rudd into boardroom power, Best Rest had five motels in and around Boston and two on the outskirts of New York, near the airport at Newark. And Morrison had been content, a paper millionaire with a business small enough for individual control and with no ambition to be publicly known beyond his own home town. His apprehension about over-extending the business and causing its collapse had been another reason, to go with all the rest, for the initial hostility. Even with the overwhelming success of the past ten years Rudd still suspected that Morrison was unhappy at their size and diversification.

"We waited," said Rudd.

His father-in-law looked at him directly for the first time. He gave an indeterminate nod of his head and seated himself at the far end of the table. After so long it was ridiculous that animosity should still exist between them, thought Rudd, as Hallett circulated files to each director. Maybe he should attempt to do something about it. He hadn't made the effort for several years.

He formally opened the meeting and invited acceptance of the minutes of the previous gathering. Böch formerly proposed and Bunch seconded. Rudd decided to concentrate first upon the outline of the stockholders' report and leave that morning's meeting in Washington until last.

"The previous year has been one of consistent and increasing profit," he began. There was a satisfied stir from Böch and Walker.

"Our declared pre-tax profit on the current year's workings will be $123,000,000 . . . ." Rudd hesitated, "and that will enable a full dividend, ten per cent commitment to reserves, and I would imagine that the announcement of such a profit will have

22

the inevitable affect upon our stock quotations. I would expect a rise of two or three points."

Rudd turned to the individual divisions.

"The airline is still insufficiently viable," he said, conscious of Ottway's head twitching towards him. "During the past year there have been substantial increases in fuel costs and increased landing charges at most airports. There's also serious cut-priced competition with the larger airlines. To combat this I am suggesting that in the coming year we move further away from direct airline competition and use the fleet for the purpose for which it was originally intended, the conveyor link between mainland America to the Caribbean, Mexico and Hawaii for our leisure complexes there. I propose our travel agencies concentrate more upon the complete package, with an all-in price to include the air fare as part of the vacation package."

"The figures seem to justify the proposal," said Walker, head bent over the balance sheet. "Belle Air is showing a loss of $350,000."

"As such, it's a small deficit," said Rudd. "But it's never been a practice of this corporation to accept any loss as inevitable."

"It will make our vacation packages appear dearer than any other," protested Morrison. "I don't think we should do it."

Rudd thought it was an ill-considered protest and was surprised. He said, "Not if the presentation is correct. I've had average statistics prepared: they show that during the past year our aircraft flew half full. At times it was considerably less than half capacity. An empty seat is a dead seat: we still have our fuel costs and our landing costs and our depreciation and crew expenditure. If we link our aircraft seats with our vacations we can undercut by at least thirty per cent even the advance bookable flights from anywhere in America to any of our resorts. And come in at least fifteen per cent below any comparable vacation outlet who have to sub-lease their aircraft seating on planes they don't own. If the comparisons were properly set out – I've already asked the advertising division to prepare a presentation – then I think we'd actually *gain* rather than lose appeal. People could read at a glance the savings they would make, flying with us. And if they fly with us, then they vacation with us; one complements the other."

23

Morrison flushed at the unarguable logic.

"I think the proposal sound. I formally recommend its acceptance," said Faysel. The Arab had a soft, occasionally sibilant-blurred voice, the English perfect after three years at the Harvard Business School, across the Charles river in Cambridge from the university Rudd had attended during a different period. Faysel was a member of the ruling Saudi family, with access to unlimited wealth, and Rudd knew from their own accountants that during their association the man had earned $3,000,000 in commission from his country's investment agency.

Faysel used his wealth, but he stopped short of hedonism. There was a string of ponies at the Epsom estate in England because he played polo at Smith's Lawn in Windsor. And the thirty-six-foot ocean racer at Rhode Island was not a playboy's toy but a yacht that he could navigate and captain, to championship level if business demands hadn't limited the time available. The tailoring was Italian, the shoes English. When the Best Rest company aircraft was unavailable, he had call upon whatever executive aircraft was available from the Royal Saudi Airlines. Rudd, who had no hobbies and considered vacations things he provided for other people, not for himself, envied the Arab his enjoyment of life.

"Seconded," said Bunch.

"I think it should be considered for a trial period," said Morrison stubbornly.

"Is that an amendment?" Rudd asked the president.

Morrison shook his head, aware that he lacked support. "An observation," he said.

"We can reverse, if it proves uneconomical," said Bunch.

"Let's vote," said Rudd briskly. When the count came, Morrison voted with the rest, making it unanimous.

Rudd turned to Faysel. "The Middle East division, under the indirect guidance of our colleague, has shown consistent profit and expansion. With the opening of the Best Rest in Amman, Jordan and Muscat, our total investment there is now fifteen hotels."

Faysel smiled and nodded his head in acceptance of the gestures of congratulation from around the table.

Rudd finally became impatient with the end-of-term report.

24

"I'd like to move on to something new," he announced. Everyone looked at him expectantly. "I think there is an opportunity for a worthwhile expansion," said Rudd.

"How?" The demand from Morrison was immediate.

The attention from every director was absolute as Rudd recounted that morning's meeting in Washington. As soon as he had finished Morrison said, "I don't like it. I think it's dangerous."

"There's nothing dangerous about buying land," said Rudd, anticipating the objection.

"Jeplow is a good man to have as a friend on Capitol Hill," said Bunch. "More influential than anyone we can rely on at the moment."

"How much would the total investment cost us?" demanded Morrison.

"There can't be any definite figures until we value the land and create a schedule," said Rudd. "I would estimate $200,000,000, over a four-year period. I've made it clear we wouldn't consider proceeding until we had either fixed term or roll-up loans. With our profitability it would make tax sense to commit ourselves to further investment."

"Where's the money coming from?" asked Morrison at once.

Rudd turned to Faysel. "I intend to structure it in a way that would have little direct effect upon Best Rest accounts," he said. "Under our contract terms with the Saudi investment trust, their cash infusion into this organization has to have positive commitment. My proposal is that it be designated to this project. . . ." He looked again at Faysel. "What investment were you considering?"

"I would expect $30,000,000 this year," said the Arab.

"My intention is that no loans should be raised immediately," said Rudd. "We can commit the Saudi investment as initial capital for land purchase, and not consider borrowing until much later."

"What happens if our profitability dips?" said Morrison.

Again Rudd was prepared. "Over the preceding five years our profitability has averaged a yearly increase of fifteen per cent. This year it's eighteen. It's inconceivable that there would be a reversal as large as that. We have an in-house audit every

25

three months, adjusting our forecasts, so there would be early warning if there was an about turn. I would not recommend proceeding unless we have tax lay-offs to cushion just such a risk. And any loss would be taxable."

Morrison frowned at another door being closed in his face.

"I think we should consider three hotels and agree the five if the terms are right," said Böch.

"Sites are to be Dallas, Houston and Corpus Christi," said Rudd. "They're all boom towns. On the most modest forecast we'd run on seventy-five per cent occupancy. That would return us a fifteen per cent profit from the second year of operation, rising to twenty-five within three."

"Seems a good deal," said Walker.

"An excellent vehicle for our investment," agreed Faysel.

Morrison shifted, angered by the easy acceptance. "Why the rush?"

"The land is being re-zoned within a month," said Rudd.

"It means moving without being fully covered on everything else," protested the older man.

"What's the risk?" said Rudd, picking up the point that had come earlier that day from the Washington meeting. "If we didn't proceed with the development we'd make a profit out of buying."

"It's a developers' dream," said Ottway, gauging the majority opinion and wanting to stay with it.

"I move," said Böch.

"Seconded," said Walker at once.

There was the slightest hesitation from Morrison and then his hand moved up, to make the vote unanimous.

Rudd, who was punctilious about everything, arrived before the others at the Four Seasons, despite the limousine becoming traffic-blocked in 52nd Street and having to walk the last few yards. On the way to the table, past the centre-piece pool, he recognized and nodded to an investment broker sitting against a banquette and a stockbroker whom he hadn't seen gestured anxiously to catch his attention. Rudd ordered a martini and sat with the stem of the glass held between both hands, disconcerted by the feeling that gripped him. The board meeting had been a catalogue of success, like every other that had preceded it for as long as he could remember; he doubted when the Wall Street analysis was made whether any other corporation could show the growth rate of Best Rest. And he was about to embark upon another expansion with an edge that meant a profit was guaranteed. So why did he feel so flat? Rudd didn't like a feeling of uncertainty: he was unaccustomed to it.

Walter Bunch arrived next, dismissing the guidance of the restaurant captain, bobbing and weaving through the tables. The man moved with college boy urgency, thought Rudd: he would have looked right carrying a football under his arm.

"I've been talking to Hallett about Texas," said the lawyer, explaining his lateness. "It's a long-distance enquiry, telephone stuff, but at the moment it looks just the way Jeplow explained it."

"I'd still like you to go down right away," said Rudd. "I want to be sure it's safe before we actually make a purchase." He saw Bunch smile and said, "What's the matter?"

"Thought it was about time we had some of the usual caution," said Bunch. "I got the impression at the meeting this afternoon that we were hurrying a bit, just like Morrison said."

Was he becoming careless? wondered Rudd. "Where's Faysel?" he said.

"Arranging a flight to Europe; he's got a meeting in London," said the lawyer. He ordered a Scotch and branch water. Rudd shook his head against another drink.

"Mary wants us to get together," announced Bunch.

"What?"

"Kids and all," enlarged Bunch. "We're all going up to Connecticut this weekend. Just cook-outs and beer and watching the mosquitoes zap themselves against the bug lamp. All you'd need is a pair of Levis."

Rudd, who normally ordered suits six at once to save fitting time, realized he didn't possess a pair of jeans. "That would be nice," he said.

"You're copping out," accused Bunch. "Mary said I wasn't to let you go without a positive date."

"Well I'm not sure. . . ." began Rudd but Bunch talked over

27

him. "I am," he said. "I checked with Hallett before I left the building. You've nothing fixed for this weekend."

"I might need to keep in touch with Jeplow about Texas," said Rudd.

"And you might not; all you're doing is opening talks. We've telephones in every room. There's no reason at all why you can't come."

The man was right. Rudd couldn't remember the last time there had been a weekend without some involvement with business. "Why don't we pencil it in?" he said.

"Why don't we make it definite?"

"Stop playing lawyers."

"Stop playing hard to get. Mary's made up her mind."

"All right," agreed Rudd.

"We're going up midday on Friday," said Bunch.

Rudd decided he could take the plane to Hartford in case there was any sudden need to move. "Friday evening then?"

"You'll enjoy it," promised Bunch.

He'd try, Rudd decided. He looked up at an approach and saw Faysel coming towards them. The Arab walked with a fluid elegance and Rudd was conscious of several women watching the man's progress towards their table.

"I've kept you waiting," said Faysel. "Forgive me."

They hailed the waiter to give their order. Rudd chose wine for himself and Bunch. Faysel stayed with orange juice.

"Going to London tonight," said Faysel.

"Walter told me."

"You know Buckland House, don't you?"

"Not for a long time. Morrison insisted I work at the Berridge for six months, on a hotel management course."

Rudd felt the long forgotten anger burn through him at the memory. Of everything Morrison had ever done or attempted to do to him, splitting him from Angela during her pregnancy was something for which he would never be able to forgive the man.

"Fabulous hotel," said Faysel.

"It was a long time ago," said Rudd. He wanted to believe that Angela had known he got there but he would never be sure.

"I'm not happy about my involvement," conceded Faysel.

"What was your last yield?" said Rudd. He knew the Arab

had moved into the English group under a scheme copied from his link-up with Best Rest.

"There wasn't one,"

Both Rudd and Bunch frowned together. "But Buckland House is the best in the world!" said Bunch.

"That's what I thought," said Faysel. "And why I'm so anxious to get to the meeting."

Three thousand five hundred miles away, two other Buckland House directors had met that same evening at L'Ecu de France in London's Jermyn Street, suffering the same anxiety.

"Condway's lying," insisted John Snaith.

"Short of making an outright accusation, what can we do about it?" said Smallwood.

"Challenge." Snaith raised his hand above his head. "I'm fed up to here with Buckland and Condway and their bloody pomposity."

"We're outnumbered," said the Buckland House finance director.

Snaith shook his head. "We'll find out tomorrow," he said.

3

The boardroom was practically a shrine to the company founder, William Buckland. Like the chairman's office it was panelled but the carving was more elaborate, intricate designs worked into the cornices and pillars. Near the fireplace there was a plinth and a bust of the old man, the heavily moustached Glaswegian features refined and faintly deified under the improving chisel of a Victorian sculptor.

Above the mantel was a sepia-grained photograph of the opening of their first hotel, the Berridge, dignitaries grouped in stiff self-consciousness, a mixture of bowler hats and frock-coats and button-sided boots. But for the fashions it could have been a picture of the present board, thought Buckland, staring around. Condway, his friend, sat to his immediate right. Next to him and already pledged to support the loan manoeuvre was Sir Richard Penhardy. He was Member of Parliament for a Cornish constituency he regarded with almost feudal propriety and whose voters, with fitting obedience, had returned him for the past twenty years with one of the safest majorities in the House of Commons. Penhardy was a recognizable parliamentary character. He wore a luxuriant moustache as a reminder of a wartime flying career that had earned him the DFC and drove vintage motorcars with personalized number plates. He shunned party office, however, preferring to remain a backbencher with time to devote to his City interests. Apart from Buckland House, he was on the board of five other companies. The next director was Henry Gore-Pelham, although Buckland didn't think of him as such. Gore-Pelham was a friend, as their fathers had been before them. They had gone to Eton together as well as Cambridge, and together made the grand tour of the overseas hotels after they had come down. Gore-Pelham was a tall, angular man, blond-haired and raucous-voiced. Buckland hadn't involved Gore-

Pelham in what was to happen because it wasn't necessary: he was sure of the man's backing. Buckland felt comfortable with people like Condway and Penhardy and Gore-Pelham. They formed part of the established society to which he belonged, the sort of men it was pleasant to invite for country weekends or be alongside on a grouse moor.

That couldn't be said for the others: and certainly not of Snaith.

It had irritated Buckland, having to concede two years earlier to the merchant bank's pressure to have Snaith on the board. He still wondered if he should have confronted the threat to withdraw liquidity funding and gone to another group of financiers. Snaith was a neat, precise banker who wore chain-store suits and drank mineral water with the lunch that was the traditional conclusion of every director's gathering, because alcohol might have risked mistakes in the calculations he always appeared to be making in small, loose-leafed notebooks. Buckland found the reason for Prince Faysel's abstinence easier to accept, although he felt the Arab's directorship was a concession, like Snaith's appointment. Probably because they had been for the same reason. A condition of the Saudi investment had been Faysel's election to the board. But the man had style, which Buckland liked, and despite his wealth and position within the Saudi hierarchy he seemed to regard himself as a working director, not a titular appointee. Buckland still wished the board had remained entirely English. He thought back to the impression with which he had begun his reflection. Faysel couldn't have appeared in the photograph over the fireplace. Outside one of the overseas holdings, perhaps, but not outside the Berridge.

Henry Smallwood sat at the end, plump and myopic. Smallwood had joined the board under his father's chairmanship and had revered the old man, imagining no one else capable of continuing the empire. That was why he'd run tittle-tattling to Condway, instead of approaching him directly. Bloody clerk.

"Shall we start?" said Buckland. He'd decided to make it appear a normal meeting, in the beginning.

The noise around the table ceased and Buckland cleared his throat. "Not a good year," he began. "From the provisional figures it would seem an £800,000 loss is likely." He was

31

consciously forceful at board meetings, like his father had always been. Except that the old man hadn't had to feign the demeanour.

Buckland was aware of Snaith's wince. He went on, "We're not alone, of course. The recession has affected everyone. And compared to some, we've done well: the overseas holdings, particularly the Far East, turned in a profit. The biggest problem is the liners: the unions insist upon a high crew complement and oil costs have risen astronomically. We can't properly run them as port-to-port vessels any more. And the cruise figures were disappointing. It's the recession spiral again, people with less money to spend."

"How much of our predicted loss comes from the ships?" asked Condway, according to the rehearsal. He had a rich, thick voice.

"About £550,000," said Buckland.

"What about economies?" said Snaith.

"We'd risk industrial action if we tried to switch to third world crews, which would reduce our salary expenditure," said Buckland. "There's nothing we can do about fuel costs, except reduce the cruise programmes. And if we cut back, we make them less attractive and risk further passenger loss."

Snaith hurried an entry into a notebook. Clerk, thought Buckland. Just like Smallwood.

"What about other economies?" said Faysel, consulting the balance sheets before him. "Our salary and administration costs seem extremely high for the London operation. . . ." He looked up, speaking directly to Buckland. "You know my association with the Best Rest chain in America. I've made a comparison against five hotels in Manhattan and Chicago. The running costs of our London units are twenty-three per cent higher."

Buckland stared hard-faced at the Arab. "Buckland House hotels are hotels, not units," he corrected. "The running costs are dictated by what they are – the best there is. People come to us because of a service and tradition they can't get anywhere else. And that decrees the administration costs. To cut that would be to destroy the very essence of what makes us different, what makes us the best."

"Surely you don't think a trading loss of £800,000 is acceptable?" said Snaith, unimpressed.

"I think it's unavoidable, considering the world conditions," said Buckland.

"Got to expect fluctuations, surely?" said Gore-Pelham supportively.

"Last year we had a royal wedding," reminded Snaith. "It inflated hotel occupancy in London artificially. We should have shown a profit, not a loss, on our London working. If we lost last year, with that advantage, then the prediction for next year must be worse."

"Why don't we put an efficiency team throughout the entire operation, not just in London but Africa and the Far East as well?" suggested Faysel.

"A what!" said Condway.

"A group of men trained in hotel operation and administration, to recommend improvements," said the Arab.

"And then introduce waitresses in cardboard caps to serve hamburgers and chips off plastic tables!" said Gore-Pelham. He looked around the table for support in the ridicule but Faysel said, "I was attempting to be constructive, not fatuous. There's nothing on these figures that suggests anything but increased and continuing losses. Are you happy with that?"

"Of course I'm not happy with it," said Gore-Pelham.

"So what's your suggestion to reverse it?"

Gore-Pelham shrugged his shoulders turning hopefully to Buckland.

"All the financial forecasts suggest the recession is bottoming out," said the chairman. "Next year there should be an upturn."

Snaith shook his head. "No upturn would be sufficient to reverse our situation, not on these figures."

"I wasn't suggesting the recovery could be accomplished in a year," said Buckland. "It'll be a process of several years."

"We didn't declare an interim dividend," reminded Snaith. "With an £800,000 deficit, what do you propose for the Full?"

"Withdrawal from reserves sufficient for a five per cent declaration," said Buckland at once.

"We drew from reserves last year," said Faysel.

"It's bad book-keeping," said Snaith making another calculation in the notebook. "Five per cent would mean £1,230,000 withdrawal from reserves. That brings us dangerously close to our support figures. And the City would recognize it. . . ." He snapped his fingers. "Just like that. It could start a share run. Worse, there could be a creditors' rush. The two together would be difficult to sustain."

"What about increasing our borrowing requirements?" suggested Penhardy, talking to Snaith. "Our overdraft is only £10,000,000, which against our assets if very small."

"We're spent up to that £10,000,000," said Snaith, pointing to the balance sheet. "At a favourable interest of 13.5 per cent, it's costing £1,350,000 a year just to service the loan. I don't think we can afford to increase our debts."

"It would remove the risk of any City speculation," said Buckland. Penhardy's suggestion was a good one.

Judging the mood, Condway said, "I'd like formally to propose the motion that we approach our bankers with the request. Another £10,000,000 is well within our asset strength."

"Seconded," said Gore-Pelham.

"Talk to the motion," invited Buckland.

"It's a panic move," said Faysel. "It buys us time but we still have to face the fact that without the proper cost control, throughout the entire chain, the losses are going to continue. There isn't sufficient support any more for the Grand Hotel concept. . . ." He turned to Gore-Pelham. "There are a lot of people who don't want hamburgers and plastic. But there are more who do. And we mustn't despise them."

"I don't despise them," said Gore-Pelham. "I just don't expect them to stay with us."

"That's the problem," said the Arab. "Too many people are staying elsewhere."

"Will you put the request to your people?" Buckland said to Snaith.

The bank nominee hesitated, looking directly at the chairman. Then he said, "It's my duty to put forward a request that has been duly voted upon by this board." The qualification was obvious.

Now it was Buckland's turn to hesitate, aware of the other man's reluctance. He said, "Any more discussion?"

From around the table came varying gestures of refusal. Confident of control, Buckland said, "Vote then."

The motion was carried four votes to three, Snaith, Smallwood and Faysel being the opposers.

"How long do you imagine it will take your people to respond?" Buckland asked Snaith.

"A week," said the man.

"Then perhaps we should meet ten days from now, for a decision upon the dividend announcement," said Buckland. There was nothing else to discuss, apart from the loan. Now the moment had come, he felt a twitch of nervousness. He'd been a bloody fool, he realized, belatedly. He stirred the papers before him, his eyes lowered. "There's another item," he said. "Something to be tidied up."

"An item of £635,000?" said Snaith at once.

Buckland's head snapped up, staring-eyed with anger. There was no way Snaith could have known about it unless Henry Smallwood had briefed him. They were a fitting pair, he thought: narrow, insular, blinkered little men who probably kept their small change in purses and carried folded-up squares of toilet paper in their top pockets and put handkerchiefs on lavatory seats. *Very* little men.

"Yes," said Buckland tightly. "Eight months ago I settled a private debt against a company cheque. It was an executive decision, involving the deputy chairman. . . ." He hesitated, grateful for Condway's nod of agreement. "Regret to say I overlooked it, until it was brought to my notice. I've repaid it, of course. But there's a need for a board minute."

"You settled a private debt against a company cheque?"

Buckland looked across the table at Snaith's question. "There seemed no point in bothering to put it through my personal account; it was for a specific purpose."

"It's illegal."

"It was an executive decision to advance me a loan."

"Which needs three directors," came in Smallwood. The man had a weak, rise-and-fall voice.

Buckland looked sideways to Penhardy.

"My agreement was sought," said Penhardy dutifully.

Buckland wished the MP had made it sound less like a recitation.

"In the draft accounts the sum is entered under investment," persisted Snaith.

"An accountancy mistake," said Buckland. "No one thought to ask."

"A mistake of over £600,000!" said Faysel. "Are sums like that often wrongly entered and then overlooked?"

"I find this embarrassing," said Buckland.

"I think I would," said the Arab unhelpfully.

"There's been adequate explanation," said Gore-Pelham.

"I don't think there has," said Snaith at once.

It was being more awkward than Buckland had expected. "I resolved a private matter through the company," he said. "I had director authority to do so. It was never my intention to avoid responsibility for the loan. I have made an adjustment through the accounts. . . ." He paused, unaccustomed to explaining himself and angered at the necessity to have to do so. "I accept an apology is justified to this board. Which I make, unhesitatingly. . . ."

Prince Faysel and Snaith were regarding him blank-faced. Smallwood was concentrating upon the accounts. Condway and Penhardy were looking away, as well. Only Gore-Pelham offered a smile of reassurance.

". . . . Just as I unhesitatingly assure the board that it is an oversight which will not be repeated," completed Buckland.

"How is it to be accounted for in the statement of account?" demanded Snaith. The three directors had made it legal and he was annoyed.

"I have already explained it was a private director's loan," said Buckland. He was sweating, the dampness glueing his shirt to his back.

"At what interest?" asked Smallwood.

Damn, thought Buckland: he should have thought of that. "Free," he said.

"For it to be free, there would have had to be shareholders' awareness and approval before the allocation," said Smallwood.

Another mistake, realized Buckland: he was being made to look extremely foolish.

"There's already been discussion about the effect of rumours upon share pressure and creditors' demands," said Penhardy. "I don't think this should come before an open shareholders' meeting." The pause was just too long. "You've already heard the

36

executive decision was within the terms of the company formation," he finished.

"I don't think there's anything here that can't be settled between the discretion of these four walls," said Condway.

"Neither do I," said Penhardy. "I think it would be a mistake to let this go to the shareholders."

"It would need a full directors' minute, properly approved by the entire board," said Snaith.

"Yes," said Buckland.

"Backdated," continued Snaith.

"Yes." The bastard was determined to make him grovel.

"I'd like to propose a retroactive minute entry, approving a temporary loan," said Gore-Pelham loyally.

"Seconded," said Condway, at once.

"When was the cheque issued?" said Snaith, refusing to be hurried.

"May last year," said Buckland. He felt as though he was explaining some lapse before a tutor.

"When was it repaid?"

"Two weeks ago."

"Base rate in May was fifteen per cent," said Snaith. "Accepting that as a preferential charge, interest on £635,000 at a full year would be £95,250."

"Are you saying you think I should pay interest!" demanded Buckland.

"I'm suggesting that shareholders might justifiably expect it as a return upon their money," said Snaith. "For a nine-month period, uncompounded, that would represent £71,437."

"This is outrageous!" said Buckland.

"So is using public money for private purposes," said Faysel.

"I think it would be wrong for this meeting to degenerate into unpleasantness," said Gore-Pelham. He looked worriedly to Condway and Penhardy for support.

"Hear, hear," said Penhardy, lapsing into the parliamentary cliché.

"Without interest payment in full, I would not be able to support any backdated minute," said Snaith. "Nor would I be able to let it pass unnoticed through any shareholders' meeting."

"Nor would I," said Faysel. "The investment fund for which I am responsible has £3,000,000 entrusted in this company."

"I accept an interest payment of £71,437," said Buckland. His voice was brittle.

"Move the vote," said Gore-Pelham. "I think we all accept a misunderstanding has arisen: there's no point in embarrassing the chairman further."

Prince Faysel, Snaith and Smallwood were the last to raise their hands.

"This meeting has gone on longer than usual," said Buckland. "I think we might have to forego the customary luncheon."

"It would have been difficult for me to have attended anyway," said Snaith.

"Me too," said Faysel.

Bastards, thought Buckland: let them go and eat their hamburgers and chips elsewhere.

Senator Warren Jeplow moved familiarly through the reception crush in the White House East Room, acknowledging the greetings and the nods of respect. It *was* respect, he knew. Respect and recognition. From the administration and the cabinet and even from the President himself. Perhaps particularly from the President. The President knew, like the campaign managers knew, that without the influence of Warren Jeplow New York wouldn't have been so solid in the last election. Or California. The big states, with the highest percentage of electoral votes. It was proper that there should be recognition, Jeplow decided; he was a kingmaker in a country which didn't have kings.

The Saudi ambassador had been manoeuvred near the window leading out on to the lawns, exactly as he'd been told to expect. The Secretary of State, Edward Bell, gestured and Jeplow feigned surprise, moving into the group. There were perfunctory and unnecessary introductions, because Jeplow knew the Arab from previous receptions, as well as from social gatherings of the Foreign Relations Committee. Jeplow considered it perfectly rehearsed; almost choreographed. The conversation continued but gradually the State Department people moved away, no one making it appear obvious, until finally there was only the Arab and one or two other Saudis forming part of the group.

Jeplow said, "We're always interested, on the Foreign Relations Committee, in how other countries regard the current administration."

"I think we've made our attitude abundantly clear, during the period of office," said the ambassador diplomatically.

"We regard Saudi Arabia as a friend," said Jeplow.

"We regard the United States of America as a friend," said the Arab.

"It's important that the friendship continues," said Jeplow.

"Vitally important," agreed the diplomat, waiting for the approach.

"Sometimes we wonder if the friendship could not be improved," said Jeplow.

"I'm sure my country would be interested in achieving an improvement, if one were possible," said the Arab.

"There are some domestic problems of concern to the government," said Jeplow.

"I'm sorry to hear of them."

"Energy costs, particularly. It's contributing greatly to our recession."

"Saudi Arabia has always regarded itself as a moderating voice against oil price increases," said the ambassador.

"For which we are grateful and which we recognize," agreed Jeplow. "Unfortunately there are other oil producers with less responsibility than yourselves."

"We do our best to achieve a unified attitude," said the Arab.

"We feel that security creates a situation where price increases can be demanded automatically at every meeting of the oil-producing countries," said Jeplow.

"Oil is a scarce commodity."

"Not for Saudi Arabia," said Jeplow. "It could afford to overproduce for a limited period."

"To what purpose?"

"To teach the less responsible producers that high prices are not automatic." Jeplow paused. "I know there would be fitting gratitude for such an attitude."

For the first time the ambassador frowned, at the sudden

39

directness. "What sort of gratitude?" he demanded, matching it.

"There is an agreement to supply thirty aircraft to Israel in the next six months," said Jeplow.

"We're aware of your arms commitment," said the Arab.

"It's no secret that the President is concerned at the belligerent attitude currently being shown by Israel," said Jeplow.

"I don't recall any recent protest," said the ambassador.

"The thought is to make it more than a verbal objection."

"Practical, you mean?"

"It could easily become practical, yes," agreed Jeplow.

The ambassador paused. "I've enjoyed our talk, senator."

"So have I, Excellency."

"It is essential for friends to understand each other."

"Essential,' agreed Jeplow. He was used to being an emissary, where direct government involvement might be embarrassing. He'd acted for administrations other than this one. Sometimes kingmaker and sometimes puppet-master, he thought. He enjoyed either role. That was why the Texas development was important: he didn't want to lose the power. Rudd would have to be taught a lesson, though. Jeplow had had to make all the concessions and he didn't like that.

Morrison colour-coded and indexed the report which Rudd had made after his Washington visit, and carefully filed it. Sighing, he went to the study window, staring out over the Common. His house was one of the oldest and best preserved on Beacon Hill, with the purple glass windows which had been the result of a defective batch of glazing but which now marked as original the houses which had it; the mauvish tint made the park look dark, like the last few moments before a storm. There hadn't been anything to storm about on what Rudd had proposed. Or at any other meeting, stretching back for years. Rudd had been lucky, Morrison decided. Efficient and clever and a good businessman, but still lucky. It couldn't last. After so long there had to be a mistake and, when it came, Morrison would be ready for it. He *had* to be ready for it; he'd waited too long and too patiently for it to slip by.

40

4

Rudd had never before been to Bunch's Connecticut estate and was surprised at its size. The house was four-storeyed and colonial-styled, white-fronted and with doric columns facing out on to a sweeping gravel drive that wound half a mile from the road through fir and rhododendron. There was a tennis court at the side of the house and the pool led off the rear patio where the barbecue pit was built. The grounds were roughly landscaped, some areas of tended grass but other parts allowed to grow wild. Yellow gorse and some blue flowers he didn't know the name of flared out.

Rudd, in his stiff new Levis, sat at a canopied table, drinking Budweizer from the can. The lawyer was trying to coax the charcoal alight and Mary was ferrying steaks and salad from the kitchen on to the outside preparation tables. Tom and Sally were in the pool, fighting for the occupation of an inflatable raft. Rudd watched them, smiling. His son would have been a year older, he calculated. He wondered if it would have been necessary for the boy's teeth to be encased in those metal braces distorting the smiles of both the Bunch children.

Bunch came away from the fire, wiping his hands on a rag. He tugged the ring off a beer can, raised it towards Rudd and said, "Isn't this great!"

"Great," agreed Rudd. Hallett knew where he was, so there was no risk of his being out of touch.

Sally won the battle in the pool and paddled hurriedly away from her brother in a churn of water. Mary finished laying out the food and came across to the table.

"What do you want to drink?" said the lawyer.

"Beer," said the woman. "But civilized, from the glass."

"These weekends are supposed to be rough," insisted the lawyer.

"Not for my fantasies they're not," said Mary.

The affection was obvious in the banter between them. They were very much in love, Rudd knew. Just as he knew that despite the opportunities the travelling and the circumstances provided, Bunch didn't fool around.

"Your health, Harry," she said. Mary Bunch was a dark-haired, thin-featured woman who looked elegant in jeans and sports shirt. She insisted on her own career and ran one of the most successful interior design agencies in Manhattan. She was a direct, honest woman and Rudd liked her.

"Cheers," he responded.

"I'm glad you came," she said.

"Walt said you insisted."

"I did," she said "Everyone should get out of New York at the weekends."

Rudd supposed he and Angela would have had a weekend place. Out on the Cape, he guessed. That's where her father had the summer-house and she'd enjoyed it there, walking on the beach and swimming and sailing.

"How do you want your meat?" asked Bunch.

"Medium," said Rudd.

"Hope you like it flavoured," said the lawyer. "I've put hickory chips on the fire."

"Hickory's fine," said Rudd.

Bunch went back to the barbecue. Smoke billowed out when he raised the cowl. He clapped his hands to disperse it and began placing the meat on the grill. He picked up a frisby, shouted to the children and skimmed it towards them. They missed it. Bunch really *did* look happy in jeans and loafers, Rudd decided.

He turned attentively to the house, listened, and then came back to Mary. Seeing her look he smiled apologetically.

"There's an extension bell," she said. "We'd hear the telephone."

"I'm sorry," he said.

"Don't you ever relax, Harry?"

"Of course I do."

She shook her head. "Surely this absolute investment isn't necessary any more?"

42

He shrugged, unoffended at the openness. "I guess it's become a habit."

"Why not try to break it?"

"I'm not sure I want to."

"Ever thought of marrying again?"

"No."

She put her head to one side at the immediacy of the answer. "Don't you think Angela might have wanted it?"

"Maybe," he said. Mary wouldn't understand he wasn't interested. He'd made arrangements for the physical side of things and that was enough.

Bunch came back to them, wet-eyed from the charcoal smoke. "Just a few minutes, " he said.

"What about Texas?" said Rudd. As it had turned out, there was good reason for him to be in Connecticut: the lawyer had come directly here from Houston.

Mary sighed theatrically. She got up and started towards the pool. "Tell me when the weekend begins," she said.

Bunch smiled after her and then said, "It's good, Harry: we could get every site for a fifth of the cost of normal development land."

"Did you put in bids?"

Bunch nodded. "We'd have our asses in a sling if the fore-knowledge ever became public," he said.

"So would Jeplow," said Rudd. "And I think he's got a very tender ass. How long do you think it will take?"

Bunch made an uncertain gesture. "Not long," he said. "No one's rushing to buy land they can't do anything with. We're going to need Faysel's money soon."

"He's given the understanding," said Rudd. "It'll be pretty much a formality."

"The steaks will be ready," said Bunch. He looked again to the pool. "Come on," he shouted to his wife and children. "We're going to eat."

The children emerged in a rush and stood, dripping wetly, around the table. Mary shooed them off towards the changing cabins. Rudd wondered if it hurt to eat with the metal devices clamped into their mouths. He realized he didn't know how to behave with the children. Would it be acceptable to give them money when he left?

"I've arranged to go back to Austin on Monday," said Bunch.

"So it could all be settled by next week?" said Rudd.

"I don't see why not."

"If you're going to be out of town, I think I'll stay up here with the kids," said Mary, "There's nothing at the office I can't handle by telephone."

"That makes sense," said Bunch. He looked at Rudd. "I'll leave Mary the car and fly back with you."

"I've been lecturing Harry on the error of his ways," she said lightly.

"What?" said her husband.

"To stop the human dynamo routine and start enjoying himself."

Rudd opened another can of beer. "This isn't exactly *Fortune* magazine's idea of the chairman at work," he said. The wind changed and he blinked against the charcoal smoke.

"How long's it been?" said Mary.

"What?"

"Since you've done anything like this?"

"Quite a while," admitted Rudd. He'd sailed with Faysel about eight months before. He hadn't enjoyed being cut off from any sort of communication apart from an open radio.

Bunch took the meat from the pit and Mary added salad to the plates before serving them.

"Do you want any wine?" asked Bunch.

"Beer's fine," said Rudd. The lawyer had used too many hickory chips, over-flavouring the steaks. "The meat's terrific," said Rudd politely. He'd eaten two mouthfuls when the telephone sounded.

"Shit!" said Mary. To her son she said, "Get it, Tom."

The extension was on the patio bar. Rudd watched, so he was ready when the boy signalled that the call was for him.

"Put it back on the grill," he said to Bunch.

It was Hallett, reporting the London call from Prince Faysel and the arrangement the personal assistant had made for the Arab to telephone him in New York at seven that evening.

"What is it?" said Rudd.

"He didn't say," said Hallett. "Just that it was important and he wanted to speak to you."

"Get back to him and say seven is OK."

Rudd cleared the line and called the airport at Hartford so that the plane would be ready. It was ten minutes before he returned to the poolside table. When Bunch brought back the steak, it was well done.

"I'll cook you another," offered the lawyer.

"Don't bother," said Rudd. "This is fine. We're going back earlier. Faysel's called from London."

"Now you're happy," accused Mary.

"What?"

"You're going to need help if you're not careful, Harry," she said. "You're at the top. Learn to enjoy the view and stop looking around for bigger mountains."

When he moved from Boston Rudd had taken an apartment on Riverside Drive, just off Cathedral Parkway, but abandoned it after six months in preference for the hotel. The Park Summit was the most prestigious of their New York holdings, on Central Park South overlooking the zoo. Originally there had been two penthouse suites but Rudd had removed the dividing wall, giving him the entire floor. It created a complex of four bedrooms, with a dining room separate from the main living area overlooking the park. There was a little used kitchen and a bar as well. Living in the hotel meant that he had staff available twenty-four hours a day without the intrusion of their presence where he actually lived, and a telephone switchboard which ensured he never missed any calls. Rudd worried about missing calls.

Mary Bunch had done the interior design, starkly modern, contrasting colours – predominantly blacks and purples – with a lot of glass for table tops and split room screening. There were five pictures of Angela in the main room, the posed professional photographs of their wedding and the grained amateur snapshots he had sought out and had copied and blown up after her death. He wished there had been more. She had been a shy girl and it had shown in the pictures; every one portrayed her wider-eyed than she'd really been, with a startled, wary look. The eyes had been deep brown, appearing almost black at times, like her hair. She hadn't inherited the red colouring of her father; when

45

they'd first met, outside the Mugar Library, he'd thought she was Italian.

There was a permanent security guard on the secondary lift from the publicly used fiftieth floor and a corridor's length to walk between one elevator and the other, so that it took five minutes from the downstairs lobby to the private apartment. As soon as he entered Rudd notified the telephonist but she said, "I've already been advised of your return, Mr Rudd."

Rudd was pleased at the efficiency.

"Mary's concerned she might have upset you," said Bunch. The laywer had returned with him to the hotel.

"How?"

"Talking about relaxing and marrying again. She didn't mean to."

"I wasn't upset," said Rudd.

"Why don't you come up more often?" said Bunch.

The over-flavoured meat had given him indigestion and although they'd left before evening, the mosquitoes had swarmed; Rudd could feel the swelling developing irritatingly on his left arm. "We'll see," he said. "I certainly enjoyed it."

Faysel's call came exactly on time. It was a long conversation, because of Rudd's concentrated interest and the questions he asked. Before it finished Rudd relayed the Texas negotiations and warned they would soon need the Saudi money if it were to be allocated under their investment agreement.

Throughout the London call Bunch sat forward on the angularly square, white chair, frowning with the effort to follow it. "Buckland House?" guessed the lawyer, when Rudd replaced the telephone.

Rudd nodded. "He says it's shaky. That it wouldn't be easy, but that there might be a way." Absent-mindedly he scratched the insect bite.

"Would it be worth it?"

"I won't know, until I've had Hallett make the analysis."

"The best," said Bunch, awe in his voice. "They'll be protected."

"Faysel doesn't think so."

"Do you want it?"

Rudd didn't reply at once. "Yes," he said. "I think I do."

"It would be another mountain," said Bunch, remembering the poolside conversation.

"The biggest," agreed Rudd. The prospect excited him.

The message from the Washington ambassador was judged sufficiently important for a full gathering of the king's council in the white palace at Riyadh. They were twelve ministers under the chairmanship of the Crown Prince, Mohammed Faoud.

"There's no doubt that this was officially inspired?" asked Abdul Hassain. He was the Finance Minister and chairman of the Saudi investment fund.

Faoud shook his head. "The ambassador was particularly careful about that," he said. "The meeting was clearly arranged by the Secretary of State and the senator has been used that way before."

"Then we should respond positively," said Khalil Mitri, the Foreign Minister.

"It will be expensive," warned Hassain. "We've sufficient reserves to create an almost immediate glut and that will certainly reduce the spot price of oil. And spot price selling, in addition to our agreed contracts, was providing the liquidity for our investment. Our guaranteed income is committed to established projects."

"Libya and Iraq might argue otherwise," said Faoud, "but we are the leaders in the Middle East. If we accept that responsibility, then we must take it seriously. The lessening of investment funds, which would be temporary anyway, is a small price to deprive the Israelis of the means of warmongering."

"And not just the practical means," said Mitri. "It can be leaked that the warplanes have been denied because of their belligerence, so there will be diplomatic gain, as well."

"I think we are decided," said Faoud. There were nods of agreement from everyone present.

5

Lord Condway had come from another company meeting, so it was convenient to use his car, even though the distance between the headquarters of Buckland House and the City offices of Samuel Haffaford and Co. was very short, hardly more than a quarter of a mile. The car, a Rolls Camargue, and the chauffeur, were provided by Buckland House.

"Didn't expect the need for this," said Condway, as Buckland entered the car. It was heavy from cigar smoke and the vice-chairman's face was more flushed than usual.

"Neither did I," admitted Buckland. He'd committed the afternoon to high stack blackjack at a private casino in Hays Mews and didn't want to arrive after it started; he liked to feel his way into the cards and gauge the strength of the other players. It was always different after play had started. He looked across at the older man, obviously contented after a celebration. "Good meeting?"

"Eighteen per cent declaration," disclosed Condway. "Company's way ahead in microchip development."

"Pity we can't drive our ships with them, instead of oil."

"Are Haffaford going to be difficult?"

"Don't see why they should be," said Buckland. Nor did he see why they had requested the meeting with both of them. In his father's day the banks had come to them.

"Don't think Snaith has the proper attitude," complained Condway. "Like a damned housewife worried about housekeeping money." He leaned forward to the cabinet recessed into the partition dividing the back from the front of the vehicle. It dropped open on the cut-glass decanters and glasses.

Buckland looked out to see how close they were to the merchant bank. "We'll be there in a moment," he said, shaking his head.

48

Condway poured himself a brandy. "Port gets tossed about too much in a car," he said.

"I regret getting tied up with these bloody people," said Buckland. "They were attractive at the time, at one and a half per cent lower than anybody else, but if I'd known it was going to be like this I'd have gone for the higher rate. Another £10,000,000 is a pittance against the company's valuation.

"Maybe it's a good idea we're going to see them," said Condway. "Opportunity to speak to somebody with some commercial sense."

Snaith was waiting in the foyer when they arrived in the Haffaford office. There had been no contact between them since the earlier meeting and Buckland said at once, "I'd hoped the request would be a formality."

"The board here didn't feel it could be," said Snaith.

"Perhaps it was badly put forward," said Condway.

"I don't think so," said the financier.

In silence they rode up through the floors in the lift and Snaith led the way into the boardroom. There were three men already waiting. Snaith's introductions were in order of seniority: first Richard Haffaford, the merchant bank's chairman, then Sir Herbert White, the vice-chairman and lastly Henry Pryke, the senior director. They were all young and Buckland regretted the red face and brandy breath of Lord Condway. There was a conference table, but Haffaford led them away from it to an area of the room arranged with easy chairs and a low coffee table. Everything was modern, light-coloured oak and rubber tree plants and smoked-glass windows.

"We've had your needs fully explained to us," said Haffaford, indicating Snaith. He paused "We felt there would be some advantage in further discussion." He was a heavy-featured man, with thick dark hair and full eyebrows which dominated his face. The spectacles were wide and horn-rimmed and he constantly pushed them back along the bridge of his prominent, aquiline nose.

"It's very simple," said Buckland. "A matter of liquidity: we need our facility extended by another £10,000,000."

"You make it seem a temporary arrangement," said White.

"That's how I regard it."

"Your trading figures don't support that," said Haffaford.

"We've subjected your workings over the last five years to a costed analysis: there's a continuing downturn. Compared to five years ago you're operating with eleven per cent losses against cost increases of twenty-two per cent."

The figures surprised Buckland. "Surely we must take account of the recession. . . .' he started, but Pryke said, "The recession was severe and obvious and we built it into our calculations: the figures we're quoting take account of it. Your losses are eleven per cent at the lowest mean average. A more reasonable figure is something like fifteen to sixteen per cent."

"Buckland House is the best and most prestigious hotel chain in the world," said Condway. "Don't you realize that?"

"Tradition has nothing to do with what we're talking about," said Haffaford. "This discussion is about loan servicing and equity and viability. . . ."

"Viability!" protested Buckland, at once.

"Your African and Far East holdings, a total of fifteen hotels, showed a minimum operating profit," said Haffaford. "They did so because labour costs are so low. In every other operation your running deficit exceeds by at least fifty per cent whatever you can expect from your income return. Each hotel appears to be run by the whim of its manager. You have no centralized cost control. There is a semblance of purchase control, but it's patchy in operation, so that if any hotel feels justified it takes its purchasing outside the group. Your ships are hopelessly uneconomical: there wasn't one voyage, even at the height of the season last year, when income compensated for operating costs. On the routes currently operated, your liners are cost defective and can only remain so, overmanned, inefficient and sailing distances ridiculous for current fuel costs. You're running services people no longer want nor will pay for."

Buckland blinked at the attack. He had expected a difficult meeting, but he hadn't anticipated this. The damned man was practically accusing them of being bankrupt. The feeling wasn't anger or outrage: it was an empty-stomached hollowness. Until this moment the thought of failure had never occurred to him. There were no hotels like theirs. They had everything. Tradition. Style, Service. Everything. Nothing could go wrong; not seriously wrong. He was sure it couldn't.

"Will your bank extend the facility for a further £10,000,000?" asked Condway, with brandy-based belligerence.

"Not unconditionally," said Haffaford at once.

"What conditions?" said Buckland, wanting to get in before Condway.

"A properly created management structure," said White. He was a thin, pedantic man with a hesitating, word-searching way of talking, as if he were frightened of saying the wrong thing. He went on, "There would obviously have to be sub-divisions, because of the worldwide spread, but we would expect to see cost control within a year, with centralized buying and distribution. Unless you can diversify into shorter, economical cruises, the liner fleet should be scrapped or sold. Staffs throughout Europe would have to be drastically reduced and in places disposed of. . . ." The man looked down at some papers before him. "Biarritz, for instance. You've got a four hundred unit hotel dating back to a thirty-year-old popularity because Edward VIII and Mrs Simpson liked it there. It's a museum piece. Converted to service flats, it could return a profit in two years."

"Service flats!" erupted Condway. "Do you know what you're suggesting!"

"Yes," said the merchant bank director, unimpressed. "I know exactly what I'm suggesting. Buckland House is relying upon a history and tradition that doesn't apply any more."

"There are other merchant banks in this City," said Condway, and Buckland wished he hadn't.

"Of course there are," agreed Haffaford. "To each of which you would have to declare your involvement with us and each of which would want to know the reason for your wish to change. And whatever the explanation, they would insist upon the sort of trading investigation we've undertaken. I'm sure their feelings would be the same as ours."

"Are we talking about the full request for £10,000,000?" said Buckland.

"No," said Haffaford. "Until there were positive indications of a trading improvement we would not feel able to offer you more than an additional £3,000,000."

"To avoid drawing upon reserves we want to declare a dividend out of existing funds," said Buckland. "Five per cent would

51

mean £1,230,000. That leaves us dangerously low on liquidity if all you allow us is £3,000,000."

Haffaford looked directly across the table at the Buckland House chairman. "There would be another condition," he said slowly. "To avoid misunderstandings about personally signed cheques being assigned to investment funding we would want a three-monthly audit period. So there would be a quarterly review for additional funding."

"This is not the sort of relationship I expected when I linked with your bank," said Buckland. He decided against a direct defence of the blasted gambling debt. "You're virtually taking management control for us."

"That is precisely what we're *not* doing," insisted Pryke. The third Haffaford director was a fat, bulging man who reminded Buckland of their own Finance Director. "We're seeking to get the management control that hasn't been in operation for several years."

They were rudely sure of themselves, decided Buckland. "I'm not satisfied that a proper case has been made out on our behalf," he said.

"I can assure you that it has," said Haffaford. "There's not one argument that's been overlooked."

"You would want your own accountants monitoring our running?" said Buckland, intent on defining the terms.

Haffaford nodded. "And properly formulated proposals, showing how your sub-divisions would be controlled through upper management here in London. Once formulated we would expect them to be discussed with us before they were put into operation."

They might deny it as much as they liked, but they *were* intruding upon the running of the company, thought Buckland. They were being dictated to, like recalcitrant children. He rose formally. "I will have to put these proposals before my board," he said.

"Of course," said Haffaford, rising with him. The merchant bank chairman extended his hand. Buckland hesitated, then accepted the gesture. "I wouldn't want there to be any misunderstanding between us," said Haffaford. "We genuinely want to help."

"I'll make that clear, too," said Buckland.

Snaith escorted them back to the foyer so it was not until they were back inside the car that they spoke.

"Didn't get a proper chance to explain ourselves," complained Condway.

"Bloody money-lenders," said Buckland.

The Haffaford directors waited until Snaith returned before beginning their discussion. To their representative on the Buckland House board Haffaford said, "Smallwood was right to warn us."

"I believe there are some good people in middle management," said Snaith. "Smallwood is a sound man: been with the firm for years. But the problem remains that there's not any decisive control."

"They didn't even offer a convincing argument!" said Pryke.

"We're already committed in overdraft to £10,000,000," reminded Haffaford.

"Which I think we've got to protect," said White, with his careful delivery.

The game was already well established when Buckland arrived and he had to wait an hour before there was a vacancy he could fill at the table. He scribbled his signature against a house docket and received £20,000 in £500 denomination chips. It was a centre seat, which Buckland didn't like. He played cautiously low, closing on fourteen. The two players to his left took risks, one actually calling for a card with eighteen showing and winning the hand when the dealer overdrew. The cards consistently went against him. He signed for another £20,000 and fought to get his money back from the two who were gambling carelessly, taking risks himself. He lost his second drawing within two hours.

Buckland pushed away from the table, obeying the gambler's edict against chasing bad luck. It wasn't until he stood that he saw Tommy Ellerby at the bar. As he approached Ellerby held out the champagne and said, "Bad run?"

With his free hand, Buckland gestured uncertainly. Ellerby
had been with him at Trinity, Cambridge; introduced him to
gambling, in fact. Ellerby had run the private house in Hays
Mews for fifteen years: it was one of Buckland's favourite gambling clubs.

"How much," said Ellerby.

"Forty thousand," said Buckland. He sipped his drink, looking around the club. It was filling up with evening gamblers, the
majority in black tie and dinner jackets.

"Glad to have the chance to speak to you," said the club
owner.

Buckland looked back to the man.

"Your account's a bit high, Ian."

"How much?"

"A hundred and twenty, with what you've lost tonight."

Buckland had thought it was half of that. He patted his empty
pockets and said, "I'll let you have a cheque tomorrow."

"I'd appreciate it," said Ellerby. "Not pressing, you understand. Damn book-keepers."

"Don't tell me," said Buckland with feeling. "I know."

"I wondered if I might find you here," said a familiar voice
behind him and Buckland turned, towards Prince Faysel.

"Playing tonight, your Highness?" said Ellerby.

"I don't think so," said the Arab.

The oil market is a volatile one and the unannounced Saudi
release of unlimited supplies had an immediate affect. Spot price
which was as high as $52 a barrel came down almost overnight,
even though countries like South Africa, deprived of oil because
of the Middle East producers' apartheid embargo, hurriedly
tried to stockpile through nominee companies.

The Washington announcement that the Israeli aircraft were
being withheld caused immediate protest in Jerusalem. There
was an emergency debate in the Knesset and the Israeli Foreign
Minister flew to America to meet the Secretary of State. Over-
confident because of their past relationship and forgetting that
the United States President still had three years of office and did
not, therefore, need to cultivate the American Jewish vote for a

further eighteen months, the Israelis scheduled a press conference during the visit, expecting to be able to announce a reversal
of the American attitude. It had to be cancelled because of
American insistence that the supply of arms could not be
resumed until there was a positive indication of Israeli intentions, particularly in the Lebanon, linked to the logic of Palesti-
nian recognition.

In Geneva, where the Saudi investment fund was headquartered, accountants calculated that the revenue loss because of
the manoeuvre would be $120,000,000 in the remaining trading
period of the current year and $210,000,000 in a full year. They
recommended investment economies over a two-year span.

6

It was intended that Prince Faysel should remain in New York for only twenty-four hours, so he used Concorde for the flight from London. There was a helicopter connection arranged, which got him to the downtown heliport by nine-thirty. A company car was waiting; from Heathrow to the Best Rest headquarters the journey timed out at three hours, forty-five minutes. The Arab entered the boardroom to find the chairman, Walter Bunch and Richard Hallett already assembled. The dossiers which Hallett had prepared were laid out in readiness, the issue limited to four restricted copies all of which Rudd insisted on retaining in the private safe in his office: only Bunch possessed a key, apart from himself.

"What's it look like?" said Faysel, indicating the file.

"Interesting," said Rudd. He turned to the personal assistant. "Why not take us through it?"

Hallett's face momentarily tightened into creases in his nervousness. He coughed, opening the folder. "Buckland House is the parent holding company for a total of four others," he said, his voice strengthening almost at once with the facts in front of him. "It's really a convenient split of countries, rather like our own. In London there are five hotels, with the Berridge being the front runner. They've all five-star ratings, but the Berridge is reckoned the leader, better than the Savoy, Claridges or the Dorchester. . . ." He hesitated, looking up at the other three men. "That's the hallmark everywhere," he emphasized. "They're always the best."

"Is London grouped with Europe?" asked Bunch.

Hallett shook his head, went back to his papers. "Page 9," he itemized. "Europe covers Paris, Rome, Venice and Cannes. A total of eight hotels. London's a separate company. . . ." He turned the pages. "There are nine throughout Africa, six in the

56

Far East and India and two here in America, the King Court in Manhattan and the Louis in San Francisco."

"A total of twenty-seven?" queried Rudd. The feeling of anticipation that had come after Faysel's telephone call from London was still with him.

Hallett nodded agreement. "And then there are the liners," he said. "A separate company again. There's a fleet of seven, the largest 65,000 tons built in 1945 and still the flagship of their commodore. Average tonnage is around 45,000. They predominantly run passenger routings across the Atlantic and to the Far East and Australia. In the last few years they've attempted the cruise market, competing with P & O and the Scandinavian carriers in the Caribbean and the Pacific, but their air-conditioning is obsolete. There have been stories in the travel papers of complaints and breakdowns. No record of any capacity booking. Their engines are old and expensive, too, designed before there was any problem with oil."

"What's the quotation?" asked Rudd.

"Wrong," said Hallett at once. "Last property valuation appears to have been carried out about ten years ago, from the publicly registered papers I've been able to find. Listing on the London exchange at close last night was 102p a share, which I'd say was too low."

"What about personal details?" asked Rudd. Morrison thought him impetuous, seeking takeovers and mergers on a whim, but the reality was that Rudd never moved without being as fully briefed as possible.

The personal assistant looked up at the Arab. "Perhaps the Prince can help there better than I can," he said. "All I've been able to get is impressions from newspaper clippings." He waited hopefully, but Faysel shook his head. Hallett went back to his file. "Sir Ian Buckland is the grandson of the founder," he said. "Took over the chairmanship five years ago on the death of his father. Married, with no children. Seems to be a keen yachtsman and something of a playboy. Lot of references to him at first nights and society events. Gambler, apparently. Lord Condway and Sir Richard Penhardy were contemporaries of his father. A third director, Gore-Pelham, went to school with Sir Ian. There was a merchant bank nominee brought in about three years ago. . . ." He hesitated, looking sideways again. "Prince Faysel went on a year later." He blinked nervously up at Rudd. "Not much, I'm afraid."

"That's fine," said Rudd. "Thank you." He turned to Faysel. "How does that square with what you think?"

The Arab looked immaculate, despite the 3500-mile flight. "It's ripe for plucking," he said. "At the meeting it was agreed to cover up an irregular gambling loan rather than create any uncertainty in the City. They're right up against their liquidity margin and the merchant bank has put its shutters up."

"Outright refusal?" intruded Rudd at once.

Faysel shook his head. "Limited availability. Just sufficient to make a dividend, but close audit and complete management restructure."

"What's wrong with management at the moment?"

Faysel considered his reply. "It hardly exists," he said. "The Buckland grandfather and father ran everything as a private empire and were strong enough to do it. Which meant that no one on the board had to do anything but rubber stamp the decisions and enjoy the profits. Buckland hasn't inherited the flair. He's tried to behave like his father without the knowledge of how to do it. As far as I can gather there hasn't been any head office scrutiny of running operations, and certainly not any visits, for three years."

"Christ!" said Rudd, who insisted on twice-yearly head office audits and personally toured each of their complexes once every twelve months.

"Are the cracks beginning to show?" said Bunch.

"Not yet," said Faysel.

"It won't take long," predicted Rudd. "We're this far away, have hardly gone further than first base with any sort of enquiry and we can see the takeover possibility. Somebody in the City will realize it, soon enough."

"Samuel Haffaford and Co. are financial advisers to Trust-house Forte and Grand Metropolitan: both would jump at a bid for Buckland House, if they thought there was a chance," said Faysel.

"So we've got to make our minds up," accepted Rudd. He listened to the howl of a police siren approach and then recede, far below; it had to be one of the most persistent sounds in the city.

"I sought out Buckland," said Faysel. "He's getting edgy."

"Did he admit the merchant bank resistance?"

"Not directly," said the Arab. "He talked vaguely about looking for alternative finance."

"Did he ask you openly?"

"Yes."

"What did you say?"

"That I would need to consult: I didn't say with whom."

"I think it's worth going for," said Rudd positively. It was a decision he had reached before the meeting began.

From Faysel and Bunch there were immediate nods of assent. To the Arab Rudd said, "It'll have to be approved, with a vote from the board. So if you're going back to London I'll need your proxy."

"Of course," said Faysel.

"Don't even hint a commitment until I get there," said Rudd, looking for a withdrawal route before he planned the attack. "We'll Trojan Horse it."

"What do you mean?" asked Bunch.

For an hour Rudd outlined the strategy he had begun to formulate within minutes of receiving Faysel's call after the Sunday in the country and determined upon once he'd considered Hallett's report.

"It would be clever if it works," said Bunch admiringly.

"It'll work," said Rudd. It would make him chairman of the biggest and best anywhere in the world. Where would he go after that? he wondered.

"If I'm going to set up the meeting in London, I won't be able to arrange the investment for the Texas hotels," warned Faysel. "It'll have to wait a week or two."

"We'll have to commit ourselves before then," said Bunch.

"Buckland House is too good an opportunity to miss," said Rudd decisively. "We've got the sufficient liquidity for the Texas sites from our own funds. We'll either adjust or reallocate the investment fund money when it comes in. It's a book-keeping entry, that's all."

"When shall I go down and sign?" asked Bunch.

"Tonight," said Rudd. "I want it all settled and you back here as soon as possible. If we go ahead for Buckland House there'll be a lot of work for you."

Herbert Morrison approached the cemetery carefully, aware that Rudd made visits. Morrison didn't want the man to know his own pilgrimages were just as frequent. The crypt in which Angela and the child were laid, alongside his wife, was on an exposed hill and Morrison shrugged deeper into the collar of his coat as he scuffed along the approach road. It was a large monument, with a small iron fence around the immaculately kept garden area. The weekly changed flowers were still fresh, but Morrison leant forward, lifting away some twigs that had been blown across, marring the tightly clipped grass. He stared at the inscription, wiping his hands across his eyes against the wetness he was sure the strength of the wind was causing.

ANGELA RUDD (*Née Morrison*)
1951–1972
Beloved wife of Harry Rudd
And Herbert, aged one day
Forever missed

Even here the bastard had tried to be ingratiatingly clever, insisting he'd given instructions for the hurried baptism from London because he'd known Angela had wanted the child to have her father's name. Morrison hadn't known then how she'd been tricked and cheated and pressured into giving away her birthright.

"Poor baby," muttered Morrison. "You poor baby."

He brought the handkerchief to his eyes and tried to get his collar up even further.

"He'll suffer, my darling," he said. "I promise he'll suffer."

Please God, he thought, don't let it take much longer.

Buckland began to quicken and looked down to where she knelt over him, hair forward like a curtain, expecting her to pull away. She didn't, instead staying crouched there holding him between her hands, draining him. He fell back, groaning. It was several minutes before he felt her release him.

"I like that," she said indistinctly. "It gives me a feeling of great power."

"It gives me a feeling of great soreness."

"Don't you want me to do it again?"

"I didn't say that."

Fiona moved up, to lie level with him on the bed. "Going home?" she said.

Outside some of the street lights had gone off, operated by a time-switch, and there were hardly any night sounds, only the occasional brief blur of a car engine.

"Maybe not," he said.

"I like it when you stay," she said. "It's nice having you next to me in the morning." She turned over on to her back and in the dim half-light he saw her pert breasts sticking directly upwards, tight little pink-topped mounds. He wondered if they had been siliconized, to be so firm.

"Do you like the house?" he said. It was in the mews off Sloane Street and very close to his London home. She'd moved in three weeks before.

"It's cute," she said. "You're very kind."

"You've given the bank instructions?"

"Of course," she said. "Why is it important?"

"It's listed against one of the company's overseas holdings," he said. He'd have to telephone Kevin Sinclair in Hong Kong, and then write, to be completely safe. That bloody business with the gambling cheque had taught him to be cautious.

"There couldn't be any trouble, could there?"

He shook his head. "I'm going to Cambridge at the weekend," he said.

Fiona gave a mew of disappointment. "I thought we could go down to the boat again: fucking in a bunk is like doing it in a drawer."

"I should go to the country this time."

"Do you make love to Margaret?"

Buckland hesitated, disconcerted by the question. Then he said, "No."

She moved away, propping herself up on her elbow. "Never!"

61

"Not for a long time. Did you make love to Peter, when you were doing it with other people?"

"Of course," she said. "He used to like me to beat him: he got very hard when I beat him. Would you like me to beat you?"

"Good heavens, no," said Buckland.

"A lot of men who've been to public school do like it," she said. "And other things."

"I don't like that either."

She grinned down at him. "Don't be boring," she said.

7

The only hobby Herbert Morrison had allowed himself, and that decreasingly with age, was fishing. He had developed the art with a determination to be good at it and briefly attained championship level. Until five years before, when the doctor had warned against such prolonged exposure, the month-long trip to the salmon-fishing rivers of Canada had been a regular calendar entry. Morrison would contentedly stand for hours up to his thighs in the freezing, rushing water, using the carefully learned expertise to lure the big ones and then play them, quietly at first, so that they hardly realized they had been hooked, and then with increasing strength until they were tired enough to be landed. His personal best, the year before Angela died, was 25lb: he'd had it stuffed and put into a glass case for pride of place over the mantelpiece of his study. He could still look at it and remember the burst of excitement that had gone through him when he'd felt the bite and seen the first flash of silver break water and realized the chance for which he'd waited so long.

It came again now, within minutes of Rudd beginning his address to the board, the same physical feeling of numbness high in his chest. Morrison bent over the papers before him on the conference table, unsure if he could keep any expression from his face; Rudd never expected him to smile and that was what Morrison felt like doing. Laughing almost. It had come, like he'd always known it would: he'd have to be careful – more careful than he'd ever been in his life – to ensure he made the strike at precisely the right moment and then let Rudd thrash and twist to exhaust himself. Not a salmon, thought Morrison, maintaining the analogy. More a predator, like a pike.

While Rudd talked Morrison made brief reminder notes, limiting the entries to single words with significance only to himself: there was a lot to be done before he could consider coming public and even then never completely. He looked around the table. How easy would it be to regain their following? Impossible with Bunch or the absent Faysel, he recognized at once. But he didn't need them all.

At the far end of the table Rudd sat back in his chair, coming to the end of his presentation, looking expectantly towards Morrison.

Even the predictable opposition would be in his favour, thought Morrison: it would be important for everything to be right from this moment, the first provable beginning.

"You actually propose that we make a purchase offer for the Buckland House shipping fleet?" he said.

Rudd sighed at the need for repetition. "That's the suggestion that Faysel is going to put forward," he said. "It's the biggest loss maker in their organization, so the appeal should be immediate. They can dispose of a financial drain and achieve the liquidity they seek from the purchase price. It should be irresistible."

"Why should we want to saddle ourselves with uneconomic, out-of-date passenger liners?" demanded Morrison. Everything would have to be available when the records were studied. He looked towards the smaller table: the tape was turning to supplement Hallett's notes.

"Because for us they wouldn't be," insisted Rudd patiently. "Buckland House are losing money because of the routes they attempt, twelve thousand-mile voyages to Australia and around-the-world cruises: even their attempts in the Caribbean fail because they've got a three to four thousand-mile journey to get there and then another three thousand miles back to England. In addition to that, they're hamstrung on manning levels by the British seamen's union. We'd have none of those problems. I'd refit the ships here in America to the sort of air-conditioning levels our customers would expect and then sail them either from one of the Florida or Texas ports. We could use them as a combination, carriers to our installations in the Caribbean or Mexico or as straight cruise liners. No cruise would extend 1500 miles in total, bringing fuel costs well down to manageable levels. We'd operate them one class, which would cut manning requirements even before we open negotiations with the union on acceptable levels. And think of the media appeal! These ships are famous, old and traditional and British, exactly the sort of nostalgia America loves. The Queen Mary makes a profit tied up on Long Beach, for God's sake! We'd have a winner, even if we went no further than a simple purchase from the British."

It was a sound, businesslike argument and Morrison sensed the approval of the other men around the table.

"What's the estimated cost?" persisted Morrison. This would all be important later.

"That's an obvious uncertainty, until we begin negotiations," said Rudd. "I've pencilled in a preliminary costing of between $4,000,000 to $6,000,000 per vessel: some will be priced more than others, but there should be an averaging out."

"Taking $5,000,000 as the average, you're anticipating a purchase commitment of $35,000,000?"

"About that," agreed Rudd.

"What about refit costs?"

"Expensive," conceded the chairman at once. "These are class vessels built to high specifications, teak and silk, not plastic and nylon. If we're going to go for traditional, bygone luxury, then we'd have to keep it that way. It would be a ridiculous economy otherwise."

"What's the estimate?" persisted Morrison.

"Maybe $1,000,000 per ship."

"What about the Texas investment?" demanded Morrison.

Rudd frowned. "What's that got to do with it?"

That would be a telling admission later, thought Morrison. "The liner purchase is only the beginning," he said. "I'm considering our total group expenditure projecting beyond this immediate year."

"I've already reported that I've committed us, by land purchase."

"I thought that was to be a Saudi investment," said Walker.

"Faysel is too involved with Buckland House at the moment. There can easily be an adjustment later."

"Even if we get tax advantages, we'll be involved in an additional total expenditure of $120,000,000?"

"That's well within our capabilities," said Walker.

Morrison turned to his original partner. "Not for the ultimate proposal that's been put to us."

"On the quoted valuation on the London stock exchange, there would still only need to be a borrowing of between $2,000,000 to $3,000,000," said Bunch.

Morrison decided he'd taken it almost far enough. "I can understand the surface attraction of wanting to acquire Buckland House," he said. "I recognize, too, that it would make this corporation the most prestigious in the world. Everything we've heard today suggests it is an out-of-date, unmanageable, collapsing organization. Even with the advantages we have through Prince Faysel, I do not think we should proceed with the suggestions that have been made."

Morrison saw the expressions settle around the table and was confident he had got it just right; he was going to enjoy the sight of them gasping, on the bank, when they realized what had happened.

"Any further discussion to the motion?" invited Rudd.

No one responded.

"I propose that the chairman open negotiations," said Bunch formally.

There were a few seconds of silence and then Ottway said, "I second."

"For?" said Rudd.

Five hands immediately went up and Rudd said, "The proxy of Prince Faysel is vested in me, for chairman's discretion. I put it in favour. Against?"

Morrison raised his hand.

"The proposal is carried," said Rudd.

Morrison was anxious to make the appointment immediately the meeting finished but held back from using the telephone from the Best Rest headquarters, wanting there to be no trace of the contact. Indeed he used a pay phone in La Guardia, letting Patrick Walker wait for him in the company Lear which Best Rest had acquired with their takeover of Belle Air. Gene Grearson had been his lawyer from the time of the tavern ownership in Boston: Morrison's request for a meeting meant re-arranging his schedule, he said, but if it were urgent they could meet at four that afternoon.

"I think you're wrong, Herb," said Walker, as the company jet headed north over the jagged, inlet-riven coastline of New England. "It's a good deal."

"It isn't even a deal yet," said Morrison.

"Rudd will make it one," said Walker. "That boy's got a burr up his ass that makes it impossible for him to stop running."

A day earlier the open admiration would have annoyed Morrison. He smiled at it but said nothing. When they arrived in Boston Walker invited him for lunch at the businessman's club but Morrison declined, wanting to prepare himself for the afternoon meeting, going straight to Beacon Hill instead. He stood for several moments gazing at the mounted stuffed fish: how long, he wondered, would it take him to land the prize this time.

Although the division of responsibility between them had put Patrick Walker in charge of accounts and finance in the tavern and in the early expansion days, Morrison had paid close attention to finance, with his constant fear of over-commitment. This was superseded by an altogether different reason after he lost control to Rudd. Since Rudd's elevation to chairmanship Morrison had monitored every statement, share issue, takeover account and financial involvement, searching for the smallest mistake he might use to attack the man. It had become his hobby, far more absorbing than fishing. He had created an indexing and cross-referencing system and believed, with good reason, that there was no one – not even Rudd himself and certainly not the company accountants working on separate, unconnected divisions of the corporation – who had a more comprehensive knowledge of Best Rest.

Rudd had insisted on retaining at headquarters the breakdown analysis of Buckland House, but Morrison had made sufficient notes and was confident enough of his memory not to regard that as a problem.

There was a master file, showing the complete spread of Best Rest throughout the world, individually tabbed with running and expansion costs, loan attachments and profit figures. The Texas hotel expansion was already annotated. Against it Morrison marked the development figures that Rudd had provided that morning.

He created a separate sheet, setting out the cost of acquiring the Buckland House liner fleet and then, ultimately, the group itself.

With the two spread side by side across his desk, Morrison drew up a simple subtraction calculation, giving himself the figure that would be needed for Best Rest to succeed, and sat back smiling with satisfaction.

Bunch had been right at the meeting in assessing their borrowing requirements at only $3,000,000. But he had been too glib. These were the requirements only if the shares of Buckland House remained at their current quoted price of 102p a share. A stock manipulation, properly timed and with the sudden effect of sending the price higher, would cut Rudd off from liquidity like a man left standing on an ice-floe suddenly breaking away from the glacier, and threatening him with just about the same amount of exposure.

Sure now that the idea that had come to him in the Best Rest boardroom was possible, Morrison returned all the papers to their immaculately kept and listed folders and put them in their cabinets. He then arranged his own stock portfolio and bank statements; like the earlier study, it was for confirmation of what he already knew. He could do it, Morrison decided.

He pushed back in his chair, looking up once more at the championship salmon, recapturing again the moment when he'd seen the flicker of silver. He supposed, at some stage, it might be possible to make out a criminal case. It was dismissed, a passing thought: it was the best chance he'd had – ever – and he wasn't going to let it go, any more than he'd considered losing the salmon that had almost broken his back to land.

Morrison arrived at the downtown offices of Gene Grearson early, but the lawyer emerged immediately, arms wide in greeting. There were handshakes and back-slapping and then Grearson led the hotelier back into the inner sanctum with an arm slung around his shoulders.

"Good to see you, Herb," said Grearson.

"And you."

"Read your stock report in the *Journal* the other day. Pretty impressive."

"We're doing well enough," said Morrison.

"Well enough! Believe me I wouldn't mind a piece of your action."

"I want you to look at these," said Morrison. He rose from the chair and placed before the lawyer his personal stock portfolio and bank statements.

Grearson looked down, briefly, to see what they were and then frowned up. "What for?"

"It's important," said Morrison. "From the portfolio you'll see that in holdings and stock options there's an equity value of nearly $8,000,000."

"Yes," said Grearson. The doubt in his voice was obvious.

"And there's $3,500,000 in the accounts."

Grearson looked up, nodding in further agreement. Morrison handed him a further document.

"Buckland House?" said Grearson.

"An English holding company, based in London, controlling the other divisions I've listed there," said Morrison. "I want stock purchases, Gene. Whenever and however any stock comes on to a market, anywhere, I want it. I'm not interested in the price, just the acquisition. That's why I wanted you to see the portfolio, as well as the available liquidity, to know how far you can go. If there isn't sufficient money, then raise equity against the stocks: I'll notify any authority that's necessary."

Grearson looked up, shaking his head again. "Why are you telling me all this, Herb? Go to your broker."

"No," said Morrison at once. "I want secrecy. Absolute secrecy."

Grearson sat back from the desk. "There's nothing wrong with this, is there?" He raised his hands at once. "Don't misunderstand me. It's just a question I've got to ask, professionally."

Until negotiations were actually concluded Morrison decided that technically he was not breaking any law. "No," he said. "There's nothing wrong."

Grearson pulled a yellow jotting pad towards him. "Nominee purchases, then?" he said.

"More protected than that, even," insisted Morrison. "I want the purchases initiated through American brokers but not made by them. The buys are to be made by European brokers."

Grearson frowned. "That's quite a shell you're making for yourself."

"It's something I've been waiting to do for a long time," said Morrison.

Rudd answered the door at her first knock, standing back for her to enter. Joanne Hinkler came familiarly into the penthouse, barely hesitating in case he wanted to kiss her. Sometimes he did, but not often. He made no movement and so she continued on. She stopped, just inside, allowing him to take her coat. She was beautiful and aware of it, but in a controlled, assured way, blond hair cut short and cowled around a perfect oval face, straight-nosed and with startling violet eyes. She wore a model silk dress, cut just sufficiently low to hint at the rise of her breasts, with the casual ease of the model she had once been before finding a better paid profession. There was little jewellery, just a slim gold chain at her throat and a single diamond ring; it was five carat.

Edward Hallett had found Joanne working through the best and most discreet house in Manhattan, just over a year ago. Even now she was unaware of the enquiries Rudd had demanded into her background, discretion and other clients before he'd made the first call.

Joanne carried only a small clasp bag; Rudd was quite straight. There were times when he didn't even take her to bed.

"Can I get you a drink?" she said. She knew the penthouse well.

"There's a pitcher of martini in the refrigerator," said Rudd. He'd responded automatically to her telephone call on the private line an hour before, but wished now he hadn't agreed to the usual visit: there were at least four calls outstanding.

The girl prepared his drink expertly, finally paring off a sliver of lemon. She added lemon to her own glass; with a considerable income dependent upon her face and figure, it was club soda. The telephone rang as she returned from the bar. It was Bunch, calling from Houston.

Joanne put Rudd's drink carefully on the coaster and then moved away to the windows overlooking Central Park, to distance herself from the conversation.

70

Bunch said he'd signed the realtors' undertaking on behalf of the company for the two sites in Houston, one in Dallas and one in Corpus Christi, and there was nothing further that needed attention for at least another month. Rudd listened, hunched forward over the low table, and agreed finally to meet the lawyer for a conference in Washington the following day.

"Sorry," he said, replacing the telephone.

"Usually happens," said the girl, moving back into the room. "How was the weekend in the country?"

Rudd smiled: they'd talked about his going to Connecticut during her previous visit. "Smoky," he said. "And I got bitten."

"Told you that you weren't a backwoodsman," she said. Sometimes they spent weekends together. She had a brownstone on 62nd Street and occasionally kept house for him. There had been times, in the early months, when she had wondered if their relationship might progress beyond a business level but she didn't think that any more.

"Actually I rather enjoyed it," he said. He wasn't sorry he'd agreed to her coming. It was easy to relax with her. It was an attribute of the profession he supposed, but what was wrong with professionalism? It suited him very well.

"I want to ask your advice, Harry," she said. She hesitated, recognizing the nearness of indiscretion, but said anyway, "I've been advised, on some investments. Told to go into either Ford or General Motors." Joanne Hinkler, who was twenty-eight, assessed her working life quite objectively at another five years, if she wanted sufficient time to marry, have children and settle down. She intended to go West, California or maybe Washington State. A complete realist, she intended by then to have a portfolio sufficient to support her for life, just in case she didn't marry or if, having done so, it didn't work out. She knew a lot of men whose marriages hadn't worked out and felt sorry for their wives.

Rudd shook his head. "Not with oil uncertainty," he said. "They're coming into compacts, but they mistimed it. Autos are never going to make a good return. What do you want, high yield or safety?"

"Safety," she said at once.

He offered his empty glass and she refilled it for him. 'Never

71

forget a basic rule of commerce," he said "People have got to buy again what they consume. Try food or maybe clothes. It's slow and it's never going to startle Wall Street. But it's safe."

She returned with the martini. "What about food commodities?"

He turned his mouth down. "Too volatile," he said. "A bad harvest in Kansas or some disease in barley and you're extended on a margin, borrowing to pay your debts." Rudd laughed suddenly, in genuine amusement. "Considering why you're here and our relationship, this is some conversation!" he said.

She laughed with him. The recollection of those weekends at 62nd street came to her after a while. She knew about the tragedy with his wife and wondered if it might have been different if he'd undergone some sort of analysis. It wasn't the proper thought for her to have and she closed her mind to it. But it took the laughter from her. Rudd was abruptly serious, too. Joanne was moving to prevent an atmosphere when there was a summons at the door and Rudd said, relieved at the interruption, "I've arranged supper."

It was the girl who admitted the waiters. They entered with discreet efficiency, pushing silver-festooned trolleys ahead of them. The table was set in the window area, complete with bud roses in silver finger stands. The sommelier from the restaurant personally brought the wine. Rudd tasted it and nodded approval. There were clams, Chateaubriand, fruit and salad. Rudd had just finished the shellfish when the telephone call came from Faysel in London.

"Very enthusiastic," reported Faysel.

"Did you fix a meeting?"

"The half-yearly investment meeting is scheduled in Zürich on Wednesday," reminded Faysel. "I said we would come to London after that."

Rudd nodded at the psychology. "So it's to our convenience?"

"Absolutely," confirmed the Arab. "I said it was a sudden idea that I hadn't even discussed with you but which I would pursue if he considered it worthwhile. He asked me to go ahead. How was it at your end?"

"Everyone enthusiastic, except Morrison."

"Whom we can discount anyway," said the Arab.

"So it's virtually unanimous," agreed Rudd. He was aware of Joanne's presence; normally he didn't find her intrusive.

"Zürich isn't going to be the normal sort of meeting," warned Faysel. "I had a briefing through the embassy here in London. Some sort of investment cut-back apparently."

Rudd didn't reply at once. Then he said, "To affect our relationship?"

"I'm going home tonight," said Faysel. "I shan't know until I get there."

To be deprived of the Saudi money would be an irritant, but no more, Rudd decided. "I'll be in Zürich on Wednesday," he said.

"I'll be there."

"I like the feel of Buckland House," said Rudd.

"So do I," concluded Faysel.

Joanne had kept the meat warm over the spirit lamp. She offered it to Rudd, who carved. She only took one slice and just a small helping of salad. The wine was French imported, a claret: she allowed herself a token sip.

"I've got to be away early tomorrow," he said. He didn't want her to stay, not now. He always felt guilty about his need, unable completely to avoid thinking of it as a betrayal. It was ridiculous, he knew, but he couldn't disregard it.

"I understand."

"I'm glad you came though."

"So am I," she said. "I always am." She hadn't meant to say that; she bent over her plate.

"And I shall be in Europe next week . . . I'm not sure for how long."

"Shall I wait for you to telephone?"

"That would be best."

"You will call, won't you?" That was wrong, too.

"Of course," he said.

Neither of them was particularly interested in eating, so they took their coffee to one of the low tables further into the room.

"It used to be fun on 62nd Street," she said. Why was she doing this! If she weren't careful, she'd screw it, like some two-buck, short-time-in-an-alley hooker.

"Yes," he agreed. It had been a mistake ever going there.

She waited and when he said nothing, she said, "We could try it again sometime."

"It would be fun," he said unconvincingly.

Joanne, who knew the rules she had broken and who was surprised by it, said "I should be going."

"There's no need, not yet. Not if you don't have to," he said politely.

"You've still got work to do . . . calls to come in," she anticipated.

"When I get back," he promised again. "I'll call when I get back."

He followed her to the vestibule, took her coat from the closet and helped her into it. As she turned he took $500 from his money clip and held it out. There had been too many lapses in her professionalism for one night; she took it immediately and said, "Thanks, Harry."

"Consumer shares," he said. "Don't forget."

"I won't."

"See you Joanne."

"I hope so."

8

Buckland turned the Rolls eastwards at Baldock, slowing not just because he was leaving the motorway but for the challenge he always set himself here, the one he'd played since he was a child, recognizing the landmarks of the shallow Cambridgeshire countryside as it flattened out for the eventual journey to the Fens. The harvest was in and the stubble ends were being burned to keep the soil pure, giving the land an unshaven look, like a five o'clock shadow. Buckland had been born here and educated at university here and this final section, just before he reached the family home, always gave him a feeling of security.

He contemplated the word, realizing its importance. He hadn't felt secure lately. He'd felt threatened. And frightened. It was an honest admission, the first he'd allowed himself and he accepted it was late coming, like so much else. He'd been complacent and careless, believing nothing could ever happen to his regulated, ordered pattern of life. And been wrong. Buckland shifted against the leather upholstery, uncomfortable at the thought. He didn't like being wrong. Thank God he'd faced the reality in time and become the businessman he was supposed to have been but wasn't. And that Prince Faysel had made it possible.

Buckland looked up at the oast-house and knew he'd missed four earlier sightings and abandoned the usual pastime, more interested in the reflections about the Arab's idea of selling the liner fleet. The family – certainly his mother – would oppose it. Just as he was reluctant. It was part of their heritage, their tradition. But he'd relied too much upon tradition. The practicalities were that the fleet was too old and too expensive but might, if Faysel were right, give him the way out of his present difficulties. He'd enjoy presenting the *fait accompli* to Smallwood

75

and Snaith and Haffaford's: showing them that almost overnight he'd reversed a bad trading position into one of positive profit and at the same time cut away the money-draining division. It had panache, the sort of entrepreneurial flair that in thirty years had taken his grandfather from a Glasgow shipping clerk to fleet owner and world hotelier. Buckland sighed. It was still going to be difficult convincing his mother.

He had his first sight of the estate from the hill at Sawston, just a flare of the lake and then the forest beyond, before the road dipped. He turned left, picking up the perimeter wall, and drove for another mile before he reached the gate lodge. He slowed and sounded the horn and waved as he passed, so the lodge-keeper would warn the main house of his arrival.

The grounds had been laid by Capability Brown. The drive, arrow straight, went between a regiment of upright elms, the fencing beyond spoiling the original effect but necessary to prevent the herds wandering across the road. To the left Buckland could just discern the mottled, nervous deer grazing close to the sanctuary of their wood. Nearer the Suffolk sheep, coats already heavy, cropped the grass to a maintainable level. The mid-afternoon sun still burned off the lake. The dower house in which his mother lived was close to the water: Buckland wondered if she were there or at the main house. It emerged from behind its screen of trees, the massively square pile that British aristocrats had erected as monuments to their importance and which had remained a talisman to success. Certainly that was how his grandfather had regarded it, and then his father and now Buckland. He shuddered, as if he were physically cold: it was inconceivable that he could lose it, just as it was inconceivable that anything serious, damagingly, harmfully serious, could ever happen to Buckland House. The business, like the house in front of him, was indestructible: in need of modernization, maybe, but absolutely indestructible.

The gravel crackled under his wheels as Buckland turned the car around the landscaped centrepiece at the end of the drive, complete with water-dribbling nymphs, and parked alongside the other cars. His wife's BMW was first, with Vanessa's Porsche too close alongside: there was a dent in the rear bumper and it was mud-caked from the drive from Yorkshire.

76

The door opened as he approached and the butler emerged to greet him. "Good afternoon, Sir."

"Afternoon Holmes."

"An easy journey?"

"Comparatively so."

"Lady Margaret is upstairs in her dressing-room," reported Holmes. "Lady Vanessa is at the dower house, with your mother. I was asked to serve tea at four, if you arrived in time."

"Fine," said Buckland. He might as well get it over with at once, he thought.

Leaving the butler to bring his things from the car, Buckland entered the house. He crossed the panelled, marble-floored hall to the wide, curving staircase to the first floor. With the canniness of a true Scot – until he died and despite immense wealth, the old man had every day set aside £1 in a savings box – his grandfather had sought good advice, and the oils lining the stairway and hallways were all genuine and good. The last insurance valuation, two years earlier, had estimated their worth at £1,000,000. Indestructible, thought Buckland again.

Margaret was reading, her feet up on a chaise-longue, when he entered her room. She looked up and smiled. "I thought I heard the car," she said.

He crossed to her and kissed her briefly on the cheek, a friendly gesture. Which is what they were, he thought, continuing the newly found honesty. Good friends: they had been for as long as he could remember. Margaret's ambassador father owned an estate at Histon. They had played together as children, spent prep school holidays in each other's homes and then, in their teens, gone to her parents' villa at Ostia for combined family holidays. She'd been at Girton, reading modern languages, when he'd been at Trinity, and weekends and long vacs had been like schooldays again, either here or at Histon. There had never been a positive decision to get married. It had always been understood by both families that they would, inevitably: never if, always when. Indeed, there were times when Buckland had imagined his father fonder of Margaret than he had been of him.

It had been a mistake, trying to turn a friendship into a marriage. It was something they never spoke about, but he believed she felt it as much as he did.

The magazine she was reading was Italian and he decided she looked Latin, dark-haired, dark-eyed and with a sallowness to her skin unusual for an English woman. She was heavy-busted but otherwise slim, someone who looked after herself with careful diet and proper exercise. There were three horses in the stable, but she didn't ride to hounds like Vanessa; Margaret was a gentle woman who thought foxhunting cruel and obscene. The two women never argued about it.

"How's London?"

Even their conversation had a friendly politeness about it, he thought. "Traffic-jammed and dirty and full of tourists."

"Which should fill the hotels."

Buckland had gone to the window, looking out towards the lake and the smaller house for the approach of his mother and sister. He turned sharply, momentarily forgetting there was no easy way she could know and that it had to be an innocent remark.

"What's the matter?" she said, frowning at his attitude.

"Nothing."

She remained doubtful. "I was thinking of coming to London next week," she said. "There's the under-privileged children's ball to arrange." Margaret took seriously her chairmanship of the organizing committee.

"That would be nice," he said. Buckland never took women to their Sloane Square house but she always warned him she was returning. "How's mother been?"

"Matriarchal," said Margaret shortly. "She's insisting that Holmes makes separate accounts for the smaller house."

"Why?"

"Something about maintaining her independence, I suppose."

"That's not necessary."

"I told her that. She said that was how she wanted it and that was the end of the conversation. She's very good at ending conversations."

From the window he caught movement and turned to see his sister and mother approaching: the old lady was using a stick and supporting herself against Vanessa's arm.

"They're coming," he said.

Margaret swung her legs off the chaise-longue. "Something worrying you?" she said. "You seem distracted."

"I'll tell you downstairs."

The other two women were already in the drawing-room when Buckland and his wife arrived. Irene, Lady Buckland was sitting stiffly on the sofa arranged before the fireplace, the stick immediately before her and both hands cupped over its handle. It was a pose, like the way she had walked through the garden. She wore a full-skirted black dress, long-sleeved and high-necked and her completely white hair was coiffured and tightly ridged in waves around her face. There was no make-up. She fixed him with sharp, blue eyes and said, "Good afternoon, Ian."

"Mother," he said. He crossed to kiss her: she even smelt slightly of lavender.

Vanessa was in the window seat, looking into the room with a faint expression of amusement. She was a yellow-haired, heavily featured woman, high cheek-boned and prominent-nosed. She was too large-breasted to wear the silk shirt without a bra; Buckland didn't know if it were fashionable, but he thought the skirt too short, as well.

"Hello brother," she said.

"How's Yorkshire, Vanessa?" Her husband, Sir Rupert Hartland, farmed one of the largest estates in the county.

"Big and boring," she said. She was aware of her mother's head turn of disapproval but she still lighted the cigarette.

The maid came in with the tea, setting it before Margaret. She poured and Vanessa handed it round. His sister should definitely have worn a bra, decided Buckland. "I'm glad we're altogether," he said. Something's arisen which we need to talk through: because of the share composition of the company, I'm going to need your approval."

Lady Buckland said, "The company! Can't the board handle it?"

"Not this," said Buckland. He put his tea aside, untouched, and explained the trading difficulties that Buckland House was confronting, aware as he spoke of his mother stiffening further and of the complete attention of Vanessa and his wife.

"Are you telling me that we're in financial difficulty?" demanded the old lady.

"No," said Buckland. "I'm saying that there have been set-backs, that we have a running problem and that to solve it I want to dispose of the liner fleet."

Red patches of anger picked out Lady Buckland's cheeks. "Your grandfather founded that fleet," she said. "Your father raised it to something greater than either Cunard or P & O!"

"Both of which have minimized and trimmed their liner commitment," said Buckland. "There's no place for passenger ships any more: not ships like ours, on routes like ours. We've got a heaven-sent opportunity to dispose of something draining us financially and settle out debts."

"No!" said his mother positively. "I shall not agree, under any circumstances. The fleet is an integral part of Buckland House and shall remain so."

"Then you're prepared to risk the entire company?" he said. Apart from himself, she held the largest single apportionment of controlling shares: her agreement was essential.

"What are you talking about?"

"What I've already explained. We need money. And the bank is insisting upon tighter control and re-structuring before they will allow us to have it. If our losses continue – and if we retain the fleet, it's inevitable that they will – then that insistence will increase."

"They can't control the company," said the woman stubbornly. "We do. And there's not a thing they can do about it."

"They control the money," said Buckland patiently, knowing it would be wrong to lose his temper. "We can't operate without their funds."

"Go to other banks."

He shook his head. "No one else will lend us working capital if they know we've already been refused by our existing merchant bank."

"Is this your fault?" demanded the old lady.

"Mother!" protested Vanessa, just ahead of Margaret.

"There was never a conversation like this in the drawing-room of my house when his father and grandfather were alive."

Buckland hesitated, confronting the question and remembering the honesty of the drive from London. He supposed the answer was yes. "I am the chairman of the board," he said. "If you want to make the accusation, then I take the responsibility." He had imagined embarrassment at the confession, but he didn't feel it.

"I'm disappointed," said his mother.

"I accept that, too," said Buckland. "What I'm trying to do is stop a worsening situation."

"They are wonderful ships," said the old lady nostalgically.

"They're a thing of the past," argued Buckland.

"Is this the only way?" said Vanessa.

"Yes," said Buckland. "It would completely reverse the situation."

"It seems common sense to me," said Margaret loyally. "The ships are only a small part of the company, anyway: getting rid of them won't affect anything, overall."

"It's the tradition," insisted the old lady. Her voice was weakening.

"Which we can no longer afford," said Buckland, deciding it was time to be forceful.

"I won't oppose it," said Vanessa.

"Neither will I," said Margaret.

Lady Buckland put her forehead against the handle of her stick, another theatrical pose. She said, "I want to think about it." She looked up at the two other women, making her choice, and then said, "Margaret, help me back to the house."

Buckland and his sister stood watching his mother leave the room on Margaret's arm. When the door closed behind the couple Vanessa turned and said, "How long has she been doing the Grande Dame?"

"I've not been as aware of it as I was today," he said.

"I suppose at seventy we must allow her an occasional eccentricity."

"Think she'll come around?"

Vanessa shrugged. "I believe her, about being disappointed: the company – every part of it – has always been a very personal thing."

"The ships should go."

"If those are the figures, then I accept that. It's still unfortunate."

"Don't you think you should wear something under that blouse?"

81

She cupped both hands, lifting her breasts. "I'm rather proud of them."

There had always been an intimacy between them in all things. "You're wobbling about like melting jelly," he said.

"Mother complained too . . ." Vanessa stopped, giggling. "She said I should wear a bodice. I don't suppose she's going senile?"

"I wondered if you'd bring someone down with you," said Buckland.

"I might be promiscuous, brother dear, but I wouldn't flaunt it quite so openly under mother's nose. . . ." She smiled again, confessionally. "There's a gorgeous lawyer just joined the hunt. You'll have to meet him soon."

"How's Rupert?"

Vanessa sighed heavily. "Full of crop yields and putting cows to bulls and wheat cultivation problems. How are things with Margaret?"

"Usual."

"She's very long suffering."

"It works. Rather well, actually. We're both happy."

"What if she met someone else; or you did?"

The question surprised Buckland. "I've not really thought about it," he admitted. "I can't imagine it happening to either of us." He couldn't think of anything he'd like less than being permanently linked with Fiona Harvey. He actually enjoyed being with Margaret during their weekends. And was looking forward to her coming to London.

"I suppose it's the same between Rupert and me," she conceded. "To change would be too much trouble."

Buckland had never contemplated a change but he didn't want to pursue the conversation with his sister. "How long are you staying down?" he said.

She shrugged. "There's a rumour that the royals are riding with us at the end of the month," she said. "I intend being back for that."

"Snob," he said.

She laughed. "I enjoy getting my picture in *Tatler*."

So did he, thought Buckland. There hadn't been one for some time. "You opening up the London house?"

"Haven't made my mind up yet," she said. "It would mean bringing staff from Yorkshire and Rupert always makes a fuss about that. My husband is bloody mean."

"Margaret's coming back with me; why not stay with us in Sloane Square?"

"I might do that," she said. "What's this rich American like who's interested in the ships?"

'I haven't met him yet," said Buckland.

"If things are as bad with the fleet as you say they are, it'll be a coup for you to pull it off," said Vanessa.

"Yes," agreed Buckland. "It will." He was looking forward to the negotiations.

The deer were being culled, so the dinner was venison. Afterwards they played bezique. Only Lady Buckland was interested and she won. Buckland escorted her back to her own house and went in with her, to ensure that the nurse would know she had returned.

"There's no way to avoid the fleet being sold?" she demanded in the hall. It was the first time it had been mentioned during the evening.

"No practicable way, no."

"This will be the end of it, won't it? There'll be no more sacrifices?"

"Yes," he said. "This will solve everything."

"I'll agree to it then," she said. "I don't want to, but I'll agree."

"Thank you."

"You said you were to blame."

"I *accepted* the blame."

"Don't play with words," she said irritably. "You were left an empire. Don't you dare risk losing it."

"I won't," said Buckland.

"I mean it: what we've got is too precious to lose."

The women had retired by the time Buckland got back to the main house. Margaret's dressing-room was between their respective bedrooms and he heard her moving around in it, so he went to the linking door: she'd taken off her dress and was wearing a thin robe, cleaning the make-up from her face. Her hair was loose and he thought she looked far more attractive than Vanessa. Fiona, too, for that matter.

"Mother's agreed," he said.

"Vanessa and I talked about it after you'd gone: we thought she would."

He went further into the room and sat on the chaise-longue she'd occupied earlier. "I do feel personally responsible," he said.

She turned away from the mirror. "Is it *very* serious?"

He smiled, trying to dispel the sudden depression. "Not if the liner sale goes through," he said.

Her movement had sagged the dressing-gown and he saw she was naked beneath. She was aware of his look and stayed as she was, waiting.

Buckland rose awkwardly. "Goodnight, Margaret," he said.

"Goodnight, Ian," she said, disappointed.

He kissed her, as fleetingly as he had done earlier in the day, and carefully closed the door behind him into his own room. He really wished he could think of her as something more than a friend.

The hierarchy – and therefore the rule – of the Saudi royal family is established through interlocking polygamous marriages, half-brother to half-brother, half-cousin to half-cousin. Had his father lived, instead of dying in an air crash at the age of forty, Faysel would have been directly in line for the throne, third behind two elder brothers. But with his father's death, his uncle's family had gained supremacy. His cousins had come ill-prepared and late to such an inheritance: the Faoud dynasty feared they could lose the throne as quickly as they had gained it, particularly now that succession was no longer an automatic right but increasingly determined by ability. Of all the challenging factions, the Faysel family was viewed as the most dangerous.

"You mustn't forget that," warned Prince Hassain. He headed another branch of the family but was separated by a tribal marriage and no direct threat; traditionally the Hassain family had backed the Faysels.

"I'm not talking about family feuds," said Faysel. "I'm talking business."

"You might not be, but the Crown Prince will," said Hassain.

He gestured and red tea was poured for both of them. Hassain and Faysel wore the white robes of Mecca pilgrims. They had both been educated in the West and spoke English to protect themselves among Hassain's staff.

"That's ridiculous."

"But understandable. And what's happened makes unarguable political sense."

"What about business sense?"

"That's debatable, I agree," said Hassain. "But for the moment one outweighs the other."

"Two years is a long time to allow uncertainty with business partners," said Faysal.

"I've checked the accountants' figures," said Hassain, like Faysel a graduate of the Harvard Business School. "That's the minimum length of time for the sort of cut-backs being imposed upon us."

Faysel rose from the floor cushions upon which he had been squatting, Arab-style. "I still think I should see Faoud."

"It won't do any good."

"I should still see him."

The protocol of Arab rule is strictly governed, with even the lowliest beggar having the unquestioned right of audience with the king, so there had been no necessity for Faysel to arrange an appointment with the Crown Prince. He did so anyway, wondering as he entered Faoud's audience chamber whether the automatic Western courtesy had been a mistake; he knew one of the many resentments was the amount of time he spent out of the country. The greetings were effusive, with much hand-holding and cheek-kissing: they were very close in status. Unlike the earlier encounter with Hassain, the discussion was automatically in Arabic.

"My father will be pleased you are well and back among us," said Faoud. Prayer beads moved slowly through his fingers.

"Regrettably only briefly," said Faysel.

"My father appreciates your dedication to the business success of our country," said Faoud.

Faysel had forgotten how the other man always avoided responsibility, even in the most inconsequential conversation. Faoud wasn't going to find it easy to follow.

"The political decision about increasing oil supplies is going to cause difficulties," said Faysel. Aware of Faoud's antipathy towards him, Faysel decided he had expressed that badly: he was conscious of a flare of satisfaction in Faoud's hooded eyes.

"You dispute the political wisdom?" said Faoud, equally badly.

"Of course not," said Faysel at once. "It was a response which had to be made and its diplomatic success is unquestionable. It is *because* of that success that I sought this audience today: I think we should consider extremely carefully the effect upon our investment programme."

Faoud frowned. "What is the connection?" he said.

"The West sees us as a country behaving responsibly, curbing the more extremist of our brothers," said Faysel. "It would be a tragedy if we were to lose that goodwill by restricting our investments too much."

"Economies have to be made."

"I'm aware of that," said Faysel. "My concern is to see that they are properly made."

"Maintained in the most influential countries and cut back in those which have little influence, you mean?"

"Yes," said Faysel. "That's precisely what I mean."

"The most influential countries are the richest," said Faoud.

"We are not debating moral right or wrong," said Faysel. "We're discussing political reality."

"The Council is well aware of political reality," said Faoud.

Not if you are guiding the discussion, thought Faysel. He said, "I'm gratified to hear that assurance." Hassain had been right; he was wasting his time.

Faoud shifted on his cushion, an indication that the audience was ending. "Continue your good work in the West," said the Crown Prince.

Was the man jealous? wondered Faysel. Until his father's accession to the throne, Faoud had maintained homes in Paris and New York and enjoyed the gambling tables and society life. "I will," he said.

"I'm sorry if your work is made more difficult by what has happened," said Faoud.

The man lied well, thought Faysel.

9

Rudd intended meeting Prince Faysel before the official session but there was a hold-up refuelling the Lear jet in the Azores, and then headwinds for the remainder of the journey, delaying him further. There were messages from the Prince when Rudd arrived at the Baur au Lac, but when he tried to return the calls Faysel was unavailable. By the time he reached the first-floor chamber overlooking the Höttingerstrasse the Arabs were already assembled, as was the practice, in an ante-chamber, so the opportunity was lost.

The meetings were rigidly formalized. As a concession to the Westerners who held minority placings, the Saudi investment board alternated its meetings between Jeddah and Europe, but arranged the sessions so that the major decisions were always taken when the venue was the Middle East, with the king and his immediate court available. Even the seating was regimented, the Saudis emphasizing their control at a separate, half-moon table, with the remainder of the board assembled at a facing table behind their named markers. Rudd's immediate neighbour was the chairman of the American Federal Reserve Bank, Alwynne Hinkley. Next to him were the chairman and vice-chairman of the Swiss Banking Corporation. The deputy governor of the Bank of England was at the end of the table. There were headsets for translation, but the discussion language was English so no one needed them.

Prince Hassain was in the chair, a bearded, wary-eyed man whom Rudd knew was regarded as a moderate within the court. Prince Faysel sat four places away from him; any indication of their closer friendship would have been improper so there was no obvious greeting between them.

"I am grateful for your attendance," began Hassain, with customary Arab politeness. "Today's session, although not one

87

at which any decisions will be reached, is regarded by my country as important."

Pens and paper were arranged before the delegates, but no one attempted notes, knowing that a simultaneous translation would be ready before they left.

"My country is being badly affected by Western inflation," resumed Hassain. "An inflation which we recognize is to a large extent caused by the uncertainty or upward price movements in oil. For that reason we are making an effort for stability, lasting, sensible, proper stability."

Rudd had received from the Best Rest intelligence division an analysis of the jump in oil supplies, because it affected their hotels as well as their airline, and he was aware of the speculation in the *Wall Street Journal* and *The New York Times*. Faysel regarded him impassively.

"We have consciously increased production," said Hassain. "Coupled with the effect of Western cut-backs, because of price and conservation policies, there is now a world surplus in oil, with refineries and tankers full and unable to make discharge. It has had the market effect of reducing the spot prices in Rotterdam from a high of $52 a barrel to something around $36. We want to see it go even lower, to a stabilized pricing of something like $30 or $28. It is that reduction for which we are going to argue at the next meeting of the oil exporting countries to be held in Vienna."

The man stopped, sipping some water. Taking advantage of the pause, the Federal Reserve bank official said, "This will surely be opposed by countries like Nigeria and Libya and Algeria?"

"But supported, I hope, by the majority," said Hassain. "There is no purpose in our being paid for our products in currency which is worthless: that has for a long time been our argument and at last it is being accepted."

"Could I ask, sir, of the effect upon this fund?"

Hassain nodded. "Which is the purpose of this session," he agreed. "Sometimes it is necessary to amputate a limb to save a body. We are not even considering amputation but severe surgery. The money available for investment through this fund and through the channels opened to us by you, our fellow board members, is being curtailed: in places, even stopped altogether. Before the oil glut policy was determined upon, it had been envisaged that this year there would be available for world-wide commitment something like $72,000,000,000, as the beginning of a five-year investment plan. This will now not be the case."

"How much will be available?" asked the Englishman at the end of the table.

"That has still to be decided and will be debated among us in Jeddah, in four months' time," said Hassain. "An estimate of $75,000,000 could be too high."

"This could have an effect upon the money markets," said the Englishman. "Certainly in London, and I would imagine in New York as well."

The Federal Reserve Bank chairman nodded agreement.

"In increased interest rates for alternative investors," agreed Hassain. "Which should delight the monetarists. We are fully conscious of the short-term difficulties that could arise but consider it necessary, for the reasons that have already been explained. Everyone – even the producers – think the wells pump money, not oil. It's an attitude that has to be corrected."

"Can we agree a commitment of investment in principle, without consultation?" asked the Swiss Bank official.

"No," refused Hassain at once. "From now on, there's no commitment without specific approval from Riyadh."

Rudd looked down at his unmarked jotting pad. So he wasn't going to get the $30,000,000 for the Texas development. Thank God they were as financially secure as they were. There was an ironic benefit: cheaper oil would mean that the ships he was considering buying would be even more economical to run. He hoped the announcement wouldn't panic the American board. The reassurance was immediate. Maybe once, he thought. But not any more.

"This is going to have a severe effect upon confidence," said Hinkley. Conscious of possible offence, he added hurriedly, "I don't mean in Saudi Arabia. I mean in money markets throughout the world."

"Which is why it is essential that what we are doing is properly explained, so that the publicity is not sensationalized," said

Hassain. "This is not a crisis. It is an attempt at rationalization."

"It could be recognized as a game of bluff," warned the Swiss chairman. "Speculators might gamble that you can't continue high production indefinitely."

"They might gamble." agreed Hassain. "And if they did they would be badly hurt. The most essential part of the strategy upon which we have decided is that there is no time limit upon it. If a speculator wants to buy an oil tanker or a refinery tank of oil and sit and wait for it to rise in price, then he's going to have to be a very rich man to sustain the interest on his money while he waits."

Rudd moved into the discussion. "We are talking about future investment," he said. "What about that which already exists? Is there any question of it being withdrawn?"

Hassain hesitated. "Subject to the most stringent examination," he said. "We want a saving of $150,000,000."

"With respect, sir, that's an ambivalent answer," said Hinkley. "And if it were given any publicity the inference could be very damaging."

Hassain nodded at the correction. "This discussion and any announcement that is likely to be made refers specifically to future commitment," he emphasized.

Rudd hoped the assurance was sustained. Best Rest were administering something like $50,000,000 of Saudi money virtually on the basis of an interest-free loan. He decided there was no point in attempting to discuss the details of the hotel development to which he had intended devoting their expected investment. Rudd looked along the table. The same thoughts appeared to be occurring to the rest of the Westerners.

"There would seem little purpose in advancing new proposals today?" said Hinkley, to be absolutely sure.

"They could be submitted for committee consideration," said Hassain.

The bankers hurried documents and prospectuses from their briefcases. Rudd added his outline to the rest, with little hope of it being accepted. The bankers would have development projects for third world countries, the sort of investment that was publicly attractive.

Normally the conferences lasted an entire day, but because no one had to talk about their schemes it finished before midday. Rudd lingered in the ante-room, waiting for Faysel.

"I'm sorry," said the Arab immediately. "I tried to get hold of you, to explain."

"The plane was delayed," said the American.

"I'm sorry, Harry. I know you went ahead with this Texas idea on my promise of investment."

"It's no big problem," dismissed Rudd.

"I gave my word," said Faysel.

"You weren't to know," said Rudd. "Texas still makes sense."

"Let's hope London does," said the Arab.

With their own aircraft available, they decided to fly directly to London and bring forward their meeting with Buckland. From the airport Rudd telephoned Hallett, already in London, to make arrangements for his arrival and telex New York about the decision of the investment board. From an adjoining booth Faysel called Buckland.

On the way to the plane Faysel said, "Buckland says he's looking forward to the meeting."

"So am I," said Rudd. Already Zürich was committed to memory. Now he was concentrating upon the meeting in England.

Buckland had been anticipating Snaith's approach but had not known that he would bring Smallwood with him. The two dissident directors sat opposite the imposing desk in the wood-lined office and Buckland thought back to his reflections on his way to the Cambridge house. He felt secure here as well, he decided: perhaps even more so than in the country. Snaith didn't appear impressed by his surroundings, but Buckland suspected that Smallwood was. Before this business was over, they'd both have reason to be impressed.

"We thought sufficient time had passed," said Snaith.

"Having heard them, I think all the proposals that Haffaford have made are extremely sound," supported Smallwood.

"I still haven't reached a decision," said Buckland.

"Isn't it one for the board, as a whole?" said Smallwood.

91

The fat little bugger was very sure of himself now, thought Buckland. "I'll present it to them when I consider it opportune," he said, consciously stressing the condescension.

"There isn't really an alternative, is there?" said the finance director.

"Isn't there?" said Buckland. He was glad the meeting with the American had been brought forward.

The London telex went first to the deputy chairman, so it was Patrick Walker who brought the news of the Saudi cut-back to Morrison: both men had office suites overlooking Wall Street and from Morrison's it was possible to see the tufted outline of Battery Park. Morrison remained head-bent over the message after he had read it; there was no cause for satisfaction but that was the feeling he had.

He looked up at last and said, "So the site purchase money comes from reserves?"

"Still a wise enough investment, when it's re-zoned," said Walker.

"What's the timing for that?" asked Morrison.

"Ten days," said Walker. "The ninth, according to Jeplow."

10

Walter Hallett had been in the lead car from the airport and was already in the reception area, completing the registration arrangements. Rudd remained just inside the door of the Berridge, gazing around and letting the memories flood back. There must have been redecoration, he supposed, but the colour seemed the same, the pale green wash on the walls pointing up the gold ormolu in the cornices and doorways. The carpet hadn't changed, either; still the rich ruby red. He stubbed his toe into it. Thick wool, not like the heavy-duty nylon he insisted upon for all their installations and for which he had established three factories in Des Moines. The reception and registration desk, still inadequately small, was to the left, with a separate desk for the cashiers, again inadequate in size. The small cocktail bar was to the right and between the bar and the reception desk, unseen behind the pale green door, was the telephone switchboard. Twenty lines, he remembered: when he'd worked here he'd volunteered for night duty and always offered to stand in for the operator when he went for supper, so that he could sneak calls to Angela in Boston without having them charged to his account.

There were five people behind the reception desk which was too cramped to accommodate them, and there was a queue at the cashiers' grille. Apart from the head porter there appeared to be at least eighteen attendants lingering in the foyer, in addition to the uniformed staff of four responding to instructions from the doorman. Rudd went to the entrance of the cocktail bar and counted five waiters and two barmen.

"You want a drink?"

Rudd turned at Hallett's surprised question. "Of course not," he said.

"There's a registration form to sign; they're sending it up to the suite."

Four porters were assembled to carry their bags; two could have managed, with a trolley, thought Rudd. The baggage man went into a separate lift. He and Hallett were taken to the fifteenth floor by a reception clerk in black jacket and striped trousers, who used the journeys to explain the amenities of the hotel. After showing them into their rooms he offered them a personalized card, with his name, in case he could help further. Rudd thought the young man was impressive. He wondered if people had thought the same about him when he'd performed the task.

"The Park Suite," identified Rudd, when the man had gone. "Ten years ago it was £15 a night, with £1 for breakfast. Now it's £250 a day and breakfast is £10 if it's continental and £18 for full English."

The decor was different from the arrival area, pale cream and yellows, and Rudd went close to the walls and saw that they were fading and chipped. The carpet, wool again, was wearing near the main door approach and the silk tapestry-covered upholstery on the furniture in the sitting-room was beginning to fur at the corners. Rudd calculated that in another six months the fray would be obvious. There were fresh flowers in four separate vases through the main room and a further display in the bedroom.

Between the bedroom and the bathroom there was a dressing-room slightly smaller in size than the regulation measurements of those in operation for the main rooms of the Best Rest motels. There were five large towels in the bathroom with a matching, full-length robe.

Rudd returned to the living-room and said, "What about the tape machine?"

"I asked for it when I booked but they haven't been able to fix it yet," said the personal assistant. "It's promised for this afternoon."

Rudd nodded behind him. "We'll put it in the dressing-room."

"Telex room closes at eleven at night and opens again at nine," said Hallett critically.

"See if we can get a machine of our own, with a tie-line," ordered Rudd. "Is Bunch here?"

Hallett nodded. "I called him from the desk; he was cleaning up after the flight and said he'd see us here in fifteen minutes."

"Why not order coffee while I unpack?" suggested Rudd. The bedroom was as large as the outer room, with a sweeping view of Hyde Park. The yellow decor had been continued; the walls were lined with yellow silk and the bed coverlet matched. There was a small table with more flowers and a bureau. Rudd opened it; every sort of writing material was available, even a small tube of ink.

The coffee was arriving when he returned to the sitting-room; two waiters where one would have been sufficient, Rudd noted. As they opened the door to leave Bunch appeared. He surged in as buoyant and fresh-faced as ever.

While Hallett served, Rudd recounted what had happened in Zürich. The lawyer sat nodding. At the end he said. "Thank God we're not dependent on the money."

"That's what I thought," said Rudd. "What about Jeplow?"

"He's putting the arm on us," announced Bunch simply.

"What do you mean?"

"I wanted to talk about development grants and tax concession and all he wanted to discuss was commission."

Rudd smiled, cynically. "How much?"

"It was all circumspect and politically voiced," said the lawyer. "At the end of a lot of words, it came down to five per cent of the overall development."

Rudd whistled. "On a total investment of $120,000,000 that's $6,000,000!"

"The best don't come cheap," said the lawyer.

"Your words or Jeplow's?"

"My words, his belief," said Bunch.

"I'd want delivery for that," insisted Rudd. "Every last damned promise, commitment and undertaking."

"I made that clear."

"What did he say?"

"He had every hope of coming through with everything he had promised," quoted Bunch.

"I don't *hope* with $6,000,000," said Rudd.

"It'll be phased," reminded Bunch.

"How much does he want up front?"

"Two hundred and fifty thousand."

Rudd sat making steeples with his fingers and then collapsing them. "How's he want it paid?"

"Offshore: maybe the Caymans but he wasn't specific about that."

"Does the account already exist?"

"We didn't discuss that either but he seemed familiar with the system so I guessed it was."

"So to make the payment, we'd have to have details?"

"Obviously."

"And once we made a deposit, we'd have a pressure point?"

Bunch looked doubtful. "We'd be breaking the law by making the payment just as much as he would be by receiving it."

"Businesses are expected to go over the edge sometimes," said Rudd. "Politicians never are. They're supposed to be honest. And certainly not cheat on their taxes."

"You want to go ahead then?"

Rudd nodded. "Lose it through the entertainment account."

"What time is Faysel due here with Buckland?" Bunch asked the question of Rudd, but it was Hallett who answered. "Four," he said. "Another thirty minutes."

"Any idea how keen the man is?" asked the lawyer.

"He responded in four days," said Rudd. "That's keen. I want you to sit through the meeting, of course, but as soon as it's over I want you to set up a complete examination into Buckland House. I want a breakdown of the holding company and each of the subsidiaries: because it's the one I shall want first, concentrate upon the shipping fleet." He looked around the suite. "This will be the office," he said. He allowed another pause, then he said, "Where else should we plan the take-over of the group but from the best hotel?"

They were men of complete contrast: Rudd slight, almost diminutive, rarely moving, the button-down man of neutral grey Dacron, Buckland flamboyant in Savile Row stripe and Royal Yacht Squadron tie, languid in the facing chair but with his hands in almost constant motion, as if offering the words for inspection. Buckland accepted whisky but Rudd remained with coffee. Hallett withdrew to the bar. Bunch sat alongide Rudd and Faysel at the corner of the small table around which they were grouped.

"I didn't expect this to be formal," said Buckland, indicating the other men in the room.

"It isn't," said Rudd. "And Prince Faysel is a director of Buckland House, so it comes to an even balance."

Buckland frowned at the qualification. "Exploratory then?" he said, wanting the terms of reference.

"Absolutely," Rudd was consciously restricting his replies so that the other man would have to take the lead.

"But you're seriously interested in acquiring the fleet?" pressed Buckland.

"I'd hardly have broken the journey here if I hadn't been."

"I've your assurance on that?"

"Yes."

"I'd need a written undertaking of intent before I could disclose detailed figures," said Buckland. He looked again the Arab sitting alongside.

Rudd held out his hand towards Hallett. The personal assistant gave him the foolscap that had been waiting on the bar top and Rudd passed it unread to the other man. "I wouldn't expect you to," he said.

Buckland read the letter, then looked up smiling. He went to his briefcase and said, "Here are the complete operating details, over the last three years. Cost and passenger breakdown, ship by ship."

The American took the file but didn't open it. "They're losing money," he said.

"Through routing and required manning," said Buckland quickly. He turned again to the man alongside him. "I understand from Prince Faysel that you are planning economical routes."

"I won't know whether they're economical or not until I fully consider the cost breakdown."

"You've my figures," said Buckland pointedly.

"I'd need to read them before I can offer mine," said Rudd. "You can't expect me to bid blind."

Disappointment crossed briefly over Buckland's face. "I'd hoped for an indication," he said.

"You have the letter," said the smaller man. "That's as far as I feel I can commit myself and my board at the moment."

"How long will you be in London?"

"For as long as necessary."

"I'd like to put proposals before my board as soon as possible."

Rudd hesitated, remembering the enquiries he had asked Bunch to make. "I will come back to you within forty-eight hours," he said. Buckland was too eager; altogether too eager.

11

The overnight stay in Switzerland had broken Rudd's journey so there was no jet-lag: he was up, as usual, by six o'clock. He ordered juice and coffee and by the time it was delivered he had showered and dressed. He had the breakfast things set on the table in front of the window overlooking the park. London was still not properly awake: the traffic was beginning up and down Park Lane, but the pavements were almost completely empty. In the park, still smoked with early morning mist, he saw a few people walking their dogs and an occasional jogger. The exercise had just caught on when he'd been here before: the rest of the staff had regarded him as some sort of craze-happy American and laughed at him.

He cleared a space for the documents that Buckland had provided, setting them out so he could create a comparison chart. They were very comprehensive and Rudd nodded approvingly: Buckland seemed to be holding nothing back. Fuel costs were by far the highest expenditure for the division, soaring over the previous three years by twenty per cent. They reflected, of course, the period when oil costs were at their highest, not what Rudd had anticipated them to be from his Zürich discussions with the Saudis. He broke each vessel down into a separate page of calculations, assessing distances against current fuel costs. Then he assessed the coming year's oil pricing at $28 a barrel, multiplied that into tonnage and set it against journeys of not more than 2000 miles, which was the maximum he intended from Florida and Texas around the Caribbean. It gave him a two per cent profit margin, before he included the cost of the capital outlay in refitting the vessels. With the extra $12,000,000 that he estimated the improvements would cost built into the assessment, the profit was reduced to a half per cent. He put aside the fuelling figures and started creating a new graph, on manning levels. Simply by reducing each liner to a single class meant that he could reduce by twelve per cent the number of crew carried and Rudd estimated that reduction could go as low as another five per cent through negotiations with the American Seaman's Union. Working on a twenty-three per cent manning reduction, Rudd checked steadily through the salary expenditure, using not the English wage minimums but those applicable to America, which Hallett had provided before they left New York. There were variations because of the differences in size between the liners, but overall the saving on crew salaries was $1,300,000.

Rudd sat back, easing the cramp from his shoulders. So the profit was better, one and a half per cent minimum, which was acceptable in the circumstances. With the bulk food-buying available through the Best Rest sub-divisions, Rudd was confident even without going into details that he could reduce victualling costs by ten per cent, particularly as he would be able to centralize it through Florida and Texas and not have to buy during voyages in various parts of the world, which Buckland House had to do at present.

Rudd finished the assessment by mid-morning, frowning at the prospect of inactivity until Bunch returned that afternoon with the company report. The idea came suddenly and he grinned at it, like a child tempted to steal sweets from a candy store. Why not? He was surprised that it hadn't occurred to him before.

Immediately outside the suite he hesitated, trying to get his sense of direction, and then went away from the main lifts towards the back of the hotel. He found the service section just behind a fire screen. He had to wait several minutes, watching the on-off progress of the indicator light, nervous of occupation when the doors opened; if it had been occupied, he couldn't have done it. He got in quickly, pressing for the fourth level. It was dirty, like all service lifts, but not unreasonably so. Rudd, who did not smoke, grimaced at the cigarette odour. He emerged curiously at the fourth floor, wondering if there had been any change. He looked expectantly to his right. It was still the staff section. The fittings were functional here, unlike the luxury of the public parts of the hotel: even the carpet was hard-wear nylon. It all looked very familiar.

Rudd went confidently along the corridor, letting the

memories wash over him, halting immediately the passage turned left. The nine of the nineteen was still slightly askew, just as it had been when he occupied it, where it had been screwed on in a hurry and never corrected. He felt out, touching it. Beyond would be a single bed. To the right, beneath the shelf of paperback books, he remembered. Above the books the ledge where he'd kept the photographs of Angela, the photographs he'd had copied and blown up and which were now displayed in the New York penthouse. At the bottom of the bed there had been a small table for the portable television, black and white and constantly blurred because of the interference. He wondered if the two easy chairs still remained: one of them had a sagging seat and a spring that had prodded into his back, like an accusing finger. The view would still be the same from the window, the air-conditioning flue perpetually spitting out grime like an old man with a cough. And the bathroom annexe was alongside, with its opaque window over the inner courtyard admitting a yellowing light. Would the tub still fill with explosive spurts of water: the plumbers had never seemed able to get the air out of the pipes.

"Can I help you?"

Rudd jumped and then turned at the question. It was a striped-trousered, dark-jacketed reception clerk, but not the one who'd escorted him to his suite the previous day. Would he be the current occupant of room number nineteen?

"I seem to have taken the wrong lift and lost my way," said Rudd. He desperately wanted to ask to be shown inside, but he bit back the question. The kid would think he was some kind of a nut and then there would be explanations and he didn't want that. He felt embarrassed: he'd gone for the candy and been caught.

The clerk didn't allow any surprise to reach his face. "Let me show you the way to the foyer," he said courteously.

Obediently Rudd followed him back to the service lift and permitted himself to be escorted down the remaining four floors. Aware of the younger man remaining at the door, looking at him, Rudd had to walk out through the doors. Hallett had established two limousines on permanent standby but Rudd ignored them, with nowhere to go. Instead he turned down Park Lane, pausing by the Dorchester and then continuing on by the Playboy Club to the Hilton and the Inn on the Park. Good sightings, he

101

decided professionally. There was a direct comparison, he supposed, with Central Park South and Fifth Avenue, because they overlooked a park, but somehow in London they seemed better. He considered going inside one of them but decided the boy would have left the foyer by now, so he turned back towards the Berridge. The feeling of embarrassment at being confronted in the service corridor had been stupid, just as it had been stupid to hold back from asking him if he could look inside.

He never did anything impulsive, thought Rudd: nothing at all.

Rudd had insisted upon a permanent Cona machine being installed in the kitchen of the suite and Bunch gratefully accepted coffee as soon as he entered: the laywer carried two briefcases and seemed bowed by weariness, which was unusual.

"It's astonishing," said Bunch, sipping his coffee. "Absolutely astonishing. I've studied company law and international law and I've never seen anything like it."

"A problem?" demanded Rudd.

Bunch took papers from the larger of the two briefcases and began talking, still looking down at them. "The Buckland House share apportionment is what is called under British company law a scheme of arrangement: it's the most amazing piece of gobbledygook from the country that's supposed to be the basis of our legal system that I've ever seen."

"Explain it," insisted Rudd.

"Voting power is split," said Bunch. "There are two superior 'A' share issues, one Preferential, the other Initial. For one vote, you need ten Preferential shares. But you only need five of the Initial holdings."

"I still don't see the significance."

"Someone, in the past, was very clever," said Bunch. "It's a block-off to any takeover because thirty-five per cent of the Initial shares are owned by the Buckland family, either personally or in the family trust."

"How many Preferential?" anticipated Rudd.

"Sixteen per cent," said Bunch. "Just the nice majority of fifty-one per cent."

Rudd sat back against the chair. "And all in the family!" he said admiringly. He looked sharply across at the lawyer, "You think Sir Ian manipulated it?"

Bunch shook his head immediately. "Dates back years," he said. "Difficult to establish exactly, but I put the creation somewhere around 1962."

"Anything significant about the date?" asked Rudd.

Bunch made an uncertain gesture. "It puts Sir Ian at eighteen: perhaps his father saw the danger signs, even then. He's supposed to have been a smart old bastard, just like his father before him."

"What's the effect?"

"Practically that of a private company which is publicly funded," said Bunch. "You heard in New York how three of the shareholders, Condway, Penhardy and Gore-Pelham, are family friends. That only leaves three other directors – Faysel one of them – in any opposition. The finance director's got a small vote, but nothing substantial. Unless there's a revolution that we can't predict, they're fireproof."

"Son of a bitch!" said Rudd vehemently. He'd expected opposition when he declared himself but not an impenetrable barrier like this. "Is it legal?" he said.

Bunch made another uncertain motion with his hand. "It must be, to have been admitted to the Registry," he said. "Obviously I'll have to take English legal adivce."

"Get an opinion," insisted Rudd. "The best. And quick. If I can't break in then he can take his fleet and sail it in his bath."

"What do the figures look like?" said Bunch.

"Good enough to go ahead," said Rudd. "Provisionally three per cent after a year."

"Isn't that good enough to take anyway?" said the lawyer.

Rudd shook his head. "It's all or nothing," he said. "I'm not interested in tidbits."

"It was looking good, too," said the lawyer.

"Too good," said Rudd, in hindsight.

Hallett answered the telephone, spoke briefly and then cupped his hand over it. "It's Buckland," he said. "A dinner invitation for tonight; black tie."

"Eager," said Bunch.

"Too eager," agreed Rudd. He hesitated. Then he said to Hallett, "Accept."

103

12

Buckland's town house was Regency, an imposing four-storey double-fronted white building in a cul-de-sac just off Sloane Square. The reception room curtains were undrawn and they saw Rudd's car arrive, so it was Buckland who opened the door to the American.

"Glad you could make it," said Buckland. "Very glad indeed."

The entrance hall was large, a checkered floor in black and white marble and dominated by a many-armed chandelier which descended through the entire length of the house from a high cupola roof. A wide staircase, with niches for plinth-mounted statuettes, spread out from the centre, up to a first-floor landing which ringed the vestibule in an open-sided, pillar-supported balcony. There were more alcoves and statues throughout the circle. The impression was of great height: it reminded Rudd of a church. Buckland cupped his arm, leading him back into the reception room. Rudd was uncomfortable at the gesture but didn't try to remove his arm. "Harry Rudd," announced Buckland, just inside the door.

Rudd had come without any idea of how many people would be at the dinner party but he had expected it to be large, maybe including some other Buckland House directors. Only two women turned towards him.

"My wife Margaret. And my sister, Vanessa Hartland," introduced Buckland.

The sister approached first, hand outstretched. Rudd saw a yellow-haired, angular woman whose make-up hadn't been applied with any particular care. She wore a long black evening skirt and a white blouse, high at the neck. From the movement as she walked she wasn't wearing anything beneath the blouse. The handshake was firm, masculine almost, and she held his eyes

104

during the greeting. Rudd broke the gaze, looking to the other woman. Lady Margaret Buckland was formally dressed, in long-skirted blue silk. The gown was off the shoulder, but discreetly so: a single diamond glittered from a gold strand at her throat. The handshake was soft and brief, almost as if she didn't welcome the physical contact. He thought she looked attractive with her dark hair short: he wondered what she looked like when it was long.

"Welcome to our house," she said. From the colour of her skin and the deepness of her eyes Rudd had expected the accent to be foreign, not cultured English.

"It was kind of you to invite me."

"Should have done it yesterday," said Buckland briskly. "Thoughtless of me."

Rudd became aware of the approaching butler; there was only champagne on the tray. Rudd took a glass and then a brief sip. He would have preferred gin; champagne gave him gas.

"How long will you be staying in England?" said Margaret, opening the polite small talk.

"I haven't decided yet," said Rudd. "Some time, I think."

"I think the theatre in London is far better than New York, don't you?" said Vanessa taking up the politeness.

Rudd made a deprecating movement with his hand. "I don't think I attend either sufficiently to be able to make a judgment," he said.

"Lincoln Centre's jolly convenient, everything grouped together like that, but I still think our National has the edge," said Vanessa.

"Perhaps I should try to go while I'm here," said Rudd. "What would you recommend?"

Vanessa blinked at the question. "Just got down from Yorkshire," she said. "Which culturally might as well be the Arctic. I don't know what the Season is." She turned to the other woman. "Do you, Margaret?"

"There have been some good reviews of Gielgud," said Margaret. "And there's a Greek production, but I understand it's very experimental."

Buckland's wife had a shy, almost retiring attitude, but Rudd didn't think she was overpowered by the other people in the room; rather it was as if she'd withdrawn as a spectator, to watch them perform. It was something he found easy to recognize because he frequently did it himself, but at gatherings larger than this.

"Don't get much time for the theatre myself," said Buckland. "Prefer something more active. Do you like gambling, Harry?"

"We've got it in Atlantic City," said Rudd. "But not legally in New York. So I don't get much opportunity, unless I go to Vegas. We've two hotels there."

"Thought we might go on after dinner. That all right with you?"

"Before Rudd could respond, Vanessa said "I *love* it!"

"Fine," accepted Rudd.

The meal was announced. Rudd put his untouched champagne glass on a side table and looked around enquiringly. Margaret offered her arm for him to take her into the dining-room: as with the handshake, it was just token contact.

"You've a lovely house," said Rudd, as they crossed the spacious hall.

"I spend most of my time in the country," she said. "But I enjoy it when I'm here."

The dining-room was big, like everything else in the house, but the main table which Rudd supposed could easily have accommodated twenty people was unlaid. The setting was at a smaller circular table, close to a window annexe. The curtains were undrawn here as well, with a view of the street. Rudd felt vaguely disconcerted at the idea of being looked in at; maybe it was something to do with spending so much time at the top of high buildings.

"Do you know London well?" asked Vanessa. She had a strident, glass-rattling voice.

"Not particularly," said Rudd. "I worked here for a couple of months, but it was a long time ago."

"Doing what?" asked Buckland. It was a casual question.

"Working at the Berridge," said Rudd.

The three other people came up from their plates practically in unison. "You *worked* at the Berridge!" said Vanessa.

"Ten years ago," said Rudd.

"But what as?"

106

"The title was assistant manager," said Rudd. "But actually I was a kind of dog's body attached to the reception desk."

"I don't understand how," said Buckland.

"My father-in-law thought it a good idea for me to learn the hotel business here." A lie, thought Rudd. Morrison had split them up to show his power, the sort of power he had intended to use throughout the rest of their married life.

"It must seem quite different to you now?" said Margaret. Unlike her husband and sister-in-law, she kept the surprise from her voice.

"Not really," said Rudd. "Not a lot seems to have changed."

"What do you think of it?" asked Buckland.

Rudd pulled back from the table for the course to be changed and more wine added to his glass. "I think it's extravagant," he said.

Buckland began to smile, imagining a compliment, but the expression faltered. "Extravagant?"

"I think the staff level is too high, I think your reception area needs completely redesigning for greater efficiency, and if you insist upon the sort of fabrics and furnishings that you're maintaining at the moment, your refurbishing costs are going to be enormous."

"The staff, design and fittings are necessary for the sort of hotel it is," said Buckland tightly.

"It's magnificent," agreed Rudd. "The service is impeccable: I was just giving a professional answer."

Rudd felt pressure against his leg from the side upon which Vanessa was sitting. He looked towards her. She smiled at him but said nothing.

Buckland was clearly irritated. Margaret attempted to cover the awkwardness, using another course change as an excuse. "Hope you like grouse?" she said.

"It's excellent," said Rudd. "Not the sort of thing we get the chance of often in New York."

"Ian shot them himself: we've a shoot in Scotland," said his wife.

"Do you have a place in the country?" said Vanessa.

"No," said Rudd. Why was he aware of sounding dull? He continued quickly, "But I often go up to Connecticut and I sometimes sail out of Rhode Island." Rudd stared down at his plate, astonished with himself: now he was lying!

"Sail!" exclaimed Buckland, his earlier offence gone. "What a coincidence. I've a yacht down on the Hamble. Twelve-metre but I don't race. Decided on comfort instead. Perhaps we can take it out?"

"We'll have to see how the time goes," said Rudd, seeking an escape. His face was burning, not so much from embarrassment but from anger at the stupidity of what he'd done.

"It would be great fun," insisted Vanessa. "We could make up a party; maybe go across to France. Why don't we make a definite date?"

Rudd had dismissed the first occasion as a mistake but he was sure the pressure this time was deliberate. He shifted his leg even further. Making a conscious effort to recover, he said, "I expect to be quite busy while I'm here; I couldn't make any positive commitment."

"Perhaps we should just keep it in mind," said Margaret.

"Of course," said Rudd. He saw she was looking directly at him and wondered if, from her spectator's position, she realized what had happened.

He was relieved when the meal ended and the women followed the English custom, leaving him and Buckland to port and cigars. The Englishman offered him the humidor but Rudd shook his head. He'd smoked at school, experimentally like everyone else, and at university fooled with marijuana and been disappointed. Buckland passed the decanter and Rudd helped himself.

"Have you had the chance to look at the figures?" said Buckland.

"Yes," said Rudd. "They were very full. Thank you."

"What did you think?"

Until they had obtained English legal opinion, the only thing he could do was keep the ball in court, decided Rudd. "They're expensive," he said. Conscious of the other man's frown, Rudd added, "But I don't think it would be impossible to run them economically."

Buckland brightened visibly. For a negotiator, the man's emotions were too near the surface, thought Rudd. He accepted the decanter again.

"I'd like to bring it to the notice of my board as soon as possible," said Buckland.

There was no legal commitment and therefore no danger, decided Rudd. "I don't see why you shouldn't say that discussions have started between us; it would be wrong at this stage to put it any stronger than that," he said.

The door from the hallway opened abruptly and Vanessa came into the room, her wrap already around her shoulders. "Time's up," she declared, in her echoing voice. "It's time to go and win a fortune."

They used Rudd's car. As he got in he wondered which one of them would be lucky. And not just tonight.

Nearly everyone was in evening dress and an effort had been made, with chandeliers and velvet drapes, but Rudd's immediate impression was of shabbiness; the casino was smaller, too, than he had expected. He was introduced to Tommy Ellerby and effusively Buckland guaranteed the credit for any cheque Rudd wanted to cash. He went with Buckland and Vanessa to the caisse: both drew £20,000. Rudd took £5000. Buckland and his sister went to separate blackjack tables. Rudd put his chips in his pocket and walked to where Margaret was standing, near the door leading to the separate bar.

"Not gambling?" he said.

She shook her head. "I can't understand the attraction," she said. "Ian loves it."

Rudd looked to where her husband sat: he was intent upon the game. "I can see," he said.

"What about you?"

"Both the hotels in Las Vegas have casinos," said Rudd. "I prefer the house odds."

"Why didn't you say so, back at the house?"

"I wanted to see what it was like in London." The roulette table was at the top of the room. "Come and give me luck," he said.

Rudd waited, watching the run of play and as soon as the colour changed, followed the ball with evens bets. There was a consecutive run for five spins of the wheel. He let his £500 ride for three turns, halved his stake and held back from playing on the turn when the colour changed from red to black, giving him a profit of £5500.

"That was done almost clinically," said Margaret. "Isn't there supposed to be a rule about quitting while you're ahead?"

She looked to where her husband sat but said nothing.

"Shall we go to the bar?" invited Rudd.

"If we're not going to gamble any more, that's about all we can do."

Instinctively he took her arm, not realizing the gesture until he touched her. He pulled away. She appeared not to notice. They walked directly behind the tables at which Buckland and Vanessa were sitting. There was a tiny wall of chips in front of Vanessa but Buckland's stake seemed to have diminished. In the bar Rudd chose brandy, but Margaret only wanted mineral water.

"Are you going to buy the ships?" she said.

"I don't know yet."

"Ian will be angry that I mentioned it; he said we shouldn't during dinner."

"Why did you?"

"It seemed a stupid pretence: that's why you're here, after all."

"I didn't mean to offend him about the Berridge," said Rudd.

"Recently he seems to have become very protective about the hotels."

"Wasn't he always?"

She made an indecisive movement but didn't reply. Instead she said, "You mustn't mind Vanessa."

"I didn't say that I did."

"You didn't have to: I saw what happened at dinner."

"Does this sort of analysis always come so quickly after a first meeting?"

"Now you're offended."

"No, really," said Rudd sincerely.

"Embarrassed then?"

"Nervous about what you might discover."

"I don't think it would be easy to discover much about you,

Mr Rudd," she said. "I've decided you're a very private man."

"What sort of person are you?" he said. Quite different from the impression he'd formed earlier, he thought.

She made another dismissive gesture. "Ordinary," she said. She sighed, looking into the casino. "This isn't very polite of Ian, is it?" she said.

"I'm content enough," he said. And he was; the realization surprised him.

"Is there a Mrs Rudd?"

"There was," he said. "She died, some time ago." Ten years, two months and three days, he thought. He hadn't visited the grave for a long time.

"Children?"

"No." He decided against telling her the circumstances of Angela's death.

"Ian and I haven't got any, either," she said. "He's very disappointed: there's a thing in the family about continuing the line. The English love their dynasties. The Bucklands regard themselves as a dynasty."

A mixture of bitterness and sorrow, he judged. Her honesty was not forced: she was utterly ingenuous. It was not often he met someone like that; hardly ever, in fact.

"About time," she said, looking beyond Rudd. The American turned to see Buckland and his sister entering the bar together.

"Champagne for me, hemlock for him," said Vanessa.

"How much did you win?" asked Rudd.

"Four and a half thousand," said Vanessa.

The excitement was obvious in her voice and Rudd thought she was the sort of person who would always want to win.

"And how much did you lose, Ian?" said his wife.

"Bad form to discuss one's gambling losses," said Buckland flippantly.

"And to abandon one's guests," she said.

"I didn't consider myself abandoned," said Rudd.

"How did you get on?" Vanessa asked him.

"I won," said Rudd.

"Let's cash up."

He let her precede him to the caisse. As he was being paid out, Vanessa said, "We should celebrate."

111

"Isn't it a bit late?" said Rudd.

"I didn't mean tonight," she said.

Rudd pocketed his winnings. "I'd like to return tonight's hospitality sometime while I'm here."

"I didn't mean that either," she said.

It took thirty minutes for Grearson and Morrison to go through the Buckland House portfolio that the Boston lawer had managed to assemble through the foreign brokers. At the end of the examination Morrison said, "In the time you've done well, *very* well. Thank you."

He had only been able to qualify for twenty Preferential on the London market, but the subsidiary purchases, through Europe and Asia, entitled him to an additional eighty Preferential on a shareholder's demand vote and he had 2000 Ordinary shares.

"This was only the loose stuff," said Grearson. "Just lying about waiting to be picked up; it isn't going to be as easy after this."

"There's a listing for Initial," said Morrison, going back to the folder. "What are they?"

"I've already made the enquiry, through Paris," said Grearson.

"How much has it cost so far?"

"Cheap," said Grearson. "A little under $500,000. Do you want to stop now?"

Morrison stared up, surprised at the question. "Good God no!" he said. "I want more. Much more."

13

Sir Ian Buckland sat almost nonchalantly in his chairman's position at the head of the table, anticipating the meeting that was to come. He supposed it might have been wise – at least courteous – to brief in advance the directors upon whose support he knew he could rely, but he had built himself up to the announcement and didn't want to diminish it, even slightly. It wouldn't have been complete if Faysel had been present. It had been sensible for the Arab to avoid the later accusation of a conflict of interest and absent himself from the meeting. Buckland went patiently through the opening formalities and while the previous minutes were being read he looked around the room. Condway and Penhardy were close together, involved in some whispered conversation. The merchant bank director was assembling files and documents before him, forever like some damned clerk about to sit an examination. From the bottom of the table Gore-Pelham smiled and then winked. Buckland smiled back. Smallwood held his eye boldly, until it was Buckland who turned away. Let's see how confident you stay in the next hour, thought Buckland.

When the formalities were finished, Buckland said, "Any business arising?"

At once Snaith said, "I think we all know that there is."

The man would have rehearsed the presentation, Buckland guessed: probably practised in front of the mirror to make sure he'd got the facial expression right. "Perhaps you'd like to take us through it?" he said to the banker. Christ he was enjoying himself!

Snaith cleared his throat. "The board will remember the decision from the previous meeting to approach the bank of which I am a director, with a request for an increase in the Buckland House overdraft facility. Subsequent to that decision there was a meeting between Haffaford and Co., the chairman and vice-chairman. . . ." The banker stopped, looking up at the people around the table. Definitely rehearsed, decided Buckland.

"Haffaford are unwilling to grant that request," Snaith declared. There was no reaction from Penhardy and Buckland guessed he'd been warned in advance during the whispered conversation with Lord Condway. Gore-Pelham stopped smiling.

"Why ever not?" said Gore-Pelham.

"An intensive examination was made of the company and its performance, and a forecast reached of its expected profitability for a three-year span. The conclusion was that an additional £10,000,000 would be an over-extension of its resources."

"An over-extension of Buckland House resources!" said Penhardy. "That's ludicrous."

"Not in the opinion of our analysts," said Snaith stubbornly.

"The opinion must be wrong," said Gore-Pelham.

"It's the opinion upon which we are basing our decision," said Snaith.

Gore-Pelham snapped his fingers. "You just can't cut us off, like that."

"Haffaford are prepared to mark up your account for a further £3,000,000," said Snaith. "For that facility we would expect a complete management restructure, to introduce cost control throughout every division of the group. And there would need to be a three-monthly audit to ensure that the economies were on target."

"Damned usury," said Condway.

"No," said Snaith. "We see these as practical business proposals to bring this company back upon course."

"I'm already involved in negotiations to do just that," said Buckland. He purposely spoke quietly, intending the maximum effect, and for a moment he feared Snaith had not heard him.

Then the man turned fully towards him and said, "What?"

Buckland spoke without notes, knowing it would increase the impression of control. "Following what I considered to be a completely unsatisfactory meeting with our merchant bankers, I decided to explore alternative proposals to resolve these temporary difficulties. The largest loss-making section of our company

114

is the liner fleet. Within the coming weeks, I have every confidence that I shall be able to negotiate its sale. The effect will be twofold: a financial drain will be stopped and the revenue from the sale will remove the existing overdraft and any need for the cap-in-hand demands that are being imposed upon us." Buckland stopped, swallowing. He hadn't intended the last part; the anger had come suddenly at his realization of the humiliation that Haffaford had attempted.

Snaith was staring along the table, tight-faced at the awareness of how he and his bank had been outmanoeuvred. "With whom are these discussions taking place?" he demanded.

"They are at the moment at the most preliminary stage," said Buckland. "If any rumour were to arise within the City, then I think they might be jeopardized."

"Are you doubting the integrity of your fellow directors!" demanded Snaith.

"No," said Buckland. "Appealing to their common sense. I seek a mandate from today's meeting to continue these discussions to the point when I can convene another meeting and put them formally before you, for a decision."

"This is monstrous!" protested Smallwood. "No board of a public company can give a chairman *carte blanche* like that."

"Let me repeat something I said earlier," asked Buckland. "If these negotiations are successful, then the Buckland House difficulties are solved overnight."

"How can you make a claim like that," demanded Smallwood. "We *must* be given details."

"None exist at the moment," said Buckland. "I've already undertaken to lay them before you the moment they're formulated."

"I've sufficient confidence in our chairman to propose that he be asked to continue these discussions," said Penhardy.

"Seconded," said Condway.

"Amendments?" invited Buckland.

Snaith spoke looking down at his carefully prepared and now useless files. "I want the record of this meeting to register my strongest protest at the conduct of the chairman and of directors who imagine that the management of a company can be conducted in this way."

"And mine," supported Smallwood.

Buckland glanced towards the secretariat table. "Notes are being taken," he said. There was a lightness to the remark which he hadn't intended.

"We're a director short," said Snaith. "A vote cannot be taken."

"Prince Faysel's proxy is vested with the chairman's discretion," said Buckland. He offered the written authorization across the table to the other man.

"My amendment is that the vote be deferred until Prince Faysel can attend and decide in person," said Snaith.

"Seconded," supported Smallwood.

"Amendment to the vote," said Buckland, sure of the outcome. Snaith and Smallwood raised their hands.

"Against?" said the Chairman, raising his hand as he spoke. Condway, Gore-Pelham and Penhardy followed.

"Original motion?" said Buckland. The voting division was the same, but reversed.

"Thank you for that expression of confidence," said Buckland, to his friends. "I repeat the earlier assurance to convene a meeting at the earliest opportunity when I have something positive to place before this board for a decision."

Snaith hurriedly gathered his papers, nodded curtly to the men around the table and walked jerkily from the room. Smallwood followed.

"Well done, Ian," said Condway. "That was as complete a counter-attack as I've seen in a long time. Bloody well done."

Buckland smiled gratefully at the praise. His father would have been proud of him today, he thought; it was an unusual reflection and Buckland confronted it. He didn't think there had been many occasions when his father would have been proud.

He wished there had.

They had to leave the car in Fleet Street and walk down the narrow, Dickensian lanes into the Inn of Court where the appointment had been arranged with the Queen's Counsel. As well as Rudd and Bunch there was Percival Berriman, the English solicitor, a plump puffing man. Berriman stopped outside the chambers and pointed to the list of occupants. Sir Henry Dray's name was the first.

"Head of chambers," said Berriman, as if the recommendation were necessary.

The corridors inside were as labyrinthine as the approach roads but Dray's office was a surprise, a bright, airy room, neat and well polished. The textbooks were behind sparkling glass and Dray's desk was large, a wide area for papers and documents. The barrister rose, coming forward to meet them. Berriman went through the introductions and Rudd decided the solicitor was given to self-importance. The barrister offered them sherry, but both the Americans declined. Neither Dray nor Berriman bothered.

"I will prepare a written opinion, of course," said Dray. "But I understood from Mr Berriman that there was some urgency, which is why I suggested this meeting."

Dray was a thin, almost skeletal man, bony-faced and bony-fingered. He kept his hands in front of him on the desk, constantly fingering a gold pencil. He spoke looking slightly beyond them, as if he were addressing a court: his voice was measured and flat.

"I need advice to enable me to decide whether or not to continue with negotiations," said Rudd.

"What sort of negotiations?"

Rudd hesitated. The man would have to know everything, if the legal opinion were to be of any use. "At the moment, merely for the purchase of the liner fleet belonging to Buckland House."

Dray lowered his eyes and looked directly at the American. "What eventually?"

"A complete takeover," said Rudd.

Dray examined his worry-bead pencil. "Negotiations for the fleet are amicable?" he said.

"Yes."

"But the takeover wouldn't be." This time it wasn't a question. Dray smiled. The expression made his face look even more skull-like. "At the moment, Mr Rudd, under the scheme of arrangement under which Buckland House is constructed, you don't stand a chance."

"That was our impression," said Bunch. "Which is why we

117

want to know if the scheme of arrangement is challengeable."

Dray indicated a red-bound law book by his right hand. "There are stated cases," he said. "It depends upon what grounds you base your challenge."

"Surely it must be against the shareholders' interests?" said Rudd.

"Not if the shareholders are getting a proper return for their investment."

"What if they're not?"

Dray nodded. "Then we're getting somewhere," he said. "If we can prove misuse or mismanagement, then we could formulate a request to the High Court Registrar. Do you have such evidence?"

"I think it might be available," said Rudd.

"How many Buckland House shares have you acquired?"

"None yet," said Rudd.

The lawyer frowned. "For someone without any holding, you seem remarkably confident," he said.

"I intend to negotiate a share exchange when I acquire the liner fleet," said Rudd.

"Will that be acceptable to the Buckland House board?"

"If it isn't then I don't want their fleet," said Rudd simply.

"Do you imagine your bargaining position sufficiently strong?"

"I won't know that until I begin negotiations."

Dray sat back in his chair, interlocking his ugly fingers. "If you can provide provable evidence of irregularities that could be shown contrary to public interest, then you would have cause for challenge," he said. "Without it, the family holding could completely baulk you, no matter how strong your other shareholder support was."

"I understand," said Rudd.

"Shareholders' fights are usually messy," warned Dray. "This one would be particularly so."

"Are you warning me against it?"

"I'm advising you to think carefully upon it, before you commit yourself."

"I always do that, sir," said Rudd.

"I'll have my written opinion available within a week," promised Dray.

"By which time I'll have decided what to do," said Rudd.

On the way back to the Berridge in the car, Bunch said, "Why didn't you mention the gambling settlement; that's precisely what he was talking about."

"I just wanted general guidance at this stage," said Rudd. "Let's see if I can get a seat on the board first."

Hallett was waiting in the suite when they entered, clipboard in hand. "Senator Jeplow has called three times from Washington. I've said we'll get back to him," announced his personal assistant.

"It'll be the commission payments," said Rudd.

"What do you want me to do?" asked the lawyer.

Rudd thought for several moments. "There's nothing more you can do here," he said. "I'll come back as soon as I've had the meeting with Buckland. You go ahead of me, direct to Washington. Set up a meeting for the day after tomorrow. . . ." He thought again. "Better make it afternoon. I'll hold a board meeting in New York in the morning." He looked to Hallett. "Better fix that, by the way. Anything else?"

"Someone called Lady Vanessa Hartland has called you twice."

Towards the end of Snaith's account of the meeting, Richard Haffaford got up from his desk and went to the panoramic window with the view of the City of London and St Paul's Cathedral. He remained there, silent for several moments, after the Buckland House director had finished. "No indication who he could be dealing with?" he asked at last.

"None."

"What's the shareholding of the funds we manage?"

"Nineteen per cent."

"Nineteen per cent of clients' money and our overdraft investment of £10,000,000 is too much to let this sort of thing go on," said Haffaford.

"What can we do?" said Snaith. "Whatever I try to do on the board, I'm blocked."

"Create a shareholders' revolt," said the merchant banker. "Have him removed from the chairmanship and get in more professional people: it's like a damned London club at the moment."

"That's exactly what it's like," said Snaith, with feeling. "It'll still be almost impossible, without boardroom help."

"How committed do you think Gore-Pelham, Condway and Penhardy are?"

"Completely loyal," judged Snaith.

Haffaford shook his head in doubt. "Condway and Penhardy are professional directors," he reminded the other man. "They've got reputations and other directorships to worry about. If we allege mismanagement and they oppose us, later to be proved wrong, that makes them look pretty silly, doesn't it?"

Snaith smiled at the cynical business logic. "What do you intend doing?"

Haffaford thought for a moment. "Perhaps give a discreet lunch at the Connaught," he suggested.

14

The Buckland House liners were named after Scottish counties, with the *Caithness* being the 65,000-ton flagship. It was mounted in the most prominent and favoured position in the display around Buckland's panelled office, followed by the *Sutherland* at 55,000 tons, then the *Ross* at 50,000. Three – the *Nairn*, *Moray* and *Inverness* – had been standardized at 45,000 and the last to be built, the *Kincardine*, had a deadweight tonnage of 40,000. Rudd knew the specifications and details of each but this was the first time he'd seen models and photographs. He walked slowly behind the English chairman, taking his time before each. He thought they looked very impressive: slightly old-fashioned, lacking the cut-away prow and raked funnels of the more modern Scandinavian cruise ships but all the more appealing because of it. Rudd saw the need for an immediate change, beyond whatever modifications had to be made internally. Black hulls were psychologically wrong in the permanent sunshine of Mexico and the West Indies; white was the colour, unless the designer came up with a more convincing argument. He decided that the names were good and that he would try to keep them.

The American turned away, purposely avoiding any interest in the other illustrations around the room of the worldwide hotel chain. The invitation came at once, as he had hoped it would. "And these are the hotels," said Buckland.

Rudd set off again, wanting to remain before each one as long as he had in front of the ships but refusing himself the time. It was interesting to see how little any of them had changed externally, apart from the occasional ventilation shaft or airconditioning tunnel: in their day they must have been regarded as extremely modern. Although architecturally dated, they were still attractive, like the ships.

Buckland stopped before one photograph and said, "The Grand Crispi, in Rome."

Rudd saw a large, typically square Italian palace-type building.

"We keep a personalized registration of every guest, throughout every one of the hotels," said Buckland proudly. "The Queen of Sweden returned to the Crispi after eighteen months to find the biography of Wellington that she had been reading on a previous visit and forgotten to take with her on the bedside table where she had left it, still with the marker in place. . . ." Buckland turned fully to the smaller man. "That's what makes Buckland House so special," he said.

And so uneconomical, thought Rudd. To maintain and update that sort of indexing system would need a small army of clerks. "That's very impressive," he said.

"It's a story we often quote in our publicity," said Buckland. "But it's quite true."

Buckland moved away from the photographs and Rudd followed, not towards the desk but to the far end of the room, to leather armchairs arranged around an open fireplace. There were fire irons in the grate and Rudd presumed it actually worked in the winter.

"I was glad to get your call," said Buckland. This was the first time he had been solely responsible for opening any sort of negotiations and certainly of something this large: before, on smaller things like land purchases or property leasing, he'd always been his father's assistant or the signatory after everything had been argued out and agreed between lawyers and accountants. Buckland felt tight with excitement. And nervous, too.

"I promised forty-eight hours," said Rudd.

"What's your decision?"

"It will have to be a decision of my board, in New York," qualified Rudd. "But I want to continue the discussions."

Buckland smiled, the relief palpably obvious. "I'm very pleased," he said.

"Did your board approve?"

Buckland nodded. "I was authorized to negotiate, if you expressed interest."

122

Rudd relaxed back against the leather, hands outstretched along each overstuffed arm. There was a ritual about negotiation, as formalized as any intricate dance routine: Rudd thought he knew every step and felt quite comfortable. "How much do you want?" he said.

Buckland blinked at the direct demand, off-balanced. "I was expecting you to make an offer," he said.

The first mis-step, thought Rudd. "There will be variations, of course," he said. "The *Caithness* is commercially more useful than, say, the *Kincardine.*"

"Of course," said Buckland. He was relieved at having avoided committing himself.

"It might even be that it would make more commercial sense for me not to buy the entire fleet, but just part of it."

Buckland frowned, feeling the concern go through him. He shook his head. "We could never consider a piecemeal purchase," he said. "The fleet goes intact or stays intact."

"You're adamant about that?"

"Absolutely."

Buckland was behaving like a dog owner determined that a much loved pet would get a good home, thought Rudd. He said. "You've adopted a very hard position."

"It's the only one from which I can offer to negotiate."

The man would imagine he was in control, thought Rudd contentedly. "The *Caithness* is old," he said. "They will all need extensive and expensive refits, if we can conclude a deal."

"I understand that," said Buckland.

"So I must allow for those additional outgoings when considering a price."

"Of course."

"For the *Caithness* I'm prepared to offer $3,000,000," said Rudd. "I put the value of the *Sutherland* at $2,500,000 and the *Ross* at $2,000,000. For the *Nairn, Moray* and *Inverness* I'll pay $1,500,000 each and the *Kincardine*, although it's the smallest, is the newest, so I assess that at $2,000,000."

Buckland did not respond immediately, quickly calculating the total offer. At $14,000,000 on the rate quoting sterling against dollar in the City that morning, the offer fell hopelessly short of what he had expected, something around £6,800,000. Which

123

would still leave them in pawn to the damned merchant bank.

"That's far less than I had in mind," said Buckland.

"What would you consider fair?" said the American. He wondered if Buckland realized they had danced completely around the floor and were back where they'd started.

"Even allowing for your refit costs, the *Caithness* must be valued at $6,000,000," said Buckland forcefully. "The *Sutherland* certainly commands $4,500,000. I would want $4,000,000 for the *Ross*, $3,000,000 each for the *Nairn*, *Moray* and *Inverness* and $4,000,000 for the *Kincardine*." He finished without faltering.

"That's almost double," said Rudd. Even costing the refit expenditure at $1,000,000 a vessel, he was still $5,500,000 below the estimate he had given to the Best Rest board. He shook his head doubtfully. "I'm not at all sure the operating figures justify that assessment."

Buckland managed to keep any expression from his face, even keeping his usually mobile hands tight in his lap, but inwardly the apprehension was numbing him. Dear God, he thought, let me not have pitched it too high!

"The operating figures aren't justified for the routings you are considering," said Buckland. "Your fuelling will be infinitesimal compared to ours. You can adjust the manning levels, too. I estimate running from Florida to Mexico would give you a break-even figure in oil costs, and lower manning a profit of maybe two per cent, after your capital outlay expenditure, within two years."

Rudd nodded approvingly. Not quite right, but then Buckland didn't have the oil figures available as he had; it was still quite impressive. "Your fleet have headquarter and administrative buildings here in London, Liverpool and Southampton," said Rudd.

Buckland nodded, feeling the apprehension lessen slightly: there hadn't been an outright rejection.

"If your fleet remains intact, then I regard that property as part of the fleet," said Rudd. "I would want that inclusive in the figures."

It would mean letting them go below market valuation, but Buckland considered the sacrifice justified. "For the property to be included the price would *have* to be that which I've indicated," he said.

In London the office block had prime sighting and Rudd estimated he could get $4,000,000 for it. He didn't know the property values of Liverpool or Southampton, but guessed each would go for around $500,000 – and that was bringing the expenditure right back into line. It was time for an exhibition step, he decided. "How do you feel about the names?" he said.

"The names?"

· "I like them," said Rudd. "If the appeal of the liners is tradition, then the names are part of it. I would like to retain them."

Where moments before there had been apprehension, there was now the warmth of satisfaction. This was small detail, Buckland recognized; the sort of fine print the lawyers squabbled about to earn their fees, after the agreement had been reached. So he wasn't going to lose him!

"I don't foresee any difficulty with that," said Buckland. He actually *liked* the idea of the titles continuing.

"Buckland House would be responsible for delivering the vessels to a designated American home port?"

"Agreed," said Buckland.

"And our purchase would take effect from that moment of delivery?"

"Yes."

"You understand that everything we have agreed today is subject to approval from my board?" said the American.

"Naturally," said Buckland. "The same restriction applies to myself."

Rudd came forward in his chair, a decisive movement. "I'm prepared to exchange letters of intent on the agreement we have reached," he announced.

"For the purchase price to be $27,500,000?" insisted Buckland.

"Yes."

"When could we exchange letters?"

"This afternoon?"

"I could be ready by then, certainly," said Buckland.

He'd got everything he wanted, thought Rudd; it had been a good day.

125

He'd got everything he wanted, thought Buckland; it had been a good day.

"More port?"

"Thank you."

Richard Haffaford handed Condway the decanter and he added to his glass. The merchant banker had watched the man's face colour change as they had progressed through the meal and the claret: now he glowed, like a traffic signal warning stop.

"I debated whether to accept," said Condway. He coughed to clear his throat but it didn't appear successful.

"Why?"

"Doubtful of the propriety."

"What's improper about the head of a merchant bank lunching with the vice-chairman of one of its clients?"

"Don't play games with me, Haffaford."

"I've not the slightest intention of playing games," said the banker. His face was serious.

"Come to the point then."

"Aren't you worried about Buckland House?"

"No," said Condway at once.

"I think you should be."

"Every company goes through setbacks," said Condway. "Seen it happen a dozen times; stupid to panic at the first sign of trouble."

"This isn't the first sign of trouble," corrected Haffaford. "Your balance sheets show a down-turn stretching back more than three years, without any effort being made to correct it. The company is in a mess and you're on enough city boards to recognize it."

Condway clipped his cigar and played the taper around the end to light it, considering what had been said. "You still haven't come to the point," he complained.

"These secret negotiations are wrong," said Haffaford. "They should never have been allowed."

"Nothing can be determined without board approval."

"He's behaved improperly before."

"Are you *warning* me?"

126

"Making the point, at least," said Haffaford. "Reputations are important, in the city."

"That's always been the case."

"How many boards do you sit on, Lord Condway?"

Condway puffed the cigar until the end glowed. "Twelve." he said.

"So you're highly respected."

Condway let his face register at the near impudence. "What does that mean?"

"That it would be a great misfortune to lose that respect through misplaced trust and loyalty," said Haffaford. He indicated the decanter. "More port?"

"Thank you," accepted Condway.

Like a man living with a congenital deformity, a livid birthmark or a limp about which he could do nothing, Rudd acknowledged that since Angela his attitude to women had been immature; practically a theatrical pretence. The grief had been honest and natural enough, just like the absorption in work to compensate for it. But it should have ended. There should have been a gradual, if reluctant acceptance of what had happened. And then a proper, adult adjustment. Instead he had created an emotional fortress with a moat and unassailable walls, into which he could run and crank up the drawbridge at the first sign of danger. So he'd become a social as well as emotional recluse. That was why he had lied and come so close to making a fool of himself at the dinner party, and why the evening was proving so difficult with Vanessa. She'd tried hard enough. When he arrived at Devonshire Mews she'd appeared almost gauche, explaining the decision to open her London house had been a hurried one and that she had no staff, impressing him to open the champagne and producing glasses that needed to be dusted before he could pour it; they couldn't find a proper cloth and had to use his handkerchief.

She asked to go to Annabel's as if she hadn't been there before, and was instantly recognized by name at the door. She kissed the head waiter. From their table she pointed out the society figures and relayed the gossip. At first it was amusing and then she

127

switched anecdotes, recounting life as the wife of a gentleman farmer in a forgotten part of England and he felt sorry for her husband. He wondered if she were as bored with him. She didn't appear so. By the time they got on to the tiny square of a dance floor, there had been the champagne at the house and two more bottles of wine at the table and the brandy. She ground her body into his, crotch against crotch, heavy, nipple-hard breasts into his chest. He didn't feel any excitement and she recognized it.

"I don't think you're enjoying yourself," she said, back at the table.

"I am," he said.

She grimaced. "Margaret said you were very controlled."

He wondered if they had spoken about him or whether it was a throw-away remark. It wasn't important. "She's a very direct woman," he said.

"So am I."

"I noticed."

"I wouldn't have guessed it."

"Would you like to dance any more?"

"No."

"More brandy?"

"No."

Rudd gestured for the bill. "It's been fun," he said.

"Sure." She let the disbelief show.

She sat withdrawn from him in the car, gazing along the width of the seat. It had rained while they were inside the club and the tyres sounded sticky against the road. Rain hadn't been forecast and people were hurrying along with their jacket collars and coats shrugged around their heads. He got out ahead of the chauffeur when they got back to Devonshire Mews, helping her out of the car. She opened the door into the house, looked back pointedly at the vehicle and then went inside, leaving the door open. He followed her.

"You haven't dismissed the car," she said.

"No."

"I see."

"I've got to go back to New York tomorrow."

"Would it have been any different if you hadn't?"

"Probably not."

128

She laughed. "I actually opened up the house," she said. "I feel stupid now."

"I enjoyed the evening."

"You already said so: I didn't believe you then."

"I shall be back in a few days. Perhaps I can repay Ian's hospitality then."

"I'm not sure I'll still be in London."

"If you are, I'd like you to come." Now he was over-compensating, Rudd thought.

"We'll see," she said.

The evening had been a mistake, Rudd accepted, slumped in the back of the car returning him to the Berridge. It had been instinctive to accept the woman's invitation, to maintain any goodwill for what was to follow. Which was ludicrous: there wouldn't be any goodwill – couldn't be any – once he made a bid. So all he'd done was embarrass both of them, for no good reason.

The rain stopped. Rudd depressed the button, lowering the window. One day, he decided, he was going to have to lower the drawbridge, like he had the window, and come out from behind the battlements. When he did, it wouldn't be for someone like Lady Vanessa Hartland.

Hallett was waiting in the suite when Rudd returned to the Berridge. "There's a problem in Washington," he said.

The connection to Bunch was established in minutes. Rudd sat listening to what the lawyer had to say and then said, "The bastard is blackmailing us."

"Right," agreed Bunch. "What shall I do?"

"Wait until I get there," said Rudd. He put the telephone down and looked up to the personal assistant. "I've been suckered," he said. There was disbelief in his voice. "Well and truly suckered," he repeated, shaking his head.

15

To avoid the concentration of Manhattan the flightpath of the helicopter from Kennedy airport followed the East River. Rudd was seated to the right, so he was able to look down upon the island. It looked what it was supposed to be, a place of castles for giants. He started to isolate the landmarks, first the rectangle of the park and from it the Park Summit and then began to concentrate, identifying the Chrysler building and the Wall Street towers and the Empire State. Ten years in the city and he'd never got to the top of the Empire State, he realized. He'd tried once, years ago, but there'd been a crowd and he hadn't bothered since. Like with so much else. He frowned at the downbeat reflection, recognizing the unusual depression. It was because things were becoming ragged, he decided. They were ragged because of the share structure controlling Buckland House and because, even if he didn't admire him professionally, he quite liked Buckland himself. And Texas was the biggest irritant of all. Texas more than England; much more. He could not have moved any other way and the Saudi decision couldn't have been foreseen. But whatever the excuses, he'd still ended up with his head over the barrel. And Harry Rudd didn't make that sort of mistake.

The helicopter started to descend as soon as it crossed the Manhattan Bridge and was quite low over the Brooklyn causeway.

Rudd looked out expectantly and saw the skyscraper block containing the Best Rest headquarters. It was the first occasion for a long time when he couldn't predict the outcome of a board meeting.

Hallett had sent a car, although the office was only a few hundred yards from the heliport, and was waiting when Rudd entered. "Everyone's waiting," he said nervously. "Mr Bunch got back from Washington on the nine o'clock shuttle."

130

Rudd handed over his briefcase and said, "So all we've got to do is wait for Morrison."

"No," said Hallett. "He's here, too."

Rudd had gone to his desk and was leaning over the appointments diary. He frowned up. "Morrison's here!"

"For more than an hour," confirmed the personal assistant.

"Can't remember the last time that happened."

Hallett smiled but said nothing.

"Ask him to stop by here, after the meeting," said Rudd. "Say there's something I'd like to talk to him about."

Hallett nodded, putting a reminder in the notebook of his fold-up case.

The rest of the board were already seated when Rudd entered. He nodded, serious-faced, at the greetings and said, standing before his chair, "Thank you all for being so prompt." He spoke directly at Morrison. His father-in-law stared back without expression. Having sat throughout the helicopter flights, Rudd remained standing.

"I've called this meeting," he began, "to report fully on the negotiations so far with Buckland House and to seek board approval both to continue and to endorse the way in which we continue."

Morrison looked pointedly at Prince Faysel's empty chair. Taking the lead, Rudd said: "I should explain that now the negotiations have reached a positive stage, Prince Faysel feels he should declare interest. He's had to return to Saudi Arabia, anyway, to prepare for a forthcoming OPEC meeting but had no intention of taking part in the discussion about the liner fleet, either here or in London. He has vested the proxy vote at my discretion and has done the same with Sir Ian Buckland."

"Seems honourable," said Ottway.

Expecting figures, Patrick Walker and Eric Böch had pulled notepads closer to them. They would have to wait, thought Rudd. First he outlined the peculiar share construction which provided the Buckland family with its power and then gave an almost verbatim account of the lawyer's opinion that it could be attacked if proper grounds could be found. He left the financial details until last. He talked of his negotiations with Buckland and finished by passing around copies of letters of intent that had been exchanged before he left London. At the end, both Walker and Böch were writing hurriedly. It was Walker who spoke first. "That's good," he said. "The initial estimate was $35,000,000 for purchase and another $7,000,000 for refit."

"And we can do more to recoup our capital expenditure," said Rudd. "I estimate that $5,000,000 is recoverable upon the property and you'll see the initialled agreement is for the vessels to be delivered by skeleton crews to us here in America. With our responsibility beginning here, we'll save ourselves redundancy payments to the existing employees. I put that at a $500,000 saving on a conservative estimate."

"They'll never agree to that, surely?" said Ottway.

"They might be concentrating on other things," said Rudd.

"Like what?" demanded Morrison, immediately suspicious.

"If you'll all look at the letter of intent you'll see that the phrase used throughout is 'purchase price' of $27,500,000. Never is it stipulated that the purchase shall be solely a cash one."

"What do you intend?" said Böch.

"Qualifying the offer," said Rudd. "Just $20,000,000 in cash and the remaining $7,500,000 in a stock exchange, Best Rest for Buckland House Preferential issue. We'll need that sort of holding at least, if we are later to make any effective take-over assault."

"Is that all?" asked Walker.

Rudd shook his head. "I shall also ask for a seat upon the board."

"That's going a long way beyond the letter of intent," said Ottway.

"Deliberately so," said Rudd. "Unless we have the seat and the stock exchange, then I don't consider the proposal worth pursuing."

Morrison stared down at the papers before him, scribbling indecipherable patterns on the paper. That morning, before flying from Boston, he'd checked with Grearson the extent of his Buckland House portfolio: at close of trading the previous day, his investment had amounted to $800,000. He felt a hollowness, deep inside, at the thought of being left with it. He tried to subdue the thought, to decide instead what sort of reaction Rudd and the rest of the board would expect from him.

"Since when have we handed around Best Rest stock like so much loose change?" he said.

Rudd sighed and Morrison knew he'd got it right. "We're not offering it like loose change," said the chairman patiently. "We're making a sound business approach, in no way endangering or diminishing the strength of the parent company here."

"What would be our percentage holding, if they agreed?" said Böch.

"Twelve Preferential voting stock," replied Rudd at once. "Faysel's Saudi investment fund has six. The Buckland family have a total of sixteen apart from their Initial holding and there's another twenty-four per cent divided between the other directors. The big insurance companies and investment funds control eighteen per cent and the rest is held by small investors."

"So with Faysel's vote, we've got eighteen per cent Preferential before we start seeking support?" said Böch, head bent over his page of figures.

"Yes," confirmed Rudd. "And before we make that bid, we will have challenged the Initial stock which locks everything up. The big funds are professional, so they should come to us. We'd pick up a lot of small stuff and there'd be defections on the board, certainly from the merchant bank people."

"You make it seem remarkably simple," said Morrison, from the far end of the table.

"It should be, once the court challenge has been made."

"Aren't you overlooking the fact that your challenge might fail?" pounced Morrison. "*Then* we'd have used our stock like loose change, made Buckland House shareholders nervous and cut our investment value with lower share prices, and gained little more than an expensive fleet of ships."

"Which can be made profitable," said Rudd, deciding upon an immediate correction. "And I'm convinced that we've proper and fitting grounds to make the legal challenge. I shall, of course, put those grounds before the lawyer we've engaged in London and I won't proceed or risk this company's holding or reputation without a positive opinion that we stand more than a fifty per cent chance of success.

Inwardly Morrison still felt nervous. He needed closer involvement, the ability to move more instant judgments than at present, dependent as he was on whenever Rudd chose to return and report. "You mentioned a reluctance in the Buckland family to dispose of the fleet?" he said, going back to Rudd's opening statement.

"Yes," said the chairman. "Like everything else in the group, it's regarded with a certain amount of nostalgia."

"The ships will form a separate division for us?" said Morrison.

"Yes."

"Under a separate, subsidiary board?"

"That's the usual practice." Rudd was studying the old man, curious at the approach.

"I have a suggestion," said Morrison. "Why not invite Sir Ian Buckland on to that board? It would continue the family association and having a titled Englishman would add prestige to our holding."

Rudd stared at his father-in-law, trying to remember the last time the man had made anything like a constructive suggestion. Perhaps the earlier impulsive thought in his office had been well founded.

"I think that's an excellent idea," said Rudd.

"And it would lessen any abruptness which might appear from our request to have our chairman sit upon the board of Buckland House," said Walker, supporting the proposal.

"It would mean the creation of a board, of course," said Morrison.

"Easily achieved?" said Böch, taking the bait.

"I would have thought so," said Ottway. "Our own chairman naturally. Prince Faysel, for added continuity both with Buckland House and Best Rest . . ."

". . . I would welcome Walter Bunch," said Rudd.

"And I propose our president, Herbert Morrison," said Walker.

"Of course," said Rudd at once. The man deserved recognition for his suggestion.

Morrison lowered his head. The momentary satisfaction concealed, he looked up and said. "I'd be happy to serve."

The man probably regarded it as a safeguard to protect what he imagined to be the proper interests of Best Rest, thought

Rudd. "We've moved ahead of ourselves," he said. "There hasn't been a decision yet about the acquisition of the ships."

"I move," said Ottway, confident of the mood of the meeting.

"Seconded," said Bunch.

"To the motion?" invited Rudd.

"The purchase must be conditional upon a board placing and share apportionment," interrupted Morrison.

"That's the assurance I've already given," said Rudd. With Faysel's proxy vote, it was unanimous. Rudd cleared his throat and said: "There's another matter that needs to be discussed," he said. "A difficulty has come up with the Texas development."

"The suspension of the Saudi funds?" anticipated Walker.

"No," said Rudd. He turned to the lawyer. "Why don't you take us through it?"

"We're the victims of a greedy man," said Bunch bluntly. "We've invested nearly $30,000,000 in open zoned land and now Jeplow says the decision to re-allocate for development isn't so definite as he understood it to be."

"What!"

The outrage came from Morrison just ahead of Walker.

"It's a poker game," said Bunch. "He's pressuring for a commission payment. When he's sure of his payment, the brake goes off."

"That's extortion," said Walker.

"If you consider it, most business commissions are exactly that," said Rudd.

"You don't seem surprised at this," accused Morrison.

"I was surprised enough when I heard about it in London," said Rudd. "Since then I've had time to think it through."

"What's the way out?" said Böch confidently.

"There isn't one," said Rudd. "We'll pay him."

"Pay a blackmailer!"

Rudd went back to his father-in-law. "Yes."

"Are you mad!"

"No," said Rudd. "Just determined not to get caught out with this."

"Isn't there any way we can withdraw from the land purchase?" asked Böch.

"Absolutely none," said Bunch. "Unless that land is re-

135

zoned, Best Rest has contributed $30,000,000 to the people of Texas."

Anxious for the maximum benefit from the totally unexpected development, Morrison said, "These negotiations seem to have been conducted with an amazing naïvety."

Rudd showed no emotion at the criticism. "There was no other way," he said.

"I warned at the time it was illegal," reminded Morrison, anxious to get the record established. "I think the whole thing should be turned over to the FBI."

"Can we really afford to do something like that?" asked Rudd.

"Of course not," said Walker at once. He stared at Rudd. "There's been an error of judgment," he said.

"Which can be reversed," said Rudd.

"At what further cost?" said Morrison.

"Two hundred and fifty thousand dollars."

"To bribe a politician!" exclaimed Morrison. "How many more laws do you intend breaking on behalf of this company?"

"A commission, not a bribe," said Rudd.

"Would you like a court of law to decide the difference?" asked Böch.

The sides were quickly forming, thought Rudd. "It's resolvable," he said.

"I don't like it," insisted Morrison. There was immediate support from Walker and Böch. Ottway hovered indeterminately.

"I'd like less losing $30,000,000," said Rudd.

"Perhaps we should have considered that earlier," said Morrison.

"I proceeded with the negotiations with the full knowledge and authority of this board," reminded Rudd.

"Were we fully informed of *all* the facts?" demanded Böch.

"Of course you were," said Rudd, letting the irritation show for the first time. "You don't imagine I would knowingly have got us trapped in this sort of situation, do you?"

"I don't think we've any alternative but to let the chairman continue negotiations," said Walker.

"What do you mean by saying it's resolvable?" Ottway asked Rudd.

Before the chairman could reply, Morrison said, "Perhaps that is better left unsaid at an open meeting."

Rudd hadn't expected any support from Morrison but he was surprised by the speed at which the others were abandoning him. "Do I have your authority to continue negotiating?" he said.

"That authority came from the previous meeting," said Morrison hurriedly again.

"Any other views?" asked Rudd, gazing around the table.

"No one spoke. Rudd walked from the boardroom with Bunch. Immediately inside the chairman's office, Bunch said, "They're frightened."

"They've got cause to be," said Rudd.

"What about you?"

"Bloody annoyed."

"Jeplow has been at it a long time," said Bunch.

"So have I," said Rudd. "I should have seen the danger."

To Hallett Rudd said, "Fix the plane to Washington for two."

"When do you intend going back to London?" asked Bunch.

"Immediately afterwards."

Bunch frowned but said nothing.

The intercom sounded and Rudd's appointments secretary reported the arrival of Herbert Morrison. Hallett and Bunch left by the main door, leaving it open for the president to enter. Morrison stopped just inside the door: Rudd doubted that the man had been in the room more than a dozen times since the move of Best Rest headquarters from Boston to New York.

"You wanted to see me?" said Morrison. The voice was more neutral than hostile.

Rudd was standing away from his chairman's desk, not wanting to irritate the other man. He indicated a chair. Morrison hesitated and then sat down.

Seeking an opening, Rudd said, "I thought the suggestion of inviting Buckland on to the liner board was a good one."

"You made that clear at the meeting."

Rudd sighed. "I thought it was worth saying again."

"You asked me here for that?"

"No."

"What then?"

137

"Don't you think it time all this ended?" demanded Rudd. He hoped the weariness hadn't sounded in his voice.

"All what ended?"

It was like arguing over a baseball mitt in a school playground, thought Rudd. "It's been ten years," he said.

Morrison's face hardened against any emotion.

Rudd went on: "Couldn't we behave towards each other like adults?"

"I'm unaware that we haven't."

Rudd knew nothing would be gained by giving way to the irritation. "When was the last time, before today, that you made a constructive suggestion at any board meeting?"

"Are you challenging my performance as a director?"

Rudd recognised his approach had been inept and he regretted it. "I'm trying to make a point," he said. "We've both of us only one interest, the company. Why don't we work together for it, instead of apart?"

"The board seems to function satisfactorily as things are."

"But it could function better," pressed Rudd, sensing a relaxation in the other man's attitude. "And now we are going to create another company and if we're going to use that as a springboard to obtain all of Buckland House, then a division between us is going to be a hindrance."

"Perhaps I should come to London for the formation?" said Morrison.

Rudd thought the man was avoiding the issue but saw the suggestion as a further concession. "I agree entirely," he said. "When would you think of coming?"

Morrison gestured uncertainly. "Almost at once," he said. "Your negotiations won't take much longer, will they?"

Now Rudd looked uncertain. "Depends upon the reaction to the changed offer," he said. "But they're in a corner. I think they'll take it, in the end."

"Within the next week or two then?" said the older man.

"We've moved away from what we were originally talking about," reminded Rudd.

"I will always hold you responsible for what happened to Angela," said Morrison.

"I know that."

138

"There could never be friendship."

"I know that, too."

Morrison rose to his feet, a ponderous, awkward movement. He hesitated, unsure, and then thrust out his hand. Rudd was so astonished that it took him several moments to respond.

"I'll work with you, with the right aim in mind," said Morrison.

Rudd was glad he'd made the effort: he should have done it years ago, instead of letting things drift.

Rudd knew the impression was practically blasphemous, which was why he didn't express it, but he rarely approached the domes of the Capitol and administration buildings of Washington without thinking the designer had worked on the side on wedding cake decorations. The car halted at Independence and First and he and Bunch went into the square office building to the right.

The attendant directed them along the echoing corridor: they were on time and a secretary was waiting, showing them immediately into Jeplow's office. It was grand, to match the man, with crossed American flags behind the desk, a bust of Abraham Lincoln on a plinth and, just as in the Georgetown house, an open catalogue of pictures with the famous, Jeplow in a group with Eisenhower, then Kennedy, then Johnson, then Ford, then Carter, and then Reagan. Rudd wondered why Nixon was still absent.

"Delighted to see you again, sir. Delighted." The handshake was forceful and as prolonged as before. Bunch's greeting was less effusive: Jeplow was a strict observer of protocol.

"I'm concerned at what appears to be the difficulty that has risen," said Rudd, at once.

The senator gestured as if waving an irritant fly from around his head. "A hiccup, sir. Nothing more than a hiccup."

"I'm relieved to hear it," said Rudd. "My company would find it extremely difficult if it were anything else."

"Simply administration," insisted the senator.

"How long before it's resolved?" pressed Rudd.

This time the gesture was one of uncertainty. "Who knows with bureaucracies and administration?" said Jeplow.

139

"My impression was that you are very close to the affairs in Austin," said Rudd.

"The state capital is still some way from here," said Jeplow.

"My company is an expanding one," said Rudd. "I've come here directly from a board meeting in New York at which we discussed expansion and development. The inconvenience I spoke about was a commitment of finance to this project when another has arisen to which we could more easily devote the money set aside for the Texas hotels." He decided it sounded convincing.

Momentarily Jeplow's complacent demeanour faltered. "You'd lose $30,000,000!" he said.

"No," said Rudd at once. "It's taxable: charitable donations are entirely deductible." Rudd indicated Bunch sitting alongside "According to the enquiries my fellow director has made there's little other land available under the sort of terms that would attract another hotel corporation: it would be a great pity to lose the opportunity to bring extra development to your state, don't you think?"

Jeplow was too practised a politician to show his concern but Rudd guessed it was there.

"I assure you, sir, it's the most minor of difficulties."

"I'd like a date when I can expect it to be settled," said Rudd, making the open demand. "There's a cut-off period for funds for the other development I've mentioned."

Jeplow hesitated, aware the control of the meeting had been taken from him.

The senator made an effort to recover. "Know Washington well, sir?" he asked.

There was time to attack and time to compromise, thought Rudd. "Not well," he said.

"Wonderful city," said Jeplow. He cupped his hand into a cornucopia. "Here we're at the very heart of things. Some great landmarks, too."

"I believe there are," said Rudd. The man was very careful.

"Walk with me in the Capitol Gardens, sir. Let me show you."

Jeplow rose and Rudd came up with him. Bunch remained in his chair, knowing he had no part in the charade.

Rudd and Jeplow went silently back along the echoing cor-

140

ridors and out on to Independence Avenue. There was good enough reason, Rudd supposed, but it still seemed like posturing and he was irritated by it. They crossed into the garden area halfway down the hill. There was a profusion of flowers, predominantly red and what looked like poppies, although Rudd wasn't sure. The wind stiffened and Rudd wished he had worn a topcoat. Jeplow continued to maintain the pretence, gesturing distractedly down the Avenue towards the White House and then needlessly pointing to the Washington monument and the Lincoln beyond. Rudd looked and nodded politely. Directly beneath the Capitol, the senator said, "I've enjoyed our business dealings, sir."

At their previous meetings, Rudd hadn't been so aware of the man's frequent use of "sir".

"So have I. I think it has been mutually advantageous to us both," said Rudd, wanting to make it easy for the man.

"Wanted to talk to you about the matter of mutual benefit," said the senator. He pointed to his right. "That's the route the English took, when they burned the White House."

"There's the matter of commission," agreed Rudd.

"Man in my position has to be careful, sir," confided Jeplow. He indicated a path that would lead them parallel with the buildings and Rudd fell into step alongside. "Washington's got a problem with gossip . . . malicious innuendo."

"I fully appreciate the need for caution," said Rudd.

"Mr Bunch gave me to understand we might be able to reach some convenient arrangement," said the politician.

Everyone had their schemes of arrangement, thought Rudd. "Entirely to your convenience," he said.

"Don't like cheques," insisted Jeplow.

"I think we can avoid that."

Jeplow nodded and gave a quick on-off smile. "You familiar with Liechtenstein, sir?"

"No," said Rudd.

"Admirable little country; admirable, discreet banking arrangements."

Jeplow was more financially sophisticated than he had imagined, conceded Rudd. "We have divisions in Europe, of course," he said.

141

"There's a firm of solicitors and accountants, in Vaduz. Handles things for me. Name of Gotwieler and Sturnden. My account number with them is 987-4457. Designation letter is F."

"Wouldn't there need to be some letter of introduction?" asked Rudd.

Jeplow got on the path leading back towards his office. "They'll be advised," he said.

"We didn't decide upon a definite date for the re-zoning," reminded Rudd.

Jeplow stopped, smiling. "Nor we did," he said, as if he were surprised at the prompting. "I'd guess it to be the 21st."

"I'd expect the commission payment to go into Liechtenstein on the 22nd," said Rudd. For a moment he thought the senator was going to argue, but then the man nodded agreement and said, "Perfect."

The path led back to Independence Avenue, facing the Madison and Cannon Buildings. Jeplow paused, waiting for the lights to change so they could cross. He said, "Isn't this a wonderful city?"

"Wonderful," agreed Rudd.

"People know what they're doing here," said the politician. "They're professionals."

Some, thought Rudd, more than others.

Because it was a limousine without a division between the driver and the passengers there was no detailed conversation between the lawyer and Rudd on the way to the airport. The flight plan for the Lear jet was already filed for the return to New York so there was no delay. Bunch leaned back in his seat, looking down at the receding city beneath them and said, "You were pretty rough."

"He deserved it," said Rudd.

"How are we going to do it?"

"We're going to need a lot of liquid money for Buckland House," said Rudd. "Put through a major transference, say $23,000,000, into London, but I want to start mopping up the loose shares throughout the group. That means broker funding in France, South Africa, England and Hong Kong for the Asian holdings. Let's say $5,000,000 apiece. Make up Jeplow's commission in sideway transfers."

"Are we really going to have to pay the whole lot over in cash?"

"That's what Jeplow wanted," said Rudd. "But I don't see why we can't provide Gotwieler and Sturnden with the bearer's cheque: that will give us a traceable number, even though Jeplow's name won't be on it. The inference would be sufficient, if his association with them became public."

"He could be useful to us in the future," said the lawyer.

Rudd nodded. "I hope he doesn't get too greedy," he said.

The two telephone calls that night were made just one hour and a little over two hundred miles apart. Herbert Morrison apologized for intruding business into the home of Gene Grearson, but explained he wanted to take advantage of the time difference with Europe. Grearson said he understood and that it didn't matter.

"I want a buying push, until Friday," said Morrison. "Anything and everything there is associated with Buckland House or any of its subsidiaries. And then on Friday, we stop."

"Any financial limit?"

"None," said Morrison. "I'll buy whatever the price."

"Why Friday closure?" demanded the lawyer.

To keep within the law, thought Morrison. He said, "By then I'll have enough."

When Joanne Hinkler didn't personally answer her telephone, there was always a crisply efficient female voice. Rudd had wondered, months before, about an answering service and Joanne had shaken her head at the lack of discretion and called the woman her secretary. Rudd had wondered the extent of that role, too, but not openly; it wasn't his business.

"I'm afraid Miss Hinkler isn't available," said the voice. "She won't be for the rest of the evening."

"It is late," agreed Rudd.

"Can she get back to you tomorrow?"

"No," said Rudd. "I'm leaving the city early, for Europe."

143

"Is there a message?" There was never a request for a name. "No," said Rudd. "No message."

Because of the summer the court had moved to Jeddah to get the benefit of the sea-wind, and it was there that Faysel and Hassain met. Faysel's palace was separate from the larger family home, really an elaborate castellated villa, pure white and built against the shore-line. For comfort both men wore robes as they relaxed on the verandah overlooking the Red Sea. The sun was low on the horizon, soft crimson after the glare of the day.

"It's been decided to announce officially what we've been doing, in advance of the OPEC meeting," said Hassain.

"Why?"

"To get a longer agreement on stability," said Hassain.

"There's a risk of it having the opposite effect, from the militants," said Faysel.

"The Council feel the risk is justified," said Hassain. He sipped his tea. "I'm sorry for the effect upon the investments allowed you," he said.

"We expected it," said Faysel.

"Will it cause you personal embarrassment?"

"It will pass," said Faysel.

"There was an irony in your American commitment being allocated to the development in Texas," said Hassain.

Faysel looked curiously across the gathering darkness at his friend, frowning as Hassain explained Jeplow's encounter with the Saudi ambassador. "Yes," Faysel agreed at the end. "An amazing irony."

16

Buckland gazed at the other directors grouped in front of him, experiencing a feeling of contentment he'd never known before. He'd come of age, he decided; even that didn't properly describe how he felt, but it was close. Never again would they doubt him, comparing him to his father. And he knew they all had, every one of them. And not just Snaith and Smallwood and the absent Faysel. Condway and Penhardy, too, for all their apparent support; even Gore-Pelham. To them all he'd been the rich man's son, silver-spooned into position by name instead of by ability. But not any longer. He'd earned the right to be where he was in this boardroom: the right to be called chairman.

It was Condway who spoke first. He looked up from the American letter of intent and said, "I think our chairman deserves a vote of thanks from this board."

"Hear, hear," said Penhardy.

"It was not without its difficulties," said Buckland, wanting to prolong the enjoyment. "But I think it's been concluded in our favour."

"Absolutely," said Gore-Pelham. "I think you've done a damned fine piece of negotiating."

"It's a letter of intent, not a formal offer," said Snaith.

Buckland smiled condescendingly at the predictable attitude of the merchant banker. "I would not have brought it before the board unless I'd been confident of it becoming one," he said. "There is a meeting arranged between myself and Rudd tomorrow. I've already had confirmation of his return from New York and there can be only one conclusion from that."

It was the perfect rebuff and Snaith looked away disconcerted.

"Was there any indication of agreement from the American board in that message?" said Smallwood.

Buckland knew he had complete control. "He'd hardly be coming back if there hadn't been, would he?"

"We're responsible for redundancy," said Snaith.

"They're our employees," said Condway, letting the irritation show.

"How much will that be?" persisted Smallwood.

"I haven't had it costed at this stage," said Buckland. "There is the statutory regulation, about which you're all aware: no doubt our industrial staff will have to negotiate with the unions. Quite clearly at this point it would be wrong to open those talks."

"They'll sell the property, of course," said Smallwood.

Buckland sighed pointedly. "I've already made it clear that the offer began at half the figure I was eventually able to get. To achieve that increase, I had to appear to make concessions. The redundancy is our liability anyway. The property will be superfluous to our needs and I considered its sacrifice justified, for the final offer.

"Quite understandable," said Penhardy. "I think it would be a good idea if members of this board recognised what has positively been achieved and stopped nitpicking at unimportant details."

"This solves our short-term needs, if it's successfully concluded" said Snaith. "What about the long term?"

"Long term?" queried Gore-Pelham.

"The uneconomical running of our hotels," said Snaith.

"I don't consider that what's being achieved with the fleet sale is just a short-term solution," said Buckland positively. "It enables us completely to settle our outstanding bank liability. And that represents a yearly saving of £1,230,000 in loan servicing and commission. Disposing of the fleet will get rid of a £550,000 loss. The combined saving is £1,780,000, against this year's deficit of £800,000. To my reckoning, we're back in profitability within a year."

Snaith frowned at the chairman. "That doesn't follow at all!" he protested. "Our hotels are losing and those losses are increasing. If we don't impose a proper management structure, then in two years' time we'll be back where we started."

"I wonder if that would be the view of the other merchant bank organizations," said Buckland. He spoke as the idea came

to him and felt a leap of satisfaction at the thought. If Haffaford's
loan was settled, they could be dispensed with and the company
could switch to another merchant bank. He had the boardroom
power to make such a move now. And he'd bloody well do it: he'd
been humiliated enough by these damned penny-pinching
Shylocks.

"I think this is extending the discussion far beyond what is
necessary," said Condway. "We were summoned to consider the
liner sale, not devise future planning structure. There's time
enough for that, if it's necessary at all, in the coming months."

Buckland and Snaith exchanged glances and Buckland knew
the banker had understood the threat. He said, "You've all had
the opportunity to consider the terms of the American offer. Do I
have the board's permission to continue?"

"I formerly propose," said Gore-Pelham.

"Seconded," said Penhardy.

The vote was unanimous, as Buckland knew it had to be. He'd
proved himself, he thought again. He couldn't remember a day
he'd enjoyed more.

Lady Margaret Buckland's involvement in charity work was
more than a compensation for the part-time relationship that she
had with her husband. She was genuinely enthusiastic about
organization. At university she had been secretary of the Cambridge Union. She had accompanied her father on two ambas-
sadorial postings, to Athens and then Madrid, and acted as his
social secretary on both occasions. Because of the old lady's
insistence, it was Margaret who divided the housekeeping bills
between the two houses in Cambridgeshire. She kept account
books of all her own expenditure, even though they were never
called for. The clothes in her wardrobes and closets were
arranged both in order of colour and season: sweaters and scarfs
and shirts and underwear had their separate drawers and each
item was precisely folded and partitioned, often with tissue
paper to avoid creasing. Invariably she found she could improve
upon her maid's work. Margaret Buckland was a very tidy
woman.

Because the children's charity ball was to be held at the

Berridge, she convened the meeting of the organizing committee there, in one of the first-floor suites. Lady Fiona Harvey was among the eight serving on the committee. They arrived to find laid out for them a complete breakdown of the previous year's working, an analysis sheet setting expenditure against income and a separate list of suggestions for improvements. Margaret ran the meeting with the precision of her report, a stopwatch prominently set before her to prevent the discussion becoming a display of public-speaking. Every one of her proposals was accepted. She scheduled three hours but the meeting only took two and a half, so even with the straggled, breaking-up conversation, she and Fiona were still in the grill room ahead of Vanessa.

"Congratulations for your usual efficiency," said Fiona.

"I enjoy detail," said Margaret. She was dutiful about it, like everything else.

"How's Ian?"

"Fine," said Margaret. "I was sorry to hear about you and Peter."

"I wasn't," said Fiona. "The marriage had been falling apart for years; he was bloody dull."

"What are you going to do?"

"Enjoy myself," said Fiona.

"Is there anyone else?"

Fiona hesitated. "I'm up to 'B' in the telephone book."

Vanessa entered proprietorially, which Margaret supposed was justified, smiling at the immediate recognition from managers and head waiters and allowing herself to be escorted to a table in a half circle of men. She flustered down into her chair, accepted the wine that Margaret had already ordered, bent forward to kiss Fiona and said, "Hell of a morning. A list of things to do as long as my arm and I've done none of it. How about you two?"

"Margaret has guided us as always, like sheep," said Fiona.

Vanessa looked at her sister-in-law. "I wish I could be like you," she said. "I bet you don't even sweat in the sun."

"I do, actually," said Margaret. "How's the house?"

"A shambles," said Vanessa. "It was a mistake to have opened it."

148

"Why not move back with us?"

"I might. I spoke to Rupert this morning and he asked me when I was coming back."

"When are you?" said Fiona.

"No sooner than I have to," said Vanessa. "Yorkshire bores me stiff. There's not a decent man for miles."

"I get bored in Cambridgeshire sometimes." Margaret was aware of both women looking at her.

"I think the world ends north of Golders Green," said Fiona. "Certainly as far as men worth taking to bed are concerned."

"What's divorce like?" said Vanessa.

"Great. I should have done it years ago: men seem to find it an aphrodisiac."

"I've been looking for an effective one for years," said Vanessa.

Margaret felt uncomfortable with the brittle conversation, unable to join in. She didn't *want* to join in. There was nothing chic or sophisticated, boasting of affairs or the virility of lovers. She thought it was cheap. She bent over her plate, embarrassed at the thought of the fantasies she sometimes had. But that's all they were, fantasies. And she was sure all women had them. At least she didn't try to put them into practice, like these two.

Aware that Vanessa was talking to her, she looked up.

"Are you going up to Cambridge this weekend?"

"Probably. Ian's thinking of inviting that American."

"I thought he had gone back to New York."

"He has. Apparently he's coming back again."

Vanessa stared around for the wine waiter and then impatiently refilled her own glass. "What did you think of him?" she said.

"He seemed pleasant enough," said Margaret.

"That's not an answer."

Margaret thought and then said, "He's not what I expected, for the sort of businessman he's supposed to be; far quieter. I think he hides away a lot."

"Did you like him?" asked Vanessa.

"Difficult to decide that, after just one meeting."

"No it's not."

"I thought he was nice," said Margaret, forced to give an

149

opinion. She realized she was looking forward to seeing him again. "What did you think?"

"Cold," judged Vanessa.

"I thought it was shyness."

Vanessa shook her head. "Cold," she insisted.

"Shan't bother with an introduction then," said Fiona.

It had been Richard Haffaford's idea to compose a loosely structured committee to decide their actions over Buckland House and to have upon it the men who had confronted Buckland and Condway when they made their overdraft request. The three men listened without interruption to Snaith's account of that morning's board meeting and then Haffaford said, "Faysel". It was right under our bloody noses and we didn't realize it!"

"What was Condway's reaction when you met him?" Snaith asked Haffaford.

"Non committal," conceded the banker.

"It's not any longer," said Smallwood. "Apart from Snaith and myself, they're fully behind him now. And they'll stay that way."

"You sure they won't consider any management reorganization?" asked Sir Herbert White.

"Any actual decision was postponed," said Snaith. "But I'm sure they won't".

"It's like selling off the family silver for gin money," said the third director, Henry Pryke.

"Do you think he'll switch his funding arrangements when they pay off the overdraft?" asked Haffaford.

"That was the obvious inference," said Smallwood.

"Perhaps we should consider ourselves lucky we got the money back,' said White.

"Our business is selling money," reminded Haffaford. "Not getting debts settled. And it doesn't end with the overdraft repayment . . . ." He looked down at some papers on his desk. "We've got something like £3,500,000 worth of clients' money invested in Buckland House and its subsidiaries."

"We could switch the portfolios," said Pryke.

150

Haffaford continued looking down at the investment advice. "Practically without exception we'd be doing so at a loss to our clients. We've a reputation to consider; what sort of money management would that be?"

"Sometimes it's better to cut losses before they worsen," said White.

Haffaford shook his head. "Properly run, Buckland House is still a good place to have our money. We decided upon a strategy and we'll stay with it. We'll get a shareholders' vote to remove Buckland. Once he's gone, the other directors will come into line. And if they don't, we'll get rid of them too."

"That involves proving Buckland's unfitness," reminded Snaith.

"The evidence is coming," promised Haffaford.

Fiona said it wouldn't be quite as good because the mews house didn't have the fittings there had been in Bangkok where it had happened to her, but that it would give him some idea of what it was like. She was already naked, waiting, when he arrived, the flowing hair tightly knotted so it wouldn't get in the way, her body lightly oiled so that her skin shone as if it were polished. Little globules of oil had gathered on her pubic puff and glistened like dew. She put rubber sheeting on the bathroom floor and near the bed and undressed him, slowly and frequently kissing him but slapping his hands away when Buckland reached for her. She made him lie on the sheet and massaged him with the oil that already covered her and then she made him put his hands above his head and lay on top of him, sliding her body up and down the complete length of his, nuzzling her face into his groin as she passed but not lingering there. He was rigid and throbbing for her and she massaged him there at last, washing her hands with him and when he began to groan she pulled away, making him stand and follow her into the bathroom. The tub was already filled and scented. She put him in and then bathed him, like she would have done a baby, ignoring his sex. Then she got in and soaped herself, so that the water was slimed with their oil. Still refusing to let him touch her, she made him get out and then dried him, enclosing the towel around the two of them. He lay on

151

the bathroom rubber and she powdered him and afterwards herself.

"I can't wait," he said.

"Soon," she said. "Soon now."

Buckland expected her to retain the dominant role when they got back into the bedroom but instead she got on to the bed and held out her hands towards him and said, "With your mouth. I want your mouth first."

He buried his head in her, lip-biting, and she moved her hips, grinding herself down against him. When her body began to arc he pulled up, stabbing into her and she screamed as he entered her. They whimpered for a rhythm and found it and began to race, belly slapping against belly. They burst together and she screamed again, a long, drawn-out sound that changed to a groan and then a sigh. Buckland fell over her, panting, too exhausted at first even to roll aside.

"Christ, that was marvellous."

"I love fucking," she said. "I really love it."

"I'd never have guessed," said Buckland.

"I had lunch with Margaret today: she said you were going to Cambridge at the weekend."

"Business," said Buckland.

"Can we go on the boat again? I enjoyed that."

"Yes," said Buckland. "I promise."

She moved over, to be on top of him. "We haven't finished yet," she said.

In the mews outside the enquiry agent made a careful notation of Buckland's car registration and then of the address. He wondered how difficult it would be to get photographs of her.

17

It had been overcast when Rudd left London, but by the time he approached Cambridge the clouds were lifting. When he entered the driveway to Buckland's country home, the soldierly elms were slicing the sunlight into wedges and he put his hand up against the sudden bursts of brightness as he drove towards the house. He thought the setting and the house were magnificent. During his travels throughout America, Rudd had seen several attempts to achieve what was laid out before him now: in Arizona and again in Virginia, the houses had been built from the actual stones of the originals which had been dismantled and shipped across. Always they had blatantly been what they were trying to avoid appearing, a copy of the original. Rudd supposed it had something to do with the feel or the ambience of the country: the tradition.

The warning had been given from the gate lodge, so Holmes was waiting when the car pulled up in front of the mansion. Rudd followed the butler into the drawing-room where Margaret was waiting. She wore jodhpurs and highly polished boots and a tailored jacket, tight against her hips and waist.

"There's been a crisis," she said lightly. "Ian's not here."

"What's the matter?"

"The electricity people want to put pylons across the home farm. The estate manager should have been able to handle it but there's an on-sight inspection with some people from the county council and they asked Ian to go along, so he has. He tried to get you in London, but you'd already left. He'll be back as soon as he can: he says he's sorry."

"It doesn't matter."

"You keep getting stuck with me, don't you?"

"I won't complain about that." Rudd thought there was a momentary uncertainty in her smile.

"Can I get you anything?"

"I had lunch on the way."

"A drink then?"

"I don't think so."

"What was the journey like?" she said, moving through the pleasantries.

"Good," said Rudd. "This is the furthest I've ever been outside of London. I thought it was very pretty."

"I do it so often I've stopped looking," she said. "Perhaps I should start again."

"Have you been riding or were you going?" said Rudd.

She looked down at the habit. "I was going, when Ian got called out. I decided to wait to see if you'd like to come."

"I don't ride," said Rudd. Every conversation with her seemed to involve a list of things he didn't do.

"Never?"

He shook his head.

"I thought all Americans rode."

"Only the ones in the cowboy pictures, and they have stand-ins," he said.

"Why don't you try?" she said, suddenly eager. "I could show you the grounds."

He was nervous, Rudd realized. Of refusing, so she would think he was scared. And of accepting and making a fool of himself in front of her. He looked down at his suit. "I haven't got anything, only jeans," he said. He didn't imagine there were going to be any cook-outs this weekend.

"We're only going to walk sedately around the grounds," said Margaret. "I guarantee we won't even break into a trot!" She looked at him, waiting.

He was caught either way, Rudd accepted. "All right," he said reluctantly.

"I'll get the stables saddling up while you change," she said. "I'll wait for you here."

The butler was waiting to show him to his room when he emerged into the hall. It was at the front of the house, with a view of the impressive, tree-lined entrance. He wished Buckland had been here, so they could have begun the discussion immediately: bearing in mind what was to happen eventually it was wrong to

154

involve himself with Margaret, just as it would have been wrong to involve himself with the man's sister. He'd rejected Vanessa. Why hadn't he refused Margaret? He hadn't wanted to, he conceded. His suitcases had been unpacked and Rudd was changed within minutes. He descended to the ground floor in the woollen shirt, jeans and loafers he'd worn in Connecticut, feeling self-conscious. Margaret Buckland looked at him but kept any expression from her face.

"Just around the grounds," she repeated, in reassurance.

Rudd's apprehension increased immediately when he saw the size of the animal; it looked enormous. The woman pulled herself easily into the saddle. A groom retained the bridle of his horse. The first time Rudd failed to get himself off the ground and then the horse shifted, so he had to hop around, one foot still in the stirrup. He managed to get on finally by laying his chest across the saddle and then swinging his leg over. He looked at her, panting and red-faced.

"I'm not at all sure this is a good idea," he said nervously.

"Grip with your thighs," she said.

Rudd tried but the horse seemed too wide: the insides of his legs ached with the effort.

"Don't hold the reins too tightly, you'll hurt his mouth. Just loose. All you need to do is indicate. He's well-trained and very docile."

She pulled her own animal easily around and clattered across the stable cobbles. Rudd made a forward motion with his body, urging his animal on. It didn't move. The groom slapped it lightly and obediently it began to walk out behind the other horse. Rudd found it difficult to move his body in time to the horse. He kept the reins slack and gripped the pommel of the saddle with both hands.

She was waiting for him just outside the stable yard. "You look terrified."

"I am."

"Do you want to go back?"

Yes, he thought. "No," he said.

The stables were next to an arbour, flowers trellised in a covered walkway; occasionally there were seats and once a table arrangement, for picnics he supposed. He wished he were down

155

there. He began to get used to the movement of the horse so the saddle stopped jarring into his back. They came out from the rear of the house. At once Margaret pointed. "There's the dower-house," she said. "Ian's mother lives there. You'll meet her tonight."

The woman continued on towards the lake, glancing quickly back to Rudd, as if judging the distance and said, "Why don't we go down there?"

"Fine," said Rudd. His horse had stopped with hers and he wondered how he was going to get it going again without the groom. He saw her thrust her feet against the side of her mount and tried to do the same: the motion threw him too far forward and he had to snatch out for the pommel to prevent himself going over the neck of the horse. As soon as Margaret's mount started moving, his picked up too. The grounds stretched away before him, without any apparent boundary or fence; far beyond the lake he could see a wooded area and gradually he became aware of deer grazing near the treeline. He wished he were able to enjoy it. The lake seemed far enough away to be a mirage.

Margaret rode slightly ahead of him, providing the lead for his horse. She sat relaxed but stiff-backed, seeming to anticipate every sway. She hadn't bothered to button her riding jacket and he was aware of the stir of her breasts. He looked away guiltily.

"Do you like it?" she said.

"It's beautiful. How big is the estate?"

"Including the farm, something like 750 acres."

"Did Ian buy it?"

She shook her head. "His grandfather."

The lake seemed to be getting closer. Thank God, he thought. He could see a jetty. There was a dinghy tied alongside and another beached, with only its stern in the water. It was larger than it appeared from the house and kidney-shaped, so that to the right it seemed to flow away as if it were a river. Near the bend there was an island, thatched with a disordered tangle of trees. Margaret rode her horse into the water and his followed. His stomach lurched as its head went down to drink.

"Why don't we dismount?"

He saw she had brought them in close to the jetty, so the distance was less if he stepped off on to the slatted wooden walkway. He did so carefully, managing to avoid stumbling and then standing away from the horse, the reins still in his hands, his legs trembling.

He smiled across at her. "I'm glad the West was already won," he said. "If it had been left to me, Geronimo would still be holding the pass."

She laughed back. "I'm sorry," she said.

Margaret hadn't dismounted. She pulled her horse's head up and said, "Don't let them drink any more; they'll get bloated."

Dismounted, this was difficult for him. The horse turned towards him when he pulled, and fleetingly Rudd thought it was going to bite out at him. Instead it allowed its head to be turned and moved unprotesting to higher ground. Margaret leapt lightly down and said, "We can tether them against the jetty rail."

She just looped her reins through: Rudd knotted his. She nodded towards the island and said, "We had a house and a camp there when we were children."

"When you were children?"

"Ian and I were what the romantics call childhood sweethearts: I seem to have known him ever since I can remember."

Rudd looked out at the tiny coppice. "What's it like out there now?"

She shrugged. "I haven't been there for years; I've no idea."

"Wouldn't you like to see?" He forced the question, consciously wanting to appear adventurous.

She looked at him hesitantly. "You mean go out there?"

"Why not?"

She looked around her, then shrugged. "No reason at all, I suppose."

Rudd went to the dinghy that was afloat; oars and rowlocks were tied together with string and stored beneath the seats. He got in, untied them, and slotted the rowlocks into their fittings. He looked up to where she stood and said, "I rode with you. Now you ride with me."

Now it was Margaret who was unsteady. She got awkwardly into the boat, stretching out her hands for balance when it rocked under her weight, and slumped down gratefully in the back.

157

Rudd thrust the boat away, fitted the oars and began to row in steady, easy movements. Insects were misting at the water's edge and in pockets further out on the lake. To the right a flotilla of ducks convoyed sedately towards the island, apparently undisturbed by their presence. Margaret put her finger over the side, tearing the water and said, "It's cold."

"How long have you been married?"

She had been looking at the trail her hand was making in the water. She brought her eyes up to him and said, "Eleven years. How long were you?"

"Seven months."

She frowned, a wincing expression.

"We were together before that, though," he said. "Almost three years. At university, in Boston."

"Was she ill?"

"She died having our baby," Rudd looked over his shoulder and saw the island was close. "Is there a landing-stage?"

"Not really," she said. "Not that I can remember anyway."

He reversed one oar against the other, bringing them parallel to the island, and began to row around it, looking for a break in the trees and shrubs that came right up to the water's edge. The ducks shuddered ashore along some familiar track.

"What was her name?"

"Angela."

"There," said Margaret, pointing suddenly. "There's where we used to land."

There was a collapsed tree, leaning into the water and creating an opening through the undergrowth with its outstretched branches. Rudd turned the boat, slightly misjudging the entry, so that the dinghy side jarred against the sloping trunk. She reached out and hauled them closer, using it for leverage, and then looped the painter around it. Margaret stood up to use it as a walkway and Rudd said, "Be careful. It looks old."

"I suppose it is," she said. She climbed agilely on to it and then tested it. It dipped slightly towards the water but seemed quite strong. Quickly, using other branches for handholds, she got ashore. Rudd waited until she was on land and then followed. It was wild and thickly overgrown, with no obvious paths. The lake must have been well drained, never flooding over the island,

158

because it was dry underfoot. There were a lot of cobwebs skeined between the shrubs and trees and Margaret picked up a stick and started to hit out at them. Rudd pushed through the undergrowth and a faint dust, pollen he supposed, rose around him. He felt her hand press against his shoulder apprehensively. Away from the shoreline, the going became slightly easier: there was no path as such, just a slight lessening of the shrub-growth. He stopped suddenly. Dangling from a tree alongside the path was a rope, frayed and tangled with some climbing plant.

"I don't remember that," said Margaret.

Rudd saw something solid-looking to their right. He had to break through more cobwebs and suddenly they were standing before a rough-built wooden hut, just a slated roof and three sides, the fourth more or less open to provide an entry. On the wooden floor there were two tins, both completely rusty. In one of them was the atrophied stem of some long dead flower. The hut was not big enough for them to go inside.

"That was our house," she said, distantly and unnecessarily. "Ian actually built it; we stole the planks from the maintenance man and shipped them across in a boat."

"You must have been young."

"About ten, I suppose: I'm not really sure. It's not at all like I remember it."

"Memories are often better left," said Rudd.

She appeared not to hear him. "It used to be big and there was grass in front, where I used to make the food. We made plans for life here." She sounded sad.

Nearby something moved noisily but unseen through the trees: probably the ducks, thought Rudd. She moved nearer to him nervously.

"Did you ever have a secret place, with Angela?"

"There wasn't time," he said. There was the one roomed apartment where they'd lived together, off campus, but he didn't think of it as Margaret seemed to regard this place.

"I wish we hadn't come," said Margaret.

"Do you want to go?"

"I suppose so."

She turned, bringing herself close to him and then stopped, looking directly up into his face. He leaned forward and kissed

159

her, not properly realizing what he was doing until his lips were against hers. For a moment she did nothing and then her lips parted, just slightly. She reached out, holding her hands against his arm.

He pulled back, so abruptly that she came forward with his movement. He said, "I'm sorry. I'm really very sorry."

"There's no need."

"I didn't mean to offend you."

"You didn't."

She was still close. He said. "I want to kiss you again."

"Why don't you?"

He felt out for her this time, conscious of her warmth beneath the silk shirt, and she let herself be pulled against him: her breasts were full against his chest and he stirred with excitement. She didn't try to move her body away. When they parted, she said, "I didn't intend coming back to London."

"Oh," he said.

"Would you like me to?"

"Yes."

There was a lot of glass in the bathroom, giving a multi-faceted reflection of the occupant. Rudd sat with the water to his chest, gazing at himself and trying to rationalize what had happened. So much for never obeying impulse! It was madness, he realized; stark, raving bloody madness. He realized something else, too, something of which he'd been worryingly aware ever since he'd met her. More forcefully than anyone before, Margaret Buckland reminded him of Angela.

Further along the same corridor as Rudd's room, Margaret Buckland stood unclothed before her dressing-room mirror, hands held tightly against her breasts as though she was surprised at their nakedness. She squeezed hard, until they hurt, feeling the warmth between her legs. She hadn't given way to the fantasy yet; not quite. But she thought she was going to. The anticipation trembled through her. She'd have to bath again, before going downstairs.

160

18

Rudd supposed the library was the most convenient place for Buckland to use as a study. It was large, like everything else in the house, books encased from floor to lofty ceiling. Running entirely around the room was an open-railed balcony, reached from either side by spiral wooden steps. There were library ladders on the ground and upper sections, and half-way along, near the circular staircases, reading tables. Hovering over each there were low-slung lights, and there were side lamps as well. At the far end there was a larger study desk, leather inlaid to match the covering of the library step platforms and the reading tables, and an alcove alongside. The furniture there was real leather and button-backed. Buckland guided Rudd towards a table already set with glasses and decanter. Slowly Rudd helped himself to whisky.

"What's wrong?" said Buckland.

"I went riding for the first time. And then took a boat on the lake."

Despite the soaking to try to ease the ache, Rudd's legs and back still hurt from the unaccustomed exercise. The physical discomfort concealed the other he felt for what had happened on the overgrown island.

"Margaret mentioned it," said Buckland. "I'm surprised she took you there; we haven't been to it for years."

"She told me." Rudd expected to feel more embarrassment than he did.

"Sorry about this afternoon."

"Margaret explained," said Rudd. It should have been him apologizing. Rudd met the man's eyes. Upstairs in his room he'd only thought about the moral implications of becoming involved with another man's wife. Here he realized it went beyond that. It wasn't any affair that mattered. It was the risk he created to the takeover. Never – ever – had Rudd allowed anything to endanger a business consideration. But never, since Angela, had he felt attracted to anyone as he felt attracted to Margaret. He knew what he *should* do. But not what he was going to do.

"I thought it was more comfortable to finalize things here, rather than in London," said Buckland. "My board approved, as I knew they would."

"Mine didn't." Rudd had planned the delivery for the maximum effect. Buckland had been reaching forward towards the decanter. He stopped, stretched forward, jerking up to the American. "What!"

"They're insisting on revisions," said Rudd.

Buckland sat back, his glass forgotten. "What sort of revisions?"

"They've imposed a liquidity limit," said Rudd. "They're refusing to allocate more than $20,000,000 for a cash purchase."

"But that's not what we agreed," protested Buckland. "You've misled me and through me the board. . . ."

Rudd held up his hands. "Please!" he said. "I know what was agreed. Hear me out. Beyond the $20,000,000 they are offering a share exchange, $7,500,000 of Best Rest stock for Buckland House Preferential Issue. Our stock quotation is currently running at twice that of Buckland House."

Buckland was sitting quite still, even his hands unmoving as he tried to analyse what Rudd was saying. At the moment they were only juggling with figures: he hadn't lost anything. "What's your dividend declaration?" demanded Buckland.

"It's not finalized yet for the full year," said Rudd. "I would expect it to be in the region of eighteen per cent overall." Like the initial announcement about the revision of terms, Rudd had rehearsed the order in which he intended to spell them out.

Buckland strained for the equation, using a rough dollar translation. Taking the conversion at £3,400,000 on an eighteen per cent declaration meant Buckland House receiving £612,000 against the £170,000 payable upon their own dividend of five. So if they agreed to the share acceptance, they'd benefit by more than £400,000 a year. Buckland tried to keep any reaction from his face. "Were there any more modifications to what we discussed?" he said.

Rudd nodded. "The liners would become a separate division of our conglomerate," he said. "It was decided to invite you to sit upon the board of that division." Rudd paused and then he said, "To maintain the tradition."

Buckland smiled. "That was a very courteous gesture."

"But practical," said Rudd. "None of the other people who are going to form the board have any experience of running ships."

Buckland recognized that it would be a peripheral involvement but nevertheless it would mean his being associated with a multinational with outlets more widely spread than his own organization. He bent forward, finally refilling his glass.

"There's one more thing," said Rudd. He decided he hadn't lost the superiority yet.

"What?" said Buckland warily.

"My board insisted that I be offered a seat with Buckland House holding company."

Buckland gave no immediate reaction, just stared across the small space that separated the two men. It would be erosion, he thought, just like having the damned merchant banker had been an erosion and even Prince Faysel. Or would it? The merchant bank claimed there was need for hotel management expertise. And who better had it than the chairman of Best Rest, plasticized and nyloned and occupancy-conscious and portion-controlled maybe. But efficient enough to declare an eighteen per cent dividend from a worldwide operation. There *were* needs for economy in some parts of the Buckland House organization. Perhaps, through Rudd, they could link up with some of the streamlining – country-to-country reservations on the same computer or bulk food-buying providing the standard was sufficiently high – and achieve those economies themselves. In many ways the proposals were better than those he'd originally presented to the board.

What was the debit balance? It was not as decisively clear-cut as before. And there would *be* a loss, an erosion. Practical good sense or not, Buckland House, holders of the awards and the rosettes, the choice of kings and queens, would be linked with Best Rest, holders of every credit card shield, the choice of the package-tripper clerk. But not inextricably linked. Again it had

163

to be an estimate, until he could get the accountants to make the calculation, but $7,500,000 would only accord about a thirteen per cent holding in Preferential shares. And Preferential didn't control anyway. The Initial issue did. And there was no danger to those.

Rudd waited patiently, conscious of the other man's inner debate. At the moment the advantages must still appear to be in favour of Buckland House.

"This is a considerable departure from our earlier discussions," said Buckland.

"Not really,' argued Rudd. "The purchase price remains unaltered in content, just adaptation." He hesitated, wondering whether to make the point. Deciding to risk it, he said, "And there could be practical advantages: basically we're in the same business, although at admittedly different levels."

"There is no question of an outright cash purchase?" demanded Buckland.

"Absolutely none," said Rudd. "Our present offer, in its entirety, is the only one with which I am empowered to proceed. If your board finds it unacceptable, in any part, then I'm afraid our negotiations must end."

"That appears to be an ultimatum," said Buckland.

"It wasn't intended as one," said Rudd. "It was intended to make absolutely clear my terms of reference. I didn't want there to be any misunderstanding so that you would have to go back again."

"You've a fresh letter of intent?"

"Of course."

"I'll present it," said Buckland.

"With a recommendation for acceptance?"

"I'll have to consider the new terms in detail before I can give a reply to that," said Buckland. What would his father have done, he wondered.

Four of them ate at a small circular table like the one in his Sloane Square house. Buckland, Margaret, Rudd and Lady Buckland. Any atmosphere between Rudd and Margaret was prevented by the old lady, who took immediate command of the conversation and made herself the focal point throughout the meal, searching for acquaintances and friends in America he might know, insisting upon discussing parts of New York and Virginia she'd visited twenty years before and refusing to accept that they had altered so much that he couldn't possibly know the places she was talking about.

When the men joined them after dinner and Rudd said he couldn't play bezique, she looked at him in disbelief.

"I thought everyone could play bezique!"

"I'm afraid I can't."

Behind his mother, Buckland raised his eyes apologetically.

"You're going to buy our ships, Mr Rudd?" said Lady Buckland.

"I hope to."

"They're very special."

"Which is why I want to buy them."

"You're not going to paint them, are you?"

Everyone regarded the old lady in surprise. "Paint them?" said Rudd.

"Garish colours. Can't stand this American insistence on painting everything like a rainbow."

"I don't think black hulls suit the Caribbean, where I intend to operate," said Rudd. "I'm considering changing to white. But apart from improved air-conditioning, they will remain exactly as they are now."

Lady Buckland stared at him, as if uncertain. Then she said, "I'm glad to hear it."

"Harry's asked me to sit upon the board that will operate the ships," said Buckland.

The old lady turned to her son. "So we'll remain associated?"

"Yes."

She came back to Rudd. "I like that," she said. "That's a very good idea." She stood up, pressing against her stick for support. "If we can't play bezique then you can take me home, Ian. Are you staying tomorrow, Mr Rudd?"

"I'm afraid that I've got to return to London early."

"Then I'll say goodbye. I'm very glad about those colours."

Rudd and Margaret stood watching her slowly walk from the room. Rudd said, "She's quite a character."

"She works hard at it," said Margaret.

Rudd turned to look at her. So much like Angela, he thought. "I've told Ian I'm coming back to London," she said.

Rudd recognized the opportunity to be sensible. Now was the time to apologize again, say it was a mistake he regretted and end anything before it began.

"It'll be better if I telephone you," he said.

"All right," she said.

Rudd and Buckland went over the terms and conditions of the sale again at breakfast, and from the other man's attitude Rudd knew Buckland considered the changes to be to his advantage. Margaret appeared as he was leaving. She shook his hand and without any self-consciousness said she hoped they'd meet again.

It was noon when Rudd got back to the Berridge. Hallett was waiting in the suite.

"Mr Bunch has gone to Paris to arrange the finance transfer for Senator Jeplow," reported the personal assistant. "Prince Faysel has cabled, saying he's arriving tomorrow. And there's a telex from New York, from Mr Morrison. He's getting here on Friday."

"I want you to do something for me," said Rudd.

Obediently Hallett opened his folder.

"I want to move into an apartment," said Rudd. "Somewhere central, as near here as possible."

Hallet sat regarding him with amazement. "An apartment!"

"I can hardly stay on here after we make the bid, can I?" he said. "It would be too awkward."

Hallett smiled, the surprise going. "I hadn't thought of that," he said.

Neither had Rudd, until just before the limousine had arrived outside the hotel.

19

The official Saudi announcement that they had purposely manipulated the oil glut affected the money and stock markets as the bankers had predicted during the investment board meeting in Zürich.

Oil and subsidiary shares dipped, rose and then dipped again in their uncertainty. Britain raised its parity rate by half a per cent and there was a brief switch in sterling, and then American banks raised their interest rates by an average of one full per cent, so the money flowed back into dollars.

The anger of the more radical producers would have been predictable anyway, but one of the chief sufferers of the Saudi investment cut-back was Nigeria, which had been dependent upon Saudi finance for the creation of a new dock and refinery at Port Harcourt. Their oil minister summoned a meeting in Lagos of Libya and Algeria, the other radicals, and succeeded in getting observer attendance from Venezuela and Iraq. It ended with a communiqué declaring that they would not be subjected to Western-influenced blackmail and insisting that they would demand a barrel price of $52, with the warning to contracted customers that if they attempted to cancel or defer their agreements for the short-term, cheaper offers, then they would be ostracized when the oil surplus was exhausted. Saudi Arabia countered with the reminder that it produced forty per cent of the West's oil and the promise it would make up any shortfall created by such victimization.

When Faysel entered the Berridge suite, Rudd thought he looked exhausted.

"We've averaged a meeting a day since the official announcement," said Faysel, confirming the American's impression.

"Did you expect these repercussions?"

"Not quite as virulent," conceded Faysel. "The Crown Prince

167

is already trying to shift responsibility for the decision on to Hassain, in case it backfires. And guess what I learned in Jeddah?"

"What?"

Faysel told Rudd of Jeplow's lobbying in Washington from which the oil embargo had emanated, intrigued by the cynical smile that developed on Rudd's face.

"Ironic, isn't it?" said the Arab.

"It may be more than that."

The reaction came from Snaith. He jerked up from the second letter of intent and said, "These are completely different terms from those already discussed."

"They're not," said Buckland, seizing upon the other man's exaggeration. "As I've already explained, they are substantially the same. If there is a difference, it is to our advantage. It was your bank who talked about the need for restructuring. Rudd would bring fresh expertise on to this board and I've already outlined the streamlining possibilities from which Buckland House might benefit from association with Best Rest."

Gauging the cause of Snaith's response, Condway said, "Would Best Rest be prepared to commit finance?"

Buckland shook his head. "At this stage, I haven't discussed it. It's a hugely rich chain, so I don't consider it out of the question. . . ." He turned back to the merchant banker. "I think our own shares will benefit, simply by the link with such an organization," he said.

"Seems to me that we gain in every way possible," said Gore-Pelham.

"Damned fine outcome," agreed Penhardy.

"I have the proxy nomination from Prince Faysel," said Buckland. "With it is the indication that he and the investment fund he represents are in favour of acceptance. I'd like a formal vote, from this board, to complete the negotiations."

"I think this might be a turning point in the affairs of this company," said Condway, after the unanimous decision.

"I think so too," said Buckland.

* * *

"It's the best short-let agency there is," said Hallett. "It's expensive."

"It's fine," said Rudd.

The apartment was half-way along Grosvenor Square, looking out over the small park and the American embassy beyond. It was on two floors, a dining-room, kitchen and lounge on the lower and three bedrooms above. The furniture was reproduction but good, and similar neither to the house off Sloane Square nor the mansion in Cambridgeshire. Rudd decided that was important.

"What about booze and food and stuff like that?" asked the personal assistant.

"Organize it," said Rudd. "I'll probably move in straight away."

"You're going to find it strange," predicted Hallett.

"Yes," said Rudd. Madness, he thought again; absolute fucking madness.

He could hardly wait to see her.

20

Margaret entered the apartment hesitantly, halting immediately inside the door. Rudd nervously gestured her further in. She smiled quickly and continued on. Rudd thought the flowers helped but the apartment still had the bare, unlived-in feeling he'd been aware of when Hallett had showed it to him. Needing a focus, Margaret went to the window with its view of Grosvenor Square.

"Its very nice," she said.

"Would you like a drink?"

"Please."

"What?"

She shrugged, her back to him. "Whatever there is."

"Wine or booze?"

"Wine. White."

Glad of the activity, Rudd went into the sectioned-off bar, took a bottle from the cooler and poured. Giving her the glass meant she had to look at him again. There was another brief smile.

"I've got some food. Just cold, until I've settled in. Salad and stuff like that," said Rudd. He couldn't remember feeling so nervous.

"I'm not really hungry."

"Neither am I. I just thought you might be."

She shook her head. "I almost didn't come."

"I wasn't sure that you would."

"I've never . . ." she started, but he felt out, putting his finger to her lips. "You haven't," he said.

There was a padded window seat and she sat down. He lowered himself beside her, then leaned forward and kissed her. Touching her, he was aware of her trembling.

"What did you tell Ian?"

"I didn't" said the woman. "He's gone gambling. Probably at Ellerby's place. He goes most evenings."

The telephone jarred into the room, making them both jump. "Damn!" said Rudd. He recognized Bunch's voice immediately.

"What the hell are you doing in an apartment?" demanded the lawyer.

"There's a reason," said Rudd.

There was silence from the other end of the line. Then Bunch said: "Do you want me to come around?"

"No."

"Oh."

"Is everything fixed?" said Rudd.

"I waited in Paris until I got confirmation from Texas of the re-zoning and then made payment of a bearer cheque against the Crédit Lyonnais. The Liechtenstein people accepted it without any argument. They were expecting me."

"So we've got him," said Rudd.

"Guess so," said Bunch. "Do you want to call him and tell him the money's deposited?"

"You do it," said Rudd.

"You all right, Harry?"

"Of course I am. The deal here's been approved."

"So Hallett told me. Suddenly it's all looking good, isn't it?"

Rudd looked across to where Margaret was sitting. She was gazing out of the window again. "There's going to be the formal business tomorrow, deposit-signing, contractual exchanges, things like that. I want surveyors' reports on all the ships and the draft contracts prepared."

"Who do you want to use?"

"Why not go on with the lawyers we've got?"

Rudd went back to where Margaret was sitting. "Sorry," he said. "Ian doesn't allow business calls at home."

"It's become some sort of habit with me. More wine?"

She nodded and he refilled both their glasses.

"So it's all going through?" she said.

"Looks like it."

"I want to tell you something."

"What?"

"That night in the casino. I. . . ." she frowned, searching for the expression. ". . . I acted up for you," she said. "I wanted to be interesting."

171

"Why?"

She humped her shoulders. "I don't know. I was as embarrassed as hell afterwards."

"It worked," he said. "I wanted to impress you, too."

She smiled. "We're not very good at this, are we?"

"No," he agreed.

They became very serious and this time it was Margaret who kissed him. "I want to," she said. "I've thought about it and I want to." Would it be like the fantasy? She wasn't positive she'd ever had a proper orgasm.

"Sure?" What if he failed her? There was no reason why he should, after Joanne. But Joanne was different. Professional. Christ, he didn't want to fail.

"I'm sure," she said, and the telephone rang.

"Shit!" he said.

He snatched it up angrily, the irritation obvious in his voice, so that Hallett said, "What's the matter?"

"Nothing," said Rudd, trying to recover. "I was thinking about something else."

He watched as Margaret stood purposefully from the seat, put her glass down and walked across the room towards the stairs that led to the upper level.

"Buckland called," said the personal assistant.

Rudd swallowed: this was getting too involved for belief! "What did he want?"

"Said it was a social call, but wondered if you'd like to have dinner with him at some casino: talk through tomorrow, he said."

"Just social?" queries Rudd. Normally he would have gone. He should go now.

"That's what he said."

"Get back to him and tell him I'm tied up. That I'll see him tomorrow," said Rudd.

"You're not going?" The surprise was obvious in Hallett's voice.

"No."

There was a pause from the other end of the line. Then Hallett said, "OK. I'll tell him."

"Hold any more calls for me," said Rudd.

There was another silence. "How long for?"

172

"I'll call you," said Rudd. He stayed for several moments by the telephone. Then he went out into the corridor and climbed the stairs, purposely loud so that she would know he was coming.

"I didn't know which was your room: I had to look in the cupboards," she said. She was already in bed, the covers pulled up completely to cover her. He couldn't see her clothes and guessed she'd undressed in the bathroom. She looked frail and lost in the bed.

It was never obvious, but there was always an eroticism when Joanne undressed. She. . . . He stopped, angry at himself. It was wrong to compare Joanne with Margaret, just as it was wrong to compare Margaret to Angela. No, that was wrong too. They should all be separate: marked-off places in his mind, boundaries that were never crossed.

"What's the matter?" she said.

"Nothing. Really." He hurried from his clothes, aware of her attention and made awkward by it. At the bedside he pulled the covering back to look at her. She lay uncomfortably, stiffly almost, arms by her side, her body tensed. She was big-breasted, the nipples brown-surrounded, her stomach soft-downed until the pubic wedge; her legs were tight together.

"You're embarrassing me."

"I want to see."

"Why?"

"I want to."

"Please don't."

He got in beside her and covered them both, leaning on his arm so he could look down at her. Their bodies were close, so close they could feel each other's nearness but not actually touching. She snatched up for him, grabbing his mouth to hers and he lay over her, her body shuddering at the physical contact. They bit and snatched at each other's faces and then he pulled his head lower over her breasts and she lay back, letting him explore her. He'd never realized Joanne's expertise, because if he had it wouldn't have been expertise: how she guided and let him think he was controlling, the pauses and the waits, the gentle touch and the brutal touch, the. . . . He slammed the door shut in his mind. Margaret's legs were still tight together, the muscles hard.

"I won't be good enough."

173

He came up to kiss her lips. "Don't be silly."

"I know I won't."

"You're beautiful."

"I don't know anything."

"I don't want you to."

She relaxed slightly and he was able to feel she was wet. He thrust suddenly hard like he'd been taught, and she mewed and parted further.

"What should I do?" she said.

"Nothing."

"I want to please you."

"You are."

He put himself over her and she parted completely. He stopped, pressed against her very entry, looking down at her. Her eyes were damp and her face was flushed, almost swollen. He felt her move, trying to pull him inside, he moved with her so they started in time. It was more than a mew, a groan, and he felt her close around him, a positive muscle movement. She relaxed and contracted, smiling up hopefully at him.

"That's wonderful." he said.

"Sure?"

"Wonderful."

"So are you." She closed her eyes and forced her head back, so that her neck corded. "Christ, you feel good."

The muscles snatched at him tighter, and she began to hurry. He wasn't ready but he tried to move with her. She rose up from the bed, her whole body coming up towards him, and then went down again, straining him into her, and he felt her warmth burst over him and then he came, quickly enough for her not to know that he had missed her.

"Oh God," she said. "That was good. That was so good."

She was completely wet now, with love and tears and sweat. "Was it good for you?" she said.

"Yes."

"Honestly?"

"Honestly." He started to move from her but she whimpered a protest, turning with him so that he stayed inside her. She gripped him, proud of her trick and said, "I'm never going to let you go."

174

"I don't want you to."

"I'm not sorry, Harry. Really I'm not."

"God."

"It's not like this between . . ."

". . . I don't want to know," he said, stopping her. "This is just us, no one else. Nothing else."

"All right," she said. She let him go but they still remained tight together.

"How often can you get away?"

"Whenever I want to." She pulled back so that she could see his face. "How often do you want me to?"

"All the time," he said.

"How long will you stay in London?"

He thought of the reason for his remaining and looked at her sweat-damp face only inches from his. What would happen, when she learned? "I don't know yet," he said.

"Make it a long time." It had been better than the fantasy; fantasies were dreams. This was better than dreaming.

"I'll try."

"What about New York, Harry?"

"What about it?"

"Who's there?"

He moved further away from her. "No one," he said.

"Don't be silly," she said. "There must be."

"No," he said uncomfortably.

Growing bold in their intimacy she said coquettishly. "Do you mean to say that you've lived a monastic, celibate existence, just waiting for Margaret Buckland!"

"No," he said shortly. He wouldn't lie: not any more than he had to. She'd remember the lies.

"So who. . . ? " she began and then stopped. She giggled, bringing her hand to her mouth and said, "You don't mean. . . ?"

He smiled back at her shyly. "It's a very practical arrangement."

She went to laugh more and then was suddenly serious. "Oh my God!" she said. "And you said it was wonderful."

"It wasn't the same."

"I bet it wasn't!"

"I didn't mean that, either."

175

Her head was down in the pillow, but turned so that she could still look at him. "I must have been awful."

"You know you weren't."

"I don't know anything of the sort."

"It was marvellous. I mean it."

"You must have compared."

"I didn't," he lied.

"Is there just one? Or lots?"

"Just one."

"What's her name?"

"Why does it matter?"

"Why are you so embarrassed?"

"I'm not embarrassed."

"Tell me her name then."

"Joanne."

"That's a pretty name," said Margaret. "Is she pretty?"

"Yes."

"Beautiful?"

"Yes."

"Better than me?"

"I told you it wasn't the same."

"What do you mean?"

"Screwing," she said. "How do you do it differently?"

"We don't."

"You must do, if she's professional. She must know everything . . . do special things."

She was excited, Rudd realized. She was moving against him, one leg over his. "The secret of being professional," he said, "is convincing the man afterwards that it was the best it had ever been, that's all."

"Was that what you were doing with me?"

"You know it wasn't."

"Will you teach me, Harry? Teach me to be really good. To do everything you want?"

"We'll teach each other," he said.

"Tell me everything you want," she insisted.

"Yes," he said. "And you."

"I promise." She was quiet for several moments and then she said, "I'm very happy."

"So am I," he said.

Margaret knew she'd never be the same as Fiona or Vanessa: she wasn't that sort of woman. But she was glad she'd done this.

Herbert Morrison had the copy sheet and was following the figures that Gene Grearson dictated from the master portfolio assembled on the desk in front of him. In his impatience the hotelier kept lifting the pages, trying to assess the total percentage of his holdings rather than progress through them pedantically. Morrison stopped at a cross-heading and interrupted the lawyer.

"There's no Initial share purchase," he said.

Grearson shook his head. "I had the enquiry made, like I said. "It's a restricted issue."

Morrison held back from showing the superior knowledge he'd learned from Rudd. "I thought there might have been some," he said.

"We did pretty well as it was," said the lawyer, imagining criticism. "We've amassed a total of 1200 Preferential holdings and more than 10,000 Ordinary."

"What does that give me, in percentage holdings in the parent company?"

Grearson made a quick calculation on a jotting pad and said, "Within a percentage point or two I work that out at something around nine."

Morrison conceded that within the time limitations, that was remarkably good. "How tight is the shell?" he demanded.

"You're absolutely protected," assured Grearson. "I placed the orders through New York brokers: none here in Boston. Everything goes from the exchanges to European brokering houses, from there to New York and then from New York to me."

"I'm indebted to you," said Morrison.

The lawyer ignored the gratitude. "But only for $2,250,000. We didn't have to go into your stock."

"I'm going to England soon," said Morrison. "But there'll be a need for us to keep in touch."

"You've got the numbers."

"If there were an emergency . . . if I had to unload in a hurry, for instance, what would be the delay?"

Grearson shook his head slowly. "A good three days, with the time difference."

"That's the risk I'll have to take," accepted Morrison.

Morrison was early for the appointment, half-way through the imported Guinness when Patrick Walker arrived at the Locke-Ober. Like Morrison he was a regular. Unasked, a bottle of Bushmills and a glass was brought, within minutes of his sitting down. Walker's face was brick-red, but that was the only indication of his intake that day: there was no slur in his voice.

"Contractual agreements tomorrow then?" said Walker.

"That was the message from London," agreed Morrison.

"And Texas is all tied up: there wasn't really any cause to worry, was there?"

Morrison didn't reply.

"The ships will be an unusual addition to what we've already got," said Walker.

"I've been looking at the figures," said Morrison, taking some notes from his pocket. "It wouldn't need a substantial reverse to affect us badly."

Walker sipped, savouring the flavour of the whisky. "What do you mean?"

"I mean that I'm not sure the board has been properly briefed about what might happen if this takeover attempt goes sour."

Walker put down his glass, concentrating upon what his friend was saying. "Why should it go sour?"

"Why does anything go sour?" said Morrison. "All we've heard about so far are the advantages if everything goes right. What happens if there's a concerted opposition to the take over?"

Walker laughed. "There's usually opposition from some people," he said.

"It would only take a four per cent margin increase on the value of Buckland House stock and we'd have to raise a loan of something like $20,000,000 to complete."

"That's peanuts," said the other Irishman.

"The Saudi investment fund isn't available," said Morrison. "And we're contractually committed in Texas."

"You worry too much, Herb. You always have done."

"This time I think there's proper cause," said Morrison.

21

It was a formal, posed occasion, of repeated handshakes and
feigned contract-signing for the benefit of the photographer who
flustered about them, arranging and grouping. Rudd obediently
took his place and obediently smiled, concealing the confusion of
feelings that had come as he'd entered the boardroom and
hardened with the initial hand contact with Buckland. The
takeover was a contrived, calculated affair but there was a
business morality and so it was acceptable. There wasn't any
justification with Margaret. He'd tried to find it, recognising the
aridness of their marriage, telling himself that what was happening couldn't worsen an already collapsed relationship, but it
hadn't worked. Cold-bloodedly, he had cuckolded a man. And
just as cold-bloodedly he intended going on doing it. As strong as
the guilt was, the balance came down on the side of his determination to carry on seeing her. It wasn't sex and the excitement of
the illicit. There was Joanne, for sex. And she *was* better than
Margaret. He wanted Margaret for . . . His thoughts went into
a cul-de-sac, unable to complete the reasoning. Or perhaps
he was frightened to complete it, too frightened of the barriers
and the walls and the locked doors to imagine himself ever able
to feel love. Was the emotion the same for Margaret as it had
been for Angela? He found it difficult now to recapture the
feeling. There were the memories and the nostalgia; but he didn't
know. So what did he know about Margaret? That he thought
she was beautiful, not because of any similarity with Angela
but in her own right. That his mind was consumed with her,
with seeing her and being with her and exploring her, not just
sexually but everything about her. That she made him laugh
and made him think. That with her he felt a complete, proper
man, not some business figurehead like the carved statues
they used to put on the front of sailing ships. That he was

179

being an absolute and utter bloody fool. And that he didn't care.

"Enough," declared Buckland, calling a halt.

Everyone drew apart and stood around uncertainly. Rudd looked to where Bunch was standing with the English lawyers and said, "Why don't you get the detailed contracts agreed?"

Looking generally around the room Buckland called out, "I think there should be the formality of completing the board meeting. There are things to be recorded."

Rudd stood back politely, watching the Buckland house directors file ahead of him. They moved in two groups, Buckland, Condway, Penhardy and Gore-Pelham first, then Snaith, Smallwood and Prince Faysel. At the door Buckland turned, extending his hand. "Come on," he said.

Rudd went in alongside the Englishman and allowed himself to be shown to a seat: it was between Gore-Pelham and the Arab.

Looking towards the separate secretariat table at which the stenographers were assembled, Buckland said, "I'd like the minutes of this meeting to record that draft contracts have been signed between Buckland House and Best Rest for the acquisition of the liner fleet. Ten per cent of the purchase price of $27,500,000 dollars has already been paid, the remainder upon completion. That full payment is to be made up of $20,000,000 cash, the remainder in share exchange between the two groups. . . ."

Buckland looked away from the secretaries towards the American. "I would like to welcome Harry Rudd, chairman of Best Rest and now, because of the earlier unanimous agreement of Buckland House directors, a member of this board."

"Thank you," said Rudd.

"I would also like this board to know that throughout the negotiations which have been concluded so successfully I have found Mr Rudd a man of fair dealing, honesty and integrity."

Rudd looked away, feeling a hollowness in his stomach. Christ! he thought.

Buckland continued. "I have every hope and expectation that this link-up will prove mutually beneficial."

"Hear, hear," said the always reliable Penhardy.

Aware that something was expected from him, Rudd said, "I,

too hope it will be mutually beneficial. I'm glad that your chairman has agreed to serve upon the board of the company to be formed to run the fleet."

"I think there should also be a record of thanks to Prince Faysel," said Buckland, continuing the congratulatory mood. "It was he who initiated the first approaches that have ended so well here today."

"Hear, hear," said Penhardy.

If his takeover were successful, there would have to be some changes, decided Rudd, looking around the table; he had the impression of sitting in a museum. One that was infrequently visited.

"Time's getting on," reminded Condway, to the chairman's right.

"Quite so," said Buckland. "I think we can agree that today is a moment for celebration. I've arranged lunch in a private room at the Berridge."

Buckland began to gather his papers from the bottom of the table, but Snaith said, "This meeting hasn't been properly concluded."

Buckland had been smiling towards Rudd. The expression went and he turned to the merchant banker. "What now!" he said impatiently.

"There's an agenda item for any other business," reminded Snaith.

Wearily Buckland leaned back over his papers and said, "Any other business?"

"Yes," said Snaith at once. "The composition and formation of this board permits, upon submission of a special request, an extraordinary board meeting being called by the signatures of two directors." From a folder before him Snaith distributed copies of the request to each director. There was one for Rudd.

"What are you talking about?" frowned Buckland.

"I am making such a request," said Snaith. "I am the signatory, supported by Smallwood. The requirements are for the meeting to be held within seven days."

"But what for?"

Snaith stared directly up the table. "For the directors to

181

discuss the suitability of Sir Ian Buckland remaining chairman and director of Buckland House," he declared.

The celebration lunch was a stilted, awkward affair, with Condway, Penhardy and Gore-Pelham over-compensating in their support for Buckland, even insisting upon embarrassing impromptu speeches and toasts. Made confident by that morning's agreement to bring Rudd on to the board and the brandy that followed the claret, the conversation was firmly geared towards disposing of Haffaford as a merchant bank and removing Snaith from a board upon which he was nothing more than an irritant.

Rudd had briefed Hallett before going in for the meal, so by the time he reached his now abandoned suite, the personal assistant had recalled Bunch from his legal meetings.

"Sorry to interrupt you," said Rudd at once.

"I'd virtually finished anyway," said the lawyer. He nodded towards Hallett. "I know what happened," he said.

"What do the company formation rules say?" asked Prince Faysel.

"That if by his behaviour a director loses the confidence of his other directors then by unanimous vote he can be asked to resign," quoted the lawyer.

"But not Buckland, surely!" said Rudd. "He's got the share strength."

"Obviously the rule was created for directors outside the family," agreed Bunch. "For him to be forced off, there would have to be a vote of no confidence from the shareholders. And not just the Initial holders, the Preferential as well."

"How can it work then?" said Rudd.

"Embarrassment," said Bunch simply. "He might prefer to resign rather than have his faults discussed in front of hundreds of shareholders."

"Then where would we be?" said Faysel.

"God knows," said Rudd. He turned to the lawyer. "Are Snaith and Smallwood powerful enough?"

"Snaith represents quite a few shareholders through his bank," said Bunch. "But I wouldn't have thought he was that strong, not unless he can persuade people like Condway, Gore-Pelham and Penhardy to change sides."

"We've just sat through three hours of maudlin promises of undying friendship," said Rudd.

"If it leaks out – and it would be good strategy for Haffafords to leak it – then it'll make the shares uncertain."

"Yes," agreed Rudd distantly, his head bowed.

"Shouldn't we set up some sort of buying operation to prevent them going too far?" suggested Faysel.

"Not immediately," decided Rudd. "We don't have a lot of liquidity if we base our takeover on cash. The lower the shares, the more attractive our offer might be."

"It'll badly affect what we've just transferred in the stock exchange," said Bunch. "An almost immediate loss."

"That's a justifiable gamble," said Rudd. "If everything works out, they'll firm up again soon enough."

"What do you want me to do about finance?" said Bunch. "In New York we judged about $3,000,000 borrowing but it works out a bit higher than that. I think that in addition to the liquidity we hold we're going to need $5,000,000."

"Where's the cheapest money market?" said Rudd.

"It's a toss-up between Germany and France," said Bunch. "Both quoting about eleven per cent for business loans."

"Roll-up?" demanded Rudd.

Bunch shook his head. "Difficult to arrange. They seem to prefer usual interest procedure rather than waiting until the end of a property transaction."

"The hotels definitely are property," said Rudd. "So we'd qualify for roll-up if we borrowed on the English market. If we got fixed-term roll-up here, we'd be three per cent better off than paying monthly at eleven per cent on the continent."

"I'll go to the city then," said Bunch.

"Stay quiet," warned Rudd. "I don't want Haffaford's getting the vaguest smell of this."

"Anything else?"

Rudd looked between Hallett and Bunch. "I want a complete breakdown of shareholding in Buckland House, individual, big investors, trusts and private. If it comes down to a shareholders' decision I want a guide to how the odds will be staked."

"This is a complication we didn't expect, isn't it?" said Faysel.

"There are too many complications," agreed Rudd. "Far too many." And just when he thought he'd solved them.

Rudd put his arm out and she put her head into his shoulder, their bodies sticking wetly together. "We fit," she said.

"We just have."

She put her hand on him and he tensed and she said, "It's mine. I want to hold it."

That's all she did and he relaxed again. Rudd wished he'd brought the wine up from the downstairs room. "I became a director of Buckland House this morning," he said.

"I know."

"What else did Ian say?"

"Nothing."

Rudd wondered what embarrassment Haffaford's intended producing; it was bound to affect her if it went beyond the boardroom. He pulled her closer and she turned her head, kissing his chest. This was going beyond fantasy, thought Margaret. She felt vaguely frightened.

"You're all greasy," she said.

"So are you."

"I like getting this way. With you."

"I felt a shit this morning," he said.

There was an almost imperceptible movement away. "Don't you think I do too? He's my friend as well as my husband."

"I like him."

"So do I. What's that got to do with it?"

"Nothing, I suppose. I just wanted to say it."

"Why?"

"I don't know."

"It's not just Ian, is it?" she said. "The guilt, I mean."

"I don't know what you're talking about," he lied.

"You feel you've let Angela down, don't you?"

Rudd wondered if it had been obvious to Joanne: perhaps it was different because she was professional. "Yes," he said.

"That's silly."

"I know. I can't help it."

"Do you mind talking about her?"

"No," he said. He never had before, he realized. Bunch knew but then Bunch had been there and seen it all. He didn't have any other friends, just acquaintances, and they'd never asked.

"What was she like?"

Rudd closed his eyes, waiting for the hurt, but no hurt came: not even discomfort at talking of his dead wife while next to him lay a woman to whom he'd just made love. He swallowed, remembering. "Quite small," he said. "And shy. She always wanted to hold my hand in a crowd. Very shy. . . ." His voice lapsed. "Dark-haired," he continued. "She used to be embarrassed about it, on her legs. She was always trying out new creams and treatments. She talked in her sleep. Not things you could understand, just odd words. She could always remember her dreams. I never can."

"Where did you meet?"

"At university in Boston. Her father didn't want her to go there. She could have gone anywhere. Yale or Vassar. But she wanted to go to Boston because Boston was home. She wasn't very adventurous. Shy, like I said."

"She set up home with you and became pregnant; that's adventurous."

"I've never thought about it like that before," admitted Rudd. It would have been so out of character that it would have been the first and perhaps the most definite indication to Morrison that he had unduly influenced her, particularly after the positive ban on their relationship. He decided he didn't want to talk about Angela any more. "What about you?" he said.

"I told you about me. Ordinary."

"If I'd believed that, we wouldn't be where we are now."

She kissed him again, on the chest. "There was never any doubt between the families that Ian and I would marry: it was like one of those arranged things that happened in the middle ages, children programmed to accept their parents' choice. We've always liked each other: respected each other, too, I suppose. But that's all. And that isn't enough. He's never been cruel or beastly to me, never once in his life. And I've tried not to be with him."

"It sounds very strange."

185

"I suppose it is. It doesn't seem so, to either of us. The English establishment have two faces: the one that everyone else sees and the one that they look at themselves, in the bathroom mirror."

"Is that what you are, English establishment?"

"Yes, I suppose we are. It's a stupid, out-of-date anachronism, I know, but despite all the banner-waving it exists and persists." She moved her hand away from his crotch, idly tracing patterns across his stomach. "I don't suppose Ian really qualifies," she said. "His grandfather was a clerk in Glasgow. Most of the titled families in England either come from kings' bastards or villains but there's the benefit of several hundred years' gap."

"You sound cynical."

"I'm not trying to be," she said, immediately honest. "I've enjoyed the advantages."

"Do you descend from a king's bastard?"

She shook her head. "There's another way," she said. "The dilligent, unquestioning servant. My family have been diplomats since Charles II. They were always opportunists, which was why they didn't choose Charles I and risk getting killed by Cromwell. We're masters of convenience."

"People of convenience and marriages of convenience," said Rudd.

"Now you're sounding cynical."

"I wasn't trying to either," he said.

"What was your father?" she asked suddenly.

"A baggage loader at Boston airport," said Rudd. "He got hit by a forklift truck when he was only forty-five and I know he died bitter as hell because never once in his life had he managed to earn ten dollars more than my mother. She was a stenographer in one of the harbour offices. I often think he suspected she got the money for doing something more than being a good secretary but I'm pretty sure she didn't."

"Would it have mattered to you like it did to him?"

"I suppose it should have done," he said reflectively. "I never really thought about it; I believed her, you see."

"You're the American dream, aren't you?" she said suddenly. "The poor boy who became a millionaire."

"I never really thought about that either."

186

"It's a funny thing about America," she said. "You could be the beginning of a new aristocracy: create a lineage for a hundred years' time. That doesn't seem to be happening in Britain. It's all backward-looking. Nothing seems to be starting fresh any more."

"I don't have a wife or a son to start a lineage." reminded Rudd.

Margaret was silent for a long time and then she said, "You could marry again, couldn't you?"

"Yes," he said.

Richard Haffaford replaced the telephone and smiled across at the men facing him in the office.

"Now there's an interesting call," he said.

"What?" asked Snaith.

"This time Condway wants to host the lunch at the Connaught."

It was a damned good job he'd written the letter to Hong Kong, Buckland decided. And telephoned Sinclair as well. The man would want a reward, but if it had anything to do with whatever move it was that Snaith was planning, then the man deserved it. Should he do anything about Fiona, he wondered. No, he decided. He'd wait to see what the attack was first.

22

It had been his father's edict to confront trouble the moment it appeared, which was why Buckland convened the special board meeting within twenty-four hours of the merchant banker's demand. Before the meeting Buckland gathered in his office the directors upon whom he knew he could rely; Rudd and Prince Faysel were included because he knew they were supporters after the link-up. Buckland was observing another inherited rule; divide and conquer. One of the early lessons to be preached, just after he'd come down from Cambridge and moved into the annexe office next door to the old man. Divide and conquer the opposition but remain unified ourselves. The share structure, making them inviolable whatever the setback, was the most positive example of that.

It was right that the American should be prepared for what was to come. Buckland said, "I'm sorry there's had to be this unpleasantness so soon after your joining us."

"How unpleasant is it going to be?" said Rudd.

"At the beginning of the year I settled a private debt, a gambling matter, from company funds," said Buckland. "I accept it was wrong, but I fully intended to rectify it. I just forgot. The thing's been settled now, of course, but the damned merchant bank is worrying it like a dog with a bone."

"Is that all there is, Ian?"

Buckland looked startled at Condway's question. "That's not the sort of thing I expected you to ask, George," he said.

"Private gambling debts being settled with company money isn't the sort of thing we expect either, " said the peer.

Buckland's attitude became uncertain at the unexpected hostility. "We've discussed this; resolved it," he said. "I've mentioned it before the meeting only to acquaint our new director with what might come up."

"I know we've settled it," said Condway. "I just want to make sure that if we're being prepared, then we're completely prepared for anything Haffaford's have to say."

"Rows are bad for public confidence," said Penhardy.

Buckland looked worriedly between the two men of whom he had been so sure and then turned towards Rudd, embarrassed. This wasn't going at all as it should have done. "Public confidence in Buckland House is unshakable," he said. "It always has been."

"Let's hope it stays that way," said Condway. "You haven't answered my question."

"I haven't been given any indication upon what Snaith and his bank are basing this demand," said Buckland. "It can only be the damned gambling matter."

Condway and Penhardy stared directly at him, waiting. Rudd and Prince Faysel were waiting too. Gore-Pelham appeared occupied in the photographs around the walls. Why the hell were they treating him with this sort of suspicion? Where was the lunch-table loyalty, after he'd single-handedly solved the biggest problem to confront the company for years? "I know of nothing upon which Haffaford's can base any accusation about my unfitness to continue as an officer of this company," he said, rigidly formal.

"Glad to hear it," said Condway. "You can understand my concern, of course."

"No, George," said Buckland stiffly. "After the years you have been associated with this company and with me, I can't."

"I don't think we should degenerate into any sort of argument, certainly not before we know what's happening," intervened Penhardy quickly.

"Essential we all keep cool heads," endorsed Gore-Pelham, turning away from his photographic study. "Nothing's going to be achieved by squabbling among ourselves."

"It was precisely to avoid that – and to advise Mr Rudd – that I asked you here before the meeting," said Buckland, still formal. "I must say I'm surprised at the attitudes that have emerged."

"Not attitudes, Ian," said Condway. "Caution. Every right to be cautious."

Buckland turned to the American. "You have my apologies,"

he said. "This can't be creating a very favourable impression."

"I'm no stranger to boardroom disputes," said Rudd. He wondered what Morrison would have done if the old man had found him with his hand in the till?

Buckland looked pointedly at his watch. "Let's hope this one can be quickly dispensed with," he said, rising. He led the way into the adjoining boardroom. Snaith and Smallwood were already there, waiting. Buckland nodded towards them. The two men nodded back. The directors who had been in Buckland's office assembled around the table and Buckland turned expectantly to Snaith.

The merchant banker rose, a bound document in his hand. "This extraordinary board meeting is called under the provision of Section 14 of the company's Articles of Formation, originally dated January 1897, and revised in May 1962." He looked up as if he were expecting some interruption and when there was none he added, "Section 14 remained unaltered in the revision. It allows a minimum of two directors to question the behaviour and fitness of any other director or directors to continue in office, if in the opinion of those directors there have been one or more actions affecting the proper running of Buckland House holding company or any of its subsidiaries."

Snaith swallowed at the end of the recitation. Then he said, "As I have already indicated, I am the complainant, supported by Smallwood. The fitness I question is that of our chairman, Sir Ian Buckland. I believe his behaviour risks bringing this board into disrepute and it is my intention to call upon him to resign."

The merchant banker spoke slowly and assuredly and Buckland felt the anger burn within him. He consciously tried to control it. If he were to rebut whatever attack Snaith intended making, then he had to remain composed. Another piece of advice from his father: if you lose your temper in a business discussion, then you lose the discussion.

"Upon what grounds?" he demanded. He was pleased at the calmness that appeared to be in his voice.

"In May of this year a company cheque for £635,000 was issued to Leinman Properties," began Snaith. "It was subsequently found to have been used to settle a gambling debt incurred by the chairman. . . ."

190

Buckland felt the relief spread through him, replacing the earlier anger; dogs worrying a bone, he thought again; a bone without any meat on it. He interrupted, ". . . who subsequently apologized to this board for an oversight, explained the bona fide circumstances, repaid it in full and in addition paid into the company something like £71,000 in full interest." Buckland stared around the boardroom table, moving the documents before him impatiently. "This has all been fully discussed at previous meetings. Does anyone here see the need for this pointless repetition?"

"The repetition isn't pointless," insisted Snaith. "You asked for the grounds and I'm setting them out, in full. Because the gambling debt was the first, I itemized it first."

Buckland felt a coldness, deep in his stomach. To his right Lord Condway shifted his position.

"As the chairman has reminded us," continued Snaith, "the sum was repaid, with interest." He hesitated raising his eyes towards Buckland. "It was accompanied by an assurance that it was an oversight, an assurance this board felt should be accepted. There was also the undertaking that such things would not occur again."

"Are you suggesting that they have?" demanded Buckland.

Snaith took up a fresh sheet of paper. "At the discussion concerning the year's trading and annual dividend, an in-term audit was agreed. Six weeks ago, that audit picked up a sum of £150,000 paid to Sir Ian Buckland, designated as director's remuneration."

"What's questionable about that?" demanded Buckland "The chairman and directors' remuneration is assessed agains the dividend to be declared, in addition to the fixed sum. The dividend was agreed and the sum in question was easily calculable." Damn Tommy Ellerby for pressing him for the settlement of that £120,000, he thought.

"It has to be determined by a directors' vote," rejected Snaith. "That vote has yet to be taken."

"An absolute technicality!" protested Gore-Pelham and Buckland nodded gratefully to his friend. Gore-Pelham went on, "He's entitled to a payment of £150,000, just as we're all entitled to our remuneration. To quibble about whether or not a minute has been properly recorded is hair-splitting. It certainly doesn't justify the embarrassment being created in this room this morning."

"Hear, hear," said Penhardy.

"It is improper," said Snaith.

"So's parking on a yellow line," said Gore-Pelham dismissively.

"I consider paying himself in advance of the directors' agreement to be a contravention of responsible directorial behaviour, whether it is a technicality or not," said Snaith stubbornly. "I make that the second ground for my demand."

Buckland regarded the merchant banker apprehensively. So far he knew the board were with him – just – but the man had indicated he wasn't finished. Snaith stared back up the table at him. "There has already been a reference to embarrassment," he said. "Perhaps the chairman would like to explain to this board the arrangements for the occupancy of the mews house off Sloane Street which is nominally assigned in the holding company records as belonging to our Far East division."

Buckland felt the flush spreading from his neck to his face. Every eye was upon him, every face expressionless. Purposely he widened his own eyes so that his colouring should be construed as outrage and said, "Have I been subjected to some sort of private enquiry . . . an investigation by some scruffy little man in a dirty raincoat!"

The response appeared to off-balance Snaith. He said awkwardly, "Information came into the hands of my bank."

"What sort of information!" shouted Buckland. The feigned outrage had been clever quick-thinking: his stomach was in turmoil. Thank God he'd decided to be careful.

"Of its occupancy by a woman. Of the presence outside, on numerous occasions, of cars registered in your name."

Snaith had spoken of holding company records: so they'd missed it! He was hanging over the biggest precipice ever, but he could still manage to claw back. He held the merchant banker's eyes, knowing this would look like the demeanour of an innocent, wrongly accused man. "I am offended," he said. "I am offended and insulted at the implication being made in this boardroom today. And I am outraged that I have obviously been the object of some guttersnipe investigation from a company, a merchant bank, that I believed to be one of integrity. . . ."

Buckland went from face to face surrounding him at the table: it was impossible to gauge their reaction but he thought he was doing well.

He continued. "The mews house referred to is being occupied by Lady Fiona Harvey. Lady Harvey is a family friend . . . ." He paused, purposely. "A friend of both myself and my wife. For the past two months she has been occupying the house while looking for accommodation in London. If people who are so intent upon investigation were to investigate properly, they would find in the Far East division file a letter dated July this year, from myself to our division chairman, advising him of that occupancy but asking him to let me know if ever it is his wish to take up the tenancy during a visit to this country, to enable her to move. They would also find his response, agreeing to the occupancy. That is dated, as far as I can recollect, in August. A further, proper, fair investigation would also reveal arrangements for a standing order payment, which I have insisted Lady Harvey makes, of a rental of £120 a week, the proper market value, into the account of the Far East division. . . ." Buckland hesitated again, watching the faces. He didn't know Rudd or Faysel sufficiently well to be sure, but he judged Condway, Penhardy and Gore-Pelham to be with him. He coughed. "There has been an obscene innuendo concerning the presence of my car outside the house. I do not consider it necessary for me to justify my private life to this board, but as the matter has been raised I have no hesitation in doing so. As I have said, Lady Harvey is a friend of the family. And as a friend, she has been allowed full access and use of vehicles belonging to my wife and I whenever she has wanted them." The halt, his voice indicating that he intended saying more but then not, was intentional, to cause Snaith the maximum inconvenience.

The merchant banker and Smallwood were in retreat, the finance director as flushed as Buckland had been earlier.

"Our information is that Lady Harvey's occupancy commenced in June this year," said Snaith.

"This is preposterous!" erupted Gore-Pelham. "I have no intention of sitting in this room while a colleague and friend is

193

being called upon to defend himself against baseless innuendo of the vilest sort. If there's condemnation to be made here today then it is against two directors who saw fit to behave in this offensive manner."

Buckland thought it was the strongest speech he'd ever heard the man make.

"I agree," said Penhardy. "I consider what has happened to be utterly disgraceful."

"The requirement of Section 14 is not for a vote of censure," said Smallwood doggedly. "It appears to have been designed to minimize company embarrassment by allowing the accused director to resign."

"Are you seriously expecting me to accept this fatuous accusation as justified and resign from this board?" demanded Buckland.

"Yes," said Snaith.

"You must be mad," said Buckland. "Utterly mad."

"There is a second alternative," said Snaith.

"What?"

"Accepting the damage it could do to this company, the matter can be brought before the public shareholders for a vote of confidence."

"Would you honestly go as far as that?" said Buckland.

"Unless you take the other course, yes, I would," said Snaith.

"Go to hell," said Buckland. It was what his father would have done: except that his father wouldn't have been caught out in the first place.

"Who is she?" said Margaret.

"Fiona."

"Fiona Harvey! Good God!" She hardly had grounds for criticism, thought Margaret. "It's often someone supposed to be a friend; I read that somewhere."

"I don't want this to become a row," he said.

"Why should it become that?" said Margaret. "I knew there was someone, of course; that was obvious. But I didn't suspect Fiona, although I knew she was cock-happy. Doesn't her voice irritate you? It does me."

194

"Where the hell did you learn an expression like cock-happy."

Margaret shrugged. "I don't know. Does it matter?"

"It's not an expression I'd expect my wife to use."

She laughed at him, genuinely. "This is an odd time and an odd conversation in which to start demanding standards from your wife!"

"It's serious," he said.

"I believe you."

"The bastards are going to bring it before the shareholders."

"You fool," she said. "You absolute bloody fool." There was no rancour in her voice. Her only feeling was disappointment.

"Don't you think I realize that?"

"No," she said. "I don't think you do."

"I'm sorry," he said.

"For what?"

"Hurting you."

She laughed again. "How have you hurt me?"

"Aren't you hurt, knowing I've kept your friend as a mistress?"

She was surprised. "You're sorry you've been caught out," she said. "Not that you had to ask me to create a cover-up. We've always been honest, Ian. Right from the time when we built wooden houses on the island. Don't insult me by attempting some pretence now."

"I thought you might care," he said.

"Do you?"

"Yes."

"What a funny way of showing it!"

"You're trying to start an argument."

"We don't argue, for Christ's sake! Stop inventing things."

"I called Vanessa."

"What did she say?"

"That they were fuckers."

"I think sometimes she uses a farmyard mouth to prove she's the wife of a farmer."

"She's coming down for the shareholders' meeting."

"The clan gathers and erects the barriers!"

"It's nothing to be cynical about."

195

"How should we be then?"

"Prepared."

"What does that mean?"

"If you're questioned you've got to say you knew. About the house and the cars: that she was a family friend we were helping out."

"People wouldn't believe this!" she said. "They wouldn't believe we're sitting here having a conversation like this."

"I'm trying to save the company," he said.

"Bullshit. You're trying to save yourself. That's all you've ever done."

"Who's using farmyard language now?"

"Don't try to avoid it, Ian. Not this time. You've been caught with your trousers down, literally. And there isn't a father to help you. There isn't anyone."

"Does that mean you won't say you knew?"

"How?" she said.

"I don't understand."

"How will I be asked?" she said.

"It won't be a direct question: it's not a court. But I've got to give an explanation to the shareholders and I want you to support it, if you're asked."

She breathed out deeply, a weary sound. "I won't let you down, Ian. Have I ever?"

"Thank you," he said.

"Have you told your mother?"

"I'm going up tomorrow."

"Will she have to attend the shareholders' meeting?"

"It won't be essential. But I expect she'll want to."

"You poor bastard," said Margaret. "She's going to despise you more than she already does."

"You've reason to be cruel, I suppose."

"That's not being cruel, my darling. That's being honest."

"I've put the company right financially."

"That's going to be forgotten after this scandal."

"It's a restricted meeting: only shareholders can attend."

"For God's sake, Ian, stop fooling yourself! Every nasty little bit of sex and gossip will leak out: it always does."

Buckland punched his right fist into the palm of his other

hand. "Just when everything was so perfect!" he said. "What the hell can Rudd be thinking now?"

"That you're a bloody fool, like I said. Which you are."

"I *am* sorry," he said. "About the embarrassment: I really didn't mean to embarrass you. It just happened."

"What's she like?"

"What?"

"Fiona. What's she like in bed? You haven't done it with me for months so I want to know."

Buckland sat before his wife, slump-shouldered. When he spoke it was as though a friend were making his confession and inwardly she winced at it. "She does a lot of funny things," he said. "I think she reads odd books or watches kinky films or something. But in the end it's just the same. That's all it can ever be, isn't it? Always the same."

"What about Fiona?" said Margaret. "What happens if the newspapers get to her?'

Buckland shuddered. "She knows her reputation would suffer if she said something wrong," he said.

Margaret shook her head. "Make sure she gets her story right," she said. "Don't worry about me. I'm part of the family; I've *got* to do it. She hasn't."

"You were right," said Buckland.

"About what?"

"Her voice. It practically drove me crazy."

Herbert Morrison felt light-limbed after his flight as if his body were wrapped in cotton wool, but he forced himself to listen to what Rudd had to say. When the younger man finished, Morrison said, "And we're trapped into it: we've bought the liners and signed a share exchange contract and we're linked?"

"You make it sound like some sort of a mistake," said Rudd.

"We've bought in high," said Morrison. "When this sort of shit gets out, it could cause a slide. We could end up low."

"Which could be to our advantage if there's a take-over."

Morrison blinked against the tiredness. He needed time to analyze properly what had happened, to see what benefit he could derive. At the moment his only thought was that a

$2,250,000 investment could be reduced to half. Which was confused thinking. He'd never bought for a profit: he'd bought for a lever. You could beat people with levers.

"What do the English lawyers say?" he asked.

"There's a meeting tomorrow."

"I'd like to attend."

"Of course," said Rudd.

Morrison decided he'd manoeuvred himself well. There couldn't be a move without his being aware of it, and by being aware of it he could thwart it. What did $2,250,000 matter? Avenging Angela was worth more than that; much more.

23

Sir Henry Dray worried the gold pencil between his fingers, like a man doing physiotherapy exercises after a hand injury. He listened to Rudd's account of the extraordinary meeting with his head on one side, occasionally making a note in a large, ledger-type book. When Rudd finished he said, "Messy. Very, very messy."

"But to our advantage or not?" said Rudd.

"Depends what you want that advantage to be."

"Acquisition of Buckland House," said Rudd. "We've got a twelve per cent holding now. An uncertain board. And shareholders who are going to hear accusations of mismanagement and even deceit involving their chairman. The shares are already undervalued and they're going to go lower. If we don't make a bid, then someone else will."

"I agree," said Dray.

"Do you consider the share drop inevitable?" The president of Best Rest had sat as intently as the lawyer, listening to what Rudd said.

Dray frowned towards Morrison. "Unquestionably so," he said. "Hardly a situation that's going to instil confidence, is it?"

"Buckland's account seemed reasonable enough at the meeting," said Rudd.

Dray stopped the pencil movement, ready to make more notes. "Do you believe him, about the house and the woman?"

"No," said Rudd. "Obviously he's maintaining a mistress, but he's covered himself well with the rental and the letters." He felt hypocritical and swallowed heavily.

"Acceptable enough for a boardroom or a shareholders' meeting perhaps," said Dray reflectively. "Not for a court of law. There the evidence is on oath and lying is perjury."

Rudd felt a sweep of uncertainty at what he was initiating. "There's no other way?"

199

Dray came up to him surprised. "Of course there's no other way. We've already discussed that. Haffaford's have made a mistake, limiting their criticism to the man and asking for a shareholders' decision. The attack has got to be upon the share structure first and Buckland's unfitness second. The two dovetail perfectly, but only in the right order."

Rudd wondered if the lawyer ever managed to get any emotion into his flat, expressionless voice. "What do you advise about the Haffaford move?"

"Do nothing," said Dray at once. "Let them do all the work and we'll sit back and pick up the pieces. They've obviously employed some firm of private enquiry agents. Why should we duplicate the expense?" He tapped the pencil against some point in the ledger. "I'd like to have proof about that house," he said. "The gambling debt is provable from the company documentation, and we can get sufficient inference from the advance payment of his dividend and fee apportionment. But the love nest is the pressure point." He smiled across at Rudd. "No way of proving that he's lying, is there?"

Would Margaret have known? Rudd felt sick at the thought that came to him, annoyed that the consideration should ever enter his mind. It was ludicrous for him to have imagined he could keep the relationship with Margaret separate from what he hoped to achieve with Buckland House, but he wouldn't – he couldn't – use it to benefit. Soon he'd have to tell her. Just as he'd have to tell her other things. But when? He had to be sure of her first. If he misjudged it by a second, he'd lose her. And he was determined not to do that. He'd lose Buckland House and their investment and a good deal more rather than lose Margaret. He went back to the barrister's remark. Rudd thought his own personal situation was a damned sight messier than Buckland's.

"Well?" encouraged Dray, head tilted at the American's hesitation.

"Not unless it comes from Haffaford's attack," said Rudd. "They're employing the enquiry agents, like you said."

"Perhaps after all we should bring in our own people," said Dray. "I know one or two excellent firms. They might do better than Haffaford's."

This wasn't business, thought Rudd. Sure, he normally

attempted to get every advantage available before opening negotiations and sometimes the line between right and wrong got a little blurred, but it had never before been like this, never personal. If the criterion for running a business came down to morals, he wasn't any better qualified than Buckland. Less so, if the two affairs were balanced side by side.

"I don't think we should," he said positively. "Absolute secrecy is still essential. Haffaford's people might stumble across our investigators and then there could only be one conclusion: leave it until after the shareholders' meeting."

The barrister regarded him doubtfully. "Ultimately it's your decision," he said. "You know what you want to achieve."

"Is that really a good idea, relying on somebody else's attack?" challenged Morrison. Although he had expected his investment to decrease in value by the manoeuvre he intended – even though he'd thought that first day in Boston he'd sacrifice it all to destroy Rudd – now that the moment was here the cautious contradiction gripped him. Morrison had always been terrified of poverty, of not having access to tangible money. That was why he ran such a surprisingly high cash account at his bank, instead of investing the money as most other businessmen would have done.

"I'm not relying on it," said Rudd. "I'm letting it take its course. You've heard from Sir Henry that Haffaford's move is wrongly aimed. We'll get the truth in a court." Hypocrite, thought Rudd again: he was only postponing the thing, like a child desperate for excuses to avoid taking an unpleasant-tasting medicine.

"There's another possibility we haven't discussed," said Dray.

"What's that?" said Morrison apprehensively.

"That somebody else *does* make a takeover move."

"They'd have to break the structure," said Rudd.

The barrister nodded. "Of course. And if they did, it would come down to a fight. Could even be more than one. What are you going to set your bid at?"

"Ten per cent over par, with the expectation of being driven up to twenty-five per cent. All cash."

"How much?"

201

"I estimate $200,000,000 worldwide."

"That would be cheap, if you could get it," said Dray. "The problem is that you're not going to have the opportunity to mount it quietly: if we go to court over the structure, then it will have to be declared. That's the purpose of the action, after all."

"What's the point you're making?" said Morrison.

"That you go to all the trouble and expense of breaking an archaic scheme of arrangement and someone can jump over your heads with a better offer and make what you've done a complete waste of time and money."

"Are you advising against it?" asked the old man.

"Just setting out the difficulties that might arise, to enable you to make the proper decision," said the barrister. "I see that as my function."

"Is that view in your written opinion?" asked Morrison.

"Of course."

It would be a vital piece of information, for later presentation to the Best Rest board. He looked sideways to Rudd; it was like setting out across a high wire without a balancing pole, he thought. He said, "Shouldn't we refer back to the board before committing ourselves?"

Rudd shook his head. "The board have approved. The decision comes down to me."

Morrison felt a jump of satisfaction; that remark couldn't have been better if it had been scripted.

"I need that decision," said Dray. "Irrespective of the shareholders' meeting that Haffaford's are bringing about, there will be a lot of preliminary work to be done: claims to lay, court allocation to arrange, things like that."

The moment of commitment, Rudd recognized. Once started, it would be unstoppable. Was the hurt and the damage that he would be risking be worth it, in the hope of becoming the owner of the best? *Of being* the best?

"Start the action," he said.

Margaret had a key so there was no need for his impatience, but Rudd was anxious to get away from the Berridge suite and back to the Grosvenor Square apartment before she arrived. He tried to curb the feeling, to drive it from his mind. Never – ever – before had anything personal come before work. Because until now there hadn't been anything personal. And there still shouldn't be now. She wouldn't expect it and he shouldn't allow it. There were still too many uncharted difficulties ahead to risk adding to the problems by carelessness.

"How about the share composition?" he asked Bunch.

The lawyer took the portfolio figures from his briefcase, setting them out on the conference table. Rudd moved irritably, wondering if the man were trying purposely to be slow.

"There's a mass of 'A' and 'B' ordinary," he said, starting from the bottom. "There's a special 'A' issue which carry small voting rights, but the others don't. The Preferential issue divides with sixteen per cent held by the Buckland family as you already know, fifteen per cent between the professionals – funds, institutions and pensions, and in that I include Haffaford's overall portfolio – our twelve per cent, thirty-one per cent in small holdings and twenty-five in shielded, nominee groupings. . . ." He coughed, turning a page of his file. "The Initial are mainly in the hands of the Buckland family, which again you know. That comes to thirty-five per cent. The big investors, funds and institutions again, have thirty per cent. Condway, Penhardy and Gore-Pelham hold five per cent each and there's twenty per cent among small investor pockets. . . ."

"Dray was right about the uncertainty," said Rudd. "There's going to be a slump, caused first by the shareholders' meeting and then by the action. If we could get in as soon as possible after the outcome, we could get a price a lot lower than 102p a share. The professionals should come to us at once. And they'll bring the small people, too; there's always a sheep complex in a panic. And I think that'll apply to Condway, Penhardy and Gore-Pelham."

"I thought you said they were loyal to Buckland."

"The story sounded good," said Rudd. "It won't, after the shit has been thrown."

"Should be all right then?"

"What about the nominee holdings?"

"No idea," said the American lawyer. "That's why they're nominee. They don't want anybody to know."

"Do your best to find out," urged Rudd. "It's a good break-down but it's incomplete unless we know it all."

"I'll try," said the lawyer. "It won't be easy."

"Nothing seems to be easy about this deal." said Rudd.

Margaret overcooked the steaks because she wasn't accustomed to cooking, but Rudd declared them excellent and hoped she believed him; he decided deceit was coming easily to him in everything. Neither wanted anything else, so they carried the remains of their wine into the larger room. She'd brought records, as well as tapes and some magazines and books: there were even some prints arranged against the most advantageous wall. She put a record on and said, "Do you like it? It's Delius. My favourite."

"It's beautiful," said Rudd.

She burrowed her way familiarly into his shoulder. He pulled her close to him, enjoying the feel of her body. He didn't want to go to bed yet and knew she didn't: they were getting another sort of intimacy by being together and exploring each other in a different way.

"Ian told me," she said suddenly.

"Why?"

"He needs me to support the story."

He wouldn't have used it, even if he could. What was happening between them was sacrosanct: it had nothing to do with takeovers and share assaults and business coups.

"What did he tell you?" asked Rudd cautiously.

"Everything. About Fiona, the house. The lot."

"You know her then?"

"Oh yes," she said easily. "I have done for years. She's a friend of mine."

"You don't sound very upset."

"That's what Ian said. I don't know what he expected me to feel."

"Aren't you worried about the embarrassment?"

"I'm worried about his mother," she said. "It'll be awful for her."

"Are you going to say you knew?"

"Of course I am," said Margaret. "I've got to, haven't I? It's my duty."

He looked sideways, curious at her attitude, but said nothing.

"And what those people did to Ian was dreadful: they treated him like some criminal."

Which technically Rudd supposed the man was. "Does his mother know?"

"He's telling her. Vanessa is coming down from Yorkshire to be at the meeting."

Rudd hesitated at the question and then decided it was justified. "What's going to happen to Ian and you?" he said.

"Happen?"

"Are you going to stay together?"

She twisted around and looked up at him. Her face was serious. "Don't," she said. "Please don't."

"I'm sorry," he said. Damn!

"It's still too new, Harry. Let's leave it as it is."

"What's that?" he said.

"I don't know yet." It wasn't a fantasy any more. But it wasn't real either. She felt confused. And frightened.

They had had to wait until Richard Haffaford returned from a bankers' meeting in Basle and the flight from Switzerland was delayed. The building around them was deserted apart from cleaners, the majority of the rooms in darkness. The city is a place that sleeps early: hardly any sound came from the streets outside.

Haffaford listened patiently to Snaith's review, towards the end shaking his head in annoyance. When the Buckland director finished, the merchant bank chairman went first to Sir Herbert White and then Pryke. "Well?" he invited.

"We didn't do it right," admitted White at once. "We hurried and took things on face value. Which was a mistake."

"That's my view, too," said Haffaford. He went back to Snaith. "That's not a criticism," he said. "I'm sorry we put you into that position."

"It's no good weeping over the mistakes," said Smallwood objectively. "What do we do now?"

"I made it clear we were going to seek a shareholders' declaration," said Snaith.

"We needn't go through with it," said White.

"We can't stay in this position," said Haffaford. "There's too much money committed."

"The explanations seemed satisfactory enough at the meeting," warned Snaith.

"That £635,000 was definitely criminal!" said Haffaford. "Condway has as good as admitted to me that he agreed to a cover-up."

"It's not illegal any longer," said Snaith. "It's been endorsed by the full board."

"I still think we've got enough," said Haffaford. "The board and that American are content to support Buckland, cap in hand. But the professionals won't be. No fund manager is going to take those explanations and be satisfied."

"But will there be sufficient support for the vote?" said Pryke. "If we try and fail, then the only effect will be to depress the prices and that'll mean our investors getting an even worse return for their money."

"It's a risk," accepted Haffaford. "But I think it's one we have to take. But this time I don't want us going off half-cocked. I want to know why it is necessary for Buckland to advance himself that money, ahead of the formal decision of the board. And I want to know all about the exchange of letters over the house. It's a bloody lie, and we all know it. Let's get enough material to prove it. Then we'll see how loyal Buckland's directors will remain."

"You still think Condway will switch?" said Pryke.

"He and Penhardy," said Haffaford. "He told me so, in as many words. If people start to run, Condway will be out in front, leading the way."

"What about the American? and Prince Faysel?"

"I don't know about the American," said Haffaford. "But Faysel's a professional, responsible for an investment fund like the other managers. He'll move quickly enough to cover himself."

"Any point in trying to find out more about this man Rudd, to get an assessment of which way he'll jump?" said White.

Haffaford considered the suggestion. "We know enough already to recognize him as a professional, but in a way different from the others," he said. "Let's concentrate on Buckland for the moment."

"So we go ahead with the shareholders' meeting?" said Snaith.

Haffaford nodded. "And create a campaign leading up to it," he said, "Lots of leaks to the financial journalists and commentators. And a printed circular to all shareholders. Be careful about it: we'd better write it on a committee basis and then get it thoroughly vetted by our lawyers. I don't want us being slapped down with a libel writ."

"It isn't going to be pleasant, is it?" said Pryke.

"No," agreed Haffaford. "But it's necessary."

24

Rudd considered the merchant bank's attack in the boardroom to have been inept, so their preparation for the shareholders' meeting surprised him. It began with media leaks, carefully timed to reach newspapers in the middle of the week and thus allow the speculation to grow and then increase towards the weekend for the Sunday newspapers, which were able to give greater coverage and attempt better explanations. It was in the Sunday newspapers that the link between Buckland House and Best Rest was established. And in the Sunday newspapers it was hinted that the argument did not only concern finance with its limited readership appeal but a sexual scandal. The effect was to take the interest beyond the financial pages and cause a continuous stream of interview requests, first from English and then American newspapers. Rudd rejected them all and then discovered reporters watching the hotels and trying to trace his movements. It was the discovery of this – and a test that proved they maintained a pursuit despite determined efforts to shake them off – that caused him to scrap a meeting with Margaret. She complained that her house, too, was under newspaper siege. The following day she postponed for the same reason.

Rudd anticipated the effect upon Buckland House shares, which dropped five points, but not upon Best Rest. The story of an American involvement in a boardroom dispute of a company the reputation and tradition of Buckland House got wide coverage in America, particularly in the *Wall Street Journal* and *The New York Times*. Fund managers are not gamblers but businessmen, content with a return of one or two per cent upon their portfolios and quick to spread an investment if they think their clients are at risk. The initial share movement in Best Rest was only the caution of big investors, but the smaller stockholders imagined the funds possessed knowledge denied them and started to offload as well. In a week there was a seven point drop in Best Rest stock. The support banks in New York sought explanations, which brought a constant flow of telex and telephone calls to Rudd from the directors in New York. On the Tuesday, a week after the Haffaford campaign started, there was a message from Senator Jeplow in Washington that in the committee stage the tax lay-off for the construction industry was meeting opposition that he hadn't expected. Rudd delayed the planned meeting with Buckland for a gathering of the Best Rest directors in London.

"That could cost us an extra $5,000,000 on the overall development," complained Morrison, when Rudd disclosed the latest problem.

"In addition to the stock drop of $4,500,000," said Bunch.

"The stock drop is temporary," snapped back Rudd. "And if we don't get the legislation we don't go ahead with the development. So where's the problem?" Rarely, even in the early days, had he lost control in any argument with his father-in-law. He was letting his annoyance at not seeing Margaret develop into a business irritation. Nothing, nothing at all was going to prevent him from seeing her today: it had been nine days. Nine days too long.

Prince Faysel was the fourth director in the Berridge suite. "I don't think anything has happened which should cause us to panic," he said.

"I'm not talking about panic," said Morrison. "I'm talking about confidence. It's confidence that keeps stock up."

"If there's any problem at all it's having the Best Rest board split by 3000 miles of water," conceded Rudd.

"If that becomes public knowledge, it could lead to some sort of speculation that we're here on a salvage operation," said Bunch.

"Is there any need for us all to stay here?" said Rudd.

"There is for me," said Faysel. "I'm responsible for the fund money in Buckland House."

"I've got to stay," said Rudd.

"I could go back," offered Morrison. "I think we should let the people in New York know what's going on." He thought it was a pity that the exchange was not being recorded for later use.

In spite of Morrison's sixty-eight years he didn't look fatigued, thought Rudd, but that didn't mean anything. "You've only just got here," he said.

"The composition of the liner board isn't as urgent now as assurance for New York," said Morrison.

"I wasn't thinking about that," said Rudd.

"What then?"

A mistake, decided Rudd. Like his irritation. If he mentioned age the man would construe the concern as some sort of criticism. "Just thought you might prefer to stay here." Even the attempted recovery was clumsy: not even a recovery, more an awkward expression of words. Rudd realized he wasn't concentrating completely upon any point that was being made.

Morrison frowned. "What are you talking about?"

Rudd ignored the question. "I think it's a good idea," he said. "You're right about the need for assurance." He was conscious of the attention of Bunch and Faysel.

To Bunch Rudd said, "You could go to Washington to see how serious this thing is with Jeplow."

"What's the strategy with Buckland?" said Faysel.

"To keep him in power until we can get the thing before a court," said Rudd at once. "I don't want the merchant bank slicing up the cake to their choice."

"You're due for the meeting with Buckland in under an hour," reminded Hallett, from the side of the room.

Rudd looked to his father-in-law. "Make it clear to New York that there's no problem," he said. "What's happening is unforeseen and irritating but it doesn't affect what we've already agreed. Tell them that the day before the shareholders' meeting I'm going to issue a statement in Best Rest's name expressing confidence in Buckland House's trading position."

"That will indicate support of Buckland," said the lawyer. "Won't that look odd when you challenge him?"

Rudd shook his head. "My opinion will be of the company, not the man," he qualified. He stood, ending the meeting. "Call me from Washington," he said.

The cars had been identified by the journalists waiting in the foyer. Rudd ignored them, leaving through the service lift and kitchen exit. He walked easily out along the alley into Mount Street and managed to get a taxi immediately. The vehicle did a

U-turn, taking him back through Grosvenor Square and he looked up towards the apartment. How would she react when he told her? There couldn't be surprise because he'd come close the last time; it had been Margaret who'd dodged, saying she didn't know how she felt. She'd had nine days to make up her mind.

The arrival at Buckland House headquarters was as rehearsed as the unseen departure from the Berridge. Rudd paid the taxi off in Bishopsgate and approached the rear of the building on foot. A commissionaire was on duty, expecting him, and the American reached Buckland's panelled office otherwise undetected.

"This is preposterous!" complained Buckland at once. "Haffaford's are doing their best to wreck the company."

"It's a point for you to make," said Rudd. "Are you having the accountants prepare figures, showing the effect of this campaign?"

Buckland blinked. "I hadn't thought of doing so," he said.

"Do it," advised Rudd. "The argument will be about management and responsibility: it's a factor in your favour, showing their irresponsibility."

Buckland made a note on a jotting pad. "Have you seen this?" he said. "That's going to be splashed all across the papers tomorrow."

Rudd took the document, looking down at it. It was the statement of Haffaford's move for shareholder distribution. There were no positive accusations, just references to the two sums of money. There were no details or location given of the Mews house.

"Damned libel!" said Buckland.

"That's exactly what it isn't," said Rudd. "It's too carefully worded for that. But it shows their concern."

"What do you mean?"

"This is obviously being circulated in advance of the meeting to all the shareholders."

"And the newspapers."

"I'm not worried about the newspapers," said Rudd, irritated at the man's refusal to look upon anything constructively. "Rebut it completely. Make your written reply to the shareholders very detailed. Give all the figures of the trading losses and

211

then balance them against the effect of the liner sale. It's the most positive proof against an accusation of mismanagement. . . ."

Buckland nodded, smiling, and made another note.

"And circularize something else," said Rudd. "Have a request printed, with a tear-off section at the bottom for replies. The shareholders' meeting is closed to anyone not holding stock in the company. Ask permission in advance of the meeting for lawyers to be present."

"What for?" said Buckland.

Rudd gestured with the Haffaford leaflet. "It's vaguely worded because it's got to be; to have printed the claims *would* have been libellous. And they know it. They'll have been warned, too, about the risk of slander at the meeting. They're shareholders so they'll automatically get the request if you make it; and there will only be one inference they can draw from it."

"So they'll be too frightened to make the accusations?" said Buckland hopefully.

"They'll have to be careful, if they think you're considering that sort of action."

"I'm indebted to you, Harry," said Buckland. "I wouldn't have thought of any of this."

Rudd hurried on, made awkward by the gratitude. "And guarantee that the meeting is closed," he insisted. "The press will try to get in if they can. Have stewards check the certificate holding of everyone and announce a press conference afterwards."

"A press conference!"

"It'll show you're confident: that you haven't got anything to hide."

"I thought we'd have the meeting at the Berridge," said Buckland. "The ballroom is big enough for the number of the people likely to attend."

"That's good," agreed Rudd. "It'll remind them of the sort of thing you're trying to protect."

"I've been following the American market," said Buckland. "I'm sorry about the effect on Best Rest."

Rudd made a dismissive gesture. "I didn't expect it, but it's not serious. Morrison is going back today to reassure them. Prices will pick up soon enough."

"Do you think they could win?" said Buckland, suddenly urgent. "Do you think they could overthrow me, Harry?"

Rudd winced at the nakedness of the man's fear. "You made some silly mistakes, Ian," he said.

"I'll promise the meeting not to do so again," said Buckland.

He was like a small boy caught stealing apples, thought Rudd. "No!" he said. "You don't apologize. You've got to convey the impression that you've nothing to apologize for: that there have been no irregularities, just misunderstandings and that Haffaford's have over-reacted to them."

Buckland laughed, a sighing sound. "Obviously you've been involved in more boardroom fights than I have, " he said. He decided against telling Rudd his intentions regarding Sinclair. He wanted to prove he had some ideas of his own.

"Any indications of support?" asked Rudd.

"Nothing positive," said Buckland.

"I'm going to issue a statement on behalf of Best Rest a day or two before the meeting, expressing our confidence in your company."

Buckland smiled again, missing the qualification. "You've been a good friend to me, Harry. A bloody good friend. I want you to know I shan't forget it."

Rudd said nothing.

Rudd was sure that he got away from Buckland House undetected, but he still changed taxis twice going westwards back across the city, finally paying the cab off in Brook Street and completing the last part of the journey on foot, inviting challenge if the apartment had been discovered, so that he would know it was unsafe for Margaret to come. He arrived unhindered. The apartment had a dusty, unused smell to it. Rudd opened the windows and discarded some dead flowers into the waste disposal unit. He tidied some records which had been left loose from their covers and moved aimlessly from room to room, anxious for her arrival. Realizing she might have had to cancel and that there was no way she could have contacted him, Rudd telephoned the Berridge and was connected at once to Hallett. There had been no messages, reported the personal assistant.

Morrison was flying out at four and Bunch had managed a direct connection to Washington, two hours later. Wall Street had opened quietly, with Best Rest still five points below par.

"I'm at the apartment," said Rudd.

There was a pause. Then Hallett said, "Can I call you there if anything comes up?"

"Of course. But don't give the number to anyone else."

Rudd made another tour of the apartment and then stood at the window, looking out over the square to watch for her arrival. When she came, he missed it. He was expecting a car and she came on foot, like he had, so his first awareness of her presence was the key going into the lock. She halted just inside the door, smiling shyly across the room to him.

"I was watching for you," he said.

"I had to dodge around a lot to get here. I'm fed up with it," she said.

He went towards her, not immediately kissing her but holding her close to him. She came gratefully to him and he could feel her shaking. "I don't like what's happening," she said. "I feel like . . . Oh, I don't know what I feel like. I just don't like it. *Why* did Ian have to be such a bloody fool!"

Rudd led her to the couch and seated her, as he would have seated someone suffering from some illness. "Would you like a drink?"

She shook her head. "I don't think so."

"I saw Ian this morning: we talked about how to fight off the attack."

"*Has* he done anything wrong? Legally I mean?"

"Yes," said Rudd. He hadn't wanted a conversation like this.

She stared at him wide-eyed. "He won't be arrested or go to prison or anything like that, will he?"

"I don't think so," said Rudd.

"He's told his mother and Vanessa that it's just a mistake."

"That's how it's going to be explained to the shareholders."

"Damn his gambling," she said. "Damn his gambling and his whoring and damn him."

"I've missed you," he said, wanting to change the direction of the talk.

She felt out for his hand. "I've missed you," she said in return.

214

"More than I thought I would." His face clouded. "Oh, that sounded awful! I didn't mean that. I meant . . ."

He leaned forward, kissing her and stopping the outburst. "You don't have to explain what you meant." So it had been the same for her! He felt hollow-stomached in his excitement. All the half-formed plans, the misty thoughts he'd refused to consider, were possible after all. He didn't imagine she would enjoy hotel life, so they could hunt for an apartment together. Maybe on Riverside Drive, like before. And a proper place for the weekends. Connecticut was the first thought but there was no reason why it should be there, if she didn't like it. He couldn't expect her to accept an upheaval as complete as this, to remove herself completely from England. And there wouldn't be the need, either. They could have homes here in England: London as well as the country. He'd wind down, Rudd decided. The complete absorption in business had had a purpose but now that purpose was past. What was it that Mary Bunch had said that weekend in Connecticut? "Learn to enjoy the view and stop looking around for bigger mountains." Now he would. He'd delegate, fully utilizing the management structure he'd carefully created but until now always insisted upon supervising. He'd still supervise, but not on the daily and weekly basis that he did at present.

"You're looking very serious," she said.

"I love you," he said.

Her smile faltered and fell away. "Don't," she said. She seemed frightened of him saying it.

"Why not?"

"I don't want to."

"I love you," he repeated. "And I don't want us to go on like this. I want us to tell Ian and I want you to get a divorce and I want to marry you."

She sat regarding him open-faced, her expression a mixture of disbelief and amazement. "Marry me!" This didn't happen in any of the fantasies.

"Of course."

"But . . ." She made a helpless flapping movement with her hands. "I mean . . . think what's involved!"

"I know what's involved," he said. "And I know it's going to

215

be more traumatic for you than for me and I wish there was something I could do to make it otherwise. But there isn't."

She jerked up, walking back and forth in front of the couch with her back to him and her head bent low. "I don't know," she said. Vanessa would never let situations develop like this.

"Don't you love me?"

She shrugged her shoulders. "I'm not sure what I feel. I know I was as miserable as hell without you." Which was true. But was it enough?

"I won't ever let you be unhappy," said Rudd. He realized it was coming out as a plea which he hadn't intended, because he never pleaded, but in his anxiety to convince her he didn't care. "We can live wherever you want, do whatever you want. I've already decided to worry less about the businesses. We'll be able to spend all the time together we want."

She shook her head against the flurry of words. "Not now," she said. "I can't decide now. Let's get this meeting over first. Whatever has happened between us I can't let Ian down like that."

How long after the shareholder confrontation would it be until the court challenge? wondered Rudd. Not long. "You're running away," he said.

"I'm not."

"You are."

"So I'm running away!" she shouted, annoyed at his persistence. "You say you know what you're asking me to do but you don't. You can't. It would mean cutting myself off from everything . . . everyone . . . abandoning everything I've ever known. . . ."

". . . But we could have homes here, as well as in America," he tried, but she cut across him.

"And who would come to them?"

"So you'd rather have the alternative," he said. "Exiled to some place in the country, companion to an old lady, allowed up here by some special dispensation and knowing damned well that all the friends by whom you set such store are laughing at you behind your back because of the affairs Ian is having." It was their first argument. He hadn't expected them to fight.

"I've told you," she said. "I don't know what I want."

216

"You've got to decide."

"Not if I don't want to," she said, in a spurt of petulance.

"We'll wait until after the meeting," said Rudd, conceding. "Decide immediately afterwards."

"Yes," she said, too quickly.

"*Immediately*," insisted Rudd.

She turned, standing over him. "I'm frightened, darling," she said. "I'm really frightened."

"I'm sure," he said. "But I know it would be all right."

"Shit!" she said, abruptly vehement. "Why are things never simple?"

Even though the house had not been identified, Buckland was still cautious, insisting that Fiona move out several days in advance of their meeting and come to the restaurant from a hotel. He used the rear exit escape from Buckland House and was already there when she came in. She looked around, with her habitual wide-eyed little-girl expression and then hurried to him. Her attitude didn't match the expression. "What the hell's all this about, Ian?" she said.

"You've read the newspapers?"

"That's why I asked the question. My friends are under siege: I've had newspapers offer money for my story."

"Oh Christ!" he said. A waiter came and took their drink and food order and she waited until he left the table.

"Well?" she said.

Haltingly he told her, aware as he spoke of her face hardening. When he stopped she said, "Bloody hell!"

"I'm sorry," he said.

"*You're* sorry! What about all this shit about me in the papers: I've actually been asked to explain it by my solicitors. Apparently Peter is trying to work some advantage out of it, to cut off my divorce allowance."

Buckland made a helpless gesture. "What can I say, except sorry?"

"Does Margaret know?"

"Yes."

"Oh fuck!"

217

"I had to tell her."

"Why?"

"To get out of this mess: she'd have learned anyway, from the papers."

She took the glass from the returning waiter and drank heavily.

"You're completely protected," insisted Buckland. "I made sure that the rent was paid in your name and that the registered owners knew all about it. You've nothing to be frightened of."

"Crap," she said. "The newspapers are crucifying me. I'm getting out."

Buckland felt the relief go through him. "It would probably be best," he said.

"I haven't got any money."

"That's no problem," said Buckland. "You can have whatever you want."

"A lot," she said. "Ten thousand."

Buckland swallowed and said, "All right."

"In cash."

She was a whore in everything, thought Buckland. "In cash," he agreed.

"That's what the papers have promised me."

"You'll get it," said Buckland, recognizing the threat.

"You look scared to death," she said.

"I am."

The waiter was approaching with the plates but she stood, waving him away. She put both hands on the table and leaned towards him, so they were very close. "You know something?" she said.

"What?"

"You were a pretty rotten fuck, too."

25

A properly convened board meeting would have involved official minutes, which Herbert Morrison wanted to avoid. Instead he took a small conference suite at the Park Summit, fifteen floors below Rudd's penthouse, and invited the three men there. To maintain the informality he had coffee and sandwiches laid out on a side table. Conscious of Patrick Walker's preference, he had also installed a mobile bar. It was his original partner who arrived first, early to learn ahead of the others what was happening, but before a conversation could begin Eric Böch puffed into the room, also early. Morrison smiled, conscious of the concern of both men. Morrison indicated the coffee and the bar but both men ignored it impatiently.

"Why here instead of the office?" demanded Böch.

"I thought it better," said Morrison.

"Why?"

"Why don't we wait until Harvey gets here?"

Walker was about to protest when the door opened and Ottway came in. Also ahead of time, Morrison noted.

"The chairman and Prince Faysel have remained in London," said Morrison to the three men. "Bunch has gone directly to Washington to sort out the problem that seems to have arisen over the Texas hotels. . . ." He looked to Böch whose question it had been. "With so many directors absent, it seemed better to meet like this."

"I would have thought a day or two could have been spared for a proper meeting," said Böch, taking offence precisely as Morrison had wanted him to. "We've been out on a limb back here."

"I know and I'm sorry," said Morrison. "That's why I returned." That remark, like everything else he intended to say, was carefully prepared to the impression that it had been a personal decision.

"What the hell's happening over this Buckland House thing?" said Walker.

"The chairman asked me to assure you there's no problem. He regards this merchant bank move as unforeseen and irritating, but it doesn't alter what we've already decided." The message had been delivered practically verbatim: there'd be no evidence, in any later analysis, of manipulating the discussion.

"What are you talking about, no problem!" demanded Böch. We've lost over $4,000,000, Jeplow's hinting he can't get the tax agreement, and we've had to commit $130,000,000 for land purchase."

"The chairman regards the stock loss as temporary uncertainty that'll resolve itself," said Morrison. "He's issuing a statement within the next few days to achieve that stability. It'll be in Best Rest's name and will express our confidence in the Buckland House trading position."

"What's your opinion?" said Ottway. "You've been involved and you know what's going on."

Morrison walked to the side table, for coffee. He didn't need the drink but he wanted to give the impression of considering an answer to a difficult question. He came back to the men in the room and said, "It is no secret to anyone here that Harry Rudd and myself have frequently disagreed. Almost invariably, my objections to the expansion proposals have been misjudged. Rudd has led this company to remarkable success. . . ." He sipped the coffee. Böch and Ottway were nodding appreciation at the praise. Only Walker was looking curious. ". . . having said that," Morrison resumed, "I think it is fair to this board to say I have the most serious misgivings about what's happening in England."

"For what reasons?" said Walker. He spoke on his way to the bar. Morrison had been careful to see that Bushmills was provided. Walker poured himself a stiff measure and returned to his seat.

"A lot," said Morrison. "Predominantly I'm concerned about the effect upon Best Rest, as the parent board. I do not consider it worth risking $4,000,000 stock value in any takeover And for what is to follow, we can expect it to drop substantially more than that."

"What do you mean, what is to follow?"

Succinctly, avoiding any personal opinion, Morrison outlined the Haffaford move and then how, if that failed, they were going to have to go to court to get the share agreement of Buckland House broken before they could consider proceeding with the takeover. He was conscious of the concern of the men around him when he finished.

"That's a can of worms," said Walker.

"Through nothing more than newspaper stories and speculation, we've dropped $4,000,000," said Morrison. "I think it will go down further whatever happens as a result of the English shareholders' meeting and, once the court move is declared, go lower still."

"I think you're right," said Böch. He clipped the end off a cigar and fitted it into its stubby holder, puffing it into life.

"We'll lose any element of surprise," said Morrison. "And by going to court, any possibility of amicable agreement to the takeover. We'll be fighting the Buckland House board and risking someone else – maybe even more than one group – coming in with counter-bids. We don't have the liquidity for a protracted, divided fight."

"What does Rudd say?" asked Böch.

"That he thinks there is the possibility of success and that it's worth continuing."

"Do you have a recommendation?" said Ottway.

"No," said Morrison cautiously. "Only the facts." And that's exactly what they were; maybe he'd been too careful in not putting the meeting on record. So far there was nothing that could have been wrongly construed against him.

"I don't think the mandate we gave the chairman extends to unlimited negotiation," said Walker. "I think there's got to be a reserve, both in time and financial commitment."

"I agree," said Böch, at once. "Our stockholders haven't entrusted their money to us for this sort of thing. And we can't count on the Saudi money, certainly not for this year."

Sensing the direction of the feeling, Ottway said, "I think there should be a full meeting of the board, including the chairman."

"It won't be possible before the shareholders' meeting in London," said Morrison.

"So there's the possibility of our stock worsening and us being unable to do anything about it?" said Böch.

"Yes," confirmed Morrison.

"Then immediately afterwards," insisted Böch. "This has got to be talked through again, in greater detail. I'm not happy about it."

Neither were quite a few other people going to be by the time he'd finished, thought Morrison.

Gene Grearson greeted him with his customary enthusiasm, emerging into the ante-room personally to lead him back into the office. As Morrison sat down, the Boston lawyer said, "Sorry to see all the movement in Best Rest stock, Herb."

"That's why I came back from England," said Morrison. "I wanted to reassure the board here."

"There's reason for reassurance then?"

"I think so," said Morrison. "You've got to expect a few reversals in business."

Grearson grimaced. "Four million is quite a reversal."

"We're pretty confident it'll adjust itself. Which is what I wanted to talk to you about."

Grearson pulled Morrison's portfolio closer to him and looked up expectantly.

"You got contacts with lawyers in London?" asked Morrison.

"Of course," said Grearson.

"There's going to be a stockholders' meeting of Buckland House, with a demand for a vote of support at the end," said Morrison. "I want to commit the shares I hold but it's got to be nominee again."

"I understand," said Grearson. "Which way do you want your shares pledged?"

"Behind Sir Ian Buckland," said Morrison. Rudd might withdraw if Buckland were displaced, so in the first round he had to back his son-in-law. It was like priming an old-fashioned flintlock pistol, carefully counting the gunpowder grains to ensure that it didn't blow up in his face.

*　　*　　*

222

Richard Haffaford threw down on his desk Buckland's request for lawyers to attend the meeting and stalked angrily about the room, his hands clasped tightly behind his back.

"Is there any point in getting a second opinion?" asked Pryke.

"None," said Haffaford positively. "The ruling is that he's gagged us."

"We must be able to say something!" protested Snaith.

Haffaford turned back into the room. "Only through carefully phrased questions," said the merchant bank chairman. "And they're so damned careful that they're practically meaningless. There are only two places with the sort of legal privilege we need, taking us clear of libel and slander. The Houses of Parliament and a court of law."

"I didn't think Buckland was this clever," said Sir Robert White.

"It could still go in our favour," suggested Snaith hopefully. "He might make a mistake. And the Americans might move against him. They can't be happy about what's happening, any more than the Saudis or any other investment fund."

Haffaford came back to his desk, slapping his hand against it in irritation as he sat down. "I didn't want there to be *any* doubt," he said. "And now there is."

"If we're not careful, we're going to emerge from this looking foolish," said White.

"And that wasn't the intention," said Haffaford. "That was supposed to be what happened to Buckland."

26

It was Rudd's idea that to avoid the gamut of press interest the Buckland family should stay the night before the shareholders' meeting at the Berridge. And his further suggestion that before going to the meeting they should assemble in the conference suite where he had stayed. Rudd stood as Hallett admitted the family. Lady Buckland led, prodding her way forward on the silver-topped cane he remembered from the weekend in Cambridgeshire, stiffly upright, rigidly coiffured and formally dressed in a long, straight-skirted black dress. Vanessa followed and Rudd saw she had dressed for the occasion, too, a severely cut grey morning suit, tight at the waist. There was a bra, as well, which was an improvement. The straw-coloured hair was strained back neatly beneath a small hat. Margaret was behind her sister-in-law, in black like Lady Buckland, a neat, inconspicuous morning dress. She avoided Rudd's eyes when he looked at her. Buckland was last, nodding and smiling the moment he entered.

"Good idea, staying here overnight," he said. "Manager says the place is under siege outside. Television, too."

There was a tension in the room, a nervousness in advance of the meeting, and Rudd was glad of it because it covered any atmosphere there might have been between him and Margaret, surrounded by the family: he realized it was the first time they had met as a group since their affair had begun. He wanted very much to reach out and touch her.

"You seem to have been giving Ian a lot of advice," said Vanessa.

"Just offering the benefit of experience," said Rudd.

Hallett came forward with coffee and everyone accepted, glad of something to occupy their attention. There were newspapers stacked upon the table and Buckland said, "Thanks for that, too."

The Best Rest statement of confidence had been the main story in all the newspaper coverage of the meeting.

"Is this going to be too distasteful?" said Lady Buckland.

"You can't expect it to be pleasant," said Rudd. "But I hope we've minimized the unpleasantness."

"Is there a strategy for the meeting?" said Buckland.

Rudd hesitated, realizing the extent of their dependence and uncomfortable because of it. He looked towards Margaret. She was gazing fixedly into her coffee cup. He spoke slowly, wanting each of them to understand, pausing when Buckland interjected questions and finally reached out towards Hallett for the typed reminder notes he'd prepared for Buckland to take with him to the meeting.

"You've taken a lot of trouble," said Vanessa. There was a vaguely challenging note in her voice.

"A lot of trouble needed to be taken, if this is to be defeated," he came back to her sharply. She frowned but said nothing.

"Are you sure the press conference is a good idea?" said Buckland.

"Keep strictly to a time limit and whenever there's a personal question turn it back to the statement," said Rudd.

"It's time," warned Hallett.

"Ready?" said Rudd, standing. From each member of the Buckland family there seemed a momentary reluctance to get up and leave the suite. Lady Buckland moved first. She paused by Rudd and said, "It would seem we have a lot to be grateful to you for, Mr Rudd."

"Perhaps we should wait until after the meeting to see if that's justified," said the American.

There was a stage area at the rear of the ballroom, linked by corridors to the staff section, so they were able to approach through the service lift and passageways and keep completely clear of any newspaper interception. As they approached the rear of the ballroom, Rudd stood back for Buckland to take the lead. There was a side room, where three men were waiting. Buckland introduced the lawyers to Rudd and said, "You'll have to wait here, until I can formally announce the result to admit you."

The men nodded and Buckland moved to rejoin his family.

There was a side door fitted with an observation window, and through it Rudd saw that the other directors were already assembled on the raised dais. The huge ballroom was crowded, every seat appearing to be occupied. Three were vacant in the front row, the section reserved for the Initial shareholders, for Lady Buckland, Margaret and Vanessa. As soon as they emerged into the public corridor a steward turned towards them, relaxing when he identified Buckland. He held the door open and Buckland entered first, followed by the family. The hubbub of noise stilled, momentarily, and then resumed again. Every face was turned towards them.

Lady Buckland followed her son, staring ahead of her. Vanessa was next, head high like her mother, but the lack of confidence in Margaret was obvious from her walk. Rudd was last. Directly inside he broke away from the line, going towards the stage with Buckland. The other five directors were already seated. Because of the accusation, Condway was in the chair; Buckland's place was immediately alongside. Rudd sat three paces away from him, next to Prince Faysel.

As he sat down the Arab whispered to him, "What does it look like?"

"Difficult to tell," said Rudd.

He watched as Buckland put the reminder notes carefully on the table in front of him. At the far side of the stage was a secretariat table with four stenographers, and next to it a second table, unoccupied.

Condway stood, gazing out at the spread of people in front of him, abruptly hammering the gavel against its rest to silence the noise, which was already diminishing anyway. Rudd was conscious of Margaret jumping slightly. He smiled and she smiled back.

"This is an extraordinary shareholders' meeting, summoned under Section 14 of the Articles of Formation of Buckland House (Holdings) by the directors John David Snaith and Henry Robert Smallwood," recited Condway formally. A copy of the convening notice had been placed on each chair and most of the shareholders stared down as Condway read from it, as if checking his accuracy.

"Cause of this summons is an allegation of mismanagement,"

resumed Condway. "Section 14 entitles the shareholders, if they consider the motion justified, to demand through a vote of no confidence the resignation of any director or directors. . . ." The man stopped. "Alternatively the shareholders may decide the allegations specious or unfounded and through a vote of confidence dismiss the summons."

There were shifts and stirring from the hall as people settled themselves. Rudd saw that Margaret was looking up at the stage, concentrating upon her husband. The chandeliers glittering overhead seemed incongruous for what was happening beneath them.

"There may be personal allegations made," said Condway. "It was for that reason, upon legal advice, that voting papers were circulated to all of you in advance of this meeting, requesting the attendance of non-shareholders: lawyers whose function it would be to protect against any character defamation. . . ." Condway went through the documents before him. "The result of that circulation was to receive approval, 3452 to 1200, for the admission of lawyers. . . ."

Condway looked across to the door through which they had entered, nodding to the stewards. "Will you invite them in?" he said. He turned to Snaith, offering him the voting figures. The merchant banker shook his head.

The three lawyers came self-consciously into the room, crossing directly in front of the stage to the place prepared alongside the secretariat table. While they seated themselves Rudd looked out into the hall, identifying the placings. Initial shareholders were to the left and immediately in front, about fifteen people other than the Buckland family. To the right and front were the investment fund managers, representing the block holdings. Behind them were the proxy entrants, all lawyers Rudd guessed, representing the nominee holders. At the back, where a far greater proportion of people had been seated, were the small individual holders.

Condway was awaiting an indication from the lawyers. One of them nodded and he turned back to the hall. "I give the floor to John David Snaith and Henry Robert Smallwood," he said and sat down.

The abrupt announcement had precisely the effect that Rudd

had planned. Snaith blinked up, confused, having expected a lengthy explanation of actions and behaviour from Buckland, not silence. He rose awkwardly, as he did so Buckland moved as Rudd had advised, turning pointedly to the lawyers again, as if to assure himself that they were ready.

Snaith began soft-voiced and there were immediate protests from the back. The merchant bank representative raised the microphone level and started again. "This action today has not been taken lightly nor without proper regard to the possible consequences," said Snaith.

He was reading pedantically from what appeared to be a carefully typed speech and the American guessed it had been vetted by Haffaford's legal advisers. "It has been taken because the merchant bank that I represent upon the board of Buckland House, a bank responsible for a considerable share investment within the group, has become worried about the running and administration of the company."

The huge room was quiet, disturbed only by an occasional cough or foot scuff. Buckland was sitting with his head hunched forward, as if he were deep in some private thought.

"That concern began with the realization earlier this year that a trading loss of at least £800,000 would be declared, with the company drawings against overdraft facilities almost reaching the agreed limit of £10,000,000. In these circumstances, Haffaford's felt unable to extend those facilities, despite a request from the chairman and vice-chairman. . . ."

It was too legal, judged Rudd: just a dry, dusty recitation of figures. They'd have to do better than this.

"During a preliminary discussion on loss-making sections of Buckland House operations, a figure of £635,000 was discovered, as a debit entered against the holding company. . . ." Snaith paused, clearly as rehearsed as Buckland, and said, "I would invite our chairman to explain that amount."

Rudd nodded at the move: there was no provable allegation of any sort. In front of him Margaret was frowning worriedly. He wanted to smile at her, in reassurance, but she wasn't looking at him.

Buckland rose slowly. "I think it is important that there should be complete accuracy," he said. "It has been said that the sum of £635,000 came to light during a boardroom discussion about loss-making sections. This is not so. I seek a correction from Mr Snaith."

Rudd decided it was masterly, as good as anything he would have done himself. The merchant banker rose flustered, his prepared speech disordered in his hand. "I agree to the correction," he said. "The amount was originally discovered by auditors. . . ."

From the hall there was sporadic murmuring and movement as people tried to follow what was happening on stage. Buckland had more to gain than lose from confusion, decided Rudd.

Buckland stood again, pitching the condescension just right and speaking initially to Snaith. "I am grateful for the correction," he said. "And I sincerely hope that the allegations to follow are better founded on fact." He turned out into the hall. "At the beginning of this year I received a director's loan of £635,000. It was an approved executive decision. It was signed by me off a company cheque and inadvertently listed against an investment. . . ." He glanced again at Snaith. "This was picked up, as has now been admitted, by the auditors, as it had to be: no such sum, unaccounted for, could have been passed without query. By the time the mistake was brought to my notice, the purpose of the loan had been served. I was able to repay it in full, together with full interest. The complainant directors were among those who agreed the loan. A record of that minute is available for examination."

Buckland sat down and Rudd waited tensely. Of everything this was the most challengeable. Snaith was in head-bent conversation with Smallwood at the far end of the table. There were movements of impatience from the hall.

Snaith hurried to his feet. He seemed to have difficulty in locating his place in the prepared speech. He did so finally, and said, "A little over two months ago an in-house audit agreed upon because of the earlier realized working deficit disclosed a payment of £150,000 to Sir Ian Buckland. I would like his comment about that."

Buckland started up, his confidence obvious. "Each year, you are circularized with details of salaries and directors' remuneration," he said. "You will find complete listings in previous years' accounts and in those that have been sent to you in advance of this meeting you will see them repeated. If you would turn to them. . . ." He stopped, and in front of him there was a sudden flutter of pages being turned and heads bent over accounts. ". . . You will see that my salary and remuneration, as chairman of Buckland House (Holdings) is £150,000 a year. This was the sum allocated to me and which Mr Snaith has commented upon. The allocation was made without the formality of a directors' vote. Once again, the figure was openly available to any examination. I agree with the technical error, of payment having been made and received in advance of boardroom approval. I do not agree it is sufficient justification for the convening of this meeting and the spate of inspired leaks about the running and behaviour of this company which in preceding weeks has cost something like £1,500,000 in share value."

Rudd had never believed Buckland capable of the performance: it exceeded anything he had hoped for. He was aware of Lady Buckland smiling admiringly up at her son.

Snaith rose determinedly. He looked at his speech, then across at the lawyers' table as if debating whether to abandon his own legal advice. Seeing the movement Smallwood quickly touched the man's arm. Snaith bent for another widespread conversation and then turned back towards the shareholders. "Listed among the assets of our Far East division is a mews house, off Sloane Street. It has been a property owned by that division for a number of years. I would invite the chairman to explain its present occupancy."

Buckland was rising, before the other man had time to sit down. "There is no present occupancy," he said. He was back in his seat seconds after Snaith. There were isolated sniggers and then laughter from the hall.

Snaith stood again, flushed. Rudd was unsure whether the colouring was irritation or embarrassment. "Then perhaps the chairman will explain the recent occupancy of a lady," said Snaith.

Buckland maintained the condescension. "As has already been patiently explained within the boardroom of this company, the house in question was occupied for a period of a little over two months by a friend of my family. A rental was paid into the accounts of the Far East company and the letting was agreed with the chairman of that holding, Mr Kevin Sinclair. There is a record of an exchange of letters between us, reaching agreement upon it. . . ."

Snaith jerked up, unable to control himself any further. "*After* the occupation commenced," he said. "To justify it."

Again Buckland's timing was perfect. He turned, looking first to the director and then beyond him to the lawyers. Then he came back to the hall and said, "Would Mr Kevin Sinclair please approach the table?"

The Hong Kong-based chairman of their Far East division stood, in the fifth row, and excused himself as he passed along the line of people to reach the aisle. Almost at once Rudd turned away to look at Snaith and Smallwood. Both men were staring fixed-faced at the man. Sinclair mounted the steps at the side and approached a microphone separate from the directors' table. He was a tall, loose-limbed man wearing a lightweight tropical suit.

Buckland remained standing too. He said, "There is a clear inference that there was some wrong – maybe even elicit – letting of the company house off Sloane Street."

"That's as I understood it from the hall," agreed Sinclair. There was a pronounced Australian accent.

"Can you tell me the date of the letter to you, arranging the letting?"

"July," said Sinclair. He took an envelope from his pocket. "I have the letter here."

"When did the occupancy begin?"

"June," said the Australian.

Snaith smiled and looked sideways at Smallwood.

"Was there any contact between us in June?" said Buckland.

"Sure," agreed Sinclair. "The telephone call, around the nine or tenth, when we agreed to it. The July letter was merely confirmation."

Buckland looked down at Snaith and Smallwood. Neither man was smiling now.

"What's happened to the tenancy now?" said Buckland.

"It was terminated," said Sinclair.

"Did the occupancy cause you or our Far East division any inconvenience?"

231

"No," said the Australian. "How could it have done? The arrangement always was that it was temporary; we had access at any time."

"What's the effect of the termination?"

Sinclair shrugged. "We lose £120 a week and the place stays empty again."

Buckland went back to Snaith. "Is there anything you'd like to ask?" he invited.

Snaith jerked his head towards Sinclair and he returned to his seat. Then Buckland continued: "This meeting was convened to consider allegations of mismanagement. You have heard the complaints. And my responses to them. You have already heard that because of the furore that has been created, a perfectly respectable, satisfactory tenancy bringing some £480 a month into the accounts of a sub-division has been lost. What you have not heard, although I hope you have understood it clearly enough from the statement of accounts which was sent to each of you in advance of this meeting, is that the losses of some £800,000 a year which were earlier mentioned no longer exist. As the result of a sale negotiated with. . . ." he turned sideways, nodding in Rudd's direction. ". . . our newest and most welcome director, the liner division of Buckland House has been sold. To us, they represented a loss of £550,000 a year. To our new associate, they will be profitable. Effect of that sale is to bring into the company a cash payment of close to £10,000,000. There has also been a share exchange, representing an infusion into Buckland House of something like a further £3,500,000. I would like these facts borne in mind when considering this allegation of bad management." He turned to Snaith. "Have you any further points to make?"

Snaith moved his head again and said, "No."

"I invite questions from the hall," said Buckland.

The response was immediate. From the seating plan before him Rudd identified the question as coming from the pension fund manager of the Prudential Insurance company. He appeared a neat, precise man. He rose with a sheet of notes before him.

"The £635,000 was debited against investment?" he said.

"I have already agreed that," said Buckland.

232

"And the £150,000 was paid before directors' agreement?"

"A technical oversight," repeated Buckland, too confidently.

"I do not consider technical oversights involving sums of £150,000 should arise. Nor that amount of £635,000 should be wrongly debited."

"Neither do I," said Buckland, trying to recover. "Perhaps I've failed properly to make clear that both these entries *had* to be corrected by auditing: that was how both were picked up. . . ." Buckland let his voice trail, then said, "The allegation being made today is one of bad management, not inability to put figures in the right columns."

Careful, thought Rudd worriedly. There was isolated laughter from the back but no amusement shown by the fund managers grouped before them. The Prudential man stayed on his feet. "Ultimate responsibility for getting figures in the right columns is the responsibility of management," said the man, turning Buckland's attempted sarcasm back at him.

Buckland set his face seriously. "Which I accept absolutely," he said. "I consider, however, that they are minimal mistakes capable of being settled internally, in the way that mistakes are settled within thousands of companies every day of the year, and not paraded for public display at such a disastrous cost to our company and your investment."

Better, thought Rudd. The first questioner sat down, followed at once by a man in the row behind. Sun Life of Canada, identified Rudd from his chart.

"There have been numerous references to technical oversight and passing errors, together with assurances that they would always have been picked up," said the man, tall and bespectacled. "I've yet to hear an assurance from the platform that steps are to be taken to ensure they don't occur again."

"Forgive me," said Buckland. "I unhesitatingly give that assurance. I would remind the questioner that during the last three months I have been engaged absolutely in the sale of the liner division, to the immediate £10,000,000 benefit of the company, which I construed of more immediate importance. But naturally this will never be allowed to arise again."

Rudd was beginning to regret the boastfulness when from the back of the room came an unidentified shout of "Well done!"

Rudd looked, trying to see who had said it, but almost immediately there was a second call of "Nothing wrong with this company."

A third man had stood from the fund section by the time Rudd looked back to the front, fair-haired, nervous, like a hen-pecked clerk. "I would like to ask the estimate of the declared dividend," said the man. His voice was weak.

Rudd swivelled sideways, concerned at Buckland's response. Hopefully there was no need to be, he thought, watching the man. Buckland remained seated, head bowed, a gesture of sadness. He rose with seeming reluctance and said, "And I would like to be able to give one to this meeting." He paused. "Having virtually erased our overdraft requirements and disposed of two-thirds of our loss drain, I had every hope of declaring this year an investment return better than ever before." Buckland allowed himself an almost imperceptible glance towards Snaith and Smallwood. "There can be no one in this room unaware of the effects upon the shares of this company over the last few weeks, pushed down by every rumour and innuendo. Our valuation has plummeted. It would be. . . ." A clever pause. ". . . . an indication of bad management for me to offer even an assessment at this stage of what the board will finally be able to recommend."

"Damned shame," came from the back of the hall. Then "Scandalous!"

"Despite the apparent nervousness, the fair-haired man was dogged. "Can I ask the representative of the support bank," he said, looking to Snaith, "about their attitude towards continuing finance, in the light of the apparent recovery from a bad trading and liquidity position that has been reported to this meeting."

Snaith came hesitatingly up from his chair. "I cannot give an answer to that, until the conclusion of this meeting," he said.

Buckland was tensed to rise. "Can I emphasize what has already been said," he reminded them. "The successful sale of the seven liners means that at the moment Buckland House is virtually free of any overdraft involvement with Samuel Haffaford and Co. I would like it understood that also subject to the decision of this meeting is, in my opinion, the continued acceptability of Haffaford's as the merchant bank with which this company should be dealing."

234

"Quite right too," said an unidentified small investor.

Caught by the run of the meeting, Rudd was concentrating upon the back of the room now. Before they had entered the hall he'd been convinced that Haffaford's assault had been wrongly pitched, but he hadn't anticipated the small investor support that was obviously behind Buckland. It was an interesting development. The professionals might be unsure but the amateurs seemed to have no doubts.

Snaith rose and said, "In the opinion of the merchant bank and the investors I represent, we do not consider the loose handling of the specified sums of money that have been mentioned satisfactory. Neither do we consider, despite the assurances that have been provided, that the letting of the house or the circumstances of that letting are above question."

The back of the room was noisy now, those in the front looking around, some in interest, others with annoyance. Condway fingered the gavel but did not use it, knowing what the sound meant. A man sitting among the Initial shareholders rose and stood patiently, waiting for the talk to subside. He was a thin, courtly-looking man, fastidiously dressed; the nervous tremor was obvious in the hand that gripped the chair-back in front of him. Reluctantly Condway hammered for order. The man said, "The calling of this meeting was extremely unusual: it has had a detrimental effect upon the company. Can I seek from the chairman the assurance that there is no danger whatsoever for those of us not attached to large investment organizations and whose capital, in many cases, is entirely trusted to this company?"

Buckland did not rise at once. When he did, it was with fitting gravity. Solemn-faced he said to the man, "Unhesitatingly I give that assurance. I have already referred to the involvement within this company of Mr Rudd, of whom many of you will have heard as chairman of a very large and very successful American conglomerate. I am confident that the expertise he is going to bring to Buckland House, in addition to the savings already mentioned, make this company what it has, throughout its history, consistently proved to be: a sound, profitable, worthwhile investment."

The reference brought Margaret's attention to Rudd at last.

235

Despite his earlier thoughts about reassurance, Rudd kept his face expressionless, aware he was a focal point. She gazed back at him, with matching blankness. Vanessa looked at him, too. She smiled.

Judging the moment, Condway stood and said, "The purpose of this meeting has already been explained. On your chairs when you entered were voting forms. I would ask you to complete them and hand them to the tellers who will move among you."

There was a rustle of papers and renewed noise, louder now than ever. From beside Rudd, Prince Faysel said, "It's been a disaster for Haffaford's."

"They'll get some professional votes," guessed Rudd.

"But not enough."

"No," agreed Rudd. "Not enough."

"Pleased?" said Faysel softly.

"I suppose so," said Rudd. He was unsettled by Margaret's attitude.

It took thirty minutes for the floor votes to be counted. When the results were handed to Condway he looked both ways along the directors' bench and said, "I'd welcome an open declaration. For those in favour of the no confidence motion?"

First Snaith's and then Smallwood's hand went up.

Condway nodded, checking the figures before him. "In terms of block votes, that represents four per cent," he said. "Those against?"

The voting from the other five directors was practically simultaneous.

Condway made another notation. "Combined with the floor vote, the figures are 3300 against the motion, with 1100 supporting it. I therefore declare the motion of no confidence against the chairman to have been lost."

There was a spontaneous outburst of applause from the floor. Condway stood and shook hands with Buckland. Gore-Pelham and Penhardy jostled around the man, eager to add their congratulations. Buckland was beaming his pleasure, laughing out towards where his family still sat. Lady Buckland made a small, waving gesture.

Buckland took the gavel from the vice-chairman, knocking for the attention of the disintegrating meeting. "Please," he said. "Please. There is more to be said."

Rudd was leaning forward, assessing the voting figures against the shareholding list. The Buckland family and directors accounted for the majority of votes in Buckland's favour. There appeared to be a substantial block of nominee votes and the remainder came almost entirely from the small shareholders. The institutions and funds had gone solidly behind Haffaford.

Buckland, in the chairman's position now, succeeded in getting order and said, "I thank you for your confidence. And now I think that confidence has to be extended outside this room. I intend keeping the assurance I have already made to meet the press. I think I should be accompanied by the other directors. Is it the wish of this meeting that we do so?"

The vote in favour was so overwhelming that there was no need for a recorded count.

"A fiasco," said Condway loudly, looking towards Snaith and Smallwood as the meeting broke up. "A complete bloody fiasco."

They used the staff corridors again to reach the conference room where the press had been assembled. The room was crowded when they entered, already too hot from the television lights which had been tested and which were switched full on the moment they came through the door. At once there was the stuttering glare of camera flashes. The directors filed to the table set out for them and all of them sat except Buckland.

"I would like to make an opening statement," said Buckland. "As you are all aware, a special shareholders' meeting has been called here today. It was convened under the democratic articles which govern the running of the Buckland House company, permitting directors to challenge the fitness of other directors. That challenge was made against me. This morning it has been fully and openly debated, before one of the largest gatherings of shareholders I can remember. The overwhelming decision of the meeting was a vote of confidence in me to continue as chairman. This whole affair has been one of misunderstanding which has now been completely resolved."

Buckland sat down and there was a momentary pause. Then the questions began in a babble and Buckland had to shout for order. The first question came from a grey-haired man, in the front. "Two sums of money have been mentioned in connection with this boardroom dispute," he said. "In total the amount is around £1,000,000. Was the suggestion that this sum has been misappropriated?"

Buckland rose, waiting for the room to quieten. "An unfortunate feature of this whole affair has been that it was based upon rumour and never upon fact. The sums involved were *not* around £1,000,000. They were precisely £785,000. They compose a properly agreed director's loan to me. And salary and fees, in my favour. There were some technical errors involving both sums which led to the misunderstanding to which I have referred."

"Wasn't it a misunderstanding that could have been resolved in the boardroom?" persisted the man.

"It was the wish of certain directors that it should be brought before the shareholders," said Buckland.

"How many directors and which ones?" someone shouted from the centre of the room.

"Another unfortunate feature of this business has been the degeneration into personalities. I have said it was a misunderstanding and that it has been resolved. The board are now completely united and I do not intend singling out individuals."

Rudd sat with his hands cupped beneath his chin. Buckland's performance here was as good as it had been in the ballroom. The persistent lights were making him squint.

Buckland gestured to a waving figure at the back near the television cameras, and an unidentified voice said, "Could you explain the misuse of the company house?"

"There was no misuse," said Buckland. "This was another misunderstanding. The house was properly let, to the knowledge of the people who needed to know, and a proper rental paid for it."

"Was the woman who occupied it a friend of yours?" demanded a woman's voice.

"She was a friend of my family," said Buckland.

A man sitting alongside the original questioner said, "Is her name Fiona Harvey, the ex-wife of Sir Peter Harvey?"

"I have no intention of naming the person," said Buckland. His voice sounded uneven and Rudd looked anxiously along the table towards the man.

"Why not?" asked someone.

"I have already made my position clear about naming individuals," said Buckland.

"Was your wife aware of the lady's use of the house?" said the woman who had asked the earlier question.

Buckland frowned against the lights, trying to identify her. "I resent the implication of that question," he said. "But I shall answer it, in the hope of reducing the amount of misinformation that has built up around my company. I repeat that the tenant of the house was a friend of my family and occupied it at all times with the full knowledge of my wife, Lady Margaret."

"Is she still the tenant?"

"No," said Buckland.

"Why not?"

"It is my understanding that she had no wish to become associated with the salacious suggestions and innuendo which have formed part of the sustained newspaper coverage of the past weeks," said Buckland.

Rudd thought the indignation justified but hoped Buckland hadn't overstressed it.

"Is there still contact between Lady Harvey and yourself?"

"What has Lady Harvey got to do with this?" avoided Buckland.

"Is Lady Harvey a friend of you and your family?" demanded the man in the front.

"Lady Harvey is known to my family, yes," said Buckland. His voice almost broke. He said, "If there are no further questions about today's meeting, then I'll consider the conference closed."

Thank Christ, thought Rudd.

There was an eruption of protest. Reluctantly Buckland isolated someone at the rear. "Can I put a question to Mr Rudd?" said an American voice. "Burr, *New York Times*. Can I ask Mr Rudd if he's happy for his company to be associated with Buckland House, in view of the recent developments?"

Rudd shaded his eyes, trying to locate the man. "If I hadn't been happy with the business potential of Buckland House I would not have allied myself to it," he said.

"What about the recent developments?" persisted the man.

"By which I assume you mean today's meeting," said Rudd. "Nothing that has happened today or since my share exchange or purchase of the Buckland House fleet has altered my original view."

"Do you, Sir Ian, foresee any directional changes on the holding company of Buckland House?" asked the man who had begun the questioning.

Buckland hesitated. "I think it is too early at this stage to forecast any board changes," he said.

"What about resignations?" called someone.

It was a bad question, easy to answer. "I've been given no intimations of any resignations," said Buckland. "Certainly I don't intend tendering mine, after the enthusiasm of this morning's meeting."

"Is Buckland House in any sort of trading difficulties?" asked someone shielded by the glare of lights.

"Absolutely and utterly not," insisted Buckland, glad of the question. "There was a working deficit, which was quite acceptable with the resources of the group, but even that has been removed by the disposal of the liners. Buckland House has always been the best and it remains the best."

It was a good reply to end upon and Rudd was relieved that Buckland realized it. He stood away from the table and the men on either side of him correctly interpreted the move and rose. Once more there was a flurry of questions but Buckland shook his head, leading the way out towards the corridors by which they had entered. Immediately beyond the doors there was a small ante-room, normally used by waiters when the public room was being used for small banquets. Buckland paused there, turning around to the other men. Buckland was limp with sweat, his suit crumpled to his body. He looked bitterly towards Snaith and Smallwood and said, "I hope you're bloody satisfied!"

Buckland invited Rudd and Prince Faysel to join the rest of the family for the celebration lunch, but Rudd excused himself, nervous of embarrassing Margaret. Faysel also made his apologies. Rudd led the way into the Berridge suite he had adopted as an office and Hallett emerged from the dressing-room in which the tape and telex machines had been installed.

"There's a message from New York," announced the personal assistant at once. "A request from the board for you to return for a full meeting."

Rudd frowned. "Morrison was supposed to have handled that."

"It doesn't look as if he has," said Hallett. "The message came from him." Hallett handed Rudd the torn-off slip.

"Get him on the telephone," he instructed.

"What did you think of today?" asked the Arab, as Hallett moved towards the telephone bank: a booster circuit had been installed for the three extra receivers.

"I thought Buckland was impressive," said Rudd honestly. "He asked for guidance and he certainly took it, but I got the impression he could have handled himself well enough without us."

"I was the only investment fund manager not to support Haffaford."

"I've already made the break-down," said Rudd.

"If they keep withdrawing from Buckland House, it'll become obvious. Today will have done nothing to make the shares pick up."

"I worked that out too," said Rudd.

Hallett gestured to him and the Best Rest chairman crossed to the desk; it was a good connection, without any distortion. "Why the request for a special meeting?" demanded Rudd at once. It was more forceful than the tone he would normally have used to his father-in-law but his mind was still occupied with the meeting. And with Margaret.

"They're not happy."

"Didn't you make it clear that it wasn't serious?"

"Of course I did. But from here it doesn't look that way. How did the meeting go?"

"Overwhelming support for Buckland."

"So we go ahead as planned?"

"Of course."

"I think you should come back," said Morrison.

"Can't you handle it?" said Rudd irritably.

241

"You're the chairman," said Morrison. "It's you they want to hear from."

"It's inconvenient."

"That's the way they feel about having $4,000,000 value wiped off Best Rest shares."

The responsibility was his, conceded Rudd. It was still a bastard. Belatedly he realized that there was none of the usual reserved hostility in his father-in-law's voice. Cupping his hand over the mouthpiece, Rudd said to Hallett, "What's the time of the lawyers' meeting tomorrow?"

"Eleven," said the personal assistant.

Into the telephone Rudd said, "I'll come out tomorrow afternoon: if they're that concerned they can come to an evening meeting, New York time."

"I'll arrange it for six," said Morrison.

Rudd replaced the receiver hastily and said, "They're getting nervous in New York."

"I can't say I blame them," said Faysel. "I'm not altogether happy myself."

Rudd frowned across at the Arab. "You think we should abandon the takeover?"

Faysel shrugged. "I know there's no practical reason why we should but it's got an unhappy feel about it."

"We've got $4,000,000 to pick up on the New York exchange," reminded Rudd.

"You're part of the board here already," said the Arab. Buckland seems to rely upon you more than people he's known for years. You can control him."

Rudd shook his head. "All or nothing," he reminded. He said to Hallett, "Any idea how we can contact Bunch?"

"I've got a Washington number," said the personal assistant.

"Get him," said Rudd. "Stop him coming directly back here. There's a board meeting in New York tomorrow. Six o'clock."

"Think we can do better than Haffaford's?" said Faysel.

"We'd better," said Rudd.

The final three editions of the *New Standard* led its front page with the Buckland House story and it was the major news coverage on television and radio. The tone of them all was of Buckland rejecting criticism and getting unanimous and overwhelming support.

Buckland began celebrating early with champagne, and continued with more wine throughout dinner and then with brandy afterwards. Lady Buckland retired early and Vanessa excused herself for a meeting with the Yorkshire solicitor who had travelled to London to meet her. Buckland sat in a wing-backed chair on the opposite side of the fireplace from Margaret, the brandy decanter easily to hand on a wine table. "Coup," he said, with an obvious effort to enunciate clearly. "That's what it's being described as. A coup in the entrepreneurial tradition of the Buckland family."

"There was nothing entrepreneurial about it," said Margaret objectively. "You were bloody lucky."

Buckland squeezed his eyes shut and then opened them as if he were having difficulty in focusing upon his wife. "I beat the bastards," he insisted.

"You were shown how to do it," she said dismissively. She was unhappy at the constant exposure to publicity.

"You don't know the half of it," he said belligerently.

"I know enough," said Margaret. "And from now on you'd better understand something, Ian. I won't do again what I did for you today. I sat in that bloody room feeling the suspicion wash over me and I dried up inside. I think you're a bastard, a stupid, silly bastard."

Buckland added more liquor to the brandy balloon, spilling some on his trousers. He regarded the stain curiously and then made ineffectual attempts to brush it off. "Got a position to maintain," he said. "Don't forget we've a position to maintain."

"I never forget it," she said. "It's about time you stopped doing so."

27

The two men went through a complete transcript of the press conference and then Rudd detailed what had occurred at the shareholders' meeting. It took more than an hour, Sir Henry Dray constantly making notes in his briefing ledger. At the end he said, "We did well to wait. Almost all the work has been done for us."

"Is there a hearing date?"

"The twenty-ninth," said the barrister.

Just under three weeks, thought Rudd. He said, "When are you going to serve notice?"

"Maybe a week," said Dray. "I'd expect Buckland's counsel to demand an immediate postponement for preparation time, but I'm pressing it as a matter of urgency so we might be able to go ahead."

"How do you consider our chances?"

"Very good," said Dray. "The summoning of the shareholders' meeting, with Initial and Preferential being lumped together instead of separately, is proof of how Buckland and his family can manipulate the structure to their advantage. The introduction of the man from Hong Kong was unexpected. . . ." He looked back to his notes. "Sinclair," he reminded himself. "Do you think he's lying about that telephone call?"

"I don't know," said Rudd.

"We'll see if he'll say the same thing on oath. And Lady Harvey."

"You intend calling her?"

"Of course," said the barrister. "Dozens of shareholders with their good money entrusted into Buckland House care have been told the occupation of that house was entirely innocent. If we prove otherwise then we prove Buckland's unfitness to remain inviolate because of the share arrangement. We've traced her already to Antibes."

"The shares opened at 90p this morning," said Rudd. "Just before I came here they were 88p."

"On the face of it," said Dray, "you haven't made a very wise investment, have you?"

"I've placed buy orders, to mop up," said Rudd. "It'll stop them going below 85p."

Dray frowned. "Company or personal purchases?" he said.

"Personal," said Rudd. "I haven't got board approval to buy in Best Rest's name."

"That could be expensive for you."

"I know," said Rudd. "It's the professionals who are getting out."

"Normally there'd be a rise when the takeover bid was declared," said Dray, "but I wouldn't expect that in this case, preceded by the court hearing."

"I don't," said Rudd. The continued slide of the Buckland House shares represented a further loss of Best Rest of $400,000; it was probably a good idea that he was going back to New York after all. It was still inconvenient. Now that there was a time limit, he wanted to get a positive decision from Margaret.

"By the time this is over, you're going to be pretty unpopular with some people." said Dray.

"I'm not in business to make friends," said Rudd. Only one, he thought.

"Under the Fair Trading laws of this country there is a panel to which your ultimate bid could be referred and declared unacceptable if it's thought to be creating an unfair monopoly," said Dray. "Fortunately you don't own other hotels here, so I don't expect it, but I think you should be warned."

"You mean legally I'd be prevented from going ahead with the takeover?"

Dray nodded.

"What would my position be then?" said Rudd.

"That's for you to judge," said the lawyer. "You have company and private investment in a group losing professional confidence and being run, according to what you already know, very badly."

"That's a pretty frightening thought," said the American.

"You could always get out."

"But at what cost?" demanded Rudd. "On the slide already the company investment is down over $4,000,000, irrespective of my personal buying."

Dray leaned back in his chair and began the habitual finger-play with his pencil. "From the outset this had to be a gamble," he said. "I think at the moment you're locked in with little choice but to go on. As I've said, the Monopolies Commission is an outside possibility."

"'There's no way we could get any indication?"

"Absolutely none," said Dray. "It could be initiated from too many different directions. Any director of Buckland House could ask for it. Or it could be an independent government decision. But let's not be depressive. I think we stand a good chance of winning the court case."

"I've still got to win the takeover after that," reminded Rudd.

Rudd used the flight from London to review everything that had happened since he began the move for Buckland House, and by the time he arrived at Kennedy airport he'd decided that the English lawyer was right; it would be wrong to become too depressive. Haffaford's action had ended in his favour, for the later court hearing. And the share drop, although outwardly bad, would make his purchase offer more attractive. Already he was formulating an idea about how he could confront the danger of the Monopolies Commission.

Prince Faysel had flown from England earlier in the day so all the directors were assembled by the time Rudd got to the down-town headquarters of Best Rest. He went straight to the board-room, taking his briefcase with him. The only smile of welcome came from Bunch.

"There's a lot of concern about what's happening in Eng-land," announced Morrison, from the other end of the table.

"You knew the facts," said Rudd. The co-operation from the other man appeared to have been temporary: the hostility was back in his voice.

"We wanted to hear them in more detail from you," said Walker. "And about the shareholders' meeting."

It took Rudd fifteen minutes, occasionally inviting comment

from Prince Faysel, to recount the confrontation and then he continued on with the meeting that morning with Sir Henry Dray.

Conscious of the attitude around the conference table, he omitted any reference to the Monopolies Commission: Dray had said it was an outside possibility anyway.

"At the London close Buckland House stock was down to 95p," said Böch. "We're currently being traded on the market here seven points under par."

"I've intervened in London," disclosed Rudd.

"With company money?"

Rudd frowned at Morrison's abrupt demand. "I think it's something we should consider, assembled as a board," he said. "But at the moment it's a personal purchase."

"How much have you committed?"

"A million," Rudd said. He wondered if the sum he had set aside with the London broker had been fully extended.

"I don't think it wise to commit any more company money: already we're down $4,400,000," said Morrison. He managed to keep from his voice the excitement he felt at Rudd risking his own fortune.

"It had to be expected," said Rudd. "It would be wrong to lose our nerve now."

"It wasn't to be expected," said Böch at once. "We had no idea Haffaford's were going to do what they did."

"All right," conceded Rudd. "So that's depressed the market and caused us an initial loss. But you heard what the lawyer said, about it benefiting our case in court."

"Before which there'll be enormous uncertainty and bigger drops, in London and here," said Ottway. It was an obvious remark but he wanted to be seen to be backing the majority.

"And in six months we could have the control and be in profit," said Rudd, letting the exasperation show.

"We shouldn't be thrown off course by a temporary reversal," supported Faysel. "And it isn't even that. Few investments can expect to show growth at once: that's common business sense."

"Would you consider putting any more of your investment fund money in Buckland House?" demanded Böch.

Faysel was discomforted by the question. "At the moment

that question doesn't arise," he said, trying to avoid an answer.

"Would you, if money were available?" pressed Morrison, welcoming the direction of the questioning.

"Because of my knowledge of what we intend, that's a difficult question to answer," said Faysel.

"Without that knowledge," pressed Morrison. "On face value does Buckland House look a good investment to you, after the bloodletting of the last few weeks."

"No," said Faysel honestly.

"Which is going to be the attitude of professional investors," said Ottway. "That's why they're withdrawing."

"And because they're professional they'll come hurrying back, when we're in control," said Rudd.

Morrison glanced to the secretarial bank. As he looked, a stenographer began changing a tape-recorder spool. The meeting was going exactly as he wanted.

"We've made a costly investment," he said. "I'd like an assurance from our chairman, with the benefit of yesterday's meeting, that our pursuit of Buckland House is still a viable proposition."

Rudd hesitated momentarily. Then he said, "If I thought otherwise, then naturally I would recommend withdrawal."

"And you don't?" said Walker.

Again there was a pause. "No," said Rudd. "I consider we should continue."

"What's the cost estimate?" said Walker.

"I intend the initial offer to be 110p. If the shares remain as low as they are at present, that'll look attractive."

"What's the ceiling?" said Böch.

"Twenty-five per cent," said Rudd.

Walker breathed in sharply, making a slight whistling sound. "What would that make the total cash offer?"

"There would be variations," said Rudd. "I estimate overall something like $200,000,000: maybe $6,000,000 more."

"Too much," said Walker at once. "We'd extend our reserves and have to consider borrowing maybe $30,000,000. I don't think we should go any higher than fifteen per cent."

"That's too tight," protested Rudd. "If there's a takeover battle with someone else, I'll need more room than that."

"There's a time to go on and a time to stop," said Böch. "I agree with Walker. Fifteen should be the top."

"And a time limit," said Walker. "In little under a month, we've seen more than $4,000,000 taken off our value. If this thing becomes protracted, then God knows how much more it could be."

"That's unreasonable!" said Rudd. "How can we possibly forecast and make a decision about how long it's going to take!"

"The court hearing is fixed for three weeks' time?" said Morrison, referring to Rudd's earlier briefing.

"Yes," said Rudd.

"To last how long?"

"I haven't been given an estimate," said Rudd. "Possibly a week, maybe less. If we're successful, as the lawyer is sure we will be, I'd make the offer immediately afterwards."

"Another month for conclusion then?" said Walker.

"It could take much longer!" pleaded Rudd. This had been the degree of opposition during his first year of chairmanship. He'd forgotten it and didn't like the re-emergence.

"A month from the date of offer," said Böch decisively.

This wasn't spontaneous, Rudd decided. It had all been prepared and rehearsed in advance. He gazed steadily at his father-in-law, sure of the manipulator. Why, he wondered?

"These conditions are intolerable," he said. "You're sending me to fight with my hands tied."

"The chairman should be allowed more latitude," said Bunch. "You're allowing him no room to manoeuvre if there's a counter-bid."

"If there's a counter-bid," said Walker, "then I think we should consider taking it and cutting our losses."

Rudd looked down at the table, running the words through in his mind. He looked up and said, "In ten years I have conducted a great many negotiations for this company. Never have I introduced any loss-making factor for any unacceptable length of time. I resent the attitude being expressed in this boardroom today."

"It's not personal," said Walker at once. "The shareholders have a right to committee decisions and the protection afforded by having more than one man to make those decisions. When the vote was taken to move upon Buckland House we expected a clean, clear-cut bid. It's proved to be anything but. It's scrappy and unglued. Had I known it was to develop like this, I would have opposed it. As it is, I want to minimize the possibility of worsening a mistake."

"I've already assured this board that I do not consider the acquisition of Buckland House to be a mistake," said Rudd.

"It's the privilege of a committee to have differing views," said Böch.

"Then let's abandon the bid before we even make it," said Rudd angrily. "The court action can still be cancelled."

"We've already decided that at this stage it would be too expensive," said Morrison.

"I'd like a vote," said Rudd. He already knew the outcome but he wanted it on record. "For continuation?"

Morrison led the voting. He was followed by Walker, Böch, Ottway and lastly Prince Faysel.

"Against?" said Rudd. He raised his hand at the same time as Bunch.

"The board decision is to continue," he said formally. "To vote on the limitation of fifteen per cent above the 110p, to offer to remain for one month after the conclusion of the court hearing."

This time Faysel voted with Rudd and Bunch but they were still outvoted.

"The decision is in favour of the limitations," said Rudd.

Perfect, thought Morrison.

Rudd, Prince Faysel and Bunch went immediately to Rudd's office after the board meeting. Bunch managed to remain silent until the door closed and then said, "You know what they've done, don't you? They've made you personally responsible."

"Yes," accepted Rudd. He was confused by the meeting, trying to understand it. His immediate thought was that for the first time in his life he didn't have an escape route.

"I've got an enormous amount of money committed in investment," apologized the Arab. "I had to vote for continuation."

"I understood," assured Rudd.

"Do you think you'll be able to pull it off with these limitations?" asked Bunch.

"I don't know," said Rudd. "You haven't told me about Washington."

"Jeplow is raving about the bearer cheque: says it's a direct breach of the agreement he had with you. There's no real problem with the legislation."

"What did you say?"

"That we favoured mutual trust: we trusted him and he should trust us."

"I like that," said Rudd.

"He didn't."

"There's fuck all he can do about it."

"He didn't like that either."

"For the sort of the money he's getting, he'll have to learn to like it. He shouldn't have tried to screw us in the first place."

"When do you want to go back?"

"Right away," decided Rudd. "We can take advantage of a night flight and be back in London in the morning. I've scheduled the formation meeting of the liner board for the following day."

"What about Morrison?"

"He's flying over tomorrow," said Rudd.

He was stabbing the point of a letter-knife into his blotter. "There was a surprise at yesterday's meeting," he said. "Almost all the small investors sided with Buckland."

"Trust in the English establishment," said Faysel.

"Maybe," said Rudd. "I wonder if that loyalty will stay, after the court hearing?"

"The investment funds will come to us soon enough," said Bunch.

Reminded, Rudd said to Bunch. "According to the estimates I made at the meeting yesterday, there was also a pretty strong nominee vote for Buckland. How did you get on with identifying the holders?"

"No luck," said Bunch. "Anonymity is anonymity."

"Try again," ordered Rudd. "I'd like to know what the groupings are."

*   *   *

Rudd's aircraft was circling Kennedy after take-off for the flight back to London when Herbert Morrison reached the office of the Boston lawyer. Grearson listened attentively to the instructions from the hotelier, his face tightening into a frown.

"You want your stock pledged *against* any takeover?" he said.

"Yes," said Morrison.

"But that doesn't make sense, Herb. You'll be fighting your own company."

"It makes perfect sense," insisted Morrison. "But it's got to work properly. I want you to go over and fix it personally."

"Go over!"

"Make sure they know what to do."

"But they know what to do," said Grearson. "It's all been set up by letter already. They've just got to change the pledge."

"I'll pay all the expenses, everything," said Morrison. "Take the wife. Make a vacation out of it."

"A trip to Europe might be nice," said Grearson.

"Do it for me, Gene."

"All right," agreed the lawyer.

28

Rudd had not announced the invitation to Sir Richard Penhardy to join the board of the liner subsidiary company. The surprise showed on the faces of the others gathered in the Berridge suite when the Buckland House director entered. The flamboyant MP looked slightly ill at ease; there had only been the brief telephone call from Rudd, the moment he arrived back from America, and an agreement meeting the previous evening.

Rudd stood to greet him and said, "I extended the invitation to Sir Richard, an invitation which I'm delighted to say he's accepted, because I felt it would complete the balance of the board we intend. It gives Buckland House two voices."

"Excellent idea," said Buckland at once.

"I'm delighted to be with you," said Penhardy.

Rudd resumed his place at the head of the conference table and said officially, "This is a formation meeting of a company to be a subsidiary of Best Rest to operate a fleet of seven lines from whatever parts of the world that board feels will be advantageous and beneficial." He gestured to Hallett and said, "Can we have the notice of registration and formation?"

As the personal assistant began going through the required announcements, Rudd looked around the table. Penhardy was still looking about him trying to settle. Buckland sat alongside, all the nervousness and anxiety of the preceding days gone, slouched languidly in his chair. Prince Faysel was bent forward over the table, appearing to write something on a pad before him. At the far end of the table Morrison returned his gaze without any expression. Rudd thought his father-in-law was standing up well under the strain of Atlantic commuting. Bunch was listening intently to what Hallett was saying, professionally determined to watch for any mistake. Hallett finished by listing the full names of everyone around the table and producing their signed agreements to serve.

"That really is the only purpose of the gathering today, but I think we can talk a little further about the intentions," said Rudd. "Being an American company it'll be quoted in the New York exchange. Best Rest will naturally take substantial share apportionment. I intend a Preferential issue, to which the directors will be offered purchase, and an Ordinary issue. The company will be headquartered from New York. Assets include the liners and of course the goodwill."

"What do you imagine to be the share capital required?" asked Morrison.

"That's a question for the accountants," said Rudd. "But from the refitting necessary and the loss-making expectation during the time they're laid up for refit and then begin operation I would say a minimum of $6,000,000. There will be administration staff to employ immediately and a sales campaign throughout America, which will be expensive."

"During our preliminary negotiations there was a suggestion about the names of the vessels," reminded Buckland.

To the others around the table Rudd said, "I consider the existing names perfectly satisfactory. Buckland House have agreed their title surrender to us and I consider we should keep them as they are."

"Seems a sensible enough idea," said Faysel.

"I think it's got sound, practical value, too," said Penhardy. "If we're headquartered in New York presumably the board will meet there?"

Rudd nodded. "Will that create a difficulty for you?"

The MP shook his head. "Not at all," he said. Like Buckland he welcomed the idea of multinational involvement.

"What about officers?" said Bunch.

"It's a matter for discussion, but I thought Herbert Morrison for chairman and Sir Ian Buckland as vice-chairman," said Rudd.

Morrison showed no reaction. Buckland smiled broadly.

"Seems perfectly satisfactory if they're prepared to accept," said Faysel, looking enquiringly between the two men.

"I'd be delighted," said Buckland at once.

254

"All right," nodded Morrison.

"The personnel and labour relations departments of Buckland House are negotiating the crew lay-offs," said Buckland. "That of course doesn't create any delay in the hand-over."

"Have you a date?" said Rudd.

"Possibly three weeks."

Rudd nodded to Bunch. "I think we should bring the senior management across, to make sure everything goes smoothly."

Bunch nodded back, making a note.

"Anyone anything else to raise?" asked Rudd.

There was a hesitation, then head shakes around the table. As the meeting disbanded, Buckland said, "I'm summoning a special directors' meeting of Buckland House to settle things after the damned shareholders' meeting. Day after tomorrow."

"Like to see a bit more life in the shares," said Penhardy.

The challenge announcement would cause a sell, thought Rudd. In margin purchases the support operation had so far cost him $45,000. In twenty-eight days he would have to settle the remaining ninety per cent, which meant an additional expenditure of $405,000. By then the rest of his broker's deposit would be exhausted. There would probably be a demand for him to increase his maintenance margin very shortly.

"They'll rise," predicted Buckland.

Rudd said nothing. After the two Englishmen left the suite, Faysel said, "Why Penhardy?"

"There might be a good reason later on."

"I'm opening the house at Ascot," said the Arab. "Why not come down? There won't be much opportunity for any relaxation after the challenge is made."

Rudd shook his head. "I don't think there will be time," he said.

Margaret was already in the apartment when he got there. She came to him and put her head against his chest. After he'd kissed her she said, "Christ I've missed you!"

"I was sorry about New York," he said. "I had to go."

She was wearing a checked town suit, open at the neck over a silk shirt, and he thought she looked beautiful. She'd brought fresh flowers and the windows were open, the wind slightly stirring the curtains. She indicated the window and said, "This time I watched you arrive. You walk very fast."

"I was in a hurry," he said. He felt nervous, the uncertainty moving through him. He led her to the couch where he'd asked her to make her mind up the last time, but didn't sit beside her. Instead he pulled a matching chair around, so that he was facing her. She looked curiously at him.

"I tried calling the house several times after the meeting. Somebody else always answered. I thought you might have called me," he said.

"There were too many people there," she said. "God, wasn't the meeting awful!"

"It could have been worse," he said.

She shook her head. "I don't think so. I've told Ian I won't do anything like that for him ever again."

Rudd felt a flicker of hope. "You've decided then?"

"Decided?" She looked away from him.

"You said after the meeting," he reminded her.

"I know."

"So what's the answer?"

"I'm still frightened, Harry," she said. "I think I know what I want to do, but I'm terribly frightened. Give me more time, please!"

Rudd swallowed. "I can't," he said.

She came back to him. "Why not? There's no hurry."

"There is, darling," he said.

"You going back to New York already?"

"Not that."

"What then?"

"Ian didn't deserve to win the shareholders' vote."

Her shoulders lifted uncertainly. "But he did," she said.

Rudd couldn't hold her eyes. He looked down to where her hands were clasped loosely in her lap and said, "I'm going to challenge him, Margaret."

She laughed unsurely. "Challenge him for what?"

"Buckland House," said Rudd. "I'm going to court, to get the share structure that gives the family its control declared illegal. And if I win I'm going to make a takeover bid."

He forced himself to look at her. She was staring at him, frowning, her head moving slowly in disbelief. "But why?" Her voice was strained and empty.

"The ship sale and the shareholders' meeting don't mean anything, not really. The company is still a mess. It'll go on failing unless someone does something to stop it happening."

"And that's you!"

"Yes," he said. He saw the colour flushing her cheeks.

"You bastard!" she said. She said it curiously, like someone making a discovery.

"No," he said quickly, trying to stop the anger, but she hurried on. "You complete and utter bastard." She gestured around the apartment. "It's all been part of it, hasn't it? The complete takeover, the business and the family and the wife."

"Don't be stupid," he said. "You know that isn't so."

Her lips were tight between her teeth as she fought for control. "How difficult was it for you to see how unhappy I was!" she demanded. "Is there some psychology involved in all that business crap that's talked in America? Chapter Five, how to gain advantage from seducing the abandoned wife."

"Stop it!" shouted Rudd. "What advantage have I tried to get from what's happened between us? It happened, that's all. I've told you I love you and I do. That's why I want everything settled before the court announcement."

"So Ian can go knowing he's already lost his family!"

"You're being ridiculous," said Rudd. "What sort of marriage have you got?"

Margaret jerked up, unable any longer to remain still. "One that worked, after a fashion."

"That's bullshit and you know it."

"I thought I loved you," she said, her back to him. "I really thought I loved you. I was frightened to death, but I was actually considering becoming the outcast, abandoning everyone and everything." She turned, hands before her, her knuckles in her mouth. "Christ!" she said. "I can't believe it!"

Rudd stood and went towards her but she said "Don't," and he stopped. He stood about two yards from her, his arms limp at his side. "You've got it wrong," he said. "All wrong."

"I don't think so."

257

"It's an excuse," accused Rudd. "You're using it as an excuse to avoid a decision."

"That's not true!"

"Stop running, Margaret, Make your mind up."

"I have," she said, moving towards the door. "You can go to hell."

Kevin Sinclair was an angular, sharp-jointed man with hair that flopped uncontrolled over his forehead. He sat relaxed, one leg crossed over the other, nodding to Buckland's gratitude.

"There but for the Grace of God go us all," he grinned. "I didn't consider it was too much for you to ask."

"I appreciate it all the same," said Buckland. "I'm going to restructure the board: I'd like you to come off the subsidiary group and sit with me on the holding company. We've just taken on the American, Rudd. We're really going to be multi-national."

"I'd like that," said Sinclair. "I'd like that very much indeed."

There had been communication between them in the past, before the request to act as nominee for Morrison, but Gene Grearson had never met the solicitor who acted as his London agent, on the reciprocal agreement for use of Grearson's facilities in Boston. Peter Coppell was exactly what he imagined an English lawyer to be, neatly suited, neatly barbered and precise to the point of being pedantic.

Coppell frowned as Grearson relayed Morrison's instructions and said, "Are you sure the man knows what he's doing?"

"Completely," assured the American.

"At the shareholders' meeting I was in the minority of nominee holders, in favour of Buckland. This reversal will mean exactly the same thing; surely Morrison would benefit from supporting the takeover. He's voting against himself!"

"I know," agreed Grearson. "I've talked it through most fully with him: those are his instructions."

"Most unusual!" said Coppell.

258

"It was originally his company," said Grearson. "He insists that to oppose the takeover would be in its best interests."

Coppell shook his head but decided against continuing the opposition. "How long will you be staying in London, Mr Grearson?"

"Only a few days," said the American. "Having come this far I've decided to extend the visit into a vacation and go on to Europe."

Margaret sat hunched in her bedroom, the door locked, arms tight around her body as if she were cold. The immediate, instinctive anger had gone now and she didn't know how she felt. Betrayed, certainly. Relieved, too. The realization surprised her. Had he been right, about her snatching for an excuse? She thought she loved him; even after what he'd said today, she thought she loved him. But enough to throw up the security of everything she knew?

29

John Snaith was the last to arrive and as the merchant banker took his place at the boardroom table Rudd had a sensation of *déjà vu*; Snaith must feel as he had felt, all those years ago, entering for the first time the Best Rest boardroom which had then been on Boston's Atlantic Avenue, knowing that some people in the room hated him and everyone else held him in suspicion. He'd had to endure it for a long time, remembered Rudd. It was going to be much briefer for Snaith.

Rudd thought that the merchant banker and Smallwood were confronting the hostility well, refusing to turn away from the looks that were being directed at them from Buckland's side of the table.

Buckland was very sure of himself, enjoying the confrontation. The opening procedures weren't hurried and when they ended Buckland allowed a gap before he spoke.

"There is only one subject for discussion today," he said. "It is into the conduct and behaviour of our merchant bankers and their representative and supporters. What was done and the effect of that action upon this company is well enough known to everyone here for it not to be necessary for me to repeat it in detail. I think it is sufficient to say that at this morning's valuation, something like £2,200,000 has been taken off the company's value, through the lack of confidence created entirely by what they did." He paused, then continued. "Despite our share loss, you are all aware that our liquidity problem has been resolved as the result of our negotiations and link-up with Best Rest. I wish formally to recommend to this meeting the sacking of Samuel Haffaford and Co. as merchant bankers for Buckland House, and for this company to switch its financing to another institution."

"Second the proposition," said Lord Condway at once.

260

Snaith fought back immediately. He said, "The action of myself and my bank was motivated entirely by the feelings expressed to you and the vice-chairman when you made your visit seeking overdraft extensions. It was to save this company . . ."

". . . by personal, unwarranted attack!" cut in Gore-Pelham.

Snaith considered his words before resuming. "The conduct of the shareholders' meeting was very clever," he said quietly. "My company and myself were completely outmanoeuvred. But that is what it is, a manoeuvre. I have no intention of repeating any allegations here this morning. You are aware of them and I invite you all, in proper honesty, to draw your own conclusions from them."

"The point has been made and should be made again that selling off a division to settle an existing debt doesn't solve our difficulties," said Smallwood, in his high voice. "In another year, eighteen months, we'll be back where we were earlier this year, going into deep deficit."

"I don't think what happens to this company in a year should be a matter of concern for either you or Mr Snaith," said Penhardy.

"You've already spoken of confidence," said Snaith. "What sort of confidence do you imagine will come from a boardroom upheaval and the disposal of your existing bankers?"

"Isn't it a little late for you to be concerned on behalf of the people whose money you've invested and then jeopardized?" said Penhardy.

"Nothing is too late if this board puts itself in order and begins properly to run its business," said Snaith, with sudden force.

"Putting this board in order is the purpose of this meeting," said Buckland.

"If this board were to move the expulsion or seek the resignation of Snaith, then I would have immediately to offer my resignation also," said Smallwood.

"That would have to be entirely a decision for you," said Buckland contentedly.

If his court action and takeover were successful, Snaith and Smallwood were exactly the sort of professionals he would want to remain upon the board, recognized Rudd. So he had to declare himself in advance of any vote. He cleared his throat and said, "There's an announcement I'd like to make to this board."

Buckland smiled towards him.

Rudd hesitated. Then, talking directly to Buckland, he said, "Tomorrow there are being served upon the members of the Buckland family and officially upon this company, writs alleging that under the Companies Acts and regulations empowered by the Registrar of Companies the Initial shareholding formation is unjust and unfair."

The stunned silence was absolute. Then the outrage gushed from Buckland. "WHAT!" he said.

"I am instituting legal action against your family control of the company," said Rudd, more simply.

"BASTARD!" shouted Buckland.

It was becoming a common accusation against him, thought Rudd.

Within two hours of the court action being announced publicly, the institutions and fund managers who had hesitated after the shareholders' meeting began to offload. Rudd's initial mop-up commitment was quickly exhausted and brokers asked him to increase his maintenance margins, to continue the purchases at 95p a share. The intervening weekend did nothing to dampen the fever. Rudd withdrew his buy orders when he reached a limit of $2,000,000. Without the automatic barrier, the slide became an avalanche. On Tuesday they opened at 60p and by midday were being marked at 45p. It was then that the Stock Exchange Council suspended dealings, for a nominal period to allow trading to calm. The action increased the pressure upon Buckland. His lawyers sought the postponement that Rudd's advisers had predicted, but the judge sitting in chambers agreed the hearing was urgent in view of the suspension and dismissed the application. There was no suspension on the New York exchange, and Best Rest suffered by its association. In a week, the stock value plunged by $6,500,000. There were daily meetings between Rudd and Sir Henry Dray and then again between Rudd, Bunch, Faysel and Morrison in the Grosvenor Square apartment. Bunch and Morrison moved from the Berridge into the Connaught and Faysel commuted daily from Ascot. The media coverage was more intense than before, squads of reporters, photographers and television men camped almost permanently in Grosvenor Square and attempting to follow Rudd wherever he went. He supposed it was the same with the Buckland family. Several times, usually late in the evening when he was alone in the apartment, Rudd stared at the telephone, dismissed the idea as ridiculous but still considered calling Margaret; once he even lifted the receiver and held it growling in his hand for several moments before replacing it again.

At the final session with Dray, the day before the court hearing, the lawyer said, "I expected interest but I never imagined it would become quite the *cause célèbre*."

"No," said Rudd.

"Would you have initiated it, if you'd thought it was going to turn out like this?"

Rudd considered the question. Then he said, "No. I don't think I would."

"Too late now for second thoughts," said Dray briskly.

"Yes," said Rudd. Would it be for Margaret? When the case was over she wouldn't be able to use it as an excuse. And he was convinced that was what she had done."

Peter Coppell delayed until the last permitted day before complying with the court's request, trying first by telex and cable and latterly by telephone to contact Gene Grearson in Boston to advise him, but the American had not returned from his European vacation and had not left forwarding addresses. He'd made every effort, Coppell decided. And it amounted to little more than a formality anyway.

"We just made it," reported the clerk, returning from the High Court.

"Damned strange business," said Coppell. "Altogether a damned strange business."

30

The court seemed strangely insufficient for the drama to be played out in it, a sombre, dark-panelled rectangle of a place, the scarlet gown of Mr Justice Godber the only colour. The judge sat high above everyone, the wooden panelling extended to form a tiny canopy over his chair. Sir Henry Dray was to his right, black-gowned and white-wigged, appearing more skeletal than ever, like some cadaverous blackbird pecking and swooping among the junior counsel who flanked him, and the solicitor Berriman and his assistants who sat immediately behind. Buckland's counsel, Sir Walter Blair, occupied the same bench as Dray, to the left. Blair was an indulgently fat, purple-faced man, a short barristers' waistcoat corsetting his ample belly. Like Bray, he led two junior counsel. The jury-box to the right was utilized to accommodate the journalists overflowing from the press benches, and the public gallery, at the back of the court, was crowded with people, some of whom had begun queueing in Fleet Street and the Strand from early morning.

Special seating had been arranged behind Blair for members of the Buckland family who were not being called upon to give evidence. Lady Buckland wore severe black, and made heavy use of her stick climbing the stairs and entering through the narrow doorway. Vanessa sat one side of her and Margaret the other. Both women wore grey, Vanessa a suit and Margaret a dress. Rudd had already been in the corridor outside when they arrived. He had looked hopefully towards them. He knew they'd seen him, Margaret first, but they'd given no sign of recognition. Behind the Buckland family sat Condway and the other Buckland House directors. Herbert Morrison and Walter Bunch were to the side, separated by court officials.

Dray rose immediately the court clerk finished the formal calling of the case, but did not speak at once. Instead he erected a tiny podium, with collapsible supports, on the bench in front of him and theatrically arranged his papers and note ledger.

"At your convenience, Mr Dray," prompted the judge.

Dray smiled up. "This case," he began, in his arid, legal monotone, "is an unusual one to be brought under the provisions of the Act, as unusual as I shall attempt to show the construction of the holding company of Buckland House to be. While the articles of formation might be complicated, my case is not. I shall seek to show that the Buckland family exercises a wholly unwarranted control over a publicly quoted company and that the control is unsound in company law and unfair upon public shareholders."

Around him the court settled down after the immediate tension of opening. Blair sprawled back, legs askance, appearing intent upon some point on the ceiling. Dray started from the Glasgow beginning of Buckland House, and at once the paper-chase of documents started between him and the judge's bench as the barrister took from his ready juniors the original articles of formation, Registrar of Company files and then a series of board-room minutes, some dating back several years, which he claimed showed the way the company could be manipulated by the Initial shareholding. The technical, labyrinthine opening took an hour. Dray's first witness was John Snaith.

The merchant banker started his evidence uncomfortably, unused to his surroundings. He detailed his bank's involvement with the company and their investment in it, and was then brought by Dray's questioning to their growing concern about its running.

"How did you express that concern?" asked Dray.

"By seeking the chairman's resignation."

"Why?"

"Because we considered him unfit to continue."

"Why?"

"Conduct involving a large sum of money and the use of a mews house in London."

"What was his response?"

"He refused."

"What did you do then?"

265

"Asked for a special shareholders' meeting."

Dray paused, indicating the importance of his question. "The meeting was held?"

"Yes."

"Just one? Or more than one?"

"I'm afraid I don't understand."

"According to the formation of the company, there should be two meetings, one of Initial shareholders, the other of Preferential and Ordinary."

"Just one meeting," said Snaith.

"Did you realize that by having just one meeting, the Buckland family was assured of a carrying vote?"

"Not at the time, no."

"Do you consider the Buckland monopoly fair?"

"No," said Snaith.

"Has anything happened to change your opinion about Sir Ian's ability to remain chairman of Buckland House?"

"Nothing," said Snaith.

"Hasn't a substantial loss-making section of the group been disposed of? And by that disposal, an extreme overdraft position reversed?"

"Yes," agreed Snaith. "But I regard that only as a temporary improvement in the affairs of the company."

Dray sat and Blair got ponderously to his feet. He searched among his papers, appearing to have lost his notes, and then said sharply, so sharply that Snaith jumped, "As a result of the shareholders' meeting, your bank stands a good chance of being fired, doesn't it?"

"It is a possibility," agreed Snaith.

"More than a possibility," insisted Blair. "The implication was made at the shareholders' meeting, was it not?"

"Yes."

"How do you feel about that?"

"Feel?"

"You're a merchant bank, selling money at an interest. To lose Buckland House will be to lose business, won't it?"

Snaith turned the question against the barrister. "Despite which," he said, "I felt strongly enough to make the protest in an effort to protect the shareholders."

Blair's face coloured further. "Are you aware of the voting figures at the shareholders' meeting?"

"Yes," said Snaith.

"Would you remind His Lordship?"

"The voting was 3300 against the motion of dismissal, with 1100 supporting it."

"Would you interpret those figures for the court?"

"Interpret them?"

"Isn't it a fact, Mr Snaith that the motion for Sir Ian's dismissal as chairman of the board would have been defeated without the use of the Buckland-held Initial share issue?"

"Yes," said the merchant banker.

"Which proves the overwhelming confidence in Sir Ian Buckland by shareholders whose interests are supposed to be in jeopardy."

"Yes," conceded Snaith again.

"Thank you," said Blair, slumping heavily into his seat.

"I call Harry Rudd," announced Dray.

Rudd's pathway from the rear of the court to the witness-box took him immediately past Margaret. He was aware of her sitting rigidly next to her mother-in-law and was seized with the sudden desire to reach out and touch her. He kept his arms stiffly to his side, actually veering away when he reached her bench, carrying on to the raised box. He took the oath and followed Dray throughout the early questioning identifying himself with Best Rest and defining his involvement with Buckland House. Once more there was a procession of documents to the judge, showing the Best Rest share apportionment with the English company and the purchase contracts for the liners. Once he looked towards the Buckland women. Lady Buckland was sitting head bowed. Vanessa stared at him, the contempt showing in her face. Margaret was looking into the well of the court, away from the witness-box.

"You are chairman of a multinational conglomerate, predominantly involved in leisure, with pre-tax profits in the current year of $123,000,000?" asked Dray.

"Yes," said Rudd.

"How extensive is your experience of hotel administration and running?"

"It is all I have ever done."

"You are an expert then?"

"I suppose so."

"Do you consider the Buckland House company efficiently run?"

"No," said Rudd shortly. He was conscious of the flurry of activity from the press benches.

"Why not?"

"In England they are catering for a demand that no longer exists," he said. "They are inefficient. There is no cost control or centralized administration. They are grossly overstaffed. The profits of some of the overseas divisions are entirely due to low labour costs, not efficiency."

"During your short period of time upon the Buckland House board, have you heard requests made for management improvements?"

"Yes."

"What has been the response?"

"Sir Ian considers that the liner sale is sufficient to resolve their problems."

"Do you?"

"No."

"As the control of Buckland House is currently constructed, is there any way the directors or shareholders can insist upon changes?"

"An attempt was made, at the shareholders' meeting. It failed."

"A previous witness has forecast that the Buckland House deficit, under its current administration, will continue to increase. What is your opinion?"

"Unless something is done to improve their running and their efficiency, increasing losses are inevitable," said Rudd.

Blair came eagerly to his feet, anxious to begin questioning the plaintiff American. Rudd was conscious of another movement just behind the barrister and realized Margaret was looking at him. Her face was completely empty, almost as if she were hypnotized and unaware of what was happening around her.

"A multinational conglomerate with profits of $123,000,000?" began Blair.

Rudd was conscious of sarcasm and guessed the barrister was attempting to undermine his temper. "Yes," he said.

"You are an expert, experienced businessman?"

Rudd hesitated. Then he said, "I hope I am."

"A self-made millionaire?"

"I am a millionaire, yes."

"Not a man to make mistakes in business then?"

Rudd wondered at the direction of the questioning. "I try to avoid them," he said cautiously.

"Is Prince Tewfik Faysel, of the Saudi investment trust, a member of the board of Best Rest?"

"Yes."

"And of Buckland House?"

"Yes."

"Was it through Prince Tewfik Faysel that you were introduced to Buckland House and negotiated the purchase of the liner fleet?"

"Yes," said Rudd.

"The original agreement, between yourself and Sir Ian Buckland, was for a cash purchase?"

"It was."

"Why did it not remain a cash purchase?"

"My board in New York decided to limit the cash purchase and negotiate part as a share exchange."

"Part as a share exchange," echoed the barrister. "You had access to Buckland House balance sheets and knew their performance, did you not?"

"Yes."

"And had the benefit of consultation with Prince Faysel, a long-time member of the Buckland House board?"

"Yes."

"Tell me, Mr Rudd, why should you, an expert businessman, a self-made millionaire, a man who tries to avoid making business mistakes, fully able to assess in advance the ability of a company, allow yourself to become involved to the extent of £7,500,000 with . . ." Blair hesitated dramatically, appearing to consult his notes, ". . . a company you deride as inefficient, with no cost control or centralized administration and with gross overstaffing!"

Rudd moved akwardly in the box. "As I have explained, my board decided to limit the cash purchase. We wanted to buy the fleet because we saw the possibility of turning it into an attractive, profit-making division. The share exchange was the way of achieving that."

"Wasn't it also a way of achieving something else, Mr Rudd?"

"Achieving something else?"

"Wasn't it a stalking manoeuvre, a way to gain a twelve per cent shareholding in Buckland House?"

"It gave us a twelve per cent shareholding, yes," agreed Rudd. He understood the point of the questioning now. Dray hadn't thought it would be possible to keep it hidden.

"If My Lord were to find in your favour and the Initial shareholding were determined unfair, what would your next action be, Mr Rudd?"

Rudd decided there was no point in attempting to dodge. "I would make a takeover bid for Buckland House, on behalf of Best Rest," he said.

A stir went throughout the court, more obviously among the press but also throughout the spectators and the people in the well. Lady Buckland was staring up at him now, looking affronted at his presumption.

"A stalking manoeuvre," repeated Blair accusingly.

Conscious that he was occupying a platform and could benefit from it, Rudd said, "I believe that with the resources and experience of my organization we could transform Buckland House from what it is now, a collapsing, decaying company, into one with a future, giving investors a proper, secure return upon their money."

"And you are seeking the assistance of this court to help you," said Blair, his voice suddenly loud.

Rudd was not overawed or nervous of the man. "I am asking this court to declare archaic and counter-productive the share structure of an organization being run in an archaic and counter-productive manner," he said, conscious of Dray's head nod of approval.

"British company law was not created to aid entrepreneurial quick profit," said Blair.

"I would hope it was created to ensure the proper running of companies," came back Rudd.

"Don't you think we are digressing into legal philosophy a little, Mr Blair," interrupted the judge.

"My apologies, my Lord," said Blair. To Rudd he said, "There has been earlier evidence alleging inefficient running of the company by Sir Ian Buckland. Do you regard him as inefficient?"

"I think there could be improvements in the running of the company."

"I didn't ask you that, Mr Rudd," said the barrister. "I asked your opinion of Sir Ian's abilities."

"I think he has allowed things to become slack."

"Why then, Mr Rudd, did you compose a subsidiary board to manage the newly purchased liner fleet with Sir Ian as vice-chairman? Is that, too, part of your stalking manoeuvre?"

"I invited Sir Ian on to the board to retain the Buckland House association with the ships, just as I invited another Buckland House director, Sir Richard Penhardy. Sir Ian will be vice-chairman and the company will be run as a board, not a fiefdom."

"Is that how you consider the present situation in Buckland House, a fiefdom?"

"Yes," said Rudd. "I do." He regretted the word.

"Were this action to succeed and were you also successful in your takeover, who would be chairman of the Buckland House board?"

Rudd was aware again of concentration of attention, especially from the Buckland family. "The boards of my companies are democratically constituted and run," said the American easily. "The chairmanship would be a board decision, not an arbitrary one."

Blair sat down, as abruptly as he had done after questioning the merchant banker. With the plans for the takeover disclosed, Dray took the American through the improvement plans he proposed for Buckland House until the judge adjourned for lunch. Because of its convenient closeness, Rudd ate at the Savoy with the prince, Bunch and Morrison. As an afterthought, as he was leaving the law courts into the glare of more photographs, he invited Penhardy to join them. The MP hesitated and then accepted, just as he accepted the invitation at the end of the meal to come that evening to Rudd's apartment. There was another press mêlée when they returned. As they approached the court,

271

they came up behind the Buckland family. Sir Ian, who still had to give evidence, broke away and stood by a corridor window, looking at them. The women ignored them and went into the courtroom. The afternoon was occupied with evidence from Faysel and Smallwood and immediately after the adjournment they walked across Fleet Street to Dray's offices for a review of the day.

"I didn't think it went well," said Rudd, as they seated themselves.

Dray shook his head. "I expected the takeover to come out. It doesn't harm our case. Don't let Blair's histrionics confuse you. I think you made a good impression upon the judge."

"How do you think the day ended on balance?" asked Bunch.

Dray made a see-sawing motion with his hands. "Fifty-fifty," he said. "Tomorrow we'll do better. We're going to win."

In the car detouring to drop Rudd off in Grosvenor Square before taking the Arab on to Ascot, Faysel said, "I'm going to have to go to Vienna next week, for the OPEC talks."

"How long will you be away?" asked Rudd.

"Maybe a week," said Faysel. "Perhaps a little longer."

"Will there be a definite barrel price?"

Faysel nodded. "There'll be a fight, but in the end it'll come down to somewhere around $28 a barrel."

"That would justify the liner purchase at least," said Rudd.

Four pages were devoted to the hearing in the *New Standard*. The Haffaford group watched the early evening television coverage and when it ended Haffaford said, "Blair got it right. It's been a stalking manoeuvre, right from the very first."

"Certainly looks that way," agreed Pryke.

"Cleverly done, too," said White. "The bloody man let us set the pace all the time and padded gently along behind us."

"We're advisers to other hotel groups," reminded Haffaford quietly. "Groups who'd keep us as their bank if we devised a successful counter-bid."

There were smiles from the other men in the room. Snaith said, "How easy would it be?"

"When was the last time there was any property or asset valuation of Buckland House?"

"Ten years ago, at least," said Snaith.

"So those will be the figures upon which Rudd is making his bid," said the merchant bank chairman. "In ten years the value of the hotels in London alone must have doubled. If we carry out a revaluation all we've got to do is wait until he submits his figures and then outprice him: we'll start low and then top him, every time."

Snaith smiled. "There'd be a piquant justice in our following in his footsteps and beating him at the last minute."

Sir Richard Penhardy swirled the brandy around the balloon, taking in the aroma, and then raised the glass to Rudd. "Cheers," he said.

"Cheers," said Rudd.

"Damned glad the shares are suspended," said the MP. "God knows what sort of helter-skelter would have happened today if they hadn't been."

"Dray thinks we can win," said Rudd.

Penhardy gazed at him over the top of his glass, waiting.

"I'm worried about everything being referred to the Monopolies Commisssion," said Rudd.

"It could ruin it," agreed Penhardy.

"You know the Trade Secretary?"

"Very well," smiled Penhardy.

"I want your help," said Rudd. "I don't want any problems from the Office of Fair Trading. If I'm successful, there'll be a lot of board changes at Buckland House. I'd be properly grateful for anything you could do."

"I understand," said Penhardy.

Margaret thought that Rudd had been impressive in court – as impressive as Ian had been at the shareholders' meeting. No, she corrected at once. More so. She'd wanted to smile when they'd looked at each other: wanted there to be a way to show him that she didn't hate him.

"Oh Christ," she said to her reflection in the mirror. "Why are you so bloody weak?"

273

31

Rudd thought the media coverage preposterous, some newspapers committing as much as three pages of photographs and reports, and with the awareness of the witness's list that day the confusion when they arrived at the court was worse than before. Rudd shouldered his way through, stiff-faced against the cameras, ignoring the shouted questions. Bunch had arranged a place for him in the well of the court, away from the Buckland family and just two seats behind the instructing solicitors. When Rudd entered his friend was in deep conversation with Berriman. Bunch saw him and came over.

"Morrison asked me to give you a message," said Bunch. "He's coming later, but he wants to stay at the hotel and talk to New York. He's anxious to see the effect of yesterday when the market opens."

Rudd frowned. "That won't be obvious for hours."

"I told him that. He said he wants to talk to Walker anyway."

Ahead of them Dray entered the court, nodded to them and erected his tiny stand in preparation for the questioning. Rudd turned to his right. Vanessa was helping Lady Buckland into her place. Margaret looked directly at him, her face as blank as before. There was the shouted demand for them to rise for the entry of the judge. Dray remained on his feet, waited until the court settled and then said, "I call Sir Ian Buckland." There was a shuffle of expectation from the press benches.

Buckland took the oath in a steady, measured voice, standing almost to attention and looking respectfully towards the judge. Rudd realized the man was wearing the yacht club tie he had worn for their first meeting. Dray began quietly, taking the man through the basic initial questioning of identity and background and entry into the family business. Then he asked, "What sort of training did you have?"

"Training?"

"You were being taken into an enormously successful business, with a yearly turnover of millions," said Dray. "Predominantly it is hotels. Did you, for instance, undergo any hotel management course?"

Buckland smiled. "No," he said.

"You've told us you attended university?"

"Trinity, Cambridge," confirmed Buckland.

"What did you read?"

"History."

"What was your degree?"

"I got a first in the first tripos," said Buckland. "Then I became ill and went down with an *aegrotat*."

"To fit yourself for the eventual inevitable chairmanship of Buckland House, a company running hotels and liners, you took a degree in history which you didn't manage to complete!" said Dray, the sarcasm perfectly pitched. "Tell me, Sir Ian, an *aegrotat* is a medical certificate accepted as evidence of ill health by the authorities, but isn't it also a recognized and convenient excuse for students who find the pleasures of luncheon clubs and punting on the Cam more attractive than lectures?"

'I was ill," insisted Buckland stubbornly. "My health gave under the pressure of work."

Dray allowed a long pause before he asked the next question. He said, "When did you enter Buckland House?"

"In 1960," said Buckland.

"As what?"

"There was no clearly defined title," said Buckland. "I suppose I was my father's personal assistant."

"To learn at your father's knee?"

"I suppose so."

Dray reached sideways and the prepared junior counsel immediately handed him some documents. From where Rudd sat they appeared old. "I have here copies of minutes of Buckland House board meetings from 1960," said Dray. "They record attendance at board meetings. I have tried and failed to find details of your attendance at more than four in that year."

"My father did not feel it was necessary for me to attend every time."

"Your choice or his?"

"His."

"Even though you were his personal assistant?"

"He was a very self-reliant man."

"Do you regard yourself as self-reliant, Sir Ian?"

Buckland paused. "Yes," he said.

"Quite capable of running the affairs of Buckland House above criticism?"

"I think it would be impossible for a business to be run without criticism from some quarter," said Buckland.

"Capable of running the business with an acceptable degree of criticism then?"

"Yes."

Dray felt out and more papers were handed to him. "According to my instructions, the scheme of arrangement investing thirty-five per cent of the 'A' Initial apportionment into the hands of the Buckland family was made in 1962?"

"I think that was the date," said Buckland.

"After you'd been with the company for two years?"

"Yes."

"As your father's personal assistant, your working life must have been fairly close. Was there much discussion between you, about this scheme?"

"No."

"No, Sir Ian!" said Dray, stressing the surprise. "With the sixteen per cent Preferential holdings, it means that Buckland House is owned by the family and yet you tell my Lord that there was little discussion about it!"

"As well as a self-reliant man, my father was self-willed. It was his way of doing things, to make decisions and then announce them afterwards."

"Did you admire your father?"

Buckland frowned, nervous of the question. "Very much," he said.

"Do you attempt to model yourself upon him?"

"I try to continue the business in the way I think he would have approved."

"Does that extend to doing things – making decisions – and then announcing them afterwards?"

"No," said Buckland positively.

"You see yourself a servant of the company?"

"Yes."

"To serve the best interests of the shareholders?"

Buckland shifted slightly in the witness-box. "Yes," he said again.

"You do not see this scheme of arrangement as jeopardizing those best interests?"

"The shareholders of Buckland House have always seen a dividend return upon their investment," said Buckland. He spoke looking directly towards the press benches. "And they always will," he added.

Dray beckoned a court usher to carry a sheet of paper to Buckland. Dray said, "That is the photostat of a cheque made out to Leinman Properties for the sum of £635,000. Is that your signature?"

"Yes," said Buckland.

"What is the date?"

"3 May."

"What is it for?"

"A loan," said Buckland. He was staring down at the paper.

"To Leinman Properties?"

"To me," said Buckland.

"If it's a director's loan to you, why isn't it made out in your name?"

"It was more convenient this way."

"Convenient?"

"It was in settlement of a debt," said Buckland. "There seemed no point in putting it through my account first." Buckland looked up at last.

"What sort of debt, Sir Ian?"

The pause lasted for several moments. Then Buckland said, "A gambling debt."

"You speak of convenience," said Dray. "Was it your intention to get this sum of £635,000 through the company books listed for some other purpose. Capital investment, perhaps?"

"No," said Buckland. "It was an officially approved loan, by the board. There is a minute to that effect."

"Was there not a need to make that minute retroactive, when the auditors questioned you about the amount?"

"There had been an oversight," said Buckland.

"Oversights seem to be a problem with the board of which you are chairman, don't they, Sir Ian? Wasn't there an oversight in the allocation of a further sum of £150,000?"

"The earlier amount and this figure were fully discussed before the shareholders' meeting and the explanation given fully accepted by the shareholders," said Buckland.

"Regretfully neither myself nor my Lord were able to be present at that meeting and it is for our benefit that I am asking these questions," said Dray. "Would you care to explain the £150,000?"

Buckland turned towards the judge. "The sum was paid to me in advance of the directors' formal vote," he said. "As soon as it was picked up, the matter was formally rectified."

"Just as the £635,000 was rectified, as soon as it was picked up," said Dray.

Buckland said nothing.

"The £150,000 was paid to you on 4 August?"

"Yes," said Buckland.

"Is there a house off Sloane Street owned by the Far East division of your company?" asked Dray.

Buckland was gripping the edge of the witness-box, his knuckles showing white. He was looking towards his family again, concentrating upon his mother. "Yes," he said.

"What is its purpose?"

"Accommodation when necessary for the president or any officers of that division," said Buckland.

"What happens to it when it is not occupied by those people?"

"Usually it stands empty."

"Has that been the case this year?"

Buckland sighed. "For two months of this year I arranged for it to be occupied by a family friend. The Far East division were fully aware of that occupation and a rental was paid."

"That is the explanation you gave to the shareholders, I believe?" said Dray.

Buckland was perspiring, swallowing heavily. "Yes," he said. "And accepted by them."

"Is that family friend Lady Fiona Harvey?"

Buckland stared around the court, as if wondering whether to reply. Then he said, quietly, "Yes."

"Thank you," said Dray and sat down. Buckland stared at the barrister, as surprised as Rudd that the questioning had ended. Rudd leaned to Bunch and said, "I was expecting him to go on."

"There's a damned good reason for not doing so," said Bunch.

Rudd turned to the rigid, taut profile of Margaret on the other side of the court. "I'm glad he stopped," he said.

Lady Fiona Harvey wore what appeared to be a beige chamois suit, beneath a flamboyant three-quarter length fox fur, ruffed at the collar and cuffs with reversed pelts. She had worn a heavily veiled hat as some protection against the photographers outside, but the covering was back now. She had a full, almost puppy-fat face and blue eyes that she was aware of: Rudd guessed the wide-eyed expression was an affectation. Compared to Margaret, Rudd thought she looked awkward and gauche. The voice in which she responded to Dray's early questions was shrilly high.

"How long have you known the Buckland family?" asked the barrister.

"Years," said the woman.

"How many years?"

"I was at Girton with Margaret."

"So the friendship is a family one?"

"Absolutely."

"Absolutely," echoed Dray. He waited for several moments and said, "There was a period this year when you were without accommodation in London?"

"Yes," she said.

"Why?"

She frowned. "Does it matter?"

"Yes, Lady Harvey," said the judge at once. "It does matter."

"I had recently been divorced."

"So what happened?"

She blinked, as if having difficulty in understanding the question and then she said, "Sir Ian and Lady Buckland allowed me to use a house off Sloane Street."

"Did you think it was their house?"

"No, theirs is nearby. I knew it was a company house."

"Who told you?"

"Ian."

"What else did he tell you?"

The woman hesitated and Rudd got the distinct impression of her attempting to remember the right words. "That it belonged to one of his overseas divisions and that I had to pay rent for it."

"Did you?"

"Of course."

"One hundred and twenty pounds a week?"

"Yes."

"Did you make arrangements to pay that amount?"

"Ian brought me a form to sign, for the payments to be made automatically."

"Earlier you said the house was made available by Sir Ian *and* Lady Buckland," reminded Dray. "Lady Margaret seems to have been dropped from your replies."

From beside Dray, Sir Walter Blair came heavily to his seat and said, "There would appear to be an obvious direction to this questioning, my Lord. This is an action under the Company provisions, nothing more. Does it have a point?"

"Sir Henry?" invited the judge.

"If the purpose of this action is to prove the unfair and possibly injurious degree of holding in a public company, then surely the fitness of the person having that holding and the use to which he exercises benefit is very apposite?"

"It would seem a valid argument, Sir Henry," said the judge. "But I would ask you to exercise constraint. This is not a court of morals."

There was a scurry of activity from the press at the court of morals comment.

To Fiona Dray said, "Was your tenancy of the house off Sloane Street agreed between both, or just Sir Ian?"

"Sir Ian," said the woman. "But Margaret knew about it."

"How do you know that?"

Fiona looked desperately towards the Buckland family and to Buckland, who was wedged on to the bench immediately alongside his wife. "He told me," she said.

"You've taken the oath, Lady Harvey," reminded Dray, in preparation of what was to follow.

The woman nodded.

"Why did you occupy the house off Sloane Street?"

"A favour, while I looked for somewhere permanent."

"Have you found somewhere permanent?"

"Not yet."

"Do you still live off Sloane Street?"

"No."

"Why did you leave?"

"I thought it best, in view of all the fuss there has been over the last few weeks."

"Explain to my Lord exactly why you thought it best."

The woman was shifting and moving in the box, as if physically aware of the corner into which she was being backed. "I didn't want there to be any embarrassment," she said. "There was a lot of rumour and innuendo circulating."

"What sort of rumour and innuendo?"

"I would have thought that was obvious," she said, her temper going.

"Nothing is obvious in a court until it has been given in evidence," said Dray. "What sort of rumour and innuendo?"

She looked again at Buckland, briefly. Then she said, "That I was having an affair."

"Were you?"

The silence stretched for several minutes. Then Fiona said, "Yes."

The entire concentration was upon Ian and Margaret Buckland, sitting tight together. Both were as stiff and upright as the bench upon which they sat, gazing straight ahead but with their eyes on no one. Rudd thought they looked as if they could have been carved from stone.

At the shareholders' meeting Kevin Sinclair's attitude had certainly been nonchalant and maybe insolent, but it wasn't his demeanour in the court. He was alertly attentive and polite. Not once, during the fifteen minutes he had given evidence after the lunchtime adjournment, had he looked towards Buckland.

"You have made available to the court the letter you received from Sir Ian Buckland?" said Dray, holding up another photocopy.

The usher carried it across the court. Sinclair looked briefly at it and said, "Yes, that's it."

"You addressed the shareholders' meeting about that letter?"

"It was the proof I had about the letting of the house," said the Australian.

"But it wasn't, was it, Mr Sinclair? Lady Harvey's occupation began in June."

Sinclair caught his lower lip between his teeth and said, "Yes, the letter was confirmation."

"Of what?"

"The arrangement about the house."

"You knew, before July?"

Sinclair nodded.

"How?"

"A telephone call."

"You spoke to the shareholders' meeting about the telephone call, I believe. . . ." Dray put out his hand, got the file and looked up again. "You told the shareholders you received it around 9 or 10 June."

"Somewhere around then."

"That won't do," said Dray, immediately forceful. "The whole point of that telephone call and the whole purpose of your travelling all the way from Hong Kong was to assure the shareholders that you knew and approved *before* the tenancy began. What was *the* date of that telephone call?"

"I can't remember," said Sinclair badly.

"You can't remember!" Dray intruded mockery into the repetition.

"No."

"You don't keep a telephone log?"

"No sir."

"Your secretary wouldn't have a record?"

"It was a private call, between Sir Ian and myself."

"There *was* a call, wasn't there, Mr Sinclair?"

"Yes," said the man tightly.

"But you don't know when?"

"Not exactly, no."

"Could it have been nearer the end rather than the beginning of June?"

"I don't think so."

"But you've told us you can't remember."

Sinclair was flushed, his hands gripping and ungripping the rail. "It could have been towards the end."

"After Lady Harvey's occupation began?"

"I don't know."

"Look at the letter you've provided," invited Dray. "It gives the date of June 18 for the commencement. Could it have been after June 18?"

Sinclair looked at Buckland at last, a forlorn, helpless gesture. "It could have been," he conceded.

32

Herbert Morrison prepared the final stages of his attack upon Rudd with the care and attention to detail that he had devoted over the years to the compilation of the company records and balance sheets in the filing cabinets in the Beacon Hill study. He created charts showing the decline and upheaval in Buckland House since the Best Rest involvement and a matching graph for the effect upon Best Rest. With all the facts before him, the old man waited impatiently until he calculated Grearson would have arrived at his Boston office and put the first call through to Massachusetts. The lawyer came immediately to the telephone and Morrison breathed out, relieved; he was tense with the excitement of what he was doing and didn't want the irritation of delay. He wasn't far away from landing the fish.

"I'm glad you're back," said Morrison.

"It doesn't look good from here," said the lawyer. "My professional advice is to get out, as soon as those damned shares come off suspension."

"What do you reckon my losses?"

"In England, about $750,000. But aggregated with the slide here I'd say your overall portfolio has gone down almost $3,000,000."

Morrison had assessed it nearer $2,800,000, but didn't consider it sufficiently important to argue. Everything had gone exactly as he had anticipated, except for the severe effect upon Best Rest: it was going to take longer for them to recover than he'd planned.

"What's the company loss?" he said.

There was the sound of paper being moved from the other end of the line and then Grearson said, "Since it all began, I'd say Best Rest have lost something approaching $12,000,000 off their share value. And that's a hell of a lot."

Which is exactly what the shareholders would think, calculated Morrison.

"The time difference between where you are and here doesn't help," said Grearson. "The whole court coverage gets a hell of a play and Wall Street is still open. What's it like today?"

Morrison had had the early edition of the evening paper delivered and looked down at the front-page display. "Bad," he said. "Worse than yesterday."

"Why don't we sell, Herb?" pleaded the lawyer. "If we don't move soon we'll be behind a queue a mile long."

"I keep the shares," said Morrison. "But they must be set against any takeover by Best Rest."

"I've told you they are," assured the lawyer. "I think you're mad. Whatever you're doing, I think you're mad. The English lawyer thinks so, too!"

"I'll be back in Boston soon," said Morrison. "We'll talk then."

The second Massachusetts connection was as efficient as the first. More sure of Patrick Walker's habits than those of the lawyer, Morrison booked the call to his partner's house in Lincoln. Walker answered personally.

"I was going to call you," said Walker at once. "We're being turned upside down by this thing."

"I put our losses at something like $12,000,000," said Morrison, with the advantage of the call to Grearson.

"I had our brokers estimate the after-hours trading," said Walker. "The more accurate figure is something like $14,300,000. I've just been listening to an early newscast from London which makes it sound as though that stupid bastard Buckland has been lying into his teeth all along."

"It looks that way."

"What the fuck are we into, Herb? I've got every banker and broker in Wall Street demanding an explanation."

"What about the stockholders?" prompted Morrison.

"That too."

"I think we need to stop the panic, before it begins," said Morrison.

"What the hell are you talking about!" demanded Walker. "It began days ago!"

"Stop it before it goes any further then."

"How?"

"You're the vice-chairman, with the majority of the board with you there in America," said Morrison. "Why don't you convene a special stockholders' meeting?"

"What for?"

"An explanation from Rudd."

There was a hesitation from Walker. "You mean a confidence meeting?"

"I mean whatever the stockholders want to make it," said Morrison. "I wouldn't think it unreasonable to ask for an explanation of a $14,300,000 loss that stands every chance of getting worse."

"Before I do that I need your guidance, Herb," said Walker. "Has it gone wrong?"

This time it was Morrison who hesitated, to convey the impression that he was reflecting on the question. "I think it's a disaster," he said. "It's almost completely out of control."

"Will you come back to say that to the meeting?" said Walker.

"Yes," said Morrison at once.

"Then I'll call it," decided Walker.

"Telephone me tonight," said Morrison.

Morrison had difficulty in replacing the telephone and then realized it was because he was shaking so much, the tremors rippling through him. He was absolutely exposed now, committed to a course from which there could be no retreat. All his life he had been a cautious, even nervous man. Not even Rudd, who knew the extent of his feelings, would have guessed what he'd done. Morrison sniggered and stopped abruptly worried at the nearness of hysteria. It was going to work; he knew it was going to work.

Only Rudd and Morrison returned for the evening conference with Dray. Bunch wanted to remain in court, Hallett went immediately to the Connaught for the business of the day, and Faysel excused himself early for the Saudi Arabian embassy and preparations for the OPEC conference.

"You seemed surprised by the day," said Dray.

Rudd shook his head. "I'm glad you stopped where you did," he said.

"I'm not interested in papers being sent to the Director of Public Prosecutions for possible perjury," said the barrister. "That won't help any takeover. I just wanted to make the lies clear, that's all."

"And were they?" asked Morrison. He'd only got to court for the last hour of the hearing.

"I think so," said Dray.

"It was still like hammering a man to the cross," said Rudd.

Dray frowned. "Buckland provided the nails," he said, unsympathetically.

"How much longer?" said Rudd.

"Blair's not happy," predicted Dray. "I don't expect him to stick to the defence he's planning. There's still some technical stuff but I don't think more than a couple of days."

"I want it over, as soon as possible," said Rudd.

"Today was ours," said Dray confidently. "I don't think you've any cause for concern."

Morrison excused himself from returning to the Grosvenor Square apartment, wanting to be at the Connaught when the call came from Walker after his meeting with the directors in New York. Hallett was waiting when Rudd entered, the telex and tape messages already collated. Bunch had beaten him back from the court, too. Seeing the expressions on their faces, Rudd said, "What's the matter?"

"Haffaford's have announced that acting on behalf of unnamed clients they are opposing any takeover bid you propose; they've issued a statement asking every shareholder to withhold from any offer we make until they've carried out a property revaluation," said Hallett.

"Son of a bitch!" said Rudd bitterly.

"And there's a message from New York saying that the board met today in emergency session following stockholders' concern," added the personal assistant. "They want you back for an explanatory meeting."

"I've only just come back from seeing them!" said Rudd exasperated.

"Not the directors," qualified Hallett. "The stockholders."

287

"What are you going to do?" asked the lawyer.

"Think of a way to fight Haffaford's," said Rudd.

"What about our stockholders?"

"Stall them," decided Rudd.

They rode unspeaking back to Sloane Square, arriving ahead of Vanessa and Lady Buckland. They had to force their way, tight-faced, past the photographers grouped around the door, Margaret ignored Buckland when he suggested a pre-dinner drink in the drawing-room, going immediately upstairs to her dressing-room. She locked the door behind her and then stood with her back to it, eyes closed, breathing deeply. It took a long time for her to recover her composure, but at last she went further into the room. Damn them! she thought. Damn Buckland and damn Rudd.

Margaret felt utterly confused, her normally ordered, reasoning mind misted with uncertainty and contradiction. She put the files entered that day in court on the bureau, with the documentation she'd produced earlier, and stood staring down at it, unfocusing for several minutes. Then she began to read, automatically at first and then with greater concentration, recalling the opening speeches of Rudd's counsel and some of the remarks made by Sir Walter Blair. By the time dinner was announced, Margaret was deeply engrossed in the Formation Articles of Buckland House and the will apportionment and restrictions that had been imposed after the death of Buckland's father. She refused to join the family for dinner, too interested in what she was reading.

33

Before he left for the court Rudd instructed Bunch to obtain an emergency valuation on the London properties and spent the morning listening to Tommy Ellerby recount details of Buckland's gambling. The casino owner admitted the issuing of the company cheque for £635,000 and then, under persistent questioning from Dray, disclosed the date of a second gambling debt sufficiently close to the unapproved withdrawal of the £150,000 to establish a suspicion.

Rudd grew bored with the procession of fund managers indicating their concern at the running of Buckland House and during the lunch adjournment told the barrister he didn't intend remaining in court for the technical arguments and summing up. When he left he saw Buckland was missing as well. The three women were in their accustomed places. They ignored him.

Everyone was waiting when Rudd arrived back at the apartment. "What's the assessment?" he demanded at once from Bunch.

"They're all pleading for more time."

"I haven't got more time, for God's sake!" said the American. "All I asked for was an estimate."

"I provided all the details we had of previous valuations," said the lawyer. "None of the hotels has changed substantially, so using the property price index they're saying seventy-five per cent."

"Jesus!" said Rudd.

Bunch went to some papers before him. "We were thinking in the region of $200,000,000 worldwide," he reminded. "If Haffaford's come in anywhere near this sort of valuation, it would bring the value of the London properties alone to something like $125,000,000."

"Which means you don't stand a chance in hell," said Morrison.

"That's defeatist," said Rudd.

"That's practical," said Morrison. "You were given a fifteen per cent ceiling by the board: you can't come anywhere near a takeover bid now. Let's be thankful we've cut our losses and get out." The revaluation would mean he'd recover most of the $2,800,000 that Grearson had been so worried about.

"They haven't even made a counter-bid yet, for Christ's sake!" said Rudd. "It could be a bluff."

"I don't think it is," said Prince Faysel. "I had a call from Penhardy. He's unsure which side to choose. Apparently Haffaford's are holding out the olive branch but at the moment, apart from ourselves, there are two separate factions, the merchant bankers and then Buckland, Condway and Gore-Pelham."

"Your responsibility is to the Best Rest stockholders now," said Morrison. "Not some personal campaign you can't possibly win."

"It is not a personal campaign," said Rudd. "And it's the stockholders I'm thinking of. We didn't start this to become subsidiary shareholders in someone else's business."

"Neither did we start it to lose over $14,000,000 which is the estimate of what we're down so far. And that doesn't make any allowance for whatever sort of uncertainty is caused in the court today."

The fund managers wouldn't provide such titillating coverage for the newspapers but their views would impress the professionals, realized Rudd. It could lead to more unloading in New York.

"If we back off now then all we've done is made it easy for someone else to move in and make the killing," said Rudd.

"Which is exactly the warning that was given to us in the written opinion by Sir Henry Dray," remembered Morrison. "A warning that was ignored."

Rudd was aware that his father-in-law had avoided the personal accusation. He didn't imagine the stockholders would: they had every reason for anger.

"I think it would make sense to go back to New York," said Bunch, showing his lawyer's caution.

"In the middle of a court case I couldn't avoid that becoming public," said Rudd. "Can you imagine the effect that would have in Wall Street!"

"There's no point in my remaining here any longer," said Morrison. In New York he could orchestrate the whole thing to a crushing finale. Christ, it had been worth it! It had been worth every cent of the expenditure and every minute of the planning. And it wasn't just Angela, he conceded, in belated honesty. It would mean that he could get Best Rest back, from the man who had stolen it.

"Do you want me here?" asked Bunch.

"Yes, while the case is going on," said Rudd.

"It will be difficult for me, immediately," said Faysel. "I've got the Vienna meeting of OPEC beginning at the weekend."

"It isn't going to look good, three directors still absent after the sort of summons that has come not only in the name of the directors, but the stockholders as well," said Morrison.

"You'll have to explain it," said Rudd.

"I didn't have much success last time," said Morrison. "And things are a lot worse now."

The old man was right, thought Rudd. Never in his life had he fouled up as badly as he had now.

It was a private, unrecorded meeting, with no aides or witnesses for either man.

"Can you tell me who you're acting for?" said Buckland.

"No," said Haffaford.

"An English company?"

"I can say that, yes."

"I could still defeat it, if the court finds in my favour."

"We realize that" said the merchant banker. "The cost to Buckland House after all the publicity would probably be disastrous though, don't you think?"

"What would my position be, if the court orders some disposal and I came over to you?"

"I don't know."

"I need some guarantee," said Buckland.

"I can't give that."

"Then I can't give a commitment to you," said Buckland, as forcefully as he could.

"I regret that," said Haffaford. "I regret that very much indeed."

34

The need to think through an effective move against any counter-bid was the predominant reason for not attending the court on the final day, but Rudd conceded to himself the secondary cause, his reluctance to sit through submissions and then judgment upon her husband with Margaret sitting only yards away. He'd never avoided business unpleasantness before. But then there had never been anything like this before. He told Bunch to summon him in time for the decision and remained in Grosvenor Square, trying to think of an answer, slumped on the couch upon which he'd once held Margaret. He remained there a long time and then decided there wasn't one. Morrison had been right. He didn't stand a chance in hell. If the counter-bid for the London property came in at $125,000,000, then worldwide his offer of the two-thirds left would have to be $150,000,000 to stand any chance of consideration, let alone success. And to be able to make that, and possibly go higher still, he couldn't work under a ceiling of fifteen per cent. He couldn't work under any ceiling at all. The only logical thing to do would be to return to America and argue the case before the other directors and if necessary the stockholders and get an agreement for it to be lifted, so he could continue. And stood about the same chance in hell for getting them to agree, after they'd seen the value chipped away from their stock, like a madman whittling a stick. The other obvious avenue would have been Faysel and the Saudi investment fund, but he knew from the Zürich meeting that there was no money available there. He'd failed. He'd tried to get the best, to be the best, and been beaten. He'd been beaten by things he couldn't have anticipated or predicted, so there was no criticism that could be levelled at him. Bullshit, he thought. Stockholders weren't going to be interested in an apologia about convoluted English share structures and unexpected moves by merchant banks. They were going to be interested in retirement pensions and biscuit-tin money they'd put into his care and seen vanish. He's never thought of himself as a man with pride, with a necessity always to prove himself. But it existed. He enjoyed the *Fortune* magazine articles and the recognition in the Four Seasons. And enjoyed, too, getting financial support from a telephone call and boarding at whim company aircraft, to which his father had only ever carried the bags, to fly off to Mexico or the Caribbean or Europe. Failure had never occurred to him. But that's what he was confronting now, he realized. Failure. Complete and abject failure with rejection by the board and by the shareholders and suspicion instead of awe from the bankers and the brokers. He didn't want to fail. It frightened him; it frightened the hell out of him. So how was he going to escape it?

The admission intercom from the street below startled him, as much as the sound of Bunch's voice.

"It's not over," said Bunch.

Rudd was at the door when the lawyer entered the flat, followed by Prince Faysel.

"What happened?" said Rudd.

"A deferred decision," said the lawyer.

"What!"

"The judge said he wanted time to consider the submissions and evidence and so he deferred judgment."

"How long for?" demanded Rudd.

"Monday is a public holiday here in England, so the full week won't be until the following Tuesday. Buckland has called a shareholders' meeting the day after."

"That's more than a week," said Rudd. "That's a week and a half, almost. Didn't Dray object?"

"You don't object to this sort of ruling by an English judge."

"Shit!" said Rudd. "You any idea how this is going to affect the market?"

"The Stock Exchange has already announced that shares remain suspended until the decision," said the Arab.

"And all that protects Buckland House," said Rudd. "What about Best Rest? The stockholders are going to see that as further uncertainty. And it gives Haffaford's perfect time to get their bid together for the Wednesday meeting."

293

"You've got to go back," said Bunch.

"To say what? – Don't worry. I can't even offer them that as reassurance."

"You stayed to think it through, Harry," reminded Faysel.

"And decided nothing," admitted the American. "We want a lever and there isn't one. Nowhere!"

Rudd was aware of the disappointment from the other two men. Pride again, he thought.

"The OPEC meeting is only scheduled for three days," said Faysel. "I'll be back on Monday or Tuesday."

Rudd recognized it as an offer of support, for whatever happened, and smiled gratefully.

"That isn't going to be an easy meeting, either," said Faysel, in an obvious effort to divert them momentarily from their own insoluble difficulties. "If we don't get an oil freeze there isn't going to be any development money available for anyone for years."

" 'Everyone – even the producers – thinks the wells pump money, not oil' " quoted Rudd abruptly.

Both men stared at him, bewildered. "What?" said Faysel.

"The remark in Zürich, by Prince Hassain," remembered Rudd, his voice growing in his excitement. "He said, 'Everyone – even the producers – thinks the wells pump money, not oil.' "

Faysel frowned. "I'm sorry, Harry," he said. "I don't see the significance."

Rudd sat forward on his chair, hands clasped to his face, not responding for several minutes while the idea hardened in his mind. Then he said to Bunch. "How many hotels have Buckland House got in Africa?"

"Eight," said the lawyer at once, without the need to consult any file.

Rudd turned to Faysel. "And which country holds the chairmanship this year of the Organization of African Unity?"

Faysel hesitated and said, "Nigeria."

Rudd became reflective again, nodding to himself in silent contradiction. "Senator Jeplow," he said to Bunch. "Is he on the committee for development aid?"

Bunch went to a file. It took several moments. "Member since 1979," he said finally.

"You going to tell us what this is all about?" demanded Faysel.

"It's about staying in the game and getting Buckland House," said Rudd eagerly. He was excited after the unexpected depression, and he laughed aloud. "I'm coming to Vienna with you for the OPEC meeting," he said to Faysel. "It's not the sessions I'm interested in but afterwards."

"Do I come?" said Bunch.

Rudd shook his head. "I want you here, monitoring the court. And I want to know about the Buckland family, too. When I get back, I want to know where they are, every one of them."

"What about New York and Best Rest?" said the lawyer. "We've got to tell them something."

"There's nothing *to* tell them, until the court decision." insisted Rudd.

"They'll dump you, you know. With every justification," warned Bunch.

"If I don't get it right, I deserve to be dumped," said Rudd.

Morrison decided he had been wrong in his assessment of the support for Rudd: he had expected irritation, anger even, but not to the concentrated degree that every one of the directors was showing towards the man. It was making it far easier than he had imagined it would be.

"It's indefensible," said Walker. "Who the hell does the man think he is?"

"You can't say I haven't warned you," said Morrison.

"You have and we were wrong in not listening," said Böch.

"We've got to be careful," said Ottway, the man who had already lost one business. "It's important the stockholders don't link us with the same discourtesy as he's showing."

"If he wants the rope, let him hang himself with it," said Walker. "I propose we circularize every stockholder with his request for a delay until after the English court decision. It will be in his name and he will be responsible, so he'll be the recognized cause for any further loss."

"That's a good idea," agreed Böch.

"And during that time I think a full report should be prepared for the stockholders, setting out the case," said Morrison. "This whole thing is a story of someone being seized by a delusion of his own grandeur."

"Rudd's got a lot to answer for," said Böch.

"And he will," said Morrison. "He will." He decided to visit Angela's grave when he got back to Boston that night. It had been a long time since he'd been there.

35

Since the embarrassing terrorist seizure in Vienna of Sheikh Yamani and other OPEC oil ministers, the security in the Austrian capital had been quadrupled. Faysel was confident he could obtain observer's permission for Rudd, but the American decided against it, unwilling to draw any attention to his presence. Instead he watched the proceedings in his suite at the Sacher hotel. Despite Faysel's extensive briefings, he was still surprised by the degree of back-up for each spokesman. It was difficult to get an accurate assessment from the television coverage, but Rudd guessed that each front man entered the baroque conference hall to take his place behind the designating national flag with a support team of thirty advisers. And unseen behind them, he knew, were analysts and accountants and bankers and a secretariat. Faysel was part of the Saudi team, with Prince Hassain the deputy to the minister, and Rudd several times caught brief glimpses of both of them during the camera sweeps. He concentrated more upon the Nigerian contingent on the far side of the rectangular table arrangement. The division between the groups was more than physical. There was the predictable plea for price restraint from the Saudis, stressing the consumer demand cut of twenty-five per cent, opposed by the equally predictable rebuttal by Libya and Algeria and Nigeria who maintained that the oil glut had been as artificially engineered as the Western cut-backs and that one would be absorbed by the other when the energy conservation relaxed.

"The man's name is Samuel Odingo," identified Faysel, at the end of the first session. "He's the deputy director of Nigeria's development fund. A tall man, third row from the front, not wearing national costume."

"What was the response?" said Rudd. They were eating in the

Frances Karna restaurant. Twice Faysel had acknowledged other people from the conference.

"Reserved," said Faysel. "The feeling between us is very strong."

"Surely there was some indication?"

"Tomorrow," said the Arab.

The following day Rudd sat again before the hotel television, able from Faysel's description to isolate the Nigerian he had come to Vienna to meet. Rudd couldn't understand the commentary and was impatient anyway at the inactivity. Hallett monitored the business tapes and calculated that the uncertainty created by the British court deferment had cost Best Rest another $1,000,000.

"Now it seems to have steadied," reported the personal assistant.

"Thank Christ for that," said Rudd. He considered calling Bunch in London, but realized it would be pointless, just time-filling. The lawyer knew where he was and if there was any need could telephone him soon enough. Faysel's summons came during the afternoon.

"Still reserved," said the Arab. "But he's agreed."

"When?"

"Tonight. You're going to him. He's at the Palais Schwarzenberg."

Rudd had judged that his approach would be sufficiently intriguing to get a meeting, but he still felt relief. And satisfaction, too, at the prospect of doing something after two wasted days. He was early arriving in the Schwarzenbergplatz and waited until just before the appointment time before announcing himself. He was still kept for a further fifteen minutes. When he was finally admitted to Odingo's suite, there were two aides and someone whom Rudd guessed was a male secretary in the room with him.

The Nigerian was a tall man, immaculately dressed in a Western-style suit, and he greeted Rudd in carefully modulated English. Oxford, Rudd remembered, from Hallett's fact sheet; the man had a triple first in economics.

"I've not been aware of you before, as part of the Saudi investment fund," said the Nigerian. The handshake had been perfunctory and he had about him an aloof, patronizing manner.

"I'm a member of the controlling board, not its finance negotiating committee," said Rudd.

"I know your credentials," smiled Odingo, wanting to show his preparation. "And there is a personal recommendation from Prince Faysel."

Rudd looked to the other people in the room. "Then Prince Faysel will have told you this was a request for a strictly private meeting."

"Yes," said the Nigerian, making no attempt to dismiss the other Africans.

"Which is why I came alone," said Rudd. He refused to become irritated by the man's arrogance.

Odingo hesitated, then gave a dismissive gesture and the three men filed out. "Were it not for Prince Faysel, I would not see you like this," said the Nigerian.

Rudd nodded. "I am not here as a member of the investment fund," he said.

"What then?"

"A private individual," said Rudd. "But I am aware from being a member of that investment fund how money committed to your country's expansion has had to be curtailed."

Odingo's face stiffened at the reminder. "Yet they sit in conference rooms lecturing on the need for fiscal maturity!" he said. "These same people who promise money with one hand and trap us into development contracts, then take it away with another. How else are we expected to meet our commitments, if it is not through increasing the price of our own oil?"

"It's a difficult problem," agreed Rudd. "There are other countries, of course, who might be prepared to fill the gap."

Odingo came forward, looking intently across the space separating them, the condescension slipping away. "There is the Soviet Union," he agreed. "But if we were to turn to the East then the assistance we already receive from America would be stopped. That's been made very clear."

"I was thinking of American, not Soviet aid," said Rudd.

Odingo's head was to one side, the expression one of curiosity. "Washington's grant was for $60,000,000, over a two-year period," he said. "Because of the Saudi cut-back, we've had to draw fully upon that. It's exhausted."

"Have you sought an increase?"

"Of course," said Odingo impatiently. "And been refused there, too."

"What if it were possible to change the American attitude?" said Rudd.

"You're an emissary?" seized Odingo.

Rudd shook his head. "A businessman with many contacts," he said.

Odingo smiled. "We live in a hard, cruel world, Mr Rudd," he said. "I abandoned any belief in altruism a long time ago."

"This approach isn't altruistic," admitted Rudd.

"So what is it you want?"

Rudd told him.

Odingo laughed, a snigger at first and then a burst of amusement. "What on earth do you want that for?"

"You have committed yourself to development and now need money to complete," said Rudd. "I have committed myself to a course of action and this would help me to complete."

"What if the countries were to take the suggestion seriously and go through with it?"

"It's a risk," conceded Rudd. "But an acceptable one, in the circumstances in which I find myself. If I'm successful I intend changing the operation throughout Africa anyway, with diversification into government participation."

"Have I your assurance on that point?"

"Absolutely," said Rudd.

"So there could be no embarrassment to Nigeria?"

"None," said the American.

"Can you guarantee an increase in the American loan?"

"I cannot guarantee it," admitted Rudd. "I can guarantee the most influential lobbying possible in Washington, lobbying that rarely fails."

Odingo looked down into his lap, considering the proposition.

"This session of OPEC is going to end in a compromise," said Rudd. "Saudi Arabia can easily afford to continue undercutting. With its reserves it can also afford to glut the market. There's not going to be any money available from them for a year, maybe two."

Odingo's head came up in immediate offence. "Are you presenting me with an ultimatum?"

300

"To present ultimatums a man has to have strength," said Rudd easily. "What strength do I have? I'm just emphasizing the facts that exist."

"And they are?"

"That you've got absolutely nothing to lose and everything to gain."

Odingo smiled, an unexpected, bright expression. "That's what I was thinking," he said. "The timing will be important?"

"Vital," agreed Rudd. "The conference opens in Lusaka on the Monday. It must come during the opening, presidential address."

Odingo nodded. "I could ensure that."

"I could go to Washington tomorrow."

"We have an understanding then?" said the Nigerian.

"We have an understanding," confirmed Rudd.

The time difference with Europe worked in their favour, so Hallett was able to trace Senator Jeplow while it was still late afternoon in Washington. Rudd took the call and arranged the meeting for the following day in the American capital. He dined again with Faysel, briefing him fully on the meeting with Odingo, while Hallett spoke to Bunch in London to warn him of their intended return to London late on Thursday. Rudd and his personal assistant took the first available flight from Vienna, staging at Switzerland before the long haul across the Atlantic.

This time it was Rudd who made the suggestion, once they got into the senator's office. "Why don't we stroll in the garden?" he said.

Rudd walked head down, speaking in even, measured tones, revealing that he knew all about Jeplow's involvement in the Saudi oil embargo and the deal which the administration had made to get the Arab agreement. The senator's control was superb. There was no outburst or reaction; not even a change in the pace that he was maintaining, by Rudd's side.

"The President could probably withstand the disclosures," said Rudd. "But the mid-term state elections are very close. I would foresee a lot of changes in states with strong Jewish votes, wouldn't you?"

301

"Yes," admitted Jeplow. His voice lacked the usual artificial exuberance.

"And the international repercussions would be severe; I doubt if the embargo could be maintained."

"Did you come to Washington to have a discussion with me about political philosophy, Mr Rudd?"

"No." They reached the edge of the rectangle and turned right.

"What is it that you want?"

In the same even voice, Rudd detailed his request. He was aware of Jeplow straightening beside him, as if in relief.

"That doesn't seem unreasonable," said Jeplow.

"I don't consider it so," agreed Rudd.

Jeplow stopped at the re-entry to the office. "We're going to have to trust each other, aren't we?"

"That's always been a requirement, senator."

"*Can* I trust you, Mr Rudd?"

"Absolutely," said Rudd. "Can I trust you, senator?"

"I think so," said Jeplow.

After the meeting with the politican Rudd drove straight back to Dulles airport, for the first available flight to London.

"How do you think they'd react in New York if they knew we'd been here?" said Hallett as the flight cleared and the pilot set course eastwards.

"Outrage," said Rudd. "And they're reacting like that anyway."

It was midnight before they got back to Grosvenor Square, sag-shouldered with fatigue. Bunch was waiting for them.

"How did it go?" said the lawyer.

"As good as I could have hoped, I suppose," said Rudd. "I shan't really know until Monday." He felt very tired.

"The slide steadied a bit in New York but it's still pretty bad."

"I know," said Rudd. "We monitored it in Vienna. And again today in Washington."

"Faysel's back," said Bunch. "He's called from Ascot. Said he's available if you want him. Oil prices were pegged for three months, by the way."

"That'll put the pressure on Nigeria," said Rudd.

"I've got virtual confirmation of the revaluation from Penhardy," said Bunch. "It's limited to the London properties and Haffaford's people are putting it at $120,000,000."

"Not quiet as bad as we predicted," said Hallett.

"Bad enough," said Rudd. "What else?"

"Penhardy is still uncertain which way to jump," said Bunch. "We talked today. According to him, Sir Ian and his wife, Vanessa and the mother are gathering at Cambridge this weekend. Some sort of conference in advance of the court decision."

Rudd stretched wearily. "I'm going to try to do a deal," he announced.

"Who with?" said Bunch.

"The Buckland family," said Rudd.

"I knew he was a swine. I always knew he was a swine." Vanessa had drunk too much wine with dinner and her words were blurring.

"Everything wrecked," said Lady Buckland. "In less than a year, everything destroyed."

"That's an exaggeration, mother," said Buckland. "We haven't lost yet."

"It'll never be the same again," said the old lady. "It can't be."

"The company will continue to exist, whatever the outcome of the hearing."

"And what part will be left for us to play in it?" demanded Lady Buckland.

"Do you know what I think!" said Vanessa. She was swirling the brandy around her glass, watching the liquor hold and form legs down the sides.

"What?" said Margaret.

"I think Rudd is homosexual, too. Doesn't he strike you as being homosexual?"

"No," said Margaret. "I didn't get that impression."

"Homosexual," she insisted drunkenly. "Definitely homosexual."

36

Rudd was waiting for the landmark, and saw the lake as the vehicle topped the hill. Then the car started to descend the other side and just as abruptly he lost it. Not long now; maybe ten minutes. Was he contravening any legal rule, coming here before the case ended? He frowned at the uncertainty. Perhaps he should have checked with Dray. But Dray would have seen it as trickery; maybe even forbidden it. Too late now, either way. He was confronting so many risks that one more didn't matter very much.

The car turned off the main road to the minor lane and immediately picked up the meandering, looping perimeter wall, yellow-bricked and mottled with moss. Beyond he could just discern the top of the trees and wondered if it were the wood against which he'd seen the deer, when he'd ridden with Margaret. There wouldn't be any unsteady horse-rides and snatched, embarrassed kisses today. How would she react at seeing him? She didn't hate him, Rudd decided. There'd had to be the stern-faced court aloofness but he knew she didn't hate him. He'd make contact, when everything was over: talk things through, quietly and sensibly. It had been natural for her to erupt as she had, when he'd told her in the apartment. Definitely didn't hate him, he thought again.

The gates were open but Rudd saw movement at the lodge window as they went through. He would have passed too quickly for any recognition, he decided. The park spread out before him on either side of the parade of trees, a soft, tranquil place where nothing harsh or brutal could ever happen. The house rose up in front of him, massively squat and sure of itself.

The notification from the gatehouse would have gone to the servants, not to the family, but there was always the possibility that one of them might look from the window out of curiosity at the approaching car. Rudd stayed deep in the back until it pulled up in front of the door and then emerged hurriedly, not waiting for the driver. The bell echoed, deep inside. Holmes answered, and for a moment there was no recognition, then the uncertainty registered in the man's face.

"Sir Ian's expecting me," lied Rudd.

"He said nothing. . ." stumbled the man.

"There's an appointment," insisted Rudd, moving forward.

Accustomed always to taking instructions, the butler moved back and Rudd gained the entry that he wanted.

"Where is he?" demanded Rudd.

"If you'll wait, sir, I'll tell him you're here," said Holmes, recovering.

Rudd stayed where he was in the huge open hallway, not moving until he saw the door towards which the man was heading. He reached it in time to hear Buckland say "He's what!" from the other side and then he was in the room. They were all there. Lady Buckland was on the settee beside Margaret and Vanessa was at the window, staring out at the car as if she expected Rudd to be in it. Buckland was standing between the women. He looked beyond the butler as Rudd entered the room, eyes bulging with outrage.

"What the hell do you think you're doing here!"

At Buckland's shout they all turned. Holmes started to move back to the door with his arm out in an ushering movement and then hesitated, looking back to Buckland.

"I want to talk," said Rudd.

"Get out!" said Buckland, voice low in his fury. "If you don't get out then I'm going to call the police and have you arrested."

"And risk even more publicity?" chanced Rudd.

"Sir?" asked Holmes.

"You bastard," said Vanessa, from the window. "You arrogant, conceited bastard."

"Listen to me," said Rudd, "Just listen."

"There's nothing we ever want to hear from you," said Lady Buckland.

Rudd looked to the woman. At their previous meeting there had been a haughty uprightness about her. Now she seemed bowed, smaller even, and very old.

"Then you'll lose Buckland House," said Rudd.

The remark got through, as he hoped it would Buckland shook his head dismissively to the butler and said, "What do you mean?"

Rudd didn't reply at once. Instead he looked from Lady Buckland to Margaret. She was gazing at him as expressionlessly as she had done every day in the courtroom, as if she couldn't see him.

"I said, what do you mean?" repeated Buckland.

Rudd broke away, going back to the man. "At the moment you *have* lost, either way," he said. "If the court ruling is that you dispose of your share apportionment, then with it goes your control. And if it isn't the ruling, then Haffaford's will make another resignation demand at the shareholders' meeting next week. And after the evidence in court, there wouldn't be the support there was last time. Not from the floor, nor from me, nor from Prince Faysel, nor from the other directors. "You'll be voted from office and Haffaford's people will go ahead with the takeover. You'll have lost everything."

"Because of you," said Vanessa venomously. "Because of what you did!"

"What I did, ultimately, will save the company," said Rudd. "Surely to God you heard enough at the shareholders' meeting and in court to realize that!"

"All I've heard is filth, dredged up and thrown by you, to disgrace this family," said the woman.

"I didn't disgrace this family," insisted Rudd quietly.

It was the old lady who intruded. "You made us think we could save the situation," she said. "All you've spoken about is losing."

"I wanted you to understand the alternative," said Rudd.

"Alternative to what?" The question came from Margaret. Her voice was neutral, the words clipped and precise.

"Our becoming friends again," said Rudd simply.

The Buckland family gazed up at him in varying degrees of astonishment: even Margaret's mask slipped. She frowned and it made her face look haggard.

"Friends! With you!" sneered Vanessa.

"Yes," said Rudd. "It's the way you can survive. The only way."

"Make yourself clear, man, for God's sake," said Buckland.

"Anticipate the court decision," said Rudd urgently. "And move ahead of it. You heard the legal arguments. I've read transcripts of them. The likelihood of the judge finding in your favour has got to be less than fifty per cent. So dispose of your controlling Initial shareholding."

"To you?" anticipated Buckland.

Rudd nodded. "To me and to Best Rest."

"Jesus!" said Vanessa. "After what you did!"

Rudd fought hard for control against her attitude. "Why don't you listen for a moment?" he said. "Why don't you stop posturing and think constructively about what I'm saying and realize what it would mean to you all?"

Vanessa flushed, her face trembling with anger, but she didn't speak.

"Where's our advantage in doing that?" said Buckland.

"We could announce it, at the shareholders' meeting. You could declare your support for the Best Rest takeover and urge the shareholders to accept it. . . ."

Buckland was shaking his head uncertainly.

". . . . and I would also announce my complete faith in you, to continue as chairman," said Rudd. "There would need to be board changes, but you could remain exactly as you are. And the name would remain, Buckland House. I'll introduce the efficiency that's been lacking and you'll run a successful business."

"You'd expect me to do all this, on your promise?"

"No," said Rudd. "On a firm contractual guarantee."

"Any conditions?"

"Only that you stop gambling. Any gambling debts laid off against the company would nullify the contract and I'd fire you."

Buckland blinked at the bluntness.

"It would not be our company any longer," said Lady Buckland.

"The family would remain major shareholders," said Rudd. "It would make no practical difference."

"Except that you'd be in control," said Vanessa, still bitter.

"If I'm not, somebody else will be," said Rudd. "And they won't make the offer to you that I am."

307

"It would not work," said Buckland. "Not unless you greatly increase your offer. Haffaford's have swamped you with their revaluation."

"That might not be insuperable," said Rudd.

"You'd top Haffaford's?"

It wasn't the time to let them know of any difficulties. "Yes," he said.

"You talked of us winning," said Margaret. "It seems to me that you do, either way."

It was a remark he would have expected from Vanessa, not from her. "So do you," he said. "You lose restrictive control, that's all."

"In many ways, Mr Rudd, you remind me of my husband," said Lady Buckland.

Her son looked sharply at her and then back to the American. "You expect us to decide at once?"

"There isn't a lot to decide," said Rudd. "And there are only two working days for the lawyers before the shareholders' meeting."

"We'd like to talk alone."

"I know the way to the library," said Rudd.

He crossed the hall and entered the book-lined room in which he'd finalized the details of the ship purchases with Buckland. It seemed a long time ago. He walked slowly along the shelves, stopping occasionally to identify a title, wondering if they had all been read or were there as room decoration, like pictures or prints. Apart from Vanessa, it hadn't been as hostile an encounter as he had expected. Margaret's look of haggardness had surprised him; she must have suffered inwardly more than them all, because of the evidence that had come out in court. There was some sort of crazy irony in hurting the person he most wanted to protect.

It was an hour before Holmes came for him, and as soon as Rudd re-entered the drawing room he was caught by the impression of a division between the family, a separation of Margaret from the others. He looked curiously between them, noticing that Margaret was flushed. So too, was Buckland. The man said, "You were right. In the end there isn't a lot to decide. We are prepared to release fifteen per cent of our Initial holdings."

"And publicly support the Best Rest takeover at the meeting?" pressed Rudd.

"Yes."

"Then we've a deal," said Rudd. He thrust out his hand. Buckland looked at it for several moments, then responded. The reluctance was obvious.

"We're placing a great deal of trust in you, Mr Rudd," said Lady Buckland. "From what's happened in the past, there seems little reason to justify it."

Rudd avoided looking at Margaret. "You won't regret it," he said.

"I'd have liked a choice," said Vanessa.

The first speech was private, before a planning division of the American Foreign Relations committee, but because it was a condition of the agreement with Rudd, Senator Jeplow ensured it was leaked for the widest possible newspaper coverage. Africa, he said, was one of the most important areas of the world, a continent in which the major proportion of the hemisphere's strategic metals were located and as such the target of Soviet expansion and manipulation. That expansionism and attempted manipulation should be confronted. America should cease to regard Africa as unimportant: rather, it should do its utmost to inculcate western – by which he meant American – ideals of freedom. The most effective way that could be achieved was to increase their aid commitment considerably. Nigeria was a case in point; unless they acted positively, a pivotal country, rich in oil, but in need of development help, was going to look elsewhere. It was a successful plea, resulting in a $50,000,000 aid increase to Lagos.

The second speech was public and because of its content received widespread publicity. In the opening address of the annual conference of the Organisation of African Unity in Lusaka, the Nigerian president launched a diatribe against capitalist organizations and companies of the West which were still able, despite their hard-won independence, to exercise influence and control within member countries. Warnings had been given and ignored. So they had been given again. Member

309

countries should oppose the rape of their resources. Hotels were a case in point. Yearly thousands of tourists visited Africa, spent their money and departed. And their money departed, too, into the profits of the western owners. There were four major hotel chains throughout the continent, all American-owned. And one British. At a penstroke of government decree they could be nationalized and the income channelled where it rightfully belonged, into the exchequers of the country for whose beauty and appeal the tourists came in the first place. Hotel nationalization became a popular subject at the conference. By the end of the first day – the Monday before the court's decision over Buckland House – delegations from four African countries had spoken in support.

The newspaper coverage of the result of the case was more intense than at any time during the hearing, so Rudd decided against attempting to put himself close to the Buckland family; it could have resulted in speculation and he wanted the surprise at the shareholders' meeting to be absolute. Mr Justice Godber's judgment was a written one and long, exploring both arguments and including an erudite review of company law, because he was a nervous man unhappy at having his decisions contested before the Court of Appeal. The conclusion, he insisted, was irrefutable upon the evidence. There had been proven serious doubts about the running of the company. And unquestionably the scheme of arrangement governing the control of Buckland House was archaic, ill-formed and detrimental to the best interests of shareholders. He ordered the family into disposal sufficient to achieve a democratic distribution.

During the crush to leave the court, Rudd managed to intrude himself next to Margaret. Confident the hubbub would cover the words, he whispered, "I want to see you."

She continued on out of the court as if she hadn't heard him.

37

The Stock Exchange Council's suspension of the Buckland House shares lifted with the end of the hearing. By the time of the shareholders' meeting, after two days of nationalization threats from Africa, the Buckland holdings were marked down to 70p a share. The selling was in Ordinary, the least powerful, and Rudd decided against any intervention.

The meeting was at the Berridge as before, and as before the Buckland family used the staff corridors to reach the ballroom, entering after everyone else was seated. From his place at the end of the directors' table, Rudd gazed down at Margaret. As she sat down she looked towards him: she appeared about to smile, her face relaxing, and then she changed her mind. He nodded but she looked away. There was a murmur of curiosity from the floor as Buckland walked steadily in front of the stage and then up the steps at the side. Snaith and Smallwood were at the far end. Then came Condway. Beyond the vice-chairman was a space for Buckland. On Buckland's left sat Gore-Pelham, then Penhardy, with Prince Faysel next to Rudd.

When Buckland reached his place he remained standing, hammering for quiet. It was several moments before it was achieved. Buckland tapped the microphone to ensure the sound was on and said, "The last few weeks of this company have not been happy ones."

There were isolated sounds from throughout the hall, laughs of sarcasm, and Rudd realized Buckland had lost the unanimity of support among the small holders that he'd enjoyed at the previous meeting. Buckland seemed aware of it, too, pausing.

He coughed and went on. "Because of what has happened, there can be no one in this hall who is unaware of the most intimate details of myself, my family and this company. It would be easy to form the impression – perhaps inevitable – that I was

311

unconcerned at the possible harm I did to this company. That would be a wrong conclusion. Difficult though it may now be to accept, at no time did I intend to jeopardize the wellbeing of Buckland House. That it has been jeopardized is obvious from today's share quotations. For that I apologize. . . ." He stopped again. At the far end of the table Snaith and Smallwood both had settled, satisfied expressions. Not long now, thought Rudd.

"I fully recognize the mistakes I have made," said Buckland. "I recognize too, that the running of Buckland House has been in recent years as archaic as a judge has declared the share structure. I am still chairman of this company and face my responsibilities in attempting to rectify what has become in a surprisingly short time a dangerous situation. Buckland House needs modernizing. It needs greater efficiency and greater management expertise. . . ."

Snaith and Smallwood were frowning now and Condway had his head twisted, looking up at the chairman.

"I would like you today to understand that this recognition was reached *before* the court decision. . . ." said Buckland. He nodded in Rudd's direction. "The court hearing was begun at the instigation of our newest director against whom I feel no personal animosity. During the hearing, he made it clear that his purpose in bringing the action was the improvement of this business. That I believe. He also made it clear that if he were successful, then he would be making a takeover bid on behalf of his American company. . . ."

The ballroom was completely quiet now, everyone conscious that he was about to say something of importance.

"I further believe," said Buckland, "that this takeover would be in the best interests of Buckland House."

The noise began, first from the hall and then along the table. Rudd heard Snaith shout, "A point of order. . . ." before being drowned by the renewed hammering of Buckland's gavel. "Everyone will have the opportunity to speak," shouted Buckland. "First give me the opportunity to finish. It is because I seek first and foremost the best interests of Buckland House that my family and myself have already disposed of the shares judged to represent an unfair holding. The Buckland family has already signed legal undertakings under which fifteen per cent of its

Initial holdings have been purchased by Mr Rudd, Prince Faysel and by Best Rest. . . ."

"Trickery!" shouted Snaith, bursting to his feet. "This is trickery, *against* the interests of shareholders and I will not be silenced!"

Buckland hesitated, moved the microphone along the table and said, "I give the floor to Mr Snaith."

The merchant banker snatched at the microphone. His other hand was opening and closing in tiny snatching movements at his side. "Today's share quotation is 70p," he said. "It has been driven that low because of the lack of confidence in the governing of this company by a man whose character and behaviour have regaled and titillated every newspaper reader in the world in recent weeks. Sir Ian talks about responsibility and having the best interests of Buckland House at heart. The only interests he has at heart are his own. We have yet to hear the financial details of the American offer, but in anticipation of that offer my bank have carried out a revaluation of Buckland House's London holdings. At today's prices, the five hotels are worth £57,000,000. I demand on behalf of the shareholders to know what price Rudd is offering."

Rudd rose, moving the microphone at his end of the table nearer to him. "I am delighted to make clear what I am offering," he said. "Buckland House is the best and most prestigious hotel chain in the world. I am offering to keep it so."

"Answer the question!" shouted Snaith.

"The accusation is of trickery," said Rudd. "Yet you are glibly asked to consider only one division of Buckland House, at £57,000,000, when considering whatever offer I might make. Trickery. . . ." he repeated. "Yet no mention is made of the predominant reason why today's valuation is 70p a share. It is not because of a recent court action. It is because of decisions now being made in Lusaka, decisions from which it seems likely that Buckland House will lose eight of its properties. My offer will be for Buckland House worldwide, not piecemeal. And it will *include* the African holdings, which may or may not be retained. If there is trickery here, then it is in putting forward an inflated figure for England and asking you to multiply it by the worldwide divisions, which is not applicable."

"A figure," Snaith called out. "Give us a figure!"

"I am prepared to offer 60p Ordinary, 140p Preferential and £10 for the Initial holdings," announced Rudd.

"Ridiculous," said Snaith at once. He grabbed the microphone. "That is at least a third below what it should be," he said urgently. "It's ludicrous."

"It is double today's valuation," said Buckland, rising. "From the chair I urge you to accept."

"I am not satisfied with the legality of the share disposal," said Snaith, with renewed urgency. "We have been assured that the court's ruling has been complied with, but no proof has been produced. And even if there were proof, then it seems to me that the power has not been distributed to the benefit of everyone, but juggled sideways to maintain the monopoly that has always existed. I propose a postponement of this meeting so that what has happened can properly be examined by independent legal experts."

Rudd had expected the support to come automatically from Smallwood but instead it was Condway who took the microphone. "I second," he said. "I do not think we can proceed with takeover discussions until this other matter has been satisfactorily concluded."

Rudd saw the divisions were being decided. Condway had come down on the side of city respectability. Which left Penhardy and Gore-Pelham. And a lot more besides.

"Proof is obviously and clearly available," said Buckland. "Share certificates are being obviously reassigned, which is why they cannot be produced here today. But I give my word of honour that there has been a fifteen per cent dispersal. This postponement request is a pointless, delaying tactic, the only result of which will be further damage to our share stability and inevitably damage to you, the shareholders."

"Why the hurry?" demanded Smallwood, coming to the microphone for the first time.

"For the stability!" said Buckland, exasperated. "We're being quoted at 70p per share, for God's sake!"

Snaith had been making a calculation in one of his inevitable notebooks. "An offer of 140p a share values the London properties at £34,000,000," he said. "That *cannot* be accepted."

"Now who's resorting to trickery!" demanded Rudd. "There is no conceivable way you can make a calculation like that. My offer is worldwide, not restricted to England."

Gore-Pelham finally got to his feet. "I agree that there should be a postponement of this meeting," he said.

Rudd stared along the table towards Penhardy, the only director yet to declare himself. The MP had his head bent over the table, looking at some scribbled notes on some papers before him. He made no move towards the microphone.

The seating arrangements were the same as they had been at the earlier meeting and from the investment fund section a man rose and said, "If the African properties are nationalized, what is the potential loss to this company?"

Buckland responded eagerly to the question, prepared for it. "The last valuation in Africa was carried out three years ago," he said. "Upon that valuation the cost would be a minimum of £24,000,000."

Another fund manager rose, addressing himself to Rudd. "Do you guarantee that your offer includes those properties? That you won't seek a reduction in share pricing if there is a takeover?"

"A firm and absolute guarantee," said Rudd. He turned along the table. "I invite a similar undertaking from anyone whom Mr Snaith's bank might be representing."

"I have said nothing about us representing counter-bidders," said Snaith.

"Aren't you?" demanded Rudd.

The exchange caught Snaith wrong-footed. He looked down to Smallwood as if expecting help from the finance director and then said, "It is possible that there might be other interests."

"Which have not been declared to this meeting!" said Rudd triumphantly.

The fund manager who had spoken first from the hall rose again and said, "If we lose the African properties, then 140p a share is a good offer."

"But not if we don't," said Condway.

It was time for pressure, Rudd decided. "I have given the guarantee," he said. "But it cannot be an open-ended one. I am restricting the tender to two weeks."

"An ultimatum," shouted someone from the hall.

"No," rejected Rudd at once. "Enough damage has been done to Buckland House. As the chairman has already said, the urgency now is for stability."

"Postponement motion to the vote," urged Snaith.

Buckland looked into the hall, inviting further comment, and when none came he moved the motion. The stewards who had maintained the privacy of the meeting acted as tellers, moving along from row to row. The voting took several minutes. Margaret and Vanessa were twisted in their seats, trying to get some assessment.

"Directors to vote," said Buckland.

Rudd was concentrating entirely upon Penhardy. The MP looked to his right for the in favour indication from Condway, Gore-Pelham, Snaith and Smallwood. He kept his hands firmly upon the table.

"Against?" said Buckland.

The directors' division was evenly split. Buckland passed the figures along to Snaith's end of the table, for the banker to see them first and then rose. He said, "The postponement motion has been lost, by 2800 votes to 1800. I repeat from the chair what I said earlier: I recommend acceptance of the Best Rest offer of 140p a share."

Snaith was already on his feet. "I intend that the disposal be questioned, before a court. I give notice that we will seek to declare invalid the agreement reached between the Buckland family and certain directors.

"Damn the man!" said Rudd quietly to Faysel.

"It was predictable," said the Arab.

"I still hoped they wouldn't think of it," said Rudd.

Walter Bunch listened patiently while Rudd gave a detailed account of the shareholders' meeting and then said. "You were wrong, setting the tender limit. All Haffaford's have got to do now is stall us beyond two weeks."

Rudd shook his head. "After then we'd have lost anyway. We can't hope the shares to stay down beyond two weeks, certainly not now that the counter-bid is public knowledge."

"There's Africa," said Faysel. "Only we know that's not a threat."

"People will be ready to gamble if it doesn't happen immediately," said Rudd. He turned to Penhardy. "What about the Monopolies Commission?"

"I'm pretty sure we're all right, unless Condway and Snaith start building up too much pressure," said the MP. "It's a two-edged sword and they realized it; we can make the same demand, against whatever hotel chain they bring in to make the other offer. But if we're not careful there's going to be Parliamentary discussion about the whole thing. It's bloody messy."

Hallett came hurriedly into the apartment from the Connaught, his face more flushed than usual. "I thought you'd want to see this right away," he said, offering Rudd the telex slip.

It was a long message and Rudd stayed bent over it for several minutes. Then he looked back up to the other men in the room and said, "I'm summoned home to explain myself before the shareholders a week from today."

"It won't be over by then," said Faysel.

"It might," said Rudd.

Hallett stood expectantly, waiting for him to continue, but Rudd said nothing.

"It would have been a bad tactic to talk about the Best Rest problems in front of Penhardy," said Rudd. "I'm still not sure of him and it would have defeated us if he'd leaked it back to Haffaford as an entry bargain for joining them."

Only Bunch and Hallett remained in the apartment now. The lawyer said, "What's it matter? Morrison and Walker and the others have castrated you." He picked up the message, looking at the section that Rudd had not read out earlier. "How can you make a takeover when they make it quite clear they won't honour the cheques you issue? You can't even take up what the Buckland family is releasing to you in the company name."

"I won't buy them in the company name," said Rudd. "I'll make it a personal purchase."

"You've already spent something like $3,500,000," reminded Hallett. "You're committed to $2,000,000, on what was going to

317

be personal holding anyway. You'll need another $3,000,000 for the company apportionment."

"Which leaves me with $500,000 liquidity," said Rudd.

"But what about the shares that are going to come on offer!" demanded Bunch. "You've committed Best Rest to 140p. It's illegal to make an offer you can't meet."

"What's the value of my stock portfolio in Best Rest?" Rudd asked Hallett.

"Ten million," said the personal assistant, at once.

"Borrow on it," said Rudd at once. "Anything offered can be bought on margin, so I'll have twenty-eight days to settle."

"And what happens if you haven't made it in a month?" said Bunch. "You'll be arrested for fraud and won't have sufficient money left to brief a lawyer! Cut out, Harry, for God's sake. Let's write it off as an expensive mistake and go back to America, where we belong."

There had never been an expensive mistake before, thought Rudd. There wasn't going to be this time. "No," he said. If he went back, Margaret would know he'd failed.

Rudd recognized her voice immediately and at once a numbness went through him, a physical sensation. The telephone felt slippery and insecure in his hand.

"You said you wanted to see me," said Margaret.

"Do you want to see me?"

"Yes," she said.

"When?"

"After Thursday."

"Why wait until then?"

"I want everything settled."

"You've made your decision then?"

There was a long hesitation from the other end. Then she said, "Yes."

Margaret replaced the telephone, seized with a sudden feeling of claustrophobia. She hurried from the house to the stables, saddled her horse and took it, too fast for safety, across the cobbles and out into the grounds. She reined back, embarrassed: she rode without any intentional direction and then recognized the hill, the high spot she usually went to, for its view. She stopped at the summit: beneath her the horse snorted and pawed, grateful for the rest. Margaret gazed around, first at the large house, then the smaller one, letting her eyes travel to the lake and the deer forest. Enduring, she thought: unchanging and safe. Beneath her the horse shifted, breaking her mood. She couldn't delay any longer her return to London. The sensation wasn't claustrophobia now. She felt sick.

38

·Haffaford's issued a statement of their intention to challenge the share dispersal and their later hope of introducing a counter-bid to top that of Best Rest, and there was wide publicity in America. Herbert Morrison read it in the *Wall Street Journal*, coupled with the press release that Buckland House had produced urging their shareholders to accept the bid that had come from Rudd. The burly man put aside the newspaper and looked across the lounge of the businessmen's club, waiting for Walker to arrive. He'd won, Morrison decided. It had been far more costly than he had anticipated and the damage to Best Rest had been greater, but he'd won. There was no way Rudd could survive the stock-holders' meeting. Morrison decided to move their withdrawal from the Buckland House negotiations at the same time. That might depress Buckland House but it would mean an immediate rise in Best Rest. Morrison calculated the recovery would take a long time, maybe even a year, but eventually they'd regain their parity. It would be quicker with Buckland House. Once they had withdrawn and the alternative bid was declared, the prices were bound to go up. And if Haffaford's clients were putting it higher than Rudd, then it would mean recovery of the personal fortune that had been so badly eroded.

Morrison saw his partner enter and waved to attract his attention. Walker crossed the lounge, gesturing to a waiter as he did so for his usual drink. It arrived at the same time as he did.

"You've seen it?" said the Best Rest vice-chairman, indicating the discarded newspaper.

Morrison nodded. "What's happened to the market?"

"We're down another two points at the threat of a fight."

"Thank God we're getting out," said Morrison. "I'm going to propose withdrawal at the stockholders' meeting."

"If you hadn't, I would have done," said Walker. He sipped

the Bushmills. "I called New York," he said. "There's been an acknowledgement from London."

"Saying what?"

"Nothing: just the acknowledgement of the meeting."

"There's not much he could say, is there?" said Morrison.

"We're going to go down further," predicted Walker. "Pulling out of the takeover might balance it a little, but getting rid of Rudd as chairman is going to cause some nervousness. He was pretty well known, with a good track record. People had come to trust him."

"Not any more," said Morrison. "Whatever we drop will pick up soon enough."

"How do you feel about a change of title, Herb?"

"Change of title?"

"Chairman instead of president. I think you should be back in control."

Morrison looked modestly down into his lap. "There's a lot of work to be done, to recover. I'd be willing to do what I could."

"I'll raise that at the meeting, too," promised Walker.

Morrison had been expecting the offer. He said, "It might be an idea to switch Best Rest back here to Boston. We own the property in Manhattan. If we sold we'd make a hell of a profit. It would go some way towards retrieving the money we've lost."

"It's something to consider," said Walker.

They'd all been shit scared of what had happened, recognized Morrison. From now on they'd follow like lambs. It was a good feeling, to be so completely in charge; far better than landing a championship fish.

Morrison emptied the old flowers into a refuse container and threw away the sour water. He rinsed the bowl several times before refilling it and set it back upon the grave before making the new arrangements. Roses. They'd always been Angela's favourites. Satisfied at last, Morrison hunched back on his heels.

"I've done it, my darling," he said softly. "I've made the bastard pay for what he did to you."

39

Margaret went into the drawing-room early, wanting to be there before Buckland arrived. Establishing territory, she thought. Animals did that; fought for it, when they thought it was being invaded. She started moving towards the drinks tray, but stopped before she reached it. Liquor wouldn't help. She felt hot and brought a handkerchief to her upper lip. The feeling of sickness had seemed permanent for days. Buckland was on time, which she hadn't expected, thrusting into the room and then stopping just inside the door, seeming surprised to find her already there.

"I haven't kept you waiting?"

"No."

"Good."

There was the politeness of strangers between them.

"Can I get you a drink?" offered Buckland.

"No thank you."

"I think I'll have one." He went to the drinks and with his back to her said, "How was the drive up?"

"Usual."

He seemed to be taking a long time making the drink she thought.

"You said it was important to see me," he said, still not looking at her.

"It is."

"What about?"

"Don't be stupid, Ian."

Buckland stood waiting.

"I'm leaving." She babbled the words out, wanting to look at him when she said them but unable to, at the last moment.

"Of course," he said empty-voiced.

It was not the reaction she'd anticipated. "You didn't expect me to stay did you?"

"I hoped you would."

"Christ!" She wished he didn't appear so pathetic.

"When?" he said.

She moved her shoulders. "I haven't decided." That sounded ridiculous. She should have had suitcases packed, the car waiting outside. This should have been brief; curt and adult and brief.

"I'm sorry."

"You've said that before," she reminded him.

"I didn't mean that . . . sorry that you're leaving."

"Because of further scandal," she said. Why wouldn't he get angry?

Buckland shook his head wearily. "There's been too much of that for any more to do any harm." He became aware of the drink in his hand. Untouched he put it on to a side table. "I'll do whatever you want . . . about the divorce, I mean . . . I . . ." He halted abruptly, snatching out for the drink and gulping heavily from it.

Margaret felt a great wash of pity.

"Please don't!" the plea burst from him, his voice anguished. "Please . . ."

Buckland scrubbed his hand across his eyes and Margaret jerked up from her chair and went to the window with her back to him so she didn't have to see him cry. She'd never seen a man cry: they weren't supposed to.

"I've made my decision," she said.

"If you go it will all be gone," he said.

"What do you mean?" She stayed at the window, wanting him fully to recover.

"I know it's make-believe, about me retaining anything except a title if Harry wins. I'll be an employee, perhaps more than anyone else. Checked and watched, told what to do and what not to do. Maybe other people won't know. I will."

She turned at last. He was sitting, the glass cupped between both hands. He wasn't looking at her. "I'll do it, of course," he said. "For the family and for what's left of the reputation . . ." He made the vaguest gesture, to indicate the house. ". . . for this and for Cambridgeshire . . . for mother, so she won't despise me completely. . . ." He turned to her at last. "You must despise me," he said. "For what I did. And now this."

She realized, surprised, that he was speaking objectively, without any self-pity. "No," she said.

"That's kind," he said disbelievingly.

"What happens if Harry doesn't win?"

"God knows," he said. "Then I really lose, I suppose."

"God!" she said exasperated. "Didn't you fuck everything up!"

"Yes," he said. "I really did." For several moments he was silent and then he said. "I'm very ashamed."

She said "It's a bit late for that."

"It wasn't an apology," said Buckland. "I wanted you to know." He looked up at her again. "I didn't ever want to hurt you: that's the most ridiculous part of the whole thing."

"A bit late," she said again.

"Yes."

"I'd like a gin," she said.

"If course."

He made a drink for her and another for himself, carrying the glass to her. "I love you," he said.

"Don't!"

"I'm . . ." he started, then stopped. He reached out and grasped her hand: consciously she did not respond. "Please," he said again.

She was glad he wasn't crying any more.

There had been a conference, of little purpose at Sir Henry Dray's chambers and afterwards they'd returned to Grosvenor Square. Hallett served drinks and they sat around with little to say: after so long, they were talked out.

"Well," said Bunch, breaking a silence. "By this time tomorrow we'll know."

"Yes," said Rudd. He wasn't thinking about the court case, he realized.

40

The hearing before Mr Justice Perivale was in chambers, which restricted the attendance. Only Buckland appeared for the family. Rudd sat immediately alongside. Again he was represented by Sir Henry Dray and Sir Walter Blair appeared for Buckland. Richard Haffaford and John Snaith were at the far end of the same bench as Rudd and Buckland. Their counsel was Arthur Jenkins. He was younger than the other two QCs, a dark, saturnine man, with a hurried, nervous way of talking as if he was afraid of being interrupted. The application was for an injunction against Buckland and his family, preventing their disposing of the Initial shares in the way they had, to enable a fuller court hearing at which an application could be sought for them to be offered on the open market. The arguments and counter-arguments comprised technical, esoteric and convoluted points of company law being disputed and then challenged and then disputed again.

Because the action only concerned the Buckland family shares, there had been three days for a market reaction to Rudd's bid. It hadn't been good. There had been a lot of trading in Ordinary shares, soaking up the money he had personally committed, but they were giving him very little voting power. The funds were almost unanimously holding back for the better offer which Haffaford's had hinted at in their announcement, and the movement in the nominee stocks was also slow. Rudd and Bunch had carried out a minute analysis of the movement at the close the previous night and calculated that without the Buckland shares, they had twenty-seven per cent. If they were allowed to keep the Buckland allocation, it would bring them up to forty. Which was still far short of what he needed.

Sellers were obviously holding back for the result of the hearing and if it were in favour he supposed it would mean the release of a few more, but it would be unrealistic to expect it to be the remaining eleven per cent that was necessary. And if the ruling were against him, then the situation was hopeless.

Either way, he'd lost.

He'd worked from pride instead of business sense, caused God knows how much damage and achieved absolutely nothing, except possibly bankrupting himself. Perhaps if there hadn't been the distraction of Margaret. . . . Rudd stopped, refusing to accept the excuse. She'd been a distraction, certainly and was still. But she hadn't affected his thinking on the takeover, not in any substantial way. Pride, he decided positively. The pride of a man who had always won refusing to accept a time had arisen when it was not going to happen. He deserved the censure that was building up in New York.

The legal submission took two hours and then there was an adjournment for Perivale to consider the written ruling of Mr Justice Godber. During the break Rudd telephoned Hallett at the Connaught. The personal assistant had just completed a round-up of the brokers with whom they had buy orders; they'd picked up more Ordinary shares, without any effect upon the voting.

"I never want to see this place again," said Buckland, when Rudd emerged from the kiosk.

"No," said Rudd. Neither did he, he thought. "There's no substantial selling."

"They're holding back for the result."

"There's still a long way to go, even if we win."

"Blair seems confident."

"He was before," reminded Rudd. "He was wrong that time."

Buckland was suddenly reminded of his secret meeting with Haffaford. The merchant banker hadn't said he would be expelled from the board; merely that he couldn't provide any guarantee. Surely he hadn't made a mistake, backing the American offer? "You meant what you said about me, if you won?" the Englishman demanded worriedly.

"The contract is being drawn," assured Rudd, conscious of the man's nervousness. How long would it be before Penhardy ran for cover? Faysel would have to switch, he supposed, to protect his investment. Even he'd have to concur in the end, in any effort to get back some of the expenditure. Surrendering at the first shots, he thought bitterly. He *wouldn't* surrender. He wouldn't go cap in hand, eager to apologize to the stockholders. He'd argue like hell to get the bid ceiling lifted, so that he could come back and bid against whatever Haffaford put forward. The urgent determination faltered, as quickly as it had come. He'd argue, because he had to. But he wouldn't get any concessions.

Perivale resumed quicker than any of them had expected, so quickly that Blair had to be summoned from another court in which he was leading but which he had left under a junior's care.

Rudd strained forward to hear the decision.

"I have studied in detail the ruling of Mr Justice Godber," said Perivale. "And I have listened in even greater detail to the arguments put before me this morning. It is true that a complaint of sharpness might be levelled at the behaviour of Mr Rudd for Best Rest in making the proposal he did in advance of the share decision, just as it could be expressed against Sir Ian Buckland and his family for their eager acceptance. But sharpness can also be astuteness and there is nothing legally reprehensible about astuteness in business. Mr Justice Godber's decision was that there should be a dispersal. There was no direction in that dispersal, nor any sought, in the earlier application. I can find nothing in any of the arguments that have been put to me today to withhold from Sir Ian Buckland and his family permission to dispossess themselves of the holdings in the manner they have chosen to do."

Rudd felt a hand gripping his arm and turned to Buckland. "We've won!" said the Englishman. Rudd thought there was a reserve to the excitement.

It took a further fifteen minutes for the proceedings to close formally. As soon as they emerged into the corridor outside, Rudd hurried to his counsel and said, "Is there going to be an appeal?"

Dray shook his head. "I was waiting for notice to be given," he admitted. "I gather from Jenkins that his people thought it would take too long."

"What then?"

"I think they're going to rely upon a counter-bid to swamp you."

*   *   *

327

The decision came at midday, with an afternoon's trading to go. Rudd had both Hallett and Bunch monitor the reaction through their brokers, going personally to the gallery of the Exchange. Hallett got back to Grosvenor Square first, with Bunch following ten minutes behind. With the previous night's analysis already available, it only took the lawyer minutes to make his calculations.

He looked up to Rudd, shaking his head. "We've committed ourselves to another $1,500,000 on margin," he said. "And as far as I can calculate we've only picked up another six per cent of the votes."

"Forty-six per cent," said Rudd reflectively.

"You're too short, Harry," said Bunch. "Way too short."

"There'll be more, on a full day's trading."

Bunch shook his head again. "One per cent, maybe two at the outside. The big holders are waiting."

"How long do you think I've got?" said Rudd.

"Talk in the City this afternoon was a week. Maybe ten days at the outside."

"I could always top Haffaford's," said Rudd. "I've still got a lot of liquidity left."

"For margins, not completion," said Bunch. "Don't dig a deeper hole for yourself than you're in already."

"And even margin buying is going to become more expensive," warned Hallett. "The Ordinary and Preferential are going up, in anticipation of Haffaford's offer."

Rudd laughed, a humourless sound. "Doesn't sound much does it, five per cent!" he said.

"As far as you're concerned, Harry, it's as wide as the Grand Canyon," said Bunch.

"I thought you'd be more excited," said Margaret.

"We won a battle, not the war," said Buckland. "He's still six per cent short."

"I'm sorry for you," said Margaret sincerely.

"It was predictable."

"Goodbye," she said.

"Goodbye."

41

Rudd moved nervously around the flat, anxious for her to arrive. There weren't any flowers, he realized; she'd liked flowers. He looked at his watch. Too late to get any now. Should he have thought about food? He didn't want to eat. What if she did? They could go out. He grimaced at the thought. They'd never been out publicly. He'd suggested it, more than once, but Margaret had always held back, nervous of their being seen. Was her decision to hold back? Or to come with him? In his anxiety Rudd began seeking omens. She could have rejected him finally on the telephone, without the need for a meeting. And she'd made the call to him. His spirits lifted. It was an obvious conclusion and he was irritated it hadn't occurred to him before. He looked at his watch again. He'd expected her before now. What if she'd changed her mind? The concern rose and fell like a leaf in the wind. There would have been some contact, if she weren't coming. She'd be there sometime. He went to the window overlooking the square, straining out to look for her. He thought he saw her once, walking down from the direction of the embassy, and smiled instinctively in anticipation before realizing it wasn't her: soon after a taxi pulled up directly outside and he leaned against the window. A man got out and went into an adjoining building. Rudd turned away, gazing back into the empty apartment. Had he lost in his effort to control Buckland House? It didn't look good, he decided objectively. The likelihood was of his picking up one or two per cent, that was all. Only a miracle could get him more and Rudd didn't believe in miracles.

The effect of this realization registered and Rudd frowned. Here he was, expecting a woman to announce she was going to leave a millionaire husband for him and what did he have to offer? Everything he owned was being committed to what now appeared to be a futile attempt to achieve the takeover and realistically he had to accept his future with Best Rest was uncertain. Was it fair to ask her to make the financial sacrifice as well as every other sacrifice that would be involved?

She didn't use her own key but rang for him to admit her from the street, from the push-button internal security lock. He stood at the door of the apartment, holding it open for her when she emerged from the lift. She was wearing one of the black dresses she had worn in court, and a hat and gloves. He thought she looked business-like and efficient and wondered if that were the intention. If it were, the hesitation in the tiny vestibule spoiled it. He smiled and said, "Hello."

"Hello," she said. She didn't smile.

He stood back for her to enter. The first time since the row, he thought; and since other things. He thought she looked beautiful and he wanted her so much.

"It's good to see you again," said Rudd. "Like this I mean."

Margaret didn't make any response.

"Can I get you something?" he said.

"No thank you." She sat down demurely, knees tight together, her hands in her lap.

"I didn't mean it to happen like it did," said Rudd, nervously apologetic. "The embarrassment . . . the publicity, all that sort of thing."

"It did though, didn't it?"

"It wouldn't have been so bad if there hadn't been the share-holders' meeting: everyone was prepared after that."

"It's immaterial now," she said dismissively.

"Not if it hurt you, it isn't," he said.

"It did," she said. "It hurt like hell."

The silence stretched between them awkwardly. Rudd tried to think of all the things he'd planned to say but the words weren't in his head any more. "Nothing's changed," he said. "As far as I'm concerned, nothing's changed."

"I tried to hate you," she said, finding it as difficult as he was. "When it was all going on I told myself it was all your fault and that all the filth was coming out because of you and I tried to hate you. But nothing came."

Rudd felt the hope deep within him, a physical sensation of

warmth; if she didn't hate him there was only one other feeling she could have.

"I love you too," he said.

She stared at him for a long time. Then she said, "Did Ian tell you what happened in Cambridge last weekend?"

Rudd shook his head. "No," he said.

"I refused to give up any of my personal Initial holdings: said I'd been abandoned enough. His mother surrendered four per cent and Vanessa three. Ian had to make over his entire personal holding of nine per cent. He's only got the joint holdings left."

"What's this got to do with us?"

"Ian says your offer isn't being taken up."

"We're short," admitted Rudd. "About six per cent."

"I've got six per cent," she said.

"I don't want to talk about shares and takeovers," he said, irritably. "You said you'd decided."

"No, Harry," she announced, simply. She was surprised her voice was so strong.

He stared at her, shaking his head in disbelief. "You don't mean that," he said.

"I do."

"You're scared."

"Right," she said at once. "I'm scared to death."

"I'd look after you," he said desperately. "I'd protect you, against any harassment . . . have people available all the time to stop you being pursued . . ."

Margaret shuddered. "I couldn't bear that," she said.

"You're running."

"Maybe I am."

"For God's sake, Angela. . . ."

The silence thundered around them.

Margaret spoke first. "Poor darling," she said "You poor darling."

"Don't twist that, like everything else," pleaded Rudd.

"Am I very like her?"

"It was a mistake; a simple mistake!"

"I won't do it Harry. I can't."

It couldn't finish like this, thought Rudd; it was too matter-of-fact, too sterile.

"Take more time," he pleaded.

"There's no point," she said. "Just take the shares."

"I don't want the bloody shares!"

"That's stupid."

It was, he realized at once. "Would it make any difference, if I take them or not? To us, I mean."

"No," she said.

"I thought you were going to come with me," he said. "I'd really made my mind up it was what you had decided."

Margaret said nothing.

"It wasn't Angela," he said. "Not the similarity. It was you."

"I believe you."

He started to reach out for her but she pulled back. "Why then?" he said. "You're not like Vanessa and the others."

"Maybe I thought I was."

"That doesn't make sense."

"I don't know why."

"Was it . . . ?"

". . . Stop it, Harry!"

They stayed gazing at each other for a long time. Then Margaret said, "Do you want the shares?"

"Yes," he said.

"They're ready, whenever you need them."

"I'll get my broker to deal directly with yours."

She nodded. "You don't hate me, do you?" she said. She hadn't meant to allow any lapse but she couldn't prevent herself.

"You don't have to ask me that," he said.

When Hallett arrived the following morning to discuss their return to America, Rudd told him to terminate the tenancy of the apartment. He spoke by telephone to Prince Faysel and agreed to take the same plane back to New York. Then he monitored the market movement overnight in Best Rest on the New York Exchange and, when it opened, Buckland House in London. Within an hour of trading, Buckland House was marked up by 15p, buoyed by the end of the legal arguments and the prospect of bid and counter-bid. It was noon when the call came from the broker, reporting the successful purchase of Lady

Margaret Buckland's six per cent. There'd been a general loosening of the market, added the man. In addition, he'd got another two per cent of the controlling shares from floor dealing.

Bunch arrived at the apartment at lunchtime, serious-faced and burdened with two briefcases.

"I've got it," declared Rudd. "Fifty-three per cent." There was no excitement; no feeling at all.

Bunch didn't react either. He opened his briefcase and offered a sheaf of documents. "I remembered what you asked me to do," he said. "I've just come from Dray's office."

Rudd stared down curiously, the frown deepening as he turned the pages. He looked up to the lawyer, shaking his head. "Jesus Christ," he said disgustedly.

"I didn't believe it either," said Bunch.

"I do," said Rudd. The sadness pressed down on him.

"What are you going to do?" asked the lawyer.

"Settle it," said Rudd. "Once and for all settle it." He still felt nothing.

42

Anticipating the attack that was to be made and determined upon an indestructible defence, Rudd arrived at the downtown offices of Best Rest at six in the morning. Hallett was already there and Bunch arrived within fifteen minutes. The personal assistant assembled all the files and together they went through the minutes and records of the directors' meetings that had been held during the English negotiations. It was Hallett who picked up the discrepancy with the dates. Bunch checked independently, for verification, and then said, 'You're right: Morrison didn't convene a proper meeting to explain what was going on when he came back from London. There's just a reference to a meeting at the Park Summit, a week afterwards."

They both turned to Rudd for reaction. The man seemed subdued. He said, "I don't want it to be protracted: I want it over quickly."

Rudd went back to the minutes he was studying. Bunch and Hallett looked at each other but said nothing. It was a further hour before anyone spoke again. Bunch said, "Walker seems to be leading the criticism: sometimes Morrison actually appears to be arguing in favour of what you were trying to do."

"That was the impression I got," said Rudd. He stretched up from his desk. Outside it was still an early sky, streaked with orange and red and then, at the very rim, the grey blackness of the disappearing night. Rudd said, "The motion before the stockholders will be for my removal."

"There is an argument for it," said Bunch. "You should have come back more than once to explain yourself."

"It wouldn't have stopped the share slide," said Rudd. "The only outcome would have been more restrictions."

"It would still have been a good tactic," insisted the lawyer.

"Too late to think about that now," said Rudd. "The damage is done."

Around them the offices began to fill. Hallett organized coffee and they sat in Rudd's office, drinking it without any conversation. Rudd provided the explanation when Prince Faysel arrived. The Arab listened without any reaction. When Rudd finished, Faysel said; "This isn't going to be pleasant."

"Nothing has been," said Rudd. "We didn't plan it this way."

"Still unpleasant," insisted the Arab.

They filed into the boardroom early, wanting to be first. Rudd carried a thick folder with him.

"I'm sorry," said the Arab, as they seated themselves. "I'm sorry for you."

"Thanks," said Rudd.

Morrison and Walker had flown together from Boston, so they arrived at the same time. They seemed surprised to find others ahead of them.

"At last!" said Walker.

"Yes," said Rudd. "At last."

The red-faced man reddened further, went as if to speak and then changed his mind, hurrying to the vice-chairman's spot. Morrison went to the far end of the table, to his accustomed place. He looked grave even managing a vague expression of sympathy as he looked towards his son-in-law; inwardly he was bubbling with the excitement of what was going to happen. He knew it was going to be a marvellous day; absolutely marvellous.

Böch was next, coming wheezily through the door and stopping just inside, staring around. He nodded and sat down at his place. As he did so, Ottway entered. There was an immediate expression of concern. "Sorry I'm late," he said.

"You're not," said Rudd.

From the other end of the table Morrison wondered how long the younger man's confidence would last: he'd always been a cocky little bastard.

Rudd picked up the summoning notice and said formally, "This is an extraordinary board meeting convened to examine the behaviour of the chairman and certain other directors in the matter of the Buckland House takeover."

As he put the document down, Walker said, "Convened at my request."

"But decided upon unanimously," added Böch.

Rudd went from one to the other: they seemed eager to attack. "Like the stockholders' meeting was convened?" he asked. He glanced to the secretariat. It all had to come out.

"The stockholders' meeting was arranged because of the responsibility we have towards the people who have trusted us with their money," said Morrison. "At the close of trading here last night, Best Rest had suffered a loss of $18,000,000 because of this business."

"And because of your conduct in it," said Walker. "There are records which show the majority view of this board on how the negotiations should have been conducted. . . ."

". . . records which will be produced this afternoon?" interrupted Rudd.

"Yes," said Walker. "Produced to show that despite the fears which had been expressed here, you carried on beyond any proper authority."

"I was given a mandate to make a takeover," insisted Rudd. "I continued because I judged that takeover still to be viable."

"At the risk to the parent company of $18,000,000 in lost confidence!" demanded Böch.

"I agree that because of the peculiar circumstances, the effects upon both Best Rest and Buckland House have been substantial. . . ."

". . . disastrous . . ." intruded Böch.

". . . substantial," repeated Rudd. "But it's paper losses, here and in London. There'll be a recovery and after they've reached par, they'll improve."

"And to whose benefit will the Buckland House improvement be?" said Morrison. "Certainly not ours."

"I think it could be," said Rudd cautiously.

Walker came up from the paper upon which he had been making a calculation. "In this boardroom there was a binding vote, restricting you to a fifteen per cent takeover ceiling. Your offer of 60p Ordinary, 140p Preferential and £10 for Initial was grossly in excess of anything discussed here. . . ."

". . . I was fighting a counter-bid suggestion. . . ." said Rudd, and Morrison brought his hand to his face to conceal his smirk at the younger man's obvious desperation.

". . . in gross excess," insisted Walker. "If you've achieved that sort of holding, you've gone beyond that ceiling, up to something like twenty-one per cent. You've treated this board and most of the directors like children, fit only to be ignored."

Rudd allowed a pause. Then he said, "A ceiling *was* imposed. A restriction against which I protested at the time as being unreasonable and impossible to observe if a counter-bid arose, which seemed likely." He stopped again, to heighten the effect. "I have *not* exceeded the fifteen per cent that this board considered sufficient but which, as I warned from the start proved utterly inadequate. To make up the shortfall I have committed my personal fortune and raised cash upon my equities."

"Buying on a margin?" said Böch.

"Yes," said Rudd.

"How much?"

"My responsibility within twenty-eight days is something approaching $40,000,000."

"Forty million!" said Walker.

Dear God, thought Morrison; oh dear God this was wonderful! Morrison knew the share divisions in Buckland House down to the last half or quarter per cent. He knew, too, how the professionals were holding back, just as he and two other nominee blocks were refusing to sell. There was no way, no way at all, that Rudd could get his control. And he'd committed himself to an impossible debt, in his conceit that he could manipulate the boardroom and the stockholders. Best Rest would have to settle the debt, of course, to preserve their integrity. And when Haffaford's offer was established, it would even make good business sense to do so. But before then Rudd would have been driven out of this and every other boardroom possible to him, shown not to be the entrepreneur with the Midas touch but a panicky gambler prepared to put the deeds of the house on the turn of a card. Morrison's feeling of pleasure was practically sensual.

"Which I ask this board to accept," said Rudd. "Just as I this afternoon intend asking the stockholders to accept it as a company responsibility."

"As a way of getting around the restrictions that were imposed upon you by this board!" demanded Böch. "That's deceit."

"No." said Rudd. "As a way of confirming our control at fifty-three per cent."

Varying degrees of astonishment registered on the faces of the four men. "Control!" said Ottway.

"Fifty-three per cent," confirmed Rudd.

"Impossible," burst out Morrison unthinkingly.

"Why is it impossible?" seized Rudd.

Morrison swallowed, searching for the words. "Yesterday's message talked of the offer blocking at forty-five per cent. You can't have achieved eight overnight: that's hundreds of votes."

"Available from Initial holdings," agreed Rudd. "Which I've got."

"You can't have," insisted Morrison. It was a trick: it had to be a trick for Rudd to get himself off the hook. The man had tricked his way into the company and was trying to hold on in the same way. He'd face the bastard down, just as he should have been faced down years ago.

Hallett was ready, from their early morning rehearsal. The personal assistant rose at once, taking the documents from the chairman and circulating the table, placing a copy before each man.

"Share certificates confirming our control," announced Rudd. Morrison, Walker, Böch and Ottway had their heads bent over the files: Walker and Böch had calculators before them, assessing share holdings against voting strength.

Walker came up first, smiling. "You've got it," he agreed. "Sure as hell you've got it!"

"There is something further," said Rudd. Again Hallett toured the table and when the man finished Rudd said, "Further share certificates. They record the purchase of roughly nine per cent equity value in Buckland House; the purchase was made early before any negotiations were disclosed, when there were still high equity shares available at low cost. And made under nominee arrangement, for secrecy. . . ."

Morrison's face flushed and then whitened at the photostats of the certificates Grearson had obtained for him. He gazed up, staring-eyed. "Not true," he said. "I know nothing. . . ."

"They're genuine," said Rudd remorselessly. "They've been checked, both in London and through brokers here in New York and then back to Boston. Before I left London yesterday I contacted the brokers and lawyer named as nominee holder, a man named Peter Coppell. I said I was representing a client of Haffaford's. I was told the shares were available for their bid but unavailable for Best Rest, whose efforts they were committed to resist. . . ."

Morrison was shaking his head, like a boxer at the point of collapse.

"With those shares made over to Best Rest a week ago, we could have stemmed a stock loss of $4,500,000," said Rudd. "The president of this corporation has conducted a share manipulation to defeat a takeover to which this board committed itself."

"How?" said Morrison, empty-voiced. "How?"

"The British courts," disclosed Rudd. "Once I challenged the share arrangement, nominee holders had to be identified in court documents, in case the judge called for them. As it happened, he didn't. But they were available for over two weeks and we didn't even know they were there."

Morrison bent over the table, with his head in his hands. He looked an old, sad man.

Rudd said forcefully. "I want authority for the shares of which I've made myself personally responsible taken over by this company, just as I want those held by the president put into company ownership. For the sake of the share stability of Best Rest, which has already suffered far more than it should have done, I am prepared for it to be announced before the stockholders as a coup, in the declaration of our control. . . ." He paused. "Oppose me and I'll make public from the platform and later in a statement to any journalist who cares to listen exactly what has happened. . . ." Another hesitation, for the threat to be fully recognized. "Do I have to spell out the effect upon this company if I did that?"

For a long time nobody spoke. Then Walker said, "No you don't have to spell out anything more."

Another sound intruded into the quietness of the room and Rudd realized that Morrison was crying.

339

Epilogue

Because the stockholders' meeting had been at the Park Summit it seemed obvious for Hallett, Bunch and Faysel to accompany Rudd up into his suite afterwards.

"I suppose it would be right to celebrate," said the Arab. "An overwhelming vote of confidence and the takeover wrapped up."

"I don't feel much like celebrating," said Rudd. He gestured to the bar and said generally. "Help yourself."

"I think you're making a mistake, insisting that Morrison remains as president," said Bunch. He poured himself scotch and handed orange juice to the Arab.

"There'll be no power," said Rudd. "He'll be stripped of any executive authority and have to assign any voting strength."

"Do you think he'd have shown any pity to you?" insisted the lawyer.

"No," agreed Rudd. But then he didn't hate Morrison, whatever the man had tried to do. And he was Angela's father: she would have wanted her father forgiven. She'd loved him very much.

"Still a mistake," said Bunch.

"It's the way I want it." Rudd spoke more harshly than he'd intended and regretted it at once. From today his power was absolute, he realized; over Best Rest and over Buckland House. He didn't feel anything at all. Just tired.

"What about Buckland?" said Faysel.

"What about him?"

"Surely you're not going to leave him with the chairmanship?"

"That was the deal," said Rudd.

"For a purpose," insisted Bunch. "That's been achieved now; we can move him sideways in a few months."

340

"He stays," ruled Rudd. "If he breaks the service contract, then OK, he's out. Otherwise, he's chairman."

Rudd was aware of Faysel and Bunch exchanging looks. "I thought you wanted it," said Bunch.

He had, thought Rudd. Like he'd wanted to so much else. He'd restrict his trips to England to the absolute minimum, just the twice-a-year visits he imposed upon the other divisions. He supposed it was inevitable that he would meet Margaret socially. But he'd try to limit it.

"I don't want it any longer," he said to the lawyer. "I can retain the ultimate responsibility well enough from here."

"What about a safeguard?" said Faysel worriedly. "There'll have to be a safeguard."

"I know," said Rudd. He looked at his personal assistant. "How would you feel about being vice-chairman?" he said.

"Me!" Hallett's face twitched nervously.

"You know as much about it as I do," said Rudd.

Hallett gave an uncertain smile. "That would be marvellous ... I mean ... thank you ..."

"Congratulations," Bunch said to Hallett. Bunch finished his drink, looked at the bottle and decided against it. "Mary and I are going up to Connecticut for the weekend," he said. "Why don't you come up, like you did before?"

Rudd shook his head. "Not this weekend," he said. "Maybe some other time."

Bunch's departure was the cue for the others. After they'd gone Rudd stood staring out over the park. It wasn't dark yet and a few joggers still felt it safe to exercise, jostling for position on the roadways around the zoo with the horse-drawn tourist buggies. Had it been an aberration, invoking Angela's name? Or had Margaret really been a mental surrogate? He'd never know. Like so much else he'd never know. Abruptly he turned back into the apartment and used the telephone on the bar. The response was as prompt as always. There was a pause, for a further connection, and Joanne came on the line.

"How have you been, Harry?"

"Busy," he said. He'd forgotten the huskiness of her voice. "How about you?"

"So so."

341

"But now I'm back in Manhattan."

"I could come over," she said.

"I'd like that." With Joanne he'd never be let down. She was a professional, like he was.

Margaret knew he was quite detached, intent only on pleasing her, not making love because he wanted to but because he thought she expected it. She lay with her eyes closed, feigning the excitement, finding it easy to whimper although not for the reasons he wanted. When the mechanical foreplay was over he thrust into her, unaware of her dryness, and she groaned and she saw him smile, pleased. He was very heavy and she found it difficult to breathe. She was glad it ended quickly because he was hurting her so much. She felt him quicken and pretended, thrusting upwards; her only relief was to shift his weight.

"I thought that was marvellous," he said.

"Yes."

"Was it for you?"

"Yes."

He lay panting beside her, the winner of a one-man race. They remained side by side for a long time and she thought he was asleep but he said suddenly, "I know you surrendered your shares to Harry to ensure I stayed chairman of Buckland House. Thank you."

She couldn't think of anything to say.

"And thank you for staying," he said. "Thank you for that most of all."

Why hadn't she been brave enough? Why, for once in her life, hadn't she done what she wanted to do, rather than what she knew would be expected of her.

"Are you going back to Cambridge tomorrow?" said Buckland.

"In the afternoon."

"Mother will be glad," he said. "She says no one plays bezique like you do."